CHIVALRY
IN THE
SHADOWS

MEG WAHLBERG

PARKWOOD MANOR PRESS

Copyright © 2024 by Meg Wahlberg
All rights reserved
Printed in the United States of America
First Edition, 2024

ISBN 979-8-9909499-0-4 (paperback)
ISBN 979-8-9909499-1-1 (hardcover)
ISBN 979-8-9909499-2-8 (ebook)
ISBN 979-8-9909499-3-5 (audiobook)

Cover artwork created with the assistance of Midjourney, Photoshop, and Photoroom, finalized by the author.

Parkwood Manor Press
An imprint of Late Bird Media, LLC
Parkwoodpress.com
Follow us on Instagram @parkwood_manor_press

In loving memory of
Jim DeAngelis (1968-2023)
advocate, friend, and mentor.

CONTENTS

Part Three
The Tournament

ACKNOWLEDGMENTS

I would like to acknowledge the scholars of literature and history whose research assisted this speculative vision of medieval Brittany. A bibliography appears at the end of the book, detailing the books I used as references when I wrote this novel.

I would also like to thank my readers and friends who have supported me and contributed to this work. Some of you provided critical feedback on this project. Some of you kept me safe on the battlefield at Pennsic 49. Others advanced my position or took a chance on me when nobody else would. Thank you for inviting me into your world of magic. Each of you inspires me.

Baron Brandubh Donnghaile
Baron Jean Phillipe Gillies
Sir Guillaume le Noir
Tracy Hall
Hilary Kamien
Kaleb Khaine Eckart
Allie Terracina
Gayle Fallon
Lauren Quoraishee
Stefanie Babb
Paul Minkovich
Mary Fan
Caroline Elyse David

Baroness Hilderun Hügelmann
Baroness Caterine de Troyes
The Honorable Lady Svava Jórudóttir
Melissa Perry
Dmitry Feller
Fenris Wolfe Grossheim
Will Kim
Daniel A. Gilmore
PJ Storm-Artis
Kurt Wahlberg
Jen Minkovich
Elizabeth Ohlmuller

PREFACE

You may be wondering why I wrote this book, or perhaps, when I had the time. For the last six years, I have been a Ph.D. student at Louisiana State University, juggling teaching, parenting, and writing my dissertation. In truth, I could not have finished my dissertation without writing this novel. History is an exercise of invention. As I wrote my dissertation, I found myself struggling to conceptualize certain aspects of medieval life. When people returned from the Third Crusade—if they returned—how had their worldview changed? How was Otherness being constructed in remote little towns? Modernity has afflicted me with the tendency to assume people were in communication all the time, and it has also instilled a bias against historical knowledge and customs. This novel began as an exercise to help me unpack and understand the dynamic world of the Middle Ages and the diverse cultures thriving across Europe and beyond.

Wanting to expand my conception of how people reacted to certain texts on chivalric conduct, I would come here to the world of thirteenth-century Brittany where my uniquely well-travelled and linguistically-capable twins reside. They encountered difficult trials and illuminated what had previously eluded me. I discovered a world that was at once influenced by and resistant to the culture of chivalry. Through this project, I have poured information from my secondary sources into a world of moving parts where I can see my characters challenging the dominant culture and narrative of their time, as many medieval poets tried to do through cleverly wrought verse.

The purpose of telling Rowen's story was also a way of processing my own struggles with my queer identity. What I love about medieval constructions of gender and sexuality is their openness and changeability, for as one who never felt entirely one thing or another, this resonated strongly with me. With this project, I hope to challenge stereotypes and imagine history through a lens of multitude and complexity. With this book, I am honoring those who have been misunderstood and underrepresented in literature.

PART ONE

ROWEN

CHAPTER 1

Only a man with means and all his limbs could be a chevalier, but at the midsummer games, beneath a moon as gold as a coin, anyone could taste a quarter of his glory. The lists, a roped enclosure divided into aisles, contained the arena where those games were played. On each side, townspeople packed themselves onto stands made of silvered lumber.

The common girls flaunted low necklines this season. They laughed like birds, and two women danced in a circle, their arms twined like an ampersand. Wreathed in the smoke of torches, men jostled as they shouted to their friends and made boasts of manliness. Others swayed on their toes to see the mounted men-at-arms catching rings on their lances.

After testing their passes, the horses thundered to either side of the tilt, a long, frilly boundary bisecting the trampled green. At one end, a fair unknown bobbed in the saddle. His belligerent howls rallied the crowd.

On the other end, Sir Edmund le Noir watched and waited. His colors were black. And so were his eyes. His expertly crafted helm seemed to absorb the light of the torches. His was Breton blood. He wore his hair long in defiance of Norman sovereignty. For this, the people called him bold, and he had been a favorite in the lists for old and young alike.

1

Amidst the populous crowds socializing beyond the stands, a bard flickered his nails over the strings of a lute, vocalizing in a soft tenor as he wove between bodies. The sin-soaked air bubbled with an intoxicating blend of languages and stories. The young man's song faded almost as quickly as it was strummed. He lost the crowd—if he ever had them—the moment the knight marshal's horn was blown.

"Joust!" he shouted.

The riders advanced.

A member of the nobility watched from her family's dais, a girl of sixteen. Adorned in a bliaut of red silk, Rowen leaned against the railing, savoring the spectacle of mortal men speeding toward impact.

They burst their lances on each other's shields. With a loud pop, the crowd recoiled. Rowen laughed at herself for jumping. She squinted to see if her friend on the other side of the lists was laughing, too.

Amarys, the Baron's eldest daughter, sat slumped in her chair. Her family glittered like a moonlit lake, their many crystals catching every angle of light. Not one member of that noble household seemed to notice that Amarys had lost interest in the steel-clad knights. Rowen tilted her head, trying to snare her friend's attention, but Amarys remained oblivious.

"Amarys la Belle," said Rowen's brother, Roland. "Why do the people call her such?"

"Because she is so finely formed," said Rowen. "They say the Graces themselves must have sculpted her from clay."

Rowen and her twin were a mirror to each other's beauty, both tall and wan with eyes like the deadened bark of winter. The cut of their hair and clothing distinguished them from one another, for while Rowen's hair fell in ripples down her back, her brother's was cropped short and neat. And while her garments made the body lithe and willowy, his accentuated his broad shoulders and dramatic angles.

"I wonder what they call me," he said.

"Roland the Fool, no doubt," their father interrupted. "Now be quiet."

Their father, Ivin, sat between them, a weak attempt to subdue their constant banter. It made no difference.

"Have they epithets for the other daughters, or do they not matter?"

"Roland," said Ivin.

"There is Beatrice the doe," answered Rowen, "and the little one, Honora, has yet to distinguish herself."

"I should cut the tongues from your throats." Ivin's wrath tapered as Sir Edmund, having won the joust in the third pass, approached their dais. He stalled his horse, bowing his head. He removed his helm and whipped his long, dark locks in a backward motion.

"Monseigneur," said Edmund to Ivin. "I came to ask if I might wear your daughter's favor."

Ivin stood and went to the rail, dragging his leg as he walked. "You would dare? After replacing my son as your squire?"

Edmund's jaw tensed. "He is still my squire. I had my reasons for withdrawing him."

"You have no reason!" interjected Roland.

Edmund flinched, a nervous glance lighting on Rowen before returning his gaze to Ivin. "Did Roland explain what happened?"

"More or less," said Ivin. "He says you passed judgment that he is not ready to squire."

Edmund adjusted his posture in the saddle and stroked his horse's neck. "In body, he is ready, but his spirit is not in it. On more than one occasion, he has evaded his training. And recently, I caught him gambling beneath the Grim Tree."

Roland jumped up like a churning sea. "I was not gambling! I was composing a canso while my friends were gambling. An important distinction."

"You compose cansos when you should be at your sword drills."

"For seven years, I have done everything you asked!"

Rowen felt her stomach yellow like an Autumn leaf. She wanted to cool her brother's temper with soft words, but in the presence of knights, a girl might as well have been made of cloth and air.

Edmund raised his voice in turn. "Since his return from Toulouse, Roland has become nothing less than a vice-ridden libertine. The townsfolk say he is a frequent patron of Lechón. A tavern, monseigneur. A place of vice. I would not see him made a knight until he has washed himself clean of such a place."

Ivin conceded, "Rest assured; my son will repent. He will take the cross like his father and grandfather before him."

"I would rather die covered in shit!"

The bang of Ivin's fist on the railing laid the promise of a clout if Roland did not relent. "You will be a knight," said Ivin definitively.

Edmund softened his tone. "We will forgive the boy. He is in that wild part of youth that resists chivalric training. By next year, he will have glory in the lists, not as my squire but as my opponent." Sir Edmund bowed his head to acknowledge Rowen next, which worried her, for it was bold to address a man's daughter at any time, especially after a quarrel. "Lady Rowen."

Rowen flinched to hear her name out loud. What was this name, anyway, but a hapless knot formed in haste to tie her to her brother? She never felt quite right in her own skin. The role of a lady had been tailored too tight, its sleeves fitted for a child's wrists.

"Sir Edmund." She closed her eyes like one walking into fire.

"Perhaps next year, you will grace me with your favor," he said, his dark eyes glinting like the flash of a blade. "By then, you might very well be my betrothed."

Betrothed. She burned sanguine at the word.

"Give him your favor, Rowen," said her father.

Rowen had known for some time that her father intended her for Edmund. The man possessed some wealth from a lifetime of winning tourneys. She was not keen on the idea, for although Edmund was still considered a youth by having never married, the man was in his thirty-eighth year.

"Rowen," her father said, reminding her.

Obediently, she untied the ribbon binding the red sleeve of her dress and slid it down and off, exposing the gauzy chemise beneath.

In her mind, her life with Edmund stretched before her. She could see herself organizing his household and sharing his bed. She imagined growing heavy with his child. Twisting her sleeve into a circle and tying the ends together, she pushed the thoughts from her mind. She went to the railing and waited for Edmund to raise the tip of his lance, and when he did, she sent the ring down to where it settled on his wrist.

Edmund slid his helm over his head. He guided his horse to the starting position at the top of the lists.

Roland shook his head, clenching his arms in a knot over his chest. "Foul work, Father."

"A fine match," corrected Ivin, "which we will announce after Edmund becomes the champion for the third year in a row."

"Edmund is at once too old and too young for Rowen."

Wearily, Ivin rubbed his temple. "Dare I ask?"

"He will steal her youth before making her a widow."

Lost in the world of her thoughts, Rowen could see the many paths of her life being overrun with vines and brambles. They had been writing her story without her for some time. Like so many women of whom the troubadours sang, she feared she would be lost beneath her duty. Lady, wife, mother. She would become a creature as faceless and ephemeral as the dolls she weaved out of rags.

The knight marshals rode out in their livery coats, shimmering with the gold and green colors of the Baron's house. The season had been dry, so the grass was dead, and dust clouds billowed under their horses' hooves. The marshals slowed their steeds, and each spoke to the people on the nearest border of the stands.

Across the lists, on the dais of the Baron, Rowen found Amarys's face again. It amazed her that her friend could remain so engrossed with nothing at all going on. She followed her line of sight. Her friend was not even looking at the men competing. Chewing the tip of her thumb, Amarys leered at a red-headed youth who had been eliminated and was using a ladle to pour water down his throat. The man's tunic had gone sheer from sweat—a result of his exertion.

A horn played a bending note, and the squires attended the racks of lances on the perimeter. There would be three passes, and each knight would carry a lance of brittle wood and try to burst it against the other man's shield.

"I have to piss," said Roland, downing more ale and taking his tankard with him.

"Good people!" bellowed a marshal, his mouth opening wide enough to swallow a pumpkin. "The joust has eliminated all but four men: the champion of last year's tourney, Sir Edmund le Noir, our Baron's nephew, Sir Harlowe de Rohan, an esteemed knight and defender of our township, Sir Jean de Rieux, and hailing from Nantes, Sir

Michel le Juste."

Rowen looked at her father. "Who do you think will win?"

"Our man, of course," he returned without pause.

"But the others are much younger than him. And Harlowe is the size of a giant."

Ivin was deep in his cups, having just finished his sixth tankard of ale. He answered, "This is a game of technique, child, not of brute force."

Rowen did not understand how that could be true with two forces colliding at full speed, but she could sense that any further questions would provoke her father's anger.

Edmund and Harlowe rode out on horseback, their shields catching the torchlight. All knights had a unique salute when they approached any contest of arms, and Edmund and Harlowe did theirs now as they passed either side of the lists. A chorus of voices shouted belligerently for each of them.

Harlowe wore a great deal of boiled leather. Being a bigger man than Edmund, he sported a heavier lance painted red and gold. It might as well have been a battering ram. Edmund's lances were painted black with a long red line traveling down their length. There were cheers for both men, though it did not escape Rowen's notice that Amarys made a point of not clapping.

"Joust!" shouted the knight marshals.

Each man spurred his horse and vaulted down the long runway, tilting at one another with such force as could break through a castle wall. Rowen did not breathe until their lances burst. Splinters flew in all directions. Three points each, and neither man was rattled. Again, they charged. The horses flew without fear, trampling a path that quaked the foundations of the dais. Lances burst again like sparks of lightning. Edmund's expertise lent itself to his agility with a lighter, swifter lance. Harlowe checked him, though, by force alone. In the final pass, they tied again.

To break the tie, both men dismounted and drew their blades. Edmund proved to be the superior swordsman. A few minutes into hand-to-hand combat, Edmund's sword slid under Harlowe's helm, carrying it off and slicing him across the neck. Blood sprayed. The crowd sighed.

"Ha! What did I tell you?" cried Ivin, clapping his hands.

Harlowe had not even flinched at the sight of his own blood. He left his helm in the grass and threw his gauntlet beside it.

Rowen had never seen such a thing. She had only heard of it in songs. Throwing down a gauntlet laid a challenge. Fight to the death or live with your shame and yield. Rowen could sense Edmund's apprehension. The danger was palpable, the circumstances daunting. Refusing a duel was illegal. He would be disqualified. Engaging in one, though, was unethical and would win him enemies. Should Edmund kill this young man, Baron Clement's—his liege lord's—nephew, he would invite the wrath of the landed gentry. Should he throw the tournament, his career might well be over.

"Do not take it up!" shouted Ivin, beating the rail with his fist.

"Where is your courage now, le Noir?" demanded Harlowe.

Rowen did not know whether to scream or hold her composure. Gripped by indecision, she bore witness in silence as Edmund removed his helm and thrust it down beside Harlowe's.

"I will not take your life," said Edmund. "But I will have your sword hand, pup."

The people in the stands thundered for blood. Their howls reached a crescendo as Edmund took up the gauntlet and lifted it high.

"Papa," whispered Rowen. "Is there nothing we can do?"

"Pray for him," said Ivin.

"Where is Roland?" She looked over her shoulder, but the throngs of spectators in the stands obscured her vision on either side of the dais.

The men paced in a circle, saluting one another with a slash of their swords. Harlowe bled from the wound on his neck but seemed not to care. They were only playing at first, exchanging clever tricks of steel. Edmund had a superior strategy, quickly gaining the upper hand and stealing more and more ground.

"He has him," said Ivin.

Rowen began to hope. Across the lists, she saw her friend, Amarys, covering her eyes, not for fear, but in resignation. "Wait," Rowen uttered, rising from her chair, rising and stepping forth. She could see it, too. It was all written out before her in the chain of their footwork.

Reeling back on the right, Harlowe swapped his sword hand and came in from Edmund's left.

Edmund went to guard the wrong side, and in one elegant throw, Harlowe swept the head from his shoulders. How he soared, his raven locks trailing, his gentle but determined eyes suspended in a look of astonishment. Rowen watched Edmund's head hit the dirt. Like a ball, it tumbled.

The carnage shocked the crowd, and all around, the sounds of horror and disgust reeled. Nobody liked wasting good men for summer games. They booed and moaned.

Rowen could not look away as Edmund's neck bloomed like a rose. His wrist still bore her favor. The medics ran in with a large canvas tarp, laying it flat and hoisting the man onto it in all his armor. One of them grabbed his head, laying it on his abdomen. Rowen shut her eyes.

The people continued to jeer at Harlowe. Blinking, Rowen saw her surroundings fade away. The torchlight seemed to dim, the world shrinking around her. She hardly remembered she was at a joust. She clasped her hand over her absent sleeve.

"Sir Edmund," she whispered.

"Look away," said Ivin.

He was dead, his body mutilated. When the whole of mankind went before God on the Day of Reckoning, how would Edmund find his way with no eyes to see?

The next combatants rode into the lists, performing the same ritual of playing to each side of the runway: Michel le Juste, a career tourney knight, and Jean, a knight who lived locally. The people did not cheer. An unsteady silence lingered.

As the horses tore down the lists and the knights broke their lances on each other's shields, the joust looked like a game again. Michel and Jean were careful with each other's bodies. Before their second pass, Jean's helm was askew, and Michel tapped his lance to his own helm to alert him. That moment spoke to what chivalry was supposed to be: something like love. Chivalry, for Rowen, was the most potent brotherhood in existence. She looked to find her own brother, whose chair still lay empty.

"I must find Roland." Rowen held the front of her skirt, her beaded belt rustling as she descended the steps of the dais. Ivin did not move to stop her.

Below the stairs, a group of men laughed raucously. One of them backed into Rowen, spilling ale over the hem of her skirt. She kept moving, passing a pair of peasants, one of whom was lacing a daisy chain around the other's wrist. Further back, a dense crowd gathered around a pair of half-naked, filth-covered youths who were each trying with all their might to pull a plow in the direction of the stables. One of them collapsed in exhaustion, crying out for water. Some men splashed him with a bucket and shouted for him to go faster.

Rowen found her brother next to a vat of beer. He was too busy to notice her, though, for he was leaning over some little peasant.

"Say it again," the girl said, sipping her ale.

"Habibi."

"Habibi," she repeated slowly, drawing out the vowels. "Saracinois is very pretty."

"You should hear it put to music," said Roland. "Perhaps I'll sing to you later." He traced a finger up her forearm.

The girl, who was petite in stature but shapely, lowered her ale and sighed. Or was it a moan? She came up on her toes and licked Roland's mouth. Not kissed. Licked. Like one cleaning his teeth, her tongue curled like a leaf. She giggled, and Roland clasped his arm around her waist. The girl's hand went limp, spilling her drink. Their eyes closed, and it appeared that all they wanted next was to taste each other's breath.

Rowen mustered her resolve. "Roland!" she called. The peasant girl ripped away from him and stole off in another direction.

Roland clamped his lips tight, shaking his head in frustration. "What is it, Rowen?"

"Did you not see?"

He was silent. Rowen could tell he had not seen anything, but his suspicions were taking shape.

"Edmund has perished," she finished. "Harlowe has killed him."

Roland stared at her, his initial shock turning stoic and numb. He took a deep breath, tilting his face skyward as he let this truth wash over him.

In a rage, he kicked over the bench with the vat, leaking its contents and spilling the pewter mugs. The hushed witness of the other revelers enclosed them. They made him remember himself.

"I despise these games."

Rowen hardly knew what to say.

Annoyed by her silence, Roland picked up his mug and left. "Find me later."

Rowen returned to the dais and asked her father who had won the last joust. It had been Michel.

The final joust should have started already, but something had delayed it. It had nothing to do with Harlowe's wound, which the medics had already stitched. Michel and Harlowe, both already mounted, waited in the lists as the knight marshals discussed something with the Baron.

Rowen wondered about that girl Roland had kissed. What kind of girl was that? Noble girls could not do such a thing with their tongues. Rowen tried it, touching the front of her teeth with the tip of her tongue. Her tongue moved more like a hinge than a scroll.

"What are you doing?" asked Ivin.

"Nothing," she said, closing her mouth.

"Did you find Roland?"

"Yes, he is upset by the news of Edmund."

Ivin nodded. More time passed. Then, the knight marshals crossed the lists to approach their family.

"Sire," said one of them. "The Baron agrees to your terms."

"Good. Thank you."

Terms? Rowen looked at her father sharply.

"His only concern is for the crowd. They will require a fair conclusion to tonight's festivities."

Ivin leaned forward, nodding. "So bring back the man who scored the highest but did not advance into the final round. Let him joust Michel for the tourney crown. He is Erec of Avenport, a squire in Clement's retinue."

"Yes, Monseigneur. Erec is a Favourite in Rieux. I will convey your message."

The knight marshals returned to the Baron.

"Father, what has happened?"

"Sir Harlowe of Rohan has broken the tournament rules by bringing an illegal weapon. At the beginning of the tournament, all weapons were inspected and approved to ensure they were blunted. Harlowe's sword was never passed. That is why it was sharp enough to cut through Edmund's spine in a single stroke. For this reason, I have demanded that Harlowe be disqualified."

"Will this not sow discord with the Baron?"

Ivin leaned his head into his hand, closing his eyes and moaning. "His nephew has cost me. We might have seen you married by the Spring. Now, Sir Edmund's lands will go to Clement."

Rowen moved her head in agreement, though in truth, she found it unsavory to lament the loss of a dead man's property. There came another back and forth with the knight marshals.

"It is agreed, Sire. Baron Clement sends his apologies and promises his nephew will atone."

"Thank you."

The knight marshals looked relieved for the first time since the negotiations began. They announced the bad news to the people, dismissing Harlowe, and inviting Erec to joust in his place.

From the stands, Rowen heard a cacophony of high-pitched screams for this Erec of Avenport when he rode in unexpectedly and held his lance aloft. It was the redhead from before, that man whose form had so captivated Lady Amarys. He looked glorious now. Herculean, even. Yes, he was long of limb, and his muscles filled every curvature of his armor, but his physical beauty was hardly what won the crowd. It was his spirit. He was beaming to have returned to the lists and shared his joy with a roar of pure happiness that left everyone jumping and cheering his name.

"Ad Deum," whispered Rowen, her skin tingling when she saw how the women of Rieux came alive for this man.

At the order of the marshals, the chevaliers advanced down the lists. In the first pass, both burst their lances on each other's shields. One cluster of men in the crowd pounded their fists and stomped in the stands, chanting, "Erec of Avenport, Clement's man, second son of the red wolf clan." Rowen had no idea what it meant, but she saw Roland among them. He glowed with the fires of inebriation.

In the second pass, Erec faltered, dropping his lance and scoring no points, while Sir Michel le Juste scored two for having split his lance tip. Two points behind, Erec rode to the start of the runway and readied himself for the final pass. Much of the crowd was invested in Erec winning, for he had chased away the dark clouds of

Harlowe's brutality. A piper began to play the "Melodie d'Avenport."

The final pass began, hooves hammering the ground like the trill of a tambourine. Erec stood in the stirrups at the last moment before collision, landing his lance on Michel so it struck the gorget protecting his throat. The hit knocked Michel sideways. He flew from his horse. His body clattered as it rolled in the dust. The horse kept running, finishing the pass and returning to its gate.

Michel removed his helm, gasping for breath before clutching his lance and thrusting it away from himself as a signal of his yield. The people leapt to their feet in riotous applause. Erec dismounted, helping his opponent up and brushing him off. They patted each other's shoulders as a sign of respect, and Michel left on foot with his squire.

One of the knight marshals came to meet Erec on the field, taking his hand and raising it high. "Our champion!" As the cheers and whistles rang out in celebration, Clement came down from his dais, laying a hand on Erec's pauldron.

When the applause began to ebb, Clement spoke to his people. "I want to congratulate this young man who holds the whole heart of Rieux this night. Erec of Avenport, tonight you will keep vigil and be knighted on the morrow."

Erec bowed his head courteously, thanking the Baron. The people showed their approval with another swell of applause. A hush fell over the crowd as the Baron's daughter stood and came down from the dais. Amarys, Maid of Rieux, descended like a specter of the otherworld, holding a wreath of laurel leaves. Her eyes were the color of the water in Antioch, brighter than handfuls of green and blue sea glass. Her gaze, possessing the sharpness of a dagger's edge, had the power to peel back the layers of one's soul. And Rowen could feel this intensity now, for her friend was looking right at her.

"My daughter, Amarys," announced Clement. "These past two years, I have received many marriage offers concerning her. Because I value her safety and hold high esteem for the prowess and piety of knights, I have decided to give her hand in marriage to he who wins the summer tourney..."

Erec brightened at those words.

Then, Clement finished, "...in one year's time." Erec subdued his exuberance, lowering his head.

"Next year, we will host a special melee for unmarried knights. The esteemed lords of this Barony and I will work to determine the most worthy candidate. Through competition and deliberation, together with God, we will choose her husband."

Erec knelt before her. He unsheathed his sword and plunged it into the earth at her feet. He bowed his head, and said, "It is my life's honor to serve you and your family."

Amarys crowned him. "Worthy knight," she said, but she was looking beyond him across the lists. Her eyes remained fixed on Rowen.

Rowen signaled to Amarys with a hand gesture that nearly mirrored her signature salute, a movement that spilled from her heart and swept over her left shoulder. Amarys copied the gesture, her elegant hand dividing the air like the wing of a dove.

"I must go," Rowen told her father, slipping away before he could inquire as to why.

Part of the magic of a summer tourney was how people broke away from routine. Noble sons and daughters could steal away from their families and servants long enough to run and play and be themselves. A maid might meet her true love on the other side of a lyre. A man might become a knight. And best of all, a highborn lady might steal away for long enough to enjoy the private company of her dearest friend.

Rowen's heart thrummed in her chest as she ran toward the barracks. As she had hoped, they were abandoned. Every knight and squire remained on the field, leaving the place empty and full of toys. Rowen lit the chambersticks within, illuminating every corner of the timbered hall. Wooden benches lined the walls between two empty fireplaces. In the center of one wall, an alcove housed a statue of Mary with her hands folded over her heart. Weapons racks lay stacked with polearms, broadswords, flails, and all manner of menacing tools. Running down the center of the room, a row of hay-stuffed pells were weighed down with bags of sand, practically begging to be struck. Rowen grabbed a wooden practice sword and struck a pell with force. Her core burned as it channeled power into every whiplike movement. A minute later, her friend Amarys came dashing in, whirling to check that nobody was behind her.

"It worked!" Amarys panted. "I knew the barracks would be empty!"

"Amarys!" Rowen embraced her, kissing her cheeks. She so loved to say her companion's name. The name whistled against the roof of the mouth, crisp as an apple sliced thin. Amarys was like the crest of a sunrise, a sound like phlogiston and fire, fleeting. Amarys banished all wickedness, baptizing the soul anew each time she was invoked. She was every nameless lady of song, christened at last.

"How much trouble will you be in on the morrow, my rose?"

"My father is so drunk; it is more likely he will hide from me in shame," said Rowen. "Pray tell, how did you slip your maids?"

"I'm not sure that I did."

Rowen grabbed a practice sword for her friend. They saluted and began their play. Rowen tried cleverly for Amarys's left shoulder, but she parried. "Are we not going to talk about what happened out there?"

"I'd rather not," said Rowen, knowing what she meant by the severity of her expression.

They circled, surmising the other's readiness.

"Dueling is a wretched business," said Amarys. "My father said Edmund would not have been charged had he refused the challenge."

"Sir Edmund was an honorable man." Rowen feinted a strike on the right and then went for the left, landing what she had believed to be a light blow.

"Ow!" Amarys quacked, using her sword's flat edge to deliver a smack on Rowen's bottom.

Rowen laughed. "Got you."

"That hurt."

"That was soft."

"Oh?" Amarys raised her eyebrows, saluting in turn.

They shared another bout, and this time, Rowen carried on deflecting Amarys's attacks instead of deliberately ending the exchange.

"Have you nothing more to say than that?" asked Amarys.

"About what?"

"Edmund."

"I hardly knew him." Rowen smacked Amarys's sword away with excessive force.

14

"But he wore your favor."

Rowen considered her response carefully, allowing her muscle memory to carry her through with the sword. "I hardly knew him," she repeated, for it was true. They had never shared more than a few pleasantries in all her years of holding his acquaintance. She pitied him for having died. She pitied Roland as well, knowing he would grieve bitterly.

"There is something so intimate in wearing a woman's favor," said Amarys. "The way one's lance penetrates and claims the trophy is not unlike how a man opens a woman on her wedding night."

"What would you know of such a thing?"

"I am no child." Amarys prodded Rowen in the ribs, which caught her by surprise. "Touché!"

"You're getting better," said Rowen, relinquishing her sword to the rack. She was not out of breath or exhausted at all, but her head was spinning, and her throat had become suddenly dry. "I require some repose."

"You look flustered."

"You are more flustering than most."

"I am a curious person. Aren't you curious about things? Men's bodies? Your own?" A demure smile pulled at the corner of her mouth. "Have you never explored yourself?" she asked.

Rowen blinked. She shook her head, even though she had hovered above a mirror once out of sheer curiosity. She took Amarys's sword and put it away. "Have you?"

"When all the house has gone to bed, and at last, I am alone with God, I sometimes imagine I am giving myself to Him."

Rowen took a seat on a wooden bench where the Virgin Mary could not see her. Amarys sat beside her, taking her by the hand. She folded her thumb in under Rowen's other fingers, lightly caressing the crease between them.

"I start like this and think of Erec of Avenport. Sometimes, I try this." She slid her index finger through the crease, turning it and caressing Rowen's palm on the inside of her folded hand.

Rowen felt seared by fire. "You have supplanted prayer with the gravest sin."

"Not sin! God fashioned this body that I might enjoy it, did He not? And so I honor

Him with my pleasure."

"How can you know it is God and not some airy interloper?" whispered Rowen.

"Do you speak of incubi? I thought you were a rational creature!"

"I speak of the devil himself."

Amarys narrowed her eyes. Her playful smile remained, but she was mildly vexed. Rowen did not mean to brew conflict between them. She conceded, "You understand flights of the heart that are foreign to me. I have never been in love, nor wished to be. Earlier this night, I saw my brother with a common girl. They were kissing. And this girl did the strangest thing with her tongue."

"What was it?"

"She licked his mouth—I mean—his teeth. Like so." Rowen tried to replicate the movement by curling her index finger. Amarys burst out laughing. She took Rowen's hand once more.

"Show me."

"I cannot. My tongue will not do that."

"Nonsense! Look. Take the tip of your tongue–" Amarys stuck out her tongue and waggled it wickedly between her teeth.

Rowen's composure cracked.

"Don't laugh!" said Amarys. "Just show me." Amarys's face came very close to Rowen's.

Rowen's giggles tapered off. Instinctively, she leaned away. "You mean to kiss you?"

"Yes! Why not?"

"My lips belong only to my future husband."

Amarys reasoned, "So as to please our future husbands, it is necessary that we practice our technique."

Rowen faced her now. She closed her eyes, leaned toward her, and waited. Her heart fluttered as she felt Amarys's lips against her own. Amarys smelled so sweetly of roses and apples, and her mouth was impossibly soft. A heavenly light seemed to envelop them, providing rapturous warmth.

"Was it like that?" asked Amarys.

"Nothing like that," said Rowen, her skin tingling. "More like this." She opened her mouth and traced the edge of her friend's teeth with her tongue.

She broke away when she heard the chinking armor on the other side of the wall. "We should stop. I am prone to unchaste thoughts."

"Of your future husband?"

"Yes," said Rowen immediately, though that wasn't it.

"Do not think of him." Amarys swept Rowen's hair to one side, trailing her thumb down her clavicle. Rowen felt her nipples hardening. "Tell me what I taste like."

Before they could continue their practice, footsteps thundered on the other side of the wall. The ladies retreated to the shadows of a bunk and peered out from behind the corner.

A man in armor came through, slamming his helm to the ground and unleashing a sound that was feral and chilling. It was the man who had been disqualified in the joust. Amarys jumped at the sound of metal and mail colliding with wood. Rowen held her fast. "It is my cousin," whispered Amarys. "We must hide."

CHAPTER 2

Rowen and Amarys could see the heir of Rohan pacing like a beast in a cage, balling his hands into fists, and mumbling incoherently to himself.

"Will he not wax wroth to find us spying on him?" asked Rowen.

"Shh."

"Those cunts!" shouted Harlowe. He ripped his padded coif from his head and pressed it to his eyes. Rowen could feel Amarys physically lurch, but Harlowe was not yelling at them. He had noticed the altar to the Virgin Mary.

In his rage, he backhanded the Holy Mother so hard that the stone crumbled from the waist up. Rowen held her breath, holding back a sob at the sight of such sacrilege. Amarys looked up, shaking her head with a fierceness that said under no condition should they reveal themselves.

"Who's there?" asked Harlowe. "Someone lit these candles."

Rowen stepped forward into the light, holding a downward gaze. "It was me." She was not afraid of Harlowe. She knew how to behave in the presence of violent men, having lived so long with her father. Amarys recoiled deeper into the dark.

"You are Sir Ivin's fae-born brat, are you not?"

Rowen looked up, brandishing the small smile of a mild maiden. "Not fae, Sire. My mother was a Turk."

19

She could see him well now. His hair, cropped close to his large head, was the color of wet sand. He was broad-featured and had an immense chin and thick, lustrous brows. He might have looked pleasing if not for his unyielding sneer.

Rowen cast her eyes downward once more. Beneath the veneer of her upright ladyship lurked the secret world of demons and fae. It was encoded in the foreign features she had inherited from her mother, traits hardly taken to account in Languedoc or Iberia but certainly noticed and remarked upon in Brittany. The place of her birth was as strange to the duchy as Avalon itself. And it was equally strange to her, for she had not lived there long enough to remember it in detail. Antioch felt like a short prologue to the action of her life, its pages mottled with age.

"What are you called?"

"Rowen," she answered.

"Is that Persian?"

"French." Rowen went to sit beside him, pulling the loose part of her hair over one shoulder and braiding it. "I am of La Flèche-de Beaugency who once ruled these lands."

"I know. Your father was with Guy de Lusignan at Acre. He served in King Richard's private guard."

"Our mighty lion."

"Is the story true? The King was killed in Châlus by a boy no older than twelve?"

"That is how my father tells it."

"I have heard it said that the king had the boy brought before him in order to congratulate him for having slain the lionheart. Before his death, he settled coin upon the lad."

"No, Sir Harlowe. The boy was flayed alive. My father saw to that."

Harlowe's whole demeanor had changed. He was sitting on one of the benches now, leaning back on one hand and producing a sneer that might as well have been his best attempt at a smile. She had projected what she assumed would look like a kindred spirit to him, doing whatever it took to usher him away.

"You should meet my father. He is just outside."

"Your father loathes me. I killed his knight."

"You killed my knight, too, but exchanging words allows us to put aside our grievances."

Harlowe searched her face. "What was he to you?"

"It no longer matters."

Harlowe knelt, unsheathing his sword and presenting the mass of steel. The blade had been wiped down, but it still held the stain of Edmund's blood. He laid the metal into her hands. "Can you forgive what I have done?"

"I forgive all things done in the lists."

"Show me. Kiss the steel, and I will believe you."

Rowen locked eyes with him. He was serious. Closing her eyes, she lifted the sword to her lips. Then, she returned his blade to him and reiterated, "I forgive you."

He smiled with something of the devil in his eyes. "Most gracious lady."

"Will you come and meet my father?"

"I will."

Together, they rose.

"If I may, I would ask a favor," she said.

"What is it?"

"Will you leave out the detail of where you found me?"

Harlowe's steel sighed as it slid back into its sheath. "Assuredly. I am good at keeping secrets." Something about the way he said it made Rowen's skin prickle.

Outside, Ivin and Clement relived the highlights of prior tournaments, gesturing and speaking boisterously. Rowen relinquished Harlowe to their suddenly silent reception.

"Sir Ivin La Flèche-de Beaugency," said Harlowe, bowing his head. "I regret my actions this evening. I deserved to be disqualified and worse. Your daughter is very noble, Sir, for she summoned me here to make peace with you. Her goodwill compels me to submit myself to your judgment. Tell me what I can do to make amends."

Ivin looked at Clement whose arms were so tightly folded that he looked like a hare bound for roasting. Ivin looked at Roland whose countenance was twisted and hard. Everyone waited for him to speak, and it came as a great surprise and relief to all but Roland when the old knight said, "Give us time, Sir Harlowe, and we will speak again another day."

"You cannot mean this," Roland hissed under his breath.

"You have cost us," said Ivin, signaling his son to hold. "Edmund was my son's instructor, my daughter's suitor. He would have paid a handsome bride price and given her a home in Rieux. I could have kept my grandchildren close."

"Whatever the scale of this loss, I will compensate you."

"We do not want your coin!" interjected Roland. "Come on, Rowen. Let us find some better company than this."

"See your sister home, Roland. The evening waxes ever sinful." Ivin then proceeded to discuss the matter of compensation with Harlowe.

Roland hooked his sister by the arm, eager to be rid of their father. As they walked, they bowed their heads to a family acquaintance, the lord and lady of Montfort. The darkening night obscured the ground where dewy earth seeped through Rowen's cloth shoes. She could smell the fortified wine on Roland's breath as he spoke.

"We need to find some revels." He spoke in the Saracinois so others would not understand him. They were not permitted to speak the language of the Arab tribes in their father's presence, but they often communicated this way when he was not around.

"I met with Amarys," said Rowen.

"Is she about? I would like to say hello."

"You will go nowhere near my friends." Rowen lacked the vocabulary to go on in Saracinois, so she reduced her voice to a whisper and said everything else in the langue d'oïl. "Your behavior this evening was reckless and uncouth. Since when are you Roland, the despoiler of maidens?"

Roland patted his sister's forearm. "Different rules apply with common folk."

"Do they? Does that girl's father know she's drinking ale and kissing you?"

Roland continued speaking in Saracinois, not caring if his sister failed to keep up. She could understand him, but it vexed her all the same. "Father drowns you in his world of violence and has taught you nothing of love. Let me show you what a tournament is really about!"

He pulled her arm, leading her in the direction of the barracks. "I know a knight who came from the isle. No one will know us in his camp. And the men in his retinue throw excellent parties."

"Someone from Rieux may be in attendance and recognize us."

Roland groaned, whirling away to face her head-on. He clasped her shoulders and said, "You are so careful; it is a wonder you take the risk of drawing breath! Come on. You will borrow my clothes, and we will call you Wendel."

"Wendel? I would not wish the name Wendel on my worst enemy. Could I not have a nicer name, like Hal or Reynald?"

"Those names are far too stalwart. They will draw attention to you. No, you are Wendel, the shepherd's boy. You go only by Wendel and have few interests beyond drinking and swaying to music."

They reached the barracks. Although Roland had a bunk, he never slept there, living so close to home. When Roland saw the broken statue of Mary, he cursed under his breath.

"Drunken bastards."

"It was Harlowe."

"The worst of them. Here, try these." Roland handed Rowen a hessian sack. Inside, she found a pair of linen hose and a sweat-stained shirt that left much to be desired. Still, she had never been to a camp party before, so she put on her clothes without complaining.

As she began to change behind the wall of the bunk, she asked, "Can you tell me what you know of Harlowe?"

"He is the piece of shit who killed Edmund. That is all I need to know."

Rowen struggled with the drawstring on the braies, squeezing it as tight as it would go to fit her waist and keep the hose snug above her hips. "I think Amarys is afraid of him."

"She is wise to keep her distance."

"He could never get away with hurting her, right? It would start a war between Clement and his late wife's brother."

"A war?" Roland coughed up a chuckle. "There's an idea. It depends on the damage. Abuse of the spirit has no legal repercussions. Perhaps he has already threatened or insulted her. He could bruise her anywhere but her face and get away with a mere scolding."

Rowen finished pulling on the shirt and came out into the candlelight. "What if he killed her?"

Roland patted his sister's arm in a kind of mocking consolation. "Clement has other daughters."

Rowen lowered her gaze, feeling queasy. Her brother draped a thin woolen capelet across her shoulders to add mass.

"Some financial compensation would be negotiated. Now, if he ravished her, the family would simply make them marry. Hardly a punishment since Amarys and Harlowe are expected to marry anyhow."

Rowen nearly jumped out of her skin when she heard Amarys groan aloud. "How is one to listen in when you insist on speaking in your Saracen tongue!" Amarys emerged from the shadows of a bunk.

"Amarys!" cried Rowen. "What are you still doing here?"

"Spying, obviously. I heard my cousin's name and mine. What are you plotting?"

"Nothing. Why haven't you returned to your ladies?"

"I was waiting for the path outside to clear." Her eyes traveled up Roland's length and lingered on his face. "Good evening, Roland."

Roland gave a nod. "Maid of Rieux."

"No need for formalities." Amarys examined Rowen, her brow furrowing. "Why have you dressed my lady so?"

To hear Amarys take possession of her made Rowen's blood warm.

Roland answered her, "Do not concern yourself with our antics."

"I have another question," she returned. "What say you of Harlowe?"

"Only that you may have to marry him if he wins next year's tourney, assuming he does not behead anyone else. As your husband, he would inherit the part of Rieux that is ours by right."

Amarys's laughter caught in her throat. "Bold words! You would never speak so if my father were here."

"It would surprise you how my tongue flies," said Roland.

Rowen could feel them connecting. The pot had found its lid. "Roland. Mind your words in the presence of a lady."

"She comes from a line of marauders, Rowen. Her chateau was built with our family's plundered wealth."

Amarys stepped close enough to him that it made Rowen feel pressed in upon.

24

She had the bearing of a conqueror as she said, "My people have held these lands longer than our fathers have been alive."

"When my father saved the life of the Lionheart—"

"—a tale you love to recount—"

Roland raised his voice over hers. "—Our gracious king restored these lands to him, and your father only yielded half."

"You got the manor. You got the forest. Half the town. Your family even owns the place where my mother is buried."

"Your father holds the best farmland, though, and profits immensely. Had King Richard lived, he would have sent his army to see you Norman dogs brought to heel. Instead, my family must scrape by while yours erects castles and hosts tournaments."

"What is it that you want, Roland? My head on a pike?" Amarys trailed a finger along the length of his collarbone. His eyebrows lifted ever so slightly. It was not easy to surprise him, but she had done it in a single stroke. "Perhaps you'll settle for my hand."

Roland choked on a laugh, stepping back from her. "I do not want your hand, Amarys."

"No. Just to breach the walls of my chateau."

Roland covered his smile with his fist. Rowen could not glean what amused him so. Was Amarys in on the joke?

"I do not want that either. For the gate is always open."

Rowen's guts churned. His teasing went too far, an effect of too much ale. But Amarys only smiled more broadly. She laughed beyond all sense, pivoting to lean against Rowen.

Rowen held her arm. "Never mind what my brother says. He is no knight. He cannot compete."

Roland took a swig from his cup. "Oh, yes. Can you imagine?" Roland cleared his throat and set down his ale. He stood upon the bench. "We hereby present the hand of Lady Amarys to the most hated man in the county: Roland the Turk!" He leaped to another bench, bowing and opening his arms to his imaginary admirers. "Thank you, my good people! I am pleased to announce that my bride and I will be converting to

25

Islam."

Amarys's mirth crinkled her eyes. "May I never eat pork again!"

Roland went on articulating to his imaginary audience, "We leave at once for Jerusalem, where the prophet ascended to Mount Olympus and performed many miracles before the gods. When we return, we will begin the construction of a university that teaches the philosophies of Avicenna and the poetics of Sappho."

Rowen snagged his sleeve and pulled him down from the bench. "Enough!" she insisted, though she smiled in spite of herself. "We must away. And Amarys, you must return to your ladies."

"Yes, my rose," said Amarys, giggling. "We will say goodnight before your brother is arrested for heresy." She glanced at Roland one last time before she slipped from the barracks. Rowen considered the idea of betrothal. Marrying Amarys to her brother might be the only way to keep her.

"With me!" cried Roland as he ducked out of the barracks. Rowen, noticing a smell of mildew and body odor, sniffed the edge of her sleeve. Roland's clothes were in dire need of laundering. It added to the masquerade, but at what cost?

Flea-bitten and pungent, Wendel, the shepherd's son, headed out under the veil of darkness, eager for adventure.

The night teemed with possibilities as the twins set off across the green. Roland skipped, springing from one leg to another, spinning mid-vault and calling for Rowen to keep up. His friend Willem intercepted them.

"Coocooricoo!" he trilled as he slammed into Roland, nearly knocking him over. Laughing, he hung from Roland's shoulder, slurring, "Have a drink with me." Willem was an even slighter lad than Roland, effeminate and freckled all over. His smile always reminded Rowen of a child's because it was so unguarded.

Willem squeezed a wineskin into Roland's maw. He was about to offer Rowen some until he saw who she was. "Why is Rowen wearing your dirty laundry?"

"I want her to see what people are like outside of court," said Roland. "Meet Wendel, the Shepherd's son!"

Willem sucked his upper lip, frowning at Rowen. "He needs a hat." Willem removed his cap and stuffed Rowen's hair into its folds, securing the strings at the base. "Better."

"I feel stupid," said Rowen.

"Lean into it, sheep-plugger," advised Willem, chuckling like a toad.

Willem and the twins set out toward the English camp. They passed a bard playing songs of the journey to Jerusalem. He sang of the glory of the Franks who settled the Christian states, the place of the twins' birth. Dressed in men's garb, Rowen felt like she could go anywhere and talk to anyone. There was a difference in how people moved aside to let her pass.

Walls of painted canvas connected the posts demarcating the perimeter of the encampment. The images of heraldry adorned each panel. Rowen's heart ignited at the idea of walking into a foreign camp like she had every right. She stalled, basking in the delight of it all.

"Come on, Wendel!" urged Willem.

At the gate, they were greeted by a man with long black curls that came down to his waist. He held a black scepter, which he touched to Rowen's chin, pulling down the capelet to see her throat.

"What have we here," he said, his teeth shining. "A runaway princess?"

Rowen swallowed.

"Relax, child. I am not here to tell a girl what to do, only to ensure that everyone going in is to the standard." The gatekeeper turned her face with the ball tip of his staff. "And you are indeed a beauty. Enjoy your evening." Roland clutched his sister's hand, hurrying inside before the next group of people came up behind them. They followed Willem as the lad swaggered through an aisle of torches. Inside, a crowd of people swayed to the music of strings and drums, all circling a large bonfire. A man played a vielle, weaving his bow back and forth over the strings. The firelight flickered across his green foliate mask. As the man made eye contact with Rowen, his lips drew back around a smile.

"They can all tell I am not a boy," she whispered.

"How do you know?" asked Roland.

Rowen indicated the musician, whose eyes conveyed a certain hunger.

"Oh, that? That's nothing."

"What's nothing?" asked Willem, horning in.

"A musician is making eyes at Wendel here. And he's confused."

Willem guffawed, his hand whacking Rowen's back. "Oh, lamb. He could be looking at any one of us. Usually, it is Roland the boys favor."

"Is coveting a member of your own sex not a grave sin?"

"It is assuredly, but this is a tourney," said Willem, though that hardly sufficed to clear Rowen's confusion. Willem leaned in, whispering, "Let's just say none of these men are missing their wives."

Roland went to the musician, tracing his fingertips across the man's abdomen as he passed. Their eyes locked in a gaze of mutual desire, and Roland grinned over his shoulder at Rowen.

Willem stifled a laugh, leaning on Rowen and shaking her up a bit.

"Oh, come now! He's only teasing!"

"Does Roland lie with men?"

"I would not be surprised if he dabbled while he was in Toulouse."

Rowen went after her brother, striving to get Willem's voice out of her head. The crowd thickened as people began to dance, clasping hands and moving in a line around the fire. The musician played to a quicker tempo, his vielle generating a sound like something between a howl and a beehive. Rowen ducked between the dancers. She found Roland filling his tankard with a stranger's golden wine. This fair-haired fellow was shirtless, many pouches strung to the belt holding up his striped hose. He sat on a narrow wooden chair with Roland supine on the ground before him. He offered a cup to Rowen, for which she thanked him. The mildest hint of sage lingered in the mead.

Rowen plopped down on the ground on the other side of the fair-haired stranger. She gazed at the people in the crowd like one seeing the world for the first time. Many of the men went bare-chested; Rowen had never seen so much of the male anatomy. Some bodies were densely corded with muscle, others wiry and lean, some with guts that hung over their belts, some with gray hair, and others as hairless as babes.

Another body stood out, an undulating shape clad in gauze ribbons. A dancer rolled her hips for the pleasure of all who watched her, draping her arms about herself and others as though these limbs were the tendrils of a flame. Threading her belt were tiny bells that whispered when she moved. The sight of her navel made Rowen feel scandalized, and as much as she knew she should look away, she could not resist watching.

As one man backed into another, a brawl broke out between them. The stumble had been unintentional, but both were so eager to fight that it became their present truth that they must destroy the other. The crowd swelled around them, and the dancer was lost.

Rowen wanted to ask Roland a question, but when she looked at him, he was holding someone—that girl from before.

"Who is your companion?" she asked.

Roland gave his little friend a peck on the lips. The girl folded in against his chest, giggling. "She has no name. She comes from the forest."

Rowen tried to remember why she looked familiar. Many people lived in Rieux, and Rowen did not know anyone from the third estate. "Is she from town?"

"Tonight, none of us are who we were. Right?"

"Roland," the girl entreated. "I want to feel your hands upon me."

"Not right now."

Whining, the girl struck his chest with her fist. "Tabby," he said firmly, catching her hand.

Tabby, thought Rowen, remembering now that there had been a wedding that Spring in which a much-too-young girl was wed to the much-too-old butcher. And that girl's name had been Tabitha.

Rowen's stomach turned, and it was not from the wine. The wine, she knew, had dulled the voice in her head telling her she should not be here with these sorts of people. She wished Amarys had come with them. Had she, they could have fled this place together and chaperoned one another back to the safety of the chateau.

The man who had given her wine tapped her shoulder. She tilted her head to face him. He spoke the same French as her father and grandmother, a different dialect from that of Brittany.

"Let's play a game." The young man pulled an apple out of his pocket and offered it to her. "Hold this apple firmly in your hand. Without touching you, I will make you drop it, and you will pay me a kiss. If you can withstand me, you keep the apple."

His smile showed a gap in his teeth. Rowen played along, gripping the apple and trying to ignore Roland's base conversation with the peasant girl.

They were whispering, but little fragments of their speech were audible. "I want to get naked with you," the girl kept saying.

"Not now."

All at once, Rowen noticed the apple felt like a hot poker pressing her bare palm. It had to be in her mind, but as she continued to hold it, the heat became unbearable. She let the apple fall and roll away.

Astonished, she examined her hand, which was beet red. "What happened?"

"Who can say?" said the youth, plucking the apple off the ground. With an air of confidence, he took a bite. "Tell me, is it me that you burn for?" Rowen tilted her head, puzzled. The lad leaned in to kiss her, and she dodged him.

"What did you do to me?"

"Nothing."

"Roland!"

Roland drew himself away from his girl's arms, peeling them off as if they had thorns. "Rowen?"

"My hand! He has disfigured me! And now he demands a kiss."

Roland scrutinized his sister's palm, which was blistering before their eyes. "What did you do to my sister?" he demanded of the youth.

"Nothing. It was some mildly poisonous sap on the pale side of the apple."

"Poisonous?" cried Rowen in alarm.

"Mildly! It will heal tomorrow."

"What plant?" demanded Roland. "Out with it."

"I can't give away my secrets! You might steal my trick."

Roland scowled, turning to see that Tabby had lost interest and wandered off. He groaned dramatically and whipped around and faced the lad head-on. "This is why I hate knights! Marring a woman's hand so you can force a kiss! Why must everything be sought through force?"

"Do you want recompense?"

Roland's expression began to resemble a gargoyle deep in loathing. "Recompense? Tell me, is it normal where you come from for a brother to pimp his own sister?"

The youth, noticing Roland's darkening mood, smiled unsurely. "I commend your chivalry, sir."

Roland nodded, baring his teeth in what had to be the most insincere grin that Rowen had ever seen. "I am no knight. Devil take your chivalry."

"Devil take your messy sister."

Not missing a beat, Roland gut-punched the youth. And like a snake spitting venom, the lad spewed vomit. Reeling in disgust, Roland spun out. Another young man came out of nowhere, shouting incoherently. He delivered a hard-impact blow to Roland's face. Roland made a sound like a firepit spitting up flame.

"Ow! Fuck!" he hissed, nose dripping with blood and snot. Pinching his septum and screwing his eyes shut, he said, "Rowen, hit him."

Other men in attendance noticed the fight breaking out and gravitated toward the scuffle.

Willem came running. Rowen felt her heart in her throat as she realized he was charging at the youth. Oh no, she thought, as their friend slammed into Roland's attacker. They stumbled into the first youth, spilling his bottle of mead. That made him especially angry. He wrestled Roland to the ground, landing blows wherever he could.

The contents of the lad's stomach were still soaking the grass, and the two of them rolled right through it. They released each other at once.

"I will have my liege lord break every bone in your bodies!" he shrieked, slicking his back and shoulders clean of his humours.

Rowen and her brother lunged into a dash for freedom. Willem moved like a cat as he bolted. The men shouted threats of retaliation, but soon, the three friends were far enough away that those curses were swallowed up by the drums and tambourines.

Willem bid them goodnight and went off to find another party. The twins cross the dew-damp field without the benefit of a torch. Roland wiped the blood from his chin. Rowen wrapped her burnt hand in her cap.

"So much for lying low! Why did you have to hit him?"

"I've been stupid." Roland held the side of his head.

"You have been. I mean, the butcher's wife. Really? He will carve you up like a bothersome rooster if he finds out!"

"I know."

"You are father's heir! You have to take your duty more seriously!"

"I have tried." Roland stopped walking. "I cannot become the man of arms that Father wants me to be, the man Edmund wanted me to be. I learned as much in Toulouse. Edmund could tell that I—I hate this—I have trained all my life to become something I hate. And to think that I was angry with him for holding me back, when really, I should have thanked him. Now, I have lost him."

Rowen seldom saw streaks of salt upon her brother's face. The last time she remembered was the day their father made them board the ship out of Antioch. Back then, when they faced the void of oblivion in the belly of the ship at night, the twins retreated to their inner world. They clung to one another in the darkness of their berth, repeating a phrase: "*Nahn yad wahida.*"

"We are one hand. I am your strength, and you are mine."

Rowen felt the grip of Roland's anguish coiling around her own heart. "His death was quick," she said. "At least now, he is at peace."

"Am I to be cut down like that? Murdered like a dog?"

The image of Sir Edmund's head lying crooked against his armored corpse still lingered in Rowen's thoughts. For years now, she had imagined her brother's death. He would be a knight cast adrift in a world of violence.

Rowen wanted to believe her life was blessed by God's Grace and that nothing terrible would ever happen to her or her brother. She wanted to hold onto the sweetness of childhood for as long as possible, gathering it into her arms like so many wildflowers. But the only certainty in life was its mutability. Nothing could last.

CHAPTER 3

The bubbled skin on her palm gradually softened into smooth, pink flesh again. Some weeks passed, and a great bounty of gifts arrived from the Viscount of Rohan. Rowen had awoken with the sun that leaked through the thin slats of her window. She donned her woolen robe, containing what heat remained in her bones. Upon opening the shutters, she discovered a procession of horses and carts trickling out of the forest.

"Roland!" she cried. "Wake up. Something is happening."

On the other side of a thin wooden panel separating their chambers, she heard her brother shifting on his mattress.

"Good or bad?" asked his pillow-muffled voice.

"Good, I think."

Moaning like a sick cat, Roland shifted again. No footsteps followed, but Rowen did not care. She called for her maid to help her dress. Once arrayed in a fine dress with a belt of moonstones and silver, Rowen presented herself alongside her father at the front of the manor. Their small staff of servants joined them as they greeted their unexpected guests.

At the front of the procession, Harlowe rode his charger. He looked very different out of his armor. His hair was in a fluff from the road, his face a little dusty. He wore a gambeson of burgundy wool that suited his amber complexion. His entourage of knights formed a perimeter around him. Two horses in the back towed a cart laden with chests.

"Sir Ivin of Antioch," projected the youth as he dismounted his horse. "I know we have already shared words regarding the loss of your man, Sir Edmund le Noir. I have expressed my regret for having killed him. As recompense for the wrong I have done you, I would like to bestow the following gifts for your daughter's dowry: two golden platters, a chest of jewels, and a bolt of wool spun by the finest artisans in Rohan."

"You are too generous, Sir Harlowe," said Ivin sternly.

"Wait, there's more," said Harlowe, gesturing to one of his men pulling two horses by the leads. He relinquished the gray one and brought the white horse forward. The animals' glistening coat filled Rowen's eyes like the sun.

"This palfrey belonged to my sister," explained Harlowe, "but she no longer rides. With your approval, Sir Ivin, I would like Rowen to have him."

"We cannot accept what—" Ivin began.

Harlowe cut him off. "Please. Allow me to settle my debt. I expect nothing in return. I intend to marry Lady Amarys, and as your daughter is my cousin's bosom friend, I extol these gifts as an extension of friendship."

Rowen rushed toward the pretty beast. She ran her hands over its neck and flank. White as a lily, the creature flinched and snuffled.

"May I ride him?"

"Go ahead," said her father.

Rowen raised her hem by folding her skirt into her belt. Harlowe's smile made her uneasy, but she accepted him as he knelt and allowed her to use his knee as a mounting block.

She climbed the stirrup, clasped the reins, and centered her weight on the animal's back. She could feel his sides expand and collapse with breath. The creature had a tenseness to his muscles she had not anticipated. She applied some pressure at the flanks, urging him to walk. The animal tossed his silvery mane as he adjusted to his new mistress.

Rowen tested his trot along the lane heading up to the forest. The palfrey was smaller than Ash and maneuvered with such swiftness and elegance that she could pivot and come charging down the lane with ease. The wind beat against her face, freezing the muscles of her smile. The way the power of the horse's body carried her like a leaf in the air instilled a feeling of flight. She had read once that the Earth shared the likeness of an egg, with the yolk as the planet's sphere, the white as the sky, and the shell as that delicate firmament between her world and the heavens. Like Icarus, she wanted to climb those airy heights and taste the outer bounds of Earth's shell. Tears formed like little stars on her eyelashes.

As much as she wanted to believe these gifts came from a place of remorse, an unsettling certainty ached in her chest. Men like Harlowe did not extend generosity without purpose. While her bloodline was eminent and her family owned half of Rieux, it was well known that her brother would inherit everything. What did he want from her?

She gazed upon what she considered a modest dwelling, the timber-fortified building spanning three floors, its roof topped with uneven chimneys and wood shingles. On one side lay a walled garden, and on the other, a workshop and stables. It was more than most people had, but Harlowe was heir to the whole glittering city of Rohan. If Amarys became his wife, she would be elevated above Rowen and require companions of a similar station. Pondering this, Rowen supposed Harlowe might be doing a service to his intended, Amarys.

His gifts might allow Rowen to fetch a better husband. She wondered—and perhaps hoped—that he was providing for her as a favor to Amarys, setting her up to marry an aristocrat in Rohan.

These contemplations soured as she saw Roland coming out of the manor. He squinted in the sun, adjusting the uneven strands of his multi-colored vest. He offered no greeting to the man who had slain his mentor, only stared fixedly the same way a man might stare at a hound unbeknownst to him. Rowen slowed her horse and dismounted with such confidence that she heard some of her servants audibly gasp.

"Roland! Look what Harlowe has given me!" She ran to her brother, pulling him by the hand. Reluctantly, he allowed himself to be dragged. Her horse had wandered toward some grass and begun to graze.

Roland examined the animal's body, stroking his velvety shoulder. "Has he a name?"

Rowen looked at Harlowe for the answer, but he only said, "He is for Lady Rowen to name as she likes."

"I will call him Biax, for I have never loved anything so much."

Ivin invited Harlowe to stay for breakfast, which was courteous given that Rohan was a day's ride from Rieux. While Roland abided by his father's courtly gesture, his steely glare never faltered, and everyone was relieved when Harlowe declined. He explained that he would be staying with his Uncle at the chateau.

Over the next few days, Roland criticized his father for accepting the bride-gift. The horse had not been well-cared for, evidenced by his lack of muscle tone and skittish temperament. One of his hooves was elongated and would require Roland's attention for weeks to come. So the name, Biax, which meant "beloved," was hardly suitable. Rowen adored Biax too much to let Roland spoil her present.

She rode every day without fail, learning the creature's idiosyncrasies and earning his trust. Agile and nervous, Biax often darted unpredictably. It took time, but eventually, he accepted Rowen's command. She came to know him like a part of herself, his long, powerful legs extensions of her own.

The day came for Rowen to visit Amarys and Roland to attend his first lesson with his new fencing instructor, Willem's father, Sir Deacon de Meu. Ivin initially wanted Roland to go to Nantes to study with a master there, but Roland stubbornly refused. Thank Mary for that, thought Rowen, who had been miserable enough the last time he left.

The sun, muted by a dark cloud, hung like an opal on the horizon. The siblings crossed the stone border into Clement's lands. Roland's horse, Ash, nipped at Biax's nape. "Hey, hey, hey!" Roland yanked the reins and spurred the beast forward.

"Keep off!" cried Rowen, stroking that part of Biax's mane that had been tugged.

Roland's charger advanced across the meadow. His mercurial temperament flared in the presence of Rowen's new palfrey. Grey with black speckles, the horse was called Ash, and he was worth more than a year's income.

The dust of the road clung to the back of Rowen's throat. She coughed to clear her airways, holding her veil, which might have flown from her head in a moment. The slate blue fabric twisted on the wind, secured to a maze of braids with silver thread. It would last the journey, she hoped.

As she and her brother neared the chateau, Rowen noticed a pair of men sparring in the middle of the open field. A breeze pulled at the leaves and branches of a nearby sheltering tree. She stalled her horse as she came in under the shadow. The two men, ruddy and panting, were drenched to the navel in sweat. They fought unarmored, swinging broadswords with alarming speed.

Roland let his eyes fall closed, apparently exhausted by the idea of watching their sport. He tugged on Ash's reins, crooning a low, "Woo there." Rowen slid down from her saddle, walking closer to observe them from the shade of the laurel tree.

To her surprise, they paused mid-bout and took a turn to acknowledge her with courtly bows before they resumed their practice. One was Erec, the champion with auburn hair and a great many spots. Erec had such agility he could dodge the other's attacks simply by leaning backward, always barely escaping the length of his opponent's blade.

The other—whose hair was brown—was unknown to her. He kept his waist tucked to one side—and his feet never rooted in one place, never ceased to dance. She tried to predict their moves by the angle of their posture. She saw it coming when Erec lunged and sliced the other man's cheek. Three strings of blood fell from his cut. The lad dropped to the ground, touched the wound, and when he saw the bright blood on his fingertips, he laughed. Rowen marveled at that.

The victor offered his hand, hoisting his friend to his feet and giving him a robust pat on the shoulder. They were smiling, admiring the blood, and the wounded said something to make the victor laugh outright.

After their second bout, Erec turned to address the siblings. "Ho, Roland," he greeted, offering a friendly salute.

Roland hung back, grazing the horses.

"Get through the tourney all right, Mohammat?" said the shorter man.

"Your mother kept me happy," Roland shot back.

All three seemed to smirk, and the one whose mother had been insulted bit his thumb at Roland.

Rowen went to her brother's side. "Friends of yours?"

"Something of the sort."

"I'm Guyon, and there's Erec," said the one she did not recognize.

"That's Sir Erec. I was knighted, ass comb."

"As you keep reminding us."

Rowen eyed Guyon unsurely. She knew his face from seeing him at Mass, though she had never distinguished him in her mind. Everyone in the township looked related and probably were.

"You are Lady Rowen of Antioch, are you not?" asked Guyon. "Roland speaks highly of you."

Rowen bent at the knee to acknowledge his address.

"The rose has bloomed," said Guyon.

Rowen wanted to respond but hesitated long enough for Roland to say what she was thinking, "She is not without her thorns."

"We played as children. Do you recall?" Guyon was still addressing Rowen.

When Sir Ivin first brought his children to Brittany, their peers, boys and girls alike, asked them questions about dromedaries and elephants.

"I recall. You wanted to know if my mother was a giantess," said Rowen, remembering him.

Guyon laughed. Erec smacked the back of his head.

"Owl!" grunted Guyon, rubbing the spot. "What was that for?"

"For being a cur."

"I was a child."

"Apologize."

"Make me."

"Grant your favor, Lady, and I shall extort his penance," said Erec.

"You have it," said Rowen, eyes wide as Erec brandished his blade anew. The men returned to sparring, their steel singing out as they dodged and clashed.

Rowen clasped her hands over her shoulders. Erec did a seamless pirouette and slashed Guyon's hand, disarming him. Guyon cried out. When he recovered, he took up a rock and tried to punch Erec in the lip. Erec captured his arm and grappled him to the earth. The rock rolled out of Guyon's palm. The fall dislocated his shoulder, which made him yowl. His sounds of anguish rang loud over the fields, starkly contrasted against the roar of Erec's robust laughter.

Erec helped Guyon to his feet, getting a firm hold of his forearm and pulling. The appendage popped back into its socket. In the heat of his suffering, Guyon spat horrible slurs.

"Whoreson! You bastard, ball-sucking, whoreson! You shed my Christian blood for that Saracen!"

Erec used the shirt off his back to make a sling, a pronounced blush coloring his face and neck.

Being called a Saracen did not bother Rowen, but Guyon had said it with a cruel inflection that suggested something foreign—something heathen. Before Rowen had the chance to check Roland's reaction, she heard his blade hissing from the sheath on his horse's flank.

Erec had just finished tying Guyon's sling when Roland came charging toward them, brandishing his blade like a spike.

Blood boiling, he shouted, "My sister is a Christian!"

Roland had a long and svelte physique. No matter how much he ate or trained, he simply could not build the oxen musculature of other boys, but his slender frame did not make him any less fearsome when he held his sword primed for battle.

Erec raised a hand. "Peace, Roland. He meant nothing by it!"

"There will be no peace until this halfwit takes back his insult."

Rowen's skin prickled to see her brother so outraged. Though she was tremulous and unsure within, she composed herself beneath a mask of calm.

Snatching up his sword, Guyon met Roland's thrust. Their steel rang like thunder. Erec shouted at them to stop, but he could not break through the noise of their shouting. Guyon had no trouble swapping sword hands, but his pain showed in his strained expression each time he deflected one of Roland's blows.

"Qadamak alyumnaa!" called Rowen, alerting him to guard his foot.

Roland slid it back in the dirt, barely escaping Guyon's plunge for his ankle. These were not practice swords. Rowen could see it all unfolding like it had at the tournament. There would be an accident. A limb would be lost, or a life. She shouted for them to stop but might as well have been shouting into a cave for all the good it did. Guyon charged Roland with his good shoulder, hitting him in the throat. Roland wheezed as he sank to the ground.

"Hot-headed heathen," spat Guyon, knocking the sword from Roland's hand. His blade came up under Roland's chin. And time seemed to stop. Rowen could imagine her brother's head leaving his shoulders like Edmund's, cleaved by a sword flown in the heat of anger. The horror of the midsummer tourney came rushing back. Edmund's limp body lay cradled in a pit of blood. His helmet was in the dirt. And his head, his head, the vessel of his soul that would never greet her again.

Rowen bent to take up Roland's sword that had fallen. She hoisted it with both arms. Desperate and terrified, she screamed as she swung. The sword seemed to fly without her. Moving with the swiftness of a bird of prey, it swooped in to clip Guyon at the shoulder.

Then, a wall of steel arrested her blade. As she felt collision with Erec's sword, she instinctively used the recoil to attack again at a new angle. He grunted, deflecting her and wrenching Guyon back by the collar.

"Holy mother!" cried Erec, his steel singing as it scraped hers away. "Has Roland been training you?"

Rowen let the sword's tip hit the earth. Flooded with shame, she dropped it and staggered back. What had she done? She did not want this to get back to her father. Guyon tried to blitz through Erec, but the knight grabbed his sore shoulder and pinned him.

"Enough," Erec snapped.

Roland sprung up to stand. He brushed the dust from his thighs and stretched his neck to each side. "You will never again use that word in reference to my sister. If you do, you will die for it, Guyon."

Rowen touched her brother's arm, compelling stillness. "Roland." Her voice was a salve to his temper, and she knew her twin would never strike at her, never shake her off. Had it been any other man, she would not have said a word, but Roland was her own flesh.

Erec tried to barter peace. "We are brothers in arms. Let us part as friends."

"Will he apologize to Rowe?" said Roland.

Guyon groaned theatrically, throwing up his good arm. "I am sorry, Lady Rowen! I know well that you are a Christian. Whatever demon possessed me to say such a thing, I know not, for I was in such agony that I could not think clearly."

"Truce?" offered Erec.

"Truce," said Roland, and he patted Guyon's wrecked shoulder.

"Agh!" Guyon bit back the pain.

"Come, Rowen. My master is waiting." Roland extended an arm and supported her as she climbed into her horse's saddle.

As they cantered over what remained of the meadow, Rowen declared loudly, "What a beautiful fight!"

"Beautiful?"

"Yes! The form. The power. Just beautiful!"

"Bah," Roland spat. "Poetry is beautiful. That's just some dullards trying to bash each other's brains in."

"There is poetry to brain-bashing!" cried Rowen.

Roland chuckled to see his sister so enthused. "There is poetry in everything, I suppose."

"Did you see me? I scared the snot out of our champion of Rieux!"

"You surprised him, that's all."

"He was rattled!"

"He was not rattled."

"He invoked the virgin!"

"Yes, but he was not rattled."

The twins neared the gatehouse and reduced their horses' speed to a gentler stride. Above its stone foundations, the timbered edifice loomed. A team of masons was building stone around one of its wooden towers, slow upgrades to turn the place into an impenetrable fortress. As they approached the chateau, Rowen felt like a ship about to capsize. It was as though some evil spirit had depleted her of breath.

Tell me what I taste like.

Those intoxicating words had fallen from Amarys's lips like little jewels. The thought made Rowen's head airy and euphoric. It stirred the rhythm of her pulse as she lingered with the memory.

CHAPTER 4

The steward led Rowen through the foyer into the inner courtyard. The cloistered garden, an area of seclusion for intimate repose with the sky, held stone arches on either side. Neatly trimmed hedges lined the perimeter of the manicured flowerbeds, bluebells blooming within. In the square's center, honeysuckle twisted around the trunk of a hazel tree. White blooms budded along its vines like lace, a striking contrast to the hazel's radiant green leaves. The ground was littered with hazelnuts. Seated upon a stone bench, Amarys plucked the strings of a lyre. Her music instructor listened on, nodding at the elegant close of the refrain.

Amarys looked up, nymphlike, her full, pink lips half-curled in a smirk. Those lips had been ensconced in Rowen's mind since she had felt them pressed against her own. She tried not to look at them. Amarys set her lyre aside and told her instructor, "Farewell, Pauline."

Pauline enclosed the instrument in a leather case, but as she was leaving, she stopped to say, "It never fails to surprise me. Are you taller than your own brother?"

Rowen tensed, saying the only thing that came to mind. "He and I are the same height."

Pauline choked on a gasp of cruel glee. "My!"

Rowen went to join Amarys on the bench, denying Pauline her attention. She

43

thought of carving knives and how it might feel to grip their cold bone handles as she dug them deep into her flesh. Were severed limbs much worse than those of a giantess?

"Ye gods," said Amarys as Pauline vanished behind the thick, steel-cased door. "What a shrew."

"Amarys, don't be unkind."

"I only wish to apologize for her."

"There is no need."

"I will not have anyone speak to my rose that way. Never mind what she says. She is jealous."

"Surely you are mistaken."

"We saw everything from my window." Amarys combed her fingers through her hair, preening haughtily as she recounted the events of the morning. "My father's men were falling all over themselves to impress you. Your brother became protective and went to fight them. When he started to lose, you took up his sword! It was quite the sight. And do you know what I saw as you and Roland rode away?"

Rowen shook her head. "I hesitate to ask."

"Sir Erec of Avenport watched you go."

"So?"

"So?!" Amarys huffed. "I am keen to ask a personal question, if I may."

Rowen knew that tone. She knew Amarys was about to try and fluster her. Swallowing, she gave a nod for her to go ahead.

"If you had your pick out of any of my father's knights, which one would you open your legs for?"

Rowen could not believe her sometimes. Unruly. Outspoken. Vulgar beyond measure in the absence of a chaperone.

"Amarys, someone could hear you."

"Every woman in Rieux would choose Sir Erec, soft in head but hard of body. What happened out there? You crossed swords with him."

"I only put a stop to their rough sport."

"Really?" she sounded more intrigued than ever. "You must tell."

"Guyon insulted me... it was a misunderstanding."

"Did he try to kiss you?"

"No."

"Did he produce a thorn in his braies?"

"No! The insult hardly matters. It gave me no offense, yet Roland was ready to kill Guyon for it, and soon, we were all caught up in this heated exchange. Erec bartered peace."

"Erec wants you. This means I'll have to fuck him sooner than later."

Rowen appraised the courtyard. She studied the stone walls to see that no windows were open. They were not, which helped to put her at ease. "You mustn't speak like this, Amarys. Even in jest."

"Why not? We are maids for an hour, and I want at least three lovers before I die," said Amarys. "At the same time if I can arrange it."

"Oh, Lord in heaven. Omnia probate, Amarys, Quod bonum est tenete—"

"My father has tried exorcism—"

"—it's a proverb! It means: Try everything but hold fast to what is good!"

"Oh, I assure you, it will be the highest good. And I mean it, Rowen. I want to try everything before I die."

Rowen crossed herself and began to pray for Amarys.

"Your brother, for instance." She emitted a melodious sigh.

"You will not bring my brother into this."

"You speak as though he were your sister! Easy now! I won't despoil Roland's virtue! I swear!"

"The way you carry on is a marvel. Does your father never threaten to disown you?"

"No. By heaven, no. He isn't your father," said Amarys, cackling and clutching her sides. "Yours would have thrown me down a well ages ago."

Amarys's Nurse, Marie, descended the stairwell. Amarys shot up from her seat, speaking as though they had been on some other subject, "Your father is right, of course. Taking the air in the gardens is very good for one's health. Ah, here is my Nurse. Marie!"

Marie approached them.

"Marie, I must take Lady Rowen through the gardens. Will you look in on my sister and report back to me?"

Marie folded her arms, her brow crinkling under her coif. "You would have me walk all those stairs just to get rid of me? Beatrice is fine, Lady Amarys. She is working her needlepoint with Marguerite, which is where you and your companion should be going."

"Please, Nurse! Rowen dislikes my sisters! She finds Bea boring and Honora irksome!"

"She jests!" Rowen assured the Nurse.

"And today is such a lovely day for walking outside."

"I like the ladies immensely," Rowen insisted.

Marie's posture eased up as she stifled a laugh. "All right, Lady Amarys. You must have some gossip to impart. Go on. Take your Lady Rowen walking. But I will not be going back up all those stairs. You will meet me in the kitchens when your walk is done."

Amarys hopped, swaying with glee. "Come, come. Let's bounce!"

The girls scurried off through the halls of rough-hewn stone. Protected by a high wall, they were well-guarded in the orchard. Clement's knights were posted along every aisle and corner. Rowen would jump a little the first time she saw one. Despite their armor, they were as stealthy as leopards, patrolling like statues. Their eyes followed the girls as they passed.

In the orchard, the girls could play how they wanted. They could climb trees or balance on stone borders. They could strap their skirts up in their belts and run at full speed as they raced down the alleys. Rowen lifted her white shawl to cover her head and protect her skin from the sun. She watched in amazement as Amarys groped the delicate branches of a mulberry tree, hoisting herself up and finding footholds where none were apparent. Her limbs tangled with the folds of her skirt. Laughing aloud, she propped herself against the innermost bough.

"Want one?" she called down. Rowen shook her head.

"No, thank you."

Amarys dropped from the tree, startling Rowen with the noise of her descent. "Have it your way," she said, eating the berries as she walked. They stained the inside of her lips crimson. A spear of red trickled down her lip as she bit into another.

Rowen drew a handkerchief and caught it fast, relinquishing the cloth. She ducked beneath the sheltering foliage of the mulberry tree, feeling suddenly out of breath. Something like euphoria had swept over her when she touched Amarys's lips.

She stepped out of the shade and took repose against the wall, holding her elbows.

"Are you all right?" asked Amarys, jarring Rowen from her thoughts.

"Yes."

Amarys spat out a stem, her brows lifting like a shrug. "What I wouldn't give for us to go beyond these walls. To ride to town without an escort."

"What would we do in town?" asked Rowen.

"Oh, I don't know. See a miracle play? Drink beer in a tavern? I was so envious of your adventure with Roland."

"You shouldn't be. It was awful."

"What marvels did you see?"

Rowen pressed the images of vomit, snot, and blood from her mind. "I cannot say. I feel we are not alone."

Amarys squinted, pursing her lips to one side. "We are quite alone."

"Not really. Never for long. There is no dodging your Nurse."

"You sound like my sister. She prefers her cocoon to fluttering about the chateau. On days that she would rather not deal with our household, I will feign a cramp, and Nurse will be fixed on me all day. Bea could return the favor."

"To what end? To sit quietly in your rooms?"

Amarys chewed the corner of her nail. "To see the marvels that come from within."

"How do you mean?"

Amarys searched between the trees for her guards. "I have heard it said that your brother is a procurer of rare plants."

Now, it was Rowen looking over her shoulder. "Who would say such a thing?"

"I am sworn to secrecy."

"Was it Willem?"

"Is it true, then?"

At this, Rowen thought her heart might burst. She had to breathe to regulate her voice before she spoke. "What is it you seek?"

Amarys's lips shone like polished coral. She came in very close—so close Rowen could smell the berries on her tongue. "The devil's cap."

Rowen drew back. She could not begin to imagine how Amarys knew of such a thing.

"Remember how I said I wanted to try everything before I died?" Her eyes glinted like the scales of a sea snake. "Will you ask him?"

"I'm not sure that I approve."

"If you do not wish to partake, I understand."

"Amarys. It turns a person mad. It is the stuff of warlocks and devilry."

"I know, but unlike you, I have never had an adventure. I have never been at sea or seen strange lands beyond the duchy. In one year's time, I will be married. Before I go to my bridal bower, I would see what magic exists in the world. I would speak to fairies and demons, and I would do it with you at my side. Say you will help me. You needn't partake. I only ask that you watch over me."

Rowen did not know what to say at first. She pressed her hand, her nose burning as her anxieties surged. "How could I forgive myself if anything happened to you?" She could tell from her friend's silence that Amarys did not want to be lectured. "All right," she said, patting her hand. "I will convey your message."

"Thank you." Amarys kissed Rowen's hands.

"You may tell Willem that he is dead to us," Rowen added dryly.

"It was not Willem!"

Whether Willem had squealed or not hardly mattered now. If Amarys knew, other people knew as well, and the only person who would have been foolish enough to spread rumor's wings was that loose-lipped oaf, Willem.

Rowen remembered how her brother had described the devil's cap some time ago, a mushroom that caused visions and made it so a person could hear the dead. He wanted to find it so he could speak to their mother. He had mentioned one of the shepherds, who was something of a mystic.

Then, all of a sudden, Roland never mentioned it again. It was as though finding the caps was all that mattered one day, and the next, they no longer existed. He retreated into his books, away from his sister, and spent a great deal of time drawing the same picture of a wreath moving in and out of verdure, half its leaves shriveled and wan and the others flowering and bursting with pollen. As children, they had shared an inner world, and now that world had been cleaved.

Something had changed in him since he went abroad. He neglected his chivalric training, shared less and less of his lessons, and seemed more interested in composing songs than honing his swordsmanship. He was changing all the time these days the way a shadow conforms to the angle of the sun or fades altogether into nightfall. They came to this country as strangers, and within each other, they had stitched together pieces of the familiar. Now, those last threads of certainty, of truly knowing and trusting her twin, were beginning to fray.

The sky darkened, transforming into a canvas of shifting hues. Streaks of fiery amber overwhelmed the fading brilliance of the sun. Amarys and Rowen, bathed in the glow of twilight, made their way through the courtyard, their figures casting elongated shadows against the castle walls. A balmy summer breeze wove through the trees lining the road to the castle gate. The groom emerged from the stables, leading Biax. The horse's pearly coat shimmered in the dwindling light.

Amarys looked about the courtyard, settling her gaze on Rowen. "Why, this is Margery's horse," she said.

"Harlowe gave him to me. He presented many gifts to apologize for—"

"He should have been charged for murder," Amarys snipped. "Ah, here is Roland."

The clattering hooves announced his arrival. Roland rode in on Ash, angling to one side to extend a greeting to Lady Amarys.

"Amarys la Belle," he said, his eyes a little too free with her.

"Roland le Diable," she teased. Roland snorted, his laughter bubbling. Her satisfaction for having amused him showed in how she jutted her chin.

The groom provided a mounting block, offering support to Rowen as she climbed the stirrup. Rowen gave Amarys a final bow of recognition and brought her velvet hood down over her forehead. Biax veered like a whip with the cluck of Rowen's tongue. She started toward the forest, her brother following behind. Rowen spurred her horse's flanks. Swiftly, they shot forth over the sleepy meadow into the woods that bordered their lands.

The siblings slowed to navigate through the wood. Less than a mile from their home, Roland dismounted to pull a mushroom from the side of a decaying log. He turned it over, bruised it, and ran his knife over the gills.

"Death bell," he said. "For a moment, I thought I had a chanterelle."

At this point in the journey, they usually spoke of the events of their days, but on this night, Rowen had urgent matters to attend.

"I need to tell you something," she said, sliding down from her horse. "It is quite serious."

Roland tossed the death bell. "Go ahead." The twins walked on either side of their horses as they conferred.

"Today, Amarys asked me to procure the devil's cap. And she seemed convinced that you knew how to get it."

"I do."

"Why did you never say?"

"You never asked."

His tone vexed her. "Well," she said, "someone has painted you as some devious apothecary. I can only imagine that Willem has been spinning tales at Lechón."

"It would not have been Willem," said Roland. "He has a sweetheart, though, and she may be an acquaintance of Amarys."

"Tell me her name. I may know her."

"Artemie. Antoine. Something like that."

"You must be more careful."

"It's no big deal."

"We are not like the other nobles here. We will always be outsiders."

Roland scoffed, and Ash seemed to mirror his reaction with a snort. "Do you want the devil's cap or not?"

"I want to help my friend."

"Of course you do. Consider this, though. If she eats the cake of the fairies, she will never be the same."

"In what way?"

"She will never be innocent again."

"She is determined to get them with or without my help. I want to be certain she procures only what is safe."

"Ah."

"Are they safe?"

"Nothing of this nature is completely safe, but they will not kill you if you only take a little."

"Why did you only take them once then?"

"Once was enough. The visions were illuminating, but they were not particularly comfortable."

"When was this?"

"Last summer, when I first returned from Toulouse. Willem and I ate the devil's cap in the forest. At first, it was lovely; the trees glowed, their moss and shadowy creases swirling inward into faces. As it got darker, everything changed. Willem vanished. I was alone. Exposed. I wanted my bed and the comforts of home. So I left, afraid that if I lingered, I would be attacked by wild beasts.

"Willem, I found out later, went walking and got lost. He thought he would be eaten by wolves or, worse, become one. He convinced himself that all wolves were men who had eaten the devil's cap and become beasts. And then, he thought the only way to survive the night was to strip naked and become an animal. So he did just that, growling at every shadow until he believed he was the most powerful beast in the wood. In his ferocity, he says he ate the moon in a single gulp and cast the world into darkness. He came to his senses at dawn. He was covered in scratches and mud, and his clothes were lost—"

"It made him wild."

"Or," proposed Roland, "It merely stripped away the illusion that he was civilized."

Roland stopped, raising his hand in alarm to signal Rowen to stop as well. Bands of outlaws came through now and again. Rowen turned her back to her brother's, surveying the forest they had left behind.

"Show yourself!" Roland boomed. "I smell your horse!"

The unseen party emerged from behind a copse.

"Roland, who is that?"

"Mount your horse."

Rowen felt the blood drain from her face. Before she could move, the stranger called to them.

"It's only me." The voice belonged to Erec.

Roland went ahead to the tight cluster of trees. He and Erec shared words, and a letter was given. At once, Erec mounted his horse and took off into the night. Head bowed in reading, Roland began to laugh. "Rowe!" he called. "Come here. You've got to see this."

Rowen walked the horses forward by the leads and joined her brother. Her mind buzzed like a hive. "What did Erec want?"

"You would not believe me if I told you."

He handed her a bouquet of wildflowers bound with twine and read the attached note aloud.

"Fair Rowen!" he emoted with a cruel inflection. Rowen tried to snatch the letter away, but Roland ducked and escaped behind the edge of a tree. "You are more beautiful than any woman I have ever laid eyes on, more beautiful than a desert rose preserved in amber. When I saw you today, I knew I could not bear to go any longer without telling you what is in my heart! I am sick with love and cannot bring myself to eat or drink. Have mercy! Release me from this torment with a word! Grant me permission to woo and win you. Your captive lover, Erec of Avenport!"

"Give it here. It is not addressed to you, Roland. You were not meant to see this."

"Erec wrote this! Can you believe it?" Roland's laughter burst forth once more. "Erec and Rowen," he sang cruelly, handing her the note.

"Enough. This is very serious."

"Hardly. You don't intend to invite his courtship."

"If father learns of this, it might not be up to me."

"Bah! Marry you to a second son? Only if you begged him."

"Well, thank heavens for that. I shall burn the letter."

Roland chuckled, incredulous. "Wait. Read the letter yourself. It is quite good."

"I do not wish to marry."

"Rowen," Roland said seriously. "Erec is the best man I know. As a suitor, he is highly desirable."

"Then you marry him! I have never even spoken to him."

"But have your eyes met? Have you exchanged smiles?"

Rowen blinked, sifting through memories. "Never. Most likely, he is teasing me."

"Stop that. You should know that you are insulting me when you insult yourself! And you are beautiful... you daft moppet."

"I am much too tall—"

"Statuesque."

"Too skinny—"

"Delicate, bird-like."

"And our origin, Roland. Our land of origin connotes heathen, churl. Saracen, remember?"

"Ah, good sister, I'm afraid only men get to claim the masks of heathens and churls. You are the exotic princess in need of rescue. These Normans want to marry you, convert you, and lop your dear brother's head off." His eyes crinkled gleefully.

"The last bit sounds agreeable enough."

Roland reached across his horse and knocked Rowen's veil off her head. It was a classic Roland retaliation. He climbed into the saddle and rode away, galloping beyond the edge of the forest. She could hear him laughing from afar.

Rowen squeezed Biax's leads as she bent to find her veil amidst the brambles. Stupid brother. He had been doing that same jest since they were children, and she still hadn't learned to expect it. All the same, she was giggling softly, like she had played the trick on herself.

CHAPTER 5

The warm breath of August brought a swell of bulbous round caps to the forest. Fairy bonnets and honey fungus lined the trails. Rowen could not help herself in reminding Roland every day. He would tell her to be patient; he was looking. Each time she saw Amarys, she would apologize for arriving empty-handed, though Amarys seemed not to mind. Her friend would thank her each time for taking up her cause.

"It is very noble of you. I am in your debt."

Such words only encouraged Rowen's idea of herself as a kind of champion for Amarys. She liked to think of herself as a knight searching for his lady's antidote, a mushroom that would break a curse. Finally, after a stretch of rainy days, Roland put a handful of caps in Rowen's palm and told her the Green Man sent his regards.

Rowen and Amarys exchanged messages back and forth, arranging for the date they could be left alone together. A leather pouch in plain sight on her hip aroused no suspicion from the steward. He led her up to the solar without a moment's hesitation. "Bon jor, ma domnizelle," a servant greeted as they passed each other in the hall. Rowen nearly flinched out of fright that she would be caught and tried for witchcraft. She returned the greeting, quickening her pace behind the steward.

They arrived at the door of Lady Amarys's chamber. Stones painted with green vines and white flowers ran up the arched door frame. The steward delivered a brisk knock. Rowen folded her arms, feeling impatient.

Perfectly safe, echoed Roland's assurance.

Rowen's heart thrummed at the thought of beholding Amarys's beauty under such a spell. Might her bright hair shine like spun gold? Or would it take a form more like Medusa's serpents? She longed to find out. And yet, a certain apprehension dogged her mind. She would have never agreed to this if it weren't safe, but she still felt unsteady. How much did Roland really know?

"Who's there?" Amarys's voice called out from beyond her door.

"Rowen of Antioch," announced the steward.

"Send her in."

Rowen straightened the laces running down her sleeves and adjusted her pearl-lined headdress, squaring the cap above her braided coif. The steward opened the door for her.

The chamber shone with the rays of the midday sun, which filtered through its tall, gabled windows. Warm mahogany furnishings glowed like burnished gold. Above the mantle of a crackling fireplace hung a tapestry of Diana at the hunt, bow at the ready, a faithful hound rushing ahead of her.

Amarys reclined on the stone bench in front of her window, holding a hoop of needlework. Her fingers appeared so dainty, threaded up with crimson. "May I see them?" she asked.

Whispering, "Yes," Rowen lifted her purse's leather flap to show Amarys the caps and stems. Amarys took them up, tilting her head when she discerned no smell. She tucked her hair behind one ear and touched a cap with the tip of her tongue.

"Tastes like parchment. Oh! I forgot the matter of payment. What is Roland's price?"

"No cost. You are a friend. And this is a gift."

"Oh, no," said Amarys. "Procuring such things is not easy or safe. I know you worry for your brother's reputation and would not see him painted as a warlock. You both risked a great deal in trusting me. Please, let me give you something in return. Perhaps this." Amarys touched a teardrop garnet pendant that hung from her throat.

"An exchange of gifts, if you insist."

Amarys brought the gem over her head and placed it in Rowen's hand. It caught the light in a way that produced a fiery gleam.

"Shall we have them now?" asked Amarys.

"How long do we have?"

"The rest of the day. My maidservants will come to prepare us for bed when it gets dark."

"How did you manage that?"

"I said we were fasting and would be deep in prayer."

"And that worked?"

"My father always fasts on this day. This year, I swore to join in solidarity."

"You are as clever as a fox," said Rowen. "Let's get started then."

Near the fireplace, Amarys had a cast iron pot full of steaming water. The round wooden table in the corner had been decorated with a pair of clay cups resting on a lace tablecloth. Amarys took the mushrooms from the pouch and stuffed them into the kettle. They waited for it to steep, and as the water turned dark and murky, Amarys added mint leaf to mask the flavor. When the brew was ready, she poured two cups and handled them carefully.

"This is completely mad, you know," said Rowen, shaking her head.

Amarys sipped, her eyes smiling over the top of her cup.

"The mint does nothing!" she cried.

"You put mint in this?"

They downed the brew all at once, hacking as the earthy flavors overpowered their senses.

"This is the cost of adventure," said Amarys. "Errantry of the mind."

"Maybe next time we could just do our embroidery?"

"Never again. Henceforth, we shall be Gawain and Yvain, and no one shall keep us from adventure."

"Not even fair damsels?" teased Rowen.

"That's right," said Amarys, poking her shoulder. "Unless they are so fair as yourself."

Rowen smiled. It was a muted smile full of uncertainty.

"I want to see the phantom island West of Ireland that rises briefly before it sinks into the sea," said Amarys. "I want to hear the selkie's song and taste St. Keiwin's medicinal white apples."

They lay prone side by side and watched the fire dancing in the hearth. They sang their song about the cycles of the Green Man, the lord of life who was born in the Spring and died again each Winter. As their voices lifted, the flames appeared to grow arms and legs and to whirl sashes of gold. Rowen could see the naked form of the dancer from the tournament, her voluptuous contours ablaze. Was the brew working?

Couldn't be. So soon? These effects—Rowen concluded—might be a result of her nervousness in the presence of Amarys. She wanted Amarys to like her. It was all she wanted, all she seemed to dwell upon. And she knew that Amarys liked her a great deal. But Rowen wanted Amarys to like her even more than that. The longing made her sick, for she always needed something she couldn't have. Endless amounts of whatever that was. Was it words she wanted? Deeds? Promises?

Why was nothing ever enough?

She usually did not listen to her thoughts so attentively. She did not like it.

Rowen dipped her finger into the cinders and drew rough images of beasts into the wood floor. A snake extended a forked tongue at a man who might have been a wodewose or werewolf. The ladies giggled over the images until something in Amarys's mind turned dark.

She shouted, smearing the soot as if she had divined some demon's face. Rowen watched her cautiously. The lady was paler than the stone walls of her chamber, and her eyes darted about the room.

"Rowen," she said. "Just now—in the soot—just now—I saw the Ankou. He was cloaked all in black. He bore a skeletal likeness. I closed my eyes, and I could feel him pulling me into his wheelbarrow."

"Do not summon him with your words."

"I will try not to—but Rowen—are we poisoned? Are we dying?"

Rowen tried not to give it away that similar anxieties had occupied her thoughts. "We took a very small amount."

"Where did Roland get these caps? Some witch of the wood?"

"No. He found them. I trust his eye on this."

Amarys tried to match Rowen's calm, but she was too stiff to be convincing.

Rowen reassured her with a line of scripture, "Et dixit illis angelus: Nolite timere. And so said the angel: Be not afraid."

Had they taken too much? Had they prepared it right?

Rowen couldn't be certain. "I won't let anything bad happen. I promise."

"I do not wish to die," whispered Amarys. "Ah, no. I am not ready to meet God!"

"You will not die. Not for a very long time." Rowen's voice felt strange in her mouth, thick like beeswax. She realized now that she had a mouth so very full of teeth.

Her stomach turned as though she were falling. The roof of her mouth tingled, and she wondered what Amarys was feeling. She had expected some descent into the weeds of her brain, but what she felt was more like a rising frenzy. Every color in the room seared her eyes, from the blinding orange flare of the hearth to the rose-red undertones in Amarys's eyelids and nail beds. The climb was forceful and fast; it continued to reach new heights like a vine hungry for sunlight.

"Oh no!" cried Amarys as she stared in amazement at something Rowen could not see. Blue dots swelled in her peripheral, and everything seemed larger than it should have been.

Rowen leaned forward, clasping Amarys against her like they were about to crash through the floor. "Courage!" said Rowen. "With me, say: I am not afraid." Amarys was trembling so hard Rowen could feel it.

"I am, though," said Amarys, clutching both sides of her head. "I fear we will be sucked into the mouth of Hell!"

"If we are, I will be consoled knowing you are with me, and I am with you." Rowen took up a discarded shawl and draped it over Amarys's shoulders.

"Do you know who you are?"

"Who?" asked Amarys.

"You are Aeneas."

"I am?"

"Yes! And I am the Sibyl of Cumae, leading you on your journey through the underworld."

Amarys, too scared to laugh, wrapped her arms around Rowen. She did not question her. She would accept any truth outside the one playing out in her own mind.

The carvings adorning every rafter and door came to life, writhing like snakes, their gaping mouths eager to devour. Rowen drew Amarys forward between immense, corrugated trees. The shadows took the shape of bears, stalking them from the corners. Amarys twined her arms ever tighter around Rowen's waist, which triggered a vision of vines wrapping over her.

Rowen screamed. Amarys tilted, pulling Rowen down. Hands clenched; they slid across the wool carpet to evade their demons. They sought escape in a distant light: the mouth of the forest. Rowen held Amarys back from the portal, rescuing her from a sharp and sudden drop.

"Amarys!" Rowen cried, catching her before she nearly fell through her bedroom window.

Amarys gasped and caught her breath. Rowen could feel the girl's heartbeat pounding beneath her embrace. They cloaked themselves within the shawl, couched against the wall beneath the window. The breath between their lips seemed to pull their spirits inward. Amarys pushed away the knit and removed Rowen's pearl-studded cap.

"You are not the Sibyl," she said. Her hands were gentle as she pulled the wooden pin from Rowen's hair. The river of her long, black hair unfurled. "You are my love, the Queen of Carthage." There was an otherworldly quality to her voice.

Her fingernails grazed Rowen's collarbone and found their way down—between her breasts, down her middle, lower and lower—until they disturbed the fabric on her thighs. Her touch cast ripples, ring after ring expanding from the point of contact. Amarys leaned forward, kissing Rowen's neck.

The room felt almost normal again, though Rowen's body hummed with magic.

"Can I trust you with my heart, Aeneas?"

Amarys only smiled. She drew herself away, moving slowly toward the bed, twirling down on it and laughing. Rowen was unsure if she should follow until Amarys called to her, "Come, Dido."

Rowen toyed with a bundle of tansy and lavender that hung from the bedpost, hesitating at the edge of the bed. Amarys swept up toward her, bringing her mouth close to Rowen's. They kissed, and every candle of sensation ignited.

Amarys unlaced Rowen's dress at the sleeves, sliding it down. Rowen covered her slender bosom with her arms.

"Don't be timid," said Amarys, removing her seed pearls and draping them around Rowen's neck. "You are my radiant prize."

Amarys laced her fingers with Rowen's, moving her hands away so she could look at her. She lay soft kisses over her throat. Rowen closed her eyes, seeing dragons of red, blue, and purple lined in thick gold borders like an illumination; they glided over what sometimes looked like vellum and sometimes like scales. The walls seemed to breathe with the smooth, wavering light of a sea cavern.

Rowen arched her back as she felt Amarys's tongue flick her nipple. Her thoughts flew from her mind. Amarys hiked her skirt up and began to stroke the little well between her legs.

Rising and falling into brocade streaked with sea dragons, Rowen could hardly fathom what was real and what was a dream. She felt like she was melting into pools of color. She grew dizzy with visions of serpents twisting, their scales bleeding bright colors that mingled into new, luminous hues.

"Amarys," she sighed. She could barely think. "It is a sin."

"Do you want me to stop?"

Rowen clung to Amarys, willing her to keep going. Near the summit, she pushed her away, rolling onto her side and exclaiming, "Such things are of the devil!"

Amarys drew back, nuzzling Rowen's ear. "Do you think I am of the devil?"

Rowen sat up, adjusting her dress. "What if we are discovered like this? Hurry. Help me dress."

When all was put back together, Amarys insisted, "We've done nothing wrong. It was only a bit of play."

Rowen could not dismiss what she had felt as what Amarys deemed a "bit of play." There was no explaining this as preparation for a husband. They certainly could never speak of it to any priest.

Outside the window, a light rain began to fall. Water droplets streaked the glass. Rowen longed to remain there, to sleep there night after night with Amarys by her side.

The devil's cap seemed to whisper every unspoken truth aloud. Rowen knew now what longings sang deep in her heart.

"I wish it would rain forever," murmured Amarys. "I wish God would see our sins and send a flood. And there would be no summer games. And we need never leave this tower again."

Remembering the terms of the next summer games, Rowen felt her heart breaking. "Knights of great renown will fight for you."

"Renown does not stir the passions."

So many thoughts swarmed Rowen's head. "If I could fight for you, I would."

Amarys's brows drew together, but there was a softness in her dismay, perceived by Rowen in the way Amarys's hand found its way to rest on hers.

"I would," said Rowen. Her eyes watered, an effect of the brew.

"I would not let you. You are too dear to me." Amarys twisted the fringed edge of her bed curtain on her finger. "You know, it is not the prospect of my duty that frightens me, only that my cousin Harlowe is projected to win. He remains undefeated in single combat."

"Perhaps he will be disqualified again."

"I can only hope."

"Why do you dislike him?"

"We bring out the worst in each other. And frankly... his heart is black."

"Surely he has some redeeming qualities," reasoned Rowen. "There are glimmers of light in everyone."

"Not in him. Those glimmers vanished long ago," Amarys insisted. "I would advise you to keep your distance, Rowen. I have known Harlowe since I was a girl— my family summers at his family's hunting castle. As the two eldest children, he and I would often play together. He had certain appetites. He would make me play games that I found loathsome."

"What sorts of games?"

"Horrid games. I cannot say."

"Amarys... Did you tell your father?"

Amarys's eyes filled with mist.

"Did you tell anyone?"

Amarys smiled, catching Rowen off guard. She pushed a strand of hair back from

Rowen's cheek, pecked her on the lips, and said, "I fear you would not understand. And I want you to be happy, always."

Rowen could not help but grow alarmed. "You must help me understand! If he has wronged you, I will not rest."

"Shh. We should speak softly. We will summon my Nurse with shouting. I will tell you everything, but you must never breathe a word to anyone, especially not Roland. You must swear, for I know you like to tell each other everything."

"Roland and I have our private lives now. I swear, I will keep your secret."

Amarys lay her arms around Rowen's neck, cuddling against her. "Harlowe's games are always games of power. He cannot derive any enjoyment unless he enacts suffering. Have you noticed this about him?"

Rowen remembered Harlowe smiling ever broader as her brother glowered at the gifts for her dowry. "I begin to," she confessed.

"As children, when we would play knights and squires, he would always be the knight. If we played dungeon, he was always the jailer. If I got to be a princess, he wanted to play my kidnapper. He would always put me beneath him, and as we got older, the games became adult in nature."

Rowen covered her mouth.

"It was only touching at first, harmless play between curious people. He wanted more and more from me, and eventually, it was more than I was willing to give. That is when he sought to punish me."

"He didn't."

"He could not have my body," Amarys assured. "At his chateau, there was a robin who nested in a tree outside my window. I would see it tending to its hatchlings, and I loved them dearly. At dinner, I told everyone how pretty the little robin was, how I loved to wake to its pretty songs each morning.

"The next day, I discovered the nest was empty. Outside, I found the hatchlings strewn about the tree, all dead. At dinner, Harlowe presented my robin on a platter just for me and boasted how he killed my 'little pest.' Since that day, I have refused all flesh. And Harlowe provokes me, promising to eat my share of fowl at every meal."

"And your father would see you married to such a man?" cried Rowen.

"My father says I am too tender-hearted. He reminds me that my shoes are made of leather, my cloaks trimmed in fur, my candles made of tallow. What can I say to that? I did not make the world what it is. My only power is controlling what I put into my mouth."

"I never knew you were opposed to flesh."

"I try not to draw attention to it. Father says God created animals to sustain and support us. That I have no idea what it is to starve. My stepmother says I do it for attention. No one understands. So I do not speak of it."

"It is hard for me to understand," said Rowen. "I have always felt so fortunate for what God provides. I also understand that it brings us closer to God to go without flesh so that others may eat. I do not think there is anything wrong with your choice. I rather admire it."

"Thank you."

"Why does Harlowe wish to marry you? Surely, he could derive pleasure from the suffering of any woman."

"I have dwelled on this very question. I believe it to be a result of our childhood attachment. With a heart as black as his, our history may be the closest thing to love that he will ever know."

"He will be defeated by a worthier knight," said Rowen.

"There is only one that I pray for."

"Who?"

"Isn't it obvious?"

They were both quiet for a long time. Or maybe it only felt long before Amarys slid out of bed and went into a chest. There, she found a jar of silver ink. She pried the wide cork from the inkwell and dipped a paintbrush inside. "Come," she called to Rowen.

Rowen sat up on her arm. "What are you doing?"

Amarys pulled a wooden stool and took a seat. "I want you to illuminate me like a book of hours."

Rowen came forward, taking the ink from her. She rolled the brush in the silver, scraping it on the edge of the bottle. "Is this a good idea?"

"Shall I paint you instead?"

Rowen took hold of Amarys's arm, bringing the brush's tip against her wrist. With its silken fibers, she formed vines of ivy, attentive to every detail in the leaves and coils. The silver spread over Amarys's skin like an enchantment; the coiling vines of ink seemed to tighten and unfurl.

Rowen hummed the melody of the Green Man as she painted fluid rivulets over the top of Amarys's hand. A fractured memory fluttered in and out of her mind. Had she done this before with red paint? No, it was henna. During a religious holiday, women in Jerusalem had painted their daughter's hands and feet with intricate decorations, waves and clouds, flowers, and tiny dots. She still remembered the journey she and her brother took as children.

These thoughts halted as Amarys slipped her dress down her shoulders, exposing her back. Rowen's hand trembled. She painted her with the stars of heaven, sprawling tendrils between the constellations of stars that had guided her ship to Brittany. The sailors spoke of them endlessly, and Rowen had listened, intent on knowing where she was going so that one day she might return to the place from which she had come. She swept her brush in reverse and then up toward the base of Amarys's skull, where she filled a crescent moon on the back of her neck.

"Do you really not know?"

"Know what?"

Painting each moon phase below the last, Rowen streamed the silver spheres down her friend's spine.

Amarys turned on the stool, causing Rowen's hand to wrap silver around her shoulder before she drew her brush away. "The one I wish would fight for me?"

Rowen knew, and here she was, painting her like a bride for him. The effects of the cap made her emotions surge. "You mean Roland?"

"Yes."

"But he is not a knight."

"He could become one. My father would see it done."

Rowen brushed the tears away and set her paintbrush aside. "Forgive these tears. I cannot say why I am crying. Please excuse me."

She returned to Amarys's bed, staunching her eyes like wounds with the backs of her hands. She fought her sorrow with everything she had, for any attempt to speak would have erupted in sobs. She fell to the mattress, the flood of her sorrow in full deluge—the darkening sky, as if in solidarity, scattered rain across the fields.

Amarys climbed into bed and hugged her from behind. "I should not have meddled with you. I have stained the love between us."

"No, you haven't," Rowen choked out. "I understand now what Roland meant. He said that if we took the devil's cap, we would never be innocent again."

A year and a day from the night of the midsummer games, Amarys would be betrothed to someone. Her marriage bower might as well have been Rowen's crypt. She was in love. She knew it now. The rain fell like a hail of arrows laying siege. Streams of water rushed rivers down the beveled glass, obscuring the world outside the dense stone walls.

"I have not been innocent... for a very long time," whispered Amarys.

The fire in the hearth had weakened, exhaling little warmth and imbuing the air with soot and the smell of smoke. Rowen craned her neck to face her, this luscious youth with the face of Venus. Longings bloomed and withered.

The brew had worn off. She was an ordinary girl again.

And now all she wanted was to run from this place.

CHAPTER 6

Rowen's soul was untethered, her mind lost to the divine flight she had taken with Amarys. She was too unsure of herself to attempt riding her horse. And as much as she wanted to ask for her brother, she worried that if she spoke to the servants, she might sound enchanted. So she left the chateau on foot like a peasant, slipping out in secret without telling anyone but Amarys. She followed the road toward the dense forest connecting their estates. Early Autumn tinged the air with a chill. Navigating this path on foot in the darkness of a rainstorm was no easy task. The world was awash in rainy twilight, everything drenched and covered in mud: her leather boots, her wool stockings, her skirt's hem, even after she'd bunched it up into her belt to keep it from dragging. The wind made a sound like a great beast roaring over the moors. Each gust tossed Rowen's hair like a flail. The winds, she knew, came in from the sea, rising like a leviathan. Strange dreams still played in her mind, brain-swelling and visceral as ever. She quickened her pace.

It had been ages since she seized the opportunity to walk anywhere alone. Alone felt very strange; with no one to talk to, she took more notice of the wind's chill and the world teeming with possibilities around her. She hopped between the mounds of slick grass, avoiding puddles as best she could, but a pocket of water caught her by surprise. Her whole foot plunged into the muck and froze her ankle to the bone.

Rowen snarled an expletive under her breath, kicking the toe of her sopping-wet boot against the ground. A noise from behind all but silenced her. It was the hooves of someone's horse. Rowen spun, staggering backward in the mud.

"Ha!" the man bellowed, coming into sight through the mist.

She half-expected to see Roland, but the register of the voice was low and resonant. Erec approached on horseback, offering his arm.

"These are no conditions for walking alone!"

"I prefer to walk. Good evening to you, Sir Erec."

Erec followed, his horse sputtering. "I must insist."

"As must I."

"I would not see you freeze or drown out here. I know a place that we might shelter, at least until the storm relents."

Rowen rolled her eyes, an unwilling participant in what felt like a love trap. Did knights venture out in the rain just hoping to find lost damsels they could rescue? "I suppose I must either acquiesce or be hounded for the rest of my journey!" she shouted over the storm.

Accepting his arms about her, she kicked up from the stirrup and settled in front of him in what hardly felt safe. They rode a short way to the mouth of a cave, a place Rowen knew well.

The cave was tucked beneath a knotted old oak tree known to locals as the Grim Tree. The Grim Tree was marred with many carvings of names and Latin phrases. "Amor Vincit Omnia" featured prominently.

Glass bottles lay discarded between the roots, roots that extended down and around the upper lip of the cave below. Little brown mushrooms grew in clusters along the edges of the cave ceiling. It was several strides deep but flat and open on the sides. The opening was tall enough for their horse to tuck its head and take shelter with them.

Erec tried to make a fire, to no avail. Rowen could not believe how exposed she had made herself. She was alone in a cave—sopping wet and still half out of her mind—with one of the few men in Rieux she couldn't overpower even if she managed to steal his sword. She sat upon a wide, flat stone, arms folded, wishing she had just run from him. The rain showed no signs of stopping. It cascaded down the cave mouth like a veil of tears, pooling into mud puddles, swelling and merging until it formed a canal barring their exit.

The knight sang softly as he tried stripping wood to get it dry. It was a pretty lyric that Rowen knew well.

Sing for the sparrow,

for summer's sweet song.

When Autumn exhales,

and the nights wax long.

Rowen, not thinking, joined him. The rain provided a resounding percussion.

The air grows too cold,

Our fires cease to burn.

Sing for the owls

that Spring may return.

Erec looked at her on the last line, allowing her to finish it alone. She drew the last note out, resuming a downcast gaze. "You sing beautifully," he said.

"My grandmother and I sing together as we weave."

"Your father's mother?"

"Yes," said Rowen. "I did not know my mother's family."

"Really? But Roland speaks the language of Saracens."

"Grandmother taught us."

"Do you speak the Saracen tongue?"

"Not as well as him."

"But you speak Latin?"

"I memorize things in Latin. I hardly speak it. Roland, though, is fluent. He can transcribe manuscripts into the langue d'oil, the langue d'oc. He even knows a little Breton."

"You are fortunate to have such a brother."

Disarmed by Erec's smile, she returned the sentiment. "You have a brother, too, no?"

"Yes. And four sisters."

"And who is your favorite among them?"

"I..." He colored. "I do not know them. Before coming here, I apprenticed under a

69

knight in Vitrès."

"How old were you when they sent you away?"

"Six."

"And that is why you fight so well."

"Yes, my lady." Erec dropped the sticks for the fire that refused to spark, sighing in frustration. "May I speak plainly?"

"Please."

Erec covered his eyes with one hand. "I suffer terribly. My skin feels clammy even now. My mind is blank as a stone. I wanted to tell you with words, not letters, but I was too afraid of what might happen if you rejected me. With all certainty, it would end me."

"End you? As in, kill you?"

"Yes."

"You are telling me that if I reject you, you will die?"

"Yes."

"I do not wish to kill you, Sir Erec, but you would force me to be false to say I share your feelings."

"I would have the truth, however painful. May we start again?"

"I was unaware we had begun at all." Rowen hugged herself, frozen stiff from the darkening eve. Erec unfastened his wool cloak and shook the rainwater from its surface. It was damp but warm as he draped it around her shoulders.

"You think me ugly," he said.

"Not at all."

"Is it my red hair?"

"You are beautiful, a truth acknowledged by many maidens known to us."

Erec brightened but he assumed a posture of performative humility. "I neither seek nor encourage such attention."

"That is wise, for it is foolish to love beauty, which will fade."

"What is it, then, that I am lacking?"

"Nothing. It is only that I do not know you. And I struggle to believe you when you say you are in love. You do not know me, either."

"I know your brother who speaks well of you. I know you through your visits to my liege lord's daughter. You are kind to servants and very devout. You are brave, too, for you came at Guyon with a sword to save your brother's life. And when I intervened, you kept fighting."

"Perhaps it was Roland who moved me to be brave. We sometimes share one mind."

"Whatever it was, I would like to pursue you... if you will let me."

Rowen watched the rain, unsure how to respond. This man's chivalric disposition could fall away if she provoked him with rejection. She was flattered, but part of her was fearful she might cause offense or provoke him to act on his lust. Roland was not here to protect her. At a loss for words, she began to hum the song once more. Erec listened attentively, humming a harmony.

As the rain let up, he said, "I admire your silence. There is strength in silence. I know that as a second son, I am a gamble. I wish I could prove to you that I have great potential. Perhaps in the summer tourney, you will see that I outmatch my peers. I hope one day, I will garner enough fame and wealth as a knight to return to you with an offer of marriage that would not demean you."

Rowen harnessed a conventionally soft voice. "My brother speaks well of you, Sir Erec. But he says our father will not approve this match."

"Will you wait for me? Will you promise not to marry someone else?"

Rowen took care before answering. She said calmly, "This is a promise I would give willingly were it up to me."

"I would know your will, lady. Not your father's. Not Roland's. Only yours."

"By my own accord, I would not marry any other man."

"Yes?" said Erec, grinning in disbelief. Rowen realized that he might have just indirectly proposed. Had she inadvertently agreed?

"Yes?" she asked, perplexed.

Erec gathered her up in his arms as a fawn might take a nymph and made several impassioned declarations, "I shall love no maiden but you! I shall fight every cause in your name!" By some miracle, he released her, perhaps because he could see in her eyes how much he frightened her. "Let me deliver you home to your father so I may make a good impression." Erec ran out under the drizzling tree cover and spun. "Fairy bride!" he shouted up at the trees.

"You must not get carried away, Sir Erec! My father is a difficult man. He will not agree."

"I rejoice for your chastity, your resolve for our love. You are truly the purest, dearest maid in all of Brittany!"

His grin was maddening. Rowen found herself matching his expression, only because she could not keep herself from laughing at his exuberance.

She had no idea how to react. Should she be happy? Should she scream for help?

Marriage certainly seemed preferable to a life of isolation and prayer in a convent, wasting away in some dreary anchorite's cell. He could give her a life at the side of a champion. And yet, something inside of her felt irrevocably shattered, like she had just traded something precious that she could never have back. The image of Amarys's vine work lingered in her eyelids. Vines that clung.

CHAPTER 7

As they rode the little distance to la Flèche manor, the rain abated to a light mist. The manor lay just ahead in all its ruinous glory. The storm shutters were drawn, except those to her father's bedroom on the second floor, which clattered in the wind.

"Is this where my beloved lays her head?" asked Erec.

"Quite modest compared to the chateau, is it not?"

"It is a lovely home. I much prefer it to Clement's hall, for you have an abundance of ivy and stone. Is that the chapel?"

"The chapel is the manor's best feature," Rowen admitted, pleased that he had noticed it.

"When Clement lived here, where did he lodge his men?"

"The barracks were in the town back then. The building is now a prison."

"I should like to live privately like this. Clement often complains that he is surrounded by gossiping servants, 'plagued by the wings of Rumor,' he says."

Rowen hesitated to say what she was thinking. Many rumors did circulate about Amarys's father. Before Rowen's family assumed ownership of the manor, a plague had ransacked Clement's household, claiming scores of servants, knights, and Amarys's mother. Some said it was contamination of the wheat, others said the well was poisoned, but the predominant narrative was that a village girl had been raped to death by Clement's men, and because Clement protected them from justice, the girl's spirit had cursed the Baron and dragged his wife to Hell.

The weathervane over the stables screeched as it spun. The amber glow of a lantern pulsed within. Erec veered his horse in its direction and came under the shelter. There, they found Roland running a brush over Ash's mottled coat. Erec held Rowen's waist as he helped her dismount, and she went running to stand behind her brother.

"You left Biax," he chided her. "You should have waited."

"I'm sorry."

Roland turned to greet their guest. "Erec, thank you for bringing her home." The men clasped arms and gave each other a hard pat on the shoulder.

Ash nickered as Rowen stroked the bridge of his nose. "Why is he damp?" she asked.

"I saw the rain clouds and decided I should come for you. The steward told me you had left without an escort. I could not find you along the road."

"I am sorry I was not there," said Rowen. "Erec had me wait out the heaviest part of the storm at the Grim Tree."

"Good man," he said, putting up the brush. "You'll want to go before my father sees you."

"I was rather hoping to make an introduction," said Erec.

"An introduction?" Roland looked between them, a faint smile tugging his lip. "I would not recommend it, friend. Our father's leg has been acting up from the cold, so he is particularly ornery today. You have my gratitude."

"It was no trouble," said Erec. Rowen kept her gaze fastened to the hay and dirt beneath her feet. She could feel Erec's eyes upon her. "Farewell, my fae. Look after your health."

Rowen gave a nod. When Erec had gone, she watched through the stable door as he rode off into the clouds of mist.

"That was odd," said Roland, leading Ash into his pen. "Did you tell him to leave you alone?"

"No," she said. "I was afraid to anger him. And now... I think I may have promised myself to him."

Roland whipped his head around. "You did what?" he cried, clawing a hand through his hair.

"It was a misunderstanding. He only asked me to promise not to marry anyone else. Seeing as I don't plan to, I said I would not. And he thought I meant a great deal more."

"Satan's twin. You just shoved love's arrow a little deeper. And I'll bet you want me to be the one to rip it out for you!"

He closed in on her. Rowen delivered a gentle clout to his shoulder, jostling his mantle. "I can fight my own battles."

"I'm not saying I won't do it. You know I will. But you, in turn, must reflect upon your true feelings! What are you doing telling him such things!"

"Well, he is not a bad choice. And with his protection, I would no longer need to rely upon Father."

Roland seized a pitchfork, working to turn the hay in Ash's pen. "Oh, what was I thinking, introducing a woman to the devil's cap? You taste color, see a few dragons, and now you're as wily as Cleopatra."

Rowen's neck tensed. Thinking of the journey she and Amarys had taken made her warm in the cheeks.

"How was it?" said Roland.

"I would rather not say."

"Even to me?"

"Many secrets were shared."

"Oh?"

"Amarys spoke very ill of her cousin, Harlowe. She made me promise not to tell you. I only pray he does not win her hand."

"He will. He is the next Viscount. Clement and Father will arrange the games to suit his strengths because—let's face it—Clement wants that title for his grandson."

"Yes," Rowen hedged, adding, "Unless Father had some conflict of interest... some other unmarried knight worthy of Amarys."

"No, no, no, stop that," said Roland, his sword arm pointing the pitchfork at her. "You can forget it."

"Amarys is your match in every aspect. You have no idea. If you married her, she would fill your days with light."

"She is not for me," said Roland. "I find her irksome."

"Will you let your chance to retake the Barony slip away?"

"Ha. He who takes the monkey for the money will end up with the monkey."

"Amarys is no monkey!" Rowen raised her hands as though she would claw his throat out. They grappled.

Roland laughed, dropping his pitchfork. "Look at you wax wroth for your friend!"

A low, rumbling groan escalated into a scream as she broke away. "A Norman-Breton marriage would sow peace for generations!"

Laughter still bubbled in Roland's throat. "I am too young to marry!"

"Amarys is the same age."

"Yes, but it is out of her control. People lose life and limb for these silly games. My answer is no. I like being alive."

"I used to think you were brave."

Roland's laughter burst forth anew. "Now you try to goad me into dying for your friend!" He put his pitchfork back on the wall, wiping the sweat from his brow. Roland closed the gate to Ash's pen and asked, "Why do you want this so much?"

"She told me what Harlowe is like. She says his heart is black. What if it were me, Roland? Would you let me marry the man who killed Edmund!"

Roland's mood darkened at the mention of his master's name. "If it came to it, I would have to duel him." He continued to stroke Ash's nose. "I would not let you marry such a man."

"Amarys has no brother to duel for her. Please, do me this one favor, and I shall never ask anything of you again."

Roland took a long breath, pressing his forehead to Ash's neck. "I already gave my answer. You press too far."

"Maybe I'll just steal your armor. Steal your name. Save her myself!"

Roland narrowed his eyes. "Would you?"

"I might. I am that desperate."

"Imagine if you were discovered. Your name and mine would be disgraced. I understand you want to protect your friend, but you cannot allow her fate to become your own burden. You have your own future to consider. And I have but one life to lose."

Rowen frowned, a bloom of black bile filling her chest.

The whine of a hinge emanated from the house. Across the yard, the iron door to their manor hung open. Her father's towering figure dwarfed the threshold as he leaned into it. He beckoned his issue with a subtle motion of his hand.

"We'd best go in," said Roland. He donned his hood and sprinted through the rain toward the house. Rowen kilted her muddy skirts and followed him.

"Twins," Ivin grumbled as his children came through. The dense walls of their home insulated the heat of the fireplace, producing an airy warmth full of undulating shadows. Thick, white candles glowed on little wood tables under mirrors and windowpanes, filling the tall ceilings with orbs of flickering light. The glass windows facing West highlighted the contours of the iron-studded linenfold panels.

Ivin displayed three suits of armor in the main hall and a dozen or more swords of various sizes and shapes mounted on the walls upon racks. He had taken one of them from a Seljuk heathen, a curved blade with a hilt encrusted in rubies. Another was a bastard sword nearly five feet long, a gift from the Lionheart himself. Ever since Rowen was a little girl, she would fawn over its glistening steel and long for arms strong enough to take it up.

Emelie, one of their domestics, brought Rowen a cup of stewed root vegetables and a hunk of rye.

"Thank you, Em. You may retire for the evening."

Emelie gave a lilt before she retreated to the servants' quarters. It was always strange moving between spheres, a chateau in which she had very little power and a manor in which she was Lady of the house.

Her grandmother dozed in her chair, her head nestled comfortably in her chins of fat. When they had first come to Brittany, Cecile managed the home, but in recent years, her mind had deteriorated, and the role had to be taken up by her granddaughter.

"We are sorry for being so late. The rain caused some delay," said Rowen, sitting on the floor before the inglenook. A fire ate at the logs there and warmed her cold fingers. Rowen untied her muddy laces and removed her boots, inserting a pair of wooden feet to prevent the leather from shrinking.

Ivin sank deeper into his deerskin armchair, groaning softly into his hand. "You should have waited for your brother to fetch you."

Rowen realized he must have seen Sir Erec. Of course, he had. Her father never missed anything. She kissed her grandmother's cheek, waking her so she and Roland would not be alone with their father's displeasure.

"O-oh!" said Cecile, perking up as she surveyed her surroundings. "Did I fall asleep?"

"Sorry to wake you. I wanted to tell you of my adventure in the rain!"

Cecile emitted a giddy chuckle. "A story! Yes, child. Go ahead."

"Well, I saw the rain coming and thought I should run home before a storm trapped me at the chateau," she began, kneeling at her grandmother's feet. She held the woman's soft hands to hold her attention and keep her from sinking back into slumber. "When anon, a terrible deluge befell!"

"Oh no! My poor girl!"

"But then, out of the mist, a great man appeared on horseback. I thought it was Roland, but no, it was our champion, Sir Erec of Avenport."

"Who?" asked Cecile.

"Champion of the summer games."

"Oh. I see."

"He rescued me, Grandmother. And he was not untoward, for he is very noble. He demonstrated every virtue of chivalry."

"Really? All of them?" teased Roland, folding his arms as he leaned against the mantle. "Did he pray as he rode with you?"

Cecile cackled, whacking her grandson on the behind. Roland jumped, guffawing in disbelief. "Grandma!"

"Let your sister finish her story, you changeling."

"That's all. He brought me home. Heroic, though, is it not?"

"And a good story. You'll have to tell me the real story later," giggled Cecile.

"You should not have left the chateau alone," said Ivin, sipping from a flask of mulled wine.

Rowen assumed a submissive posture, bowing her head. "I made a mistake, Papa. I am sorry."

"Sir Erec strikes me as a fortune hunter," said Ivin. "Do not mistake his heroics for an interest. I imagine he will try to win your Amarys next summer."

Rowen rolled down her stockings and hung them off the edge of the mantle. "I imagine you are right."

"Once broken, a heart is never fully mended."

"Yes, Papa." She knelt and leaned her head against her grandmother's knee, her mind exhausted from its journey to the Otherworld.

Ivin tossed a knit blanket to them, which Cecile laid over Rowen's shoulders. She could have fallen asleep there, but the flames were so lovely. She wanted to watch them as they danced themselves down into embers.

"Father," said Rowen. "Tell us of the siege of Acre! The Crusade of Kings!"

The old knight handed his flask to his daughter and sighed. "It was nothing so glorious as what the poets sing."

Rowen sipped the spiced wine, passing it back. "No matter. I prefer your stories, as I prefer chronicle to song." Rowen's father had lived a life that almost everyone she'd ever met could only imagine. He had traveled far afield, to strange and undocumented lands, crossed numerous borders, carried armor and steel over seemingly endless foreign plains, relied upon supply trains, surviving encounters with all manner of beasts. He was a true embodiment of a legendary figure like Lancelot or Yvain.

"I will tell you how the Lionheart fell sick, and how I saved his life."

Rowen straightened and leaned forward, hugging her knees.

"First of all, you must remember the siege of Acre lasted a very long time and we were beset with scarcity. Under the leadership of Guy de Lusignan, we endured terrible conditions."

Roland, having no interest in their father's stories, said, "Grandmother, can I help you upstairs?"

"Yes, dear." Roland took her arm. They said goodnight and gradually moved in the directions of their chambers.

Ivin went on, "Saladin's forces surrounded us and blocked our supply chains. The men had to slay their horses for meat, but I would not put my horse to death for anything or anyone. Godwin had served me well in battle. I had raised him from a foal.

"In 1191, King Richard arrived at Acre. His presence filled us with the spirit of hope, for he had been at war for most of his life and was seldom defeated. Soon after his arrival, though, he fell sick. His skin became hard like leather; he lost teeth and hair and nails. No one understood what was wrong with him. Except me. Some weeks before, the French King, Phillip, had suffered the same affliction. His recovery was only a matter of finding a curative food."

"Not horse, I gather."

"Not horse. But because my horse had been spared and I spoke perfect Saracinois, I was able to ride to Saladin's camp and persuade him to let me fill my satchel with the two things the Lionheart needed. Limes and rose-snow.

"Saladin had honor. He granted me these items and prayed for the king's recovery. As I anticipated, it worked. Richard recovered in a matter of days, stronger than ever. And straightaway, he sent for me. He said I would be rewarded with anything I asked." Ivin gestured to the hall in which they reposed. "So I asked for this."

Rowen knew it well that this manor had belonged to Clement and that Amarys spent her childhood playing in its halls before Clement expedited the construction of his chateau.

"Limes and rose-snow? You must tell me true, Father. What was it? The tongue of a dromedary? An actual lion's heart?"

"I always speak true, Daughter. Now, tell me, what is this quarrel between you and Roland?"

"Quarrel?"

"I heard you shouting in the barn."

"Oh, that." Rowen hugged her knees a little tighter. "I want him to enter the tournament. Would Amarys not make a fine bride for Roland?"

Her father perked up in his chair. The two of them chuckled, but neither had any genuine mirth.

"Nothing would make me happier than to see all our lands restored to us. Our house once pried these lands from Norman tyranny. But Roland is in this wretched phase, thinking he will be a troubadour to spite me."

"You must persuade him."

Ivin waved his hand like one lazily swatting a fly. "He only listens to you."

"Could you speak to Clement? Perhaps he would change the terms of the tourney if you suggested the alliance through marriage?"

"No. That would lower me in Clement's esteem. Better Roland proves himself on the field."

"Yet he refuses."

"I know. While you have sown roots in the Baron's household, I fear Roland takes after your mother."

"How so?"

Ivin's mouth thinned to a hard line. He stared into the fire, slumped in his chair, and said nothing.

"How was Roland like her?" she pressed.

Ivin exhaled heavily. "Both were born to wander." He threw his head back as he finished his wine.

Rowen knew very little of her mother. Her father never spoke of how they met or why he had married her. Whenever she had asked, it always angered him, and he would either retreat upstairs or order her not to dwell in the past.

"Sometimes I miss Antioch," said Rowen. "I still remember it, the ruins, the mosaics and fountains, the mail that glittered like dragon skin."

"Your mother hated Antioch."

"Why did she hate it, Father?"

"The people spread rumors that she was a witch."

"How could they?"

"Maybe it was true. She was a woman of the desert who came out of nowhere."

"I thought she came from Damascus."

"She did, but she did not want anyone to know. She had run away from her family. So we told them nothing." His eyes closed hard. "I have said too much."

"Father, she was my mother, and I know almost nothing about her. Grandmother says she was a lady of high standing. She was educated and could play a great many instruments. She knew fantastical stories and conveyed them beautifully. But I do not care about any of that. I only want to know where I come from."

"Here is the truth, Daughter. Beyond Damascus, I know nothing of your mother's past. Whenever I asked, she would tell me fantastical tales as though she herself had come from the land of djinns."

"Do you remember any of them?"

"Yes. One in particular has stayed with me all these years. It was about a boy and a girl with strange powers. The boy could make people forget, and the girl could make people dream. Suppose there was a soldier tormented by the nightmares of the war. The boy would simply place his hands on each side of the man's head, and all those nightmares would fly like ashes in the wind. Now, the girl... all she had to do to make a person dream was to meet their gaze as she passed them in the street... and the most beautiful dreams would unfurl in their minds. These dreams could change a man's fate. They could change his very nature. And every now and again, these dreams could change the world. When your mother finished this tale, she would ask me: who had the greater worth? The boy or the girl?"

Rowen tucked loose strands of hair behind her ears, worried that if she answered wrong, he would cease to speak of her mother. "I do not know, Father."

"The girl, of course."

"Father," she said abruptly, a lump forming in her throat. "How could that be? How could a girl have more worth than a boy?"

"Women have incredible power, Rowen, of bringing life into the world. It surpasses everything. And if you know just one thing about your mother, it should be this: that she wanted more than anything to be a mother. Your mother." Her father's black and gray mustache was damp with humours. Never had Rowen expected to hear her father open up about her mother; a river of emotions swept her up. She took his hand, feeling its warmth, perhaps for the first time.

"After meeting her, I decided I was done with war. I wanted a life of peace—a life with her. And when she—." He buried his face in his hand, quaking softly.

He composed himself with the rugged clearing of his throat. "I have shirked the responsibility of finding you a husband because I am fearful of losing you in the same way. You may serve in a convent if that is your wish."

"Father," began Rowen tremulously, "It is my wish to go on Crusade. I remember you told me of the women who washed your clothes and healed the wounded."

Sir Ivin's face paled. "Old women, Rowen. The young women, many of them, cavorted with the men. You have been sheltered from the ways of the world. I would sooner die than see my daughter so degraded. Now, change out of those damp clothes and pin them up. The night is waning fast."

"But, Father, there is another matter." She wanted to tell him of Sir Erec.

"Tomorrow, Rowen. I am tired."

It was better this way, she decided. She wished she could reveal everything to the man and get his true opinion on whether she should marry one of Clement's knights. Even if she dared to ask him, her father had already lost himself in his wine. He rubbed his forehead and leaned to one side. Rowen made slow, deliberate strides up the stairs and retired for the evening.

CHAPTER 8

The air permeating the second floor was musty from a faint presence of mildew in the carpets. Rowen's bedroom smelled more like the forest with its tall, gabled window and wood floors. The shutters were drawn, which made the room look black as pitch. Lines of faded light came in through the slits of the wood, shimmering with the shadows of rain. Her candle flickered dimly, its glow fluctuating across the cluttered chamber.

She sat on the edge of her bed, clumsily pulling the strings on the back of her dress until they hung loose. She pulled the damp garment over her head, shimmying furiously against its snug trappings.

When she had exchanged her garment for a warm, woolen bliaut, she went behind the headboard to slide away the panel that divided her room from her brother's.

"Do you have more of that wine from Giraut?" she asked.

Roland sighed. He rustled around in his room. Then he passed a long black bottle through the port. "It is a strong drink. Take small sips."

Rowen twisted the cork and yanked it out with a pop. Only a sip later, her head rushed with euphoria. "What is in this?"

"Giraut's regards."

Rowen set the bottle on her nightstand, curling up on her side under the warm fleece.

"If you want to marry Erec, I need to know. Right now. Not tomorrow, not some days from today. Now."

Rowen clenched her jaw to keep her teeth from clicking in her mouth. "I would marry him."

"Erec is my friend. Are you only choosing him to choose someone?"

Nothing in her head eluded him for long. He knew her mind like a corner of his own, having been forged in the same element of their mother's womb.

"I am falling asleep."

"We will speak on this tomorrow." Roland slid the little door shut.

The port between their rooms had not always been there. It began with a chilling episode, an event Rowen wished to forget and could not. One night, she awoke to feel cold about her thighs, and upon removing her coverlet, she discovered blood on the linens. Rowen screamed, thinking she was in grave danger, running to her brother's room. Roland, seeing only blood, went running to fetch their father. Ivin had already come out of his room, looking fear-struck and disheveled.

"I'll fetch Constance to explain it all."

Rowen had never seen her father show fear of anything before that day. He had seen all manner of gore on the battlefield, but a mere spattering of menstrual blood had sent him running to seek help from their servant.

Instead of laundering the sheets, Constance burned them, creating a dense, black smoke that filled the house with an offensive smell. The whole experience left Rowen feeling repulsed by her own flesh. She asked to bathe each day of the bleed, requesting basins of fresh water to her chamber so she could clean herself each time her garments swelled with blood.

When it came time for Constance to sit down with her, even the wise old servant grew squeamish discussing the female condition. She avoided words like 'blood,' 'bleeding,' and anything remotely relating to the female anatomy. Even the word 'spotting' offended her by the end of the lesson.

"When your... 'time' comes each month, you must... keep yourself clean, using these." She presented strips of crimson cloth.

"How must I use them?" asked Rowen.

Constance frowned. "You will understand in time."

Time came and went. Her many questions remained. Roland brought reading materials, Latin question-and-answer texts that were supposed to enlighten Rowen on this rite of passage into womanhood. They were meant to console, but they only made her more confused. They spoke of menses as "superfluities from different parts of the body attracted to the womb by the force of nature." It became her understanding that her body was colder than her brother's and that some defect in her gender caused her stomach not to digest food properly.

"What if I eat something with too much heat and bleed to death in my sleep?" Each night, she would creep into her brother's room and wake him with her latest concern. Roland reassured and consoled her, and the twins had no inkling that the opening of their chamber doors sent vibrations through the manor.

The following day, Ivin had his daughter whipped with a switch made of birch. Constance delivered the beating in a dark little room of the servants' quarters where nobody could hear her scream or see how hard the old woman struck. The fiendish little tool left welts that stung for days.

When Roland saw the welts on his sister's back, he tried to fight his father. He brandished his fists, succeeding only in getting himself locked in his chamber. In an absolute rage, Roland drove his boot through the timbered wall and made a substantial hole. The twins disguised it with a panel and used it well, exchanging notes and whispers with care not to disturb the house.

Sorry for the damage, the first note had said. Rowen smiled to see it. Roland passed another note.

Why must this happen to you? When will it be over?

"It will happen every month until I am an old woman," Rowen whispered back to him. "Constance says this happens to all women."

A third note came.

You are brave to endure it.

These words stayed with her for years. In this simple phrase, he had given her something powerful. She—like her father and Constance—had only seen how her monthlies revealed inferiority. But Roland saw them as a gauntlet to be endured.

Thenceforth, Rowen concealed it from her father, never using it as an excuse not to go to dinner or attend a ball, never giving him the privilege of isolating her again.

A pale spider wriggled as it descended a thin line of silk, floating like a pearl in front of the rain-streaked window. Rowen watched it sway.

She pulled Amarys's garnet from her purse, turning it over in the moonlight. A vibrant, blood-colored fire seemed to flicker deep within.

Closing her eyes, Rowen recited a psalm in Latin. The rain swallowed up her words, trickling down the stones of the estate, running like blood from the veins of Christ to feed the black soil of Rieux. The verse gave her comfort. These were verses she had known all her life, having memorized them since before she could remember.

While the twins had vastly different feelings about the Church, both could agree that Christ embodied all that was good and wise. Love thy neighbor and thy enemies. Do unto others what you would have done unto you. Let he who is without sin cast the first stone. Forgive. Forgive. And forgive again. And most importantly, confess or be condemned.

Rowen would never confess to anyone what she knew could incur the most perilous consequences if the wrong people found out.

They know God's justice requires that those who do these things deserve to die, yet they do them anyway.

There was a danger to her play with Amarys. Now, the full weight of its cost bore down on her. She had seen enough bodies burned and quartered in the square to know that some sins required blood to be absolved. And Clement, as Roland had so astutely pointed out, had other daughters.

CHAPTER 9

Amarys maintained that she was fasting in remembrance of her mother. Something about Rowen's departure always left her feeling empty, and tonight, it stung. Amarys stewed in guilt for having corrupted one so pure.

"My rose," she whispered, tracing over the cut glass of her window. "So much rain. Will it be enough to wash you clean of my touch?"

She knew she did not have to worry about her getting lost out there. Rowen had courage and sense enough to keep her safe. If only she could lend her some.

When her three chambermaids came to prepare her for bed, Amarys remained at the window. She stared at the water droplets trickling down the glass.

"My lady? Are you not well?"

"My mother is dead. Why should I ever be well again?"

The women hurried in, shutting the door. They surrounded her, framing her like a wreath. They recited verses about heaven and its many rooms and said everything they could to calm her, and each of them, piece by piece, provided a picture of the mother she had lost. She could breathe now. She had to.

Amarys sat up straight, trying to appear in control of her mind's mad wanderings. The ladies brought her to sit, where they brushed the dust and sweat from her hair.

"My lady, what is all of this staining your skin?"

Amarys looked down, remembering the silvery stars that Rowen had painted over her shoulders.

The ladies prepared a bath for her and scrubbed the silver ink from her back and arms. When they were done, the bathwater glittered. They dried her with towels and dressed her in a clean bedgown. They tucked her blanket in around her and said goodnight without a kiss.

Amarys watched the window. How she wanted to follow Rowen into the rain. Most days, she felt as though all her life was winter until Rowen returned and made it Spring again. She wanted nothing more than to lie in bed with her, counting raindrops, singing songs, hearing the pretty verses of forbidden lovers and djinns.

She wished she were a spirit flying between worlds, visiting the waters that Rowen had said were so clear, the people of Antioch called it the White Sea. If she were a spirit, she would chase her now through the rain, lift her like a feather in her arms, and carry her to the sparkling vistas of far-off places.

She wanted deep connections with all of the people in her life, from the women who touched and undressed her each day to the doughty knights who guarded every hall. Sometimes, craving connection so intensely, she considered grabbing them, pulling them out of their daily motions, and shocking them to life with a kiss. Sometimes, she went through with it, and they either ran from her or took her to her father to be punished. Amarys would laugh hysterically as though it had been a jest, which, in turn, made her father laugh. He would shake his head and dismiss her with a mild scolding.

It all began when she was twelve years old, shortly after her father remarried. They had relocated to the chateau, away from the memories of her mother, away from the manor and its dark histories. The servants whispered that her father had done unspeakable acts, allowing his tenants to starve while he hosted lavish parties for his knights. Tales of violence in town and food insecurity were lies, of course, lies born of resent. The small folk of Rieux lived well because they were well-protected, and the sacrifice endured by Clement's warriors deserved reward. Amarys knew her father to be a good man who loved his family, so she gave the stories no credence.

One night, she wandered out of bed and discovered that the guard posted outside her door had fallen asleep. Seeing a rare opportunity to explore the chateau, she shrouded herself in a blanket and went barefoot through the halls.

Without fires raging or candles glittering in the margins, the rooms were quiet and cold. At times, she had to navigate blind. Every few steps, she would trip into the shadows. She used the wall as her guide, pressing on as best she could. Some halls were simply too dark to penetrate. And Amarys had to be careful of guards. She managed, though, to see a great many parts of her chateau that had always been off-limits.

She found the library, and while it was too dark to read, its enormous windows let in enough moonlight that she could see it was full of treasures. She saw a trove of statues and artifacts that her family had accumulated over centuries of conquering throughout Brittany.

She went on to find the kitchens and, being only a child, did not think about the presence of tapers as an indication that anyone would be in there so late at night.

Believing herself to be alone in the bakehouse, she squeaked when she heard a hinge scraping behind her. She made a dash for the drying shed, crept inside, and closed the door without latching it. The light of a lone taper pierced the narrow opening.

One of the staff came through and placed it on the kneading counter. The girl was only a little older than Amarys yet had been graced with a woman's figure. She had bright red hair that fell in soft, voluminous waves. She retrieved what she needed from the dough box and dusted her fingers with flour. Amarys watched as she folded and pressed her ball of dough with intention and care.

The drying shed brimmed with the aromas of herbs and spices. Something peppery induced Amarys to sneeze. As well as she stifled the sound, she could not prevent the girl's notice.

"Is someone there?"

Amarys held her breath. The girl came toward the shed. She opened the door the rest of the way and discovered Amarys in the shadows.

"My lady!" she cried. "What are you doing in there?"

"I'm sorry! I only—well—I was so impressed with the bread that comes out of this kitchen that I simply had to know how it was made."

She felt quite silly hearing herself say that aloud. It had sounded better in her head.

"My lady, I will be in trouble if you are found here."

"I know. I will go, but before I do, may I ask, what is your name?"

She blinked, bobbing in what was supposed to be a curtsy. The back-of-house girls always did them so clumsily. Amarys often thought they were in the middle of fainting when they started. "I am called Vivien," said the girl softly.

"Vivien. If you will show me how to knead bread, I will see your station raised."

Vivien led Amarys over to the kneading table. She powdered her hands and sprinkled flecks of white over the worn wooden surface, resuming her folding of the dough. "I do it the way my mother taught me," she said. "Coat it once in flour. Fold in. Turn. Fold in."

Amarys pretended to be exceedingly uncertain in every motion, effectively getting the girl to put her hands on hers.

"Like this, my lady."

People said girls of her ilk had hands that were ruddy and hardened from work, but that was not true of Vivien. Her hands were impossibly soft, her nails long and clean. They left featherlike tingles on Amarys's wrists when she accidentally scraped her.

After the lesson, Amarys slipped from the kitchens. She darted through darkness, squealing with delight at the adventure she had just experienced. In doing so, she bumped into a number of tables and benches, and a guard finally discovered her. He apprehended her, taking her to her father to be punished.

It had been worth it.

From that day forward, she tried to steal more glimpses of the red-headed kitchen girl. It wasn't easy. Kitchen staff were not often seen. Most days, the girl kept her hair hidden beneath a kerchief, which made it hard to find her. Once Amarys learned her schedule, though, she could glimpse Vivien on her way to and from the dairy cow. She loved to look at her, memorizing every detail of her full lips, her white teeth, and her long, blonde eyelashes. When her hair was up, Amarys would look for faint traces of it that fell in wisps at the back of her neck. She would think about touching her there. Whenever she smelled freshly baked bread, she thought of Vivien's soft hands and the soft ways she would hold her. Sometimes, at night, she would touch herself and imagine it was Vivien's fingers working her to climax like a ball of dough.

Amarys despaired when Vivien's lovely hands became ruddy and coarse like those of all the other kitchen maids. She persuaded her father to elevate the girl to a chambermaid, and they shared a single night in each other's arms. Amarys pretended to be afraid of the dark. She claimed she needed someone to hold her. Vivien accommodated her, of course, and all through the night, Amarys contemplated how she might venture to kiss her. She could not go through with it, though, for the simple reason that Vivien could not have denied her if she wanted to.

Soon after her promotion, Vivien was lost to Amarys. She married another servant who put her to work bearing his children. She would spend the rest of her days as a wife and mother in a cottage on the edge of town, and this thought greatly bothered Amarys. How could a person ever be satisfied with only one lover?

Amarys found other muses. Her next object was a courier from Aquitaine, a youth whose broad shoulders made him stand out in a room. When he delivered his message to Amarys's father, she made a point to hold his gaze unflinchingly. Clement put him up for the night, and Amarys seized the chance to go to him. She disguised herself as a laundress with a basket of linens. She was proud of herself for walking right past the guards without alerting them.

When she reached the boy's room, he was at once fearful. He said he could be put to death for this, and she should go at once. Amarys was aware of the risk, but she had hoped she could persuade him to kiss her once before she left. The courier, whose name was Henri, was innocent like her. He had never kissed anyone outside his family.

Amarys promised to be patient and suggested they might help each other get more acquainted with the art of love. In the darkness of his room, the courier and the Baron's daughter practiced their craft. First, they kissed for hours, asking one another what they liked and what sensations it induced. Like a pair of scholars recording cause and effect, their curiosity led them toward new and ever-distant horizons. Amarys wanted to study his anatomy and observe how he was the same and how he was different. They took turns removing articles of clothing. He liked to look at her. At his request, she took a number of poses on his bed, lying passively as he pleasured himself. She watched how he squeezed and tugged his member, how he spat in his hand and tended gently to the tip. She was surprised by the size of the male organ, for she had only ever seen it represented on statues where it was no bigger than a man's thumb. The example now jutting out from her new friend's pelvis was long enough to spear a fish. When he came close to her, she ran her fingers over the muscles on his abdomen, watching how his ribs flickered when his core contracted.

"If you really want to learn to kiss," she said, "You must learn to kiss each part differently."

Amarys knelt before him like one at prayer, holding his erection and demonstrating what she meant. He found that agreeable enough and consented to kissing her in the same way.

The two devised a system. If she liked what he was doing, she would pull his hair. And if she did not like it, she would beat down on his shoulder. He laid her back on his bed and knelt at the foot of it, placing her thighs on either side of his neck. At first, he kissed her opening with too much fervor. She pushed him back and had him start again. Softly, he breathed and moaned against her, compelling her to twist a lock of his hair with her middle finger. When he made his mouth more supple, she wove her fingers deeply into his curls. She pulled his hair as though it would keep her from drowning in the feeling she knew on every stroke and thrust of his tongue.

All her life, Amarys had been told to wait for her husband to teach her the role she would play in the bedroom. For a time, after Henri had left Rieux and returned to Aquitaine, Amarys felt like a bruised flower. People continued to see her as a paragon of chastity, but Amarys knew her priest would have deemed her sullied. So be it, she thought, convinced that God would not have put the thoughts in her head if He did not want her to experience pleasure. For a time, she became enamored with Erec of Avenport, that glorious Adonis, and considered how she might gain access to the barracks. Alas, the man would never be found alone, and she had not the power to arrange for him to be brought to her in her chambers. Anyway, it was around the time that Amarys met Rowen, and her fancy for Erec all but vanished.

They met at the parish Church to visit the dead. When Ivin of Antioch presented his daughter, Amarys finally understood the notion of loving just one person for an entire lifetime. Rowen had the kind of beauty that would have angered Aphrodite.

She had worn a dress of vermillion silk with sleeves that trailed in ribbons to the stones below. She stood tall as an Amazon, her head crowned in braids interwoven with gold threads. She was soft-spoken and pious, possessing all the elegance of a queen. The girls had been left alone in a somber cloister, where they circled the crypts.

"Is your mother buried here?"

"Just there," said Amarys, gesturing to the sarcophagus bearing the likeness of a lady in stone. "Sometimes, I come here and talk to her. It gives me some small comfort to tell her of my life. Your mother is also lost?"

"Yes. Her bones are in Antioch."

"Do you ever speak to her?"

Rowen's face grew still. "No. She was a stranger to me." Amarys reached out, taking her hand.

"Speak to mine," she suggested. "It's all right. She is a very good listener. Mother, this is Rowen. Our fathers want us to be friends because we are the same age, and they don't know what else to do with us. And so we shall be friends."

Rowen squeezed Amarys's hand, taking her lead. "Good day to thee, Lady Margaret." She curtsied. She actually curtsied.

Amarys giggled at the sight. She loved her at once. She could not say why, but something about Rowen's open heart had made everything so easy.

In the early days of their kinship, Amarys begged for stories of Antioch, anything Rowen could tell her about its seaside castles and local legends. Rowen claimed not to remember much, but sometimes, without trying to remember, she would mention things she deemed inconsequential that were the stuff of marvel to a girl like Amarys. Imagining new worlds through Rowen, Amarys's longings intensified.

With the threat of betrothal only a year away, she was beginning to panic. Shutting her eyes, she tried to use the remnants of the devil's cap to carry her abroad. Anywhere. She would go anywhere if it had stories to unearth and new terrains to explore.

She breathed in the aroma on her pillow. The taste of rose oil permeated her senses. Amarys remembered Rowen bravely leading her out of the labyrinth of her fears. The toxins stripped away her sense of herself and her place in the world, but Rowen had a way of restoring her confidence. What had Rowen been feeling that made her burst into tears? Had Amarys ruined their friendship with her lust?

She pressed her fists to her forehead, sorrow breaching her chest in the shape of a moan. All through her journey with the devil's cap, she had been thinking only of herself. Her longings. Her needs. All she really wanted was to hold her friend and listen to the rain, and she had tarnished everything with sin. Now, she found within herself a well of love much deeper than she knew existed. She had buried it after her mother died. And here it was, every fathom of its depths for Rowen.

PART TWO

ROLAND

CHAPTER 10

Winter came and quieted the revels of summer. The only time Roland saw Rowen happy was at Mass. He could not say if it was because she loved God or because this was the only time she could see her friend. Amarys always came to sit with them, though she never spoke a word. Rowen continued to pester Roland, seizing his gaze with pleading eyes. Fight for her, she seemed to say. Roland pretended not to notice.

Everyone in Rieux gathered in the parish church, their whispers hissing on the edges of the nave as they lit candles and made prayers. Rowen clasped Roland's hand with icy fingers, draping it with an even icier rosary made of silver. Everyone was seated at the appointed time, their voices dimming into silence.

Father Gerard approached the altar and arranged the chalice and paten. In Latin, he commenced with the introductory rites. Roland took this chance to observe his sister. There was something about her friendship with Amarys that put him on edge. Ever since he went to Toulouse, the two seemed closer than ever before. He knew his sister was impressionable, and he worried that Amarys was using her somehow, perhaps manipulating her to get to him. There was something of the fox about that lady.

Father Gerard read from Ad Galatas, followed by Apocalypsis, and every verse was about the heavenly Jerusalem and the abomination of heresy. Roland could tell from his selections that his sermon would emphasize the importance of Crusade. Rowen appeared utterly absorbed by the priest's delivery, the passion with which he read, and the resonance of his enormous voice. Amarys, not so much. On the contrary, when Roland looked at her, she returned his gaze with an air of prim satisfaction he had noticed her.

"Brothers and sisters in Christ, some of you have already sacrificed so much. Others strive to achieve the yoke of knighthood that you might one day retake the kingdom of heaven from the heathen menace."

Knew it, thought Roland. Crusades again.

"I am sad to say it is not enough. We have not done enough."

Roland felt exhausted. He could barely keep his eyes open. His sister remained enthralled as ever, and Amarys was looking straight ahead. By her smile though, he knew that she knew he was watching her. Roland folded his hands over his cross and tried to pay attention to the sermon, or at least appear like one paying attention.

The consecration followed by communion went well enough, except that Rowen did not take the sacrament. Standing and walking to take the sacrament woke Roland sufficiently enough to last until the priest dismissed the congregation with the closing phrase: "Ite, missa est."

After Mass, Rowen went to seek confession. Roland was caught off guard when Amarys followed him to the margin of the vestibule.

She slid her fingertips down the chain hanging from his neck, stalling over the bright, blue stone flecked with gold.

"You wear the stone of a prince," said Amarys.

"It was my mother's."

"I know. Rowen told me. When your mother died, you got the lapis lazuli, and she got the silks."

"Is there some way I might be of service to you, Lady, or may I go?"

Amarys came closer. "I could ask the same question of the man who stared at me throughout the liturgy of the word."

Roland tried not to look down. Her bosom featured a golden cross that drew the eye to her cleavage. "I was only pondering how such a dress could be comfortable in the snow." He lingered on the last syllable. He expected her to gasp and storm away, but she did not. She only smiled, took his hand, and had him hold the cross he had been eyeing. His knuckles brushed the tops of her breasts. She stepped in against him, whispering a prayer for the dead. Roland joined her as he felt both their fathers noticing them together.

"Réquiem æternam dona ei, Dómine. Et lux perpétua lúceat ei. Requiéstcat in pace. Amen."

"For Edmund?" said Roland.

"May his murderer meet a similar end," said Amarys.

She was good at what she did, concealing the finesse of a courtier beneath a masque of moral principle. A man could climb to the highest office with such a wife pulling the strings of court. If such a thing had ever made his blood race, he might have fallen for her. But no. Roland preferred the company of girls who liked to riot and dance and went barefoot on the green. His ideal wore ragged skirts and flailed her hair like the fae folk. Good attempt, fair one, he thought to himself. Amarys might have found a way to control Rowen, but Roland would not fall prey to her sorcery.

As winter stretched on, Roland made great efforts to honor his deceased mentor by composing a song about Edmund's adventures as a younger man. He refused all libations, even in the coldest months when their servant Emelie brewed mulled wine fragrant with figs and cinnamon. More and more, he committed himself to his writings and sketches, ever dreaming of a life of errantry filled with muses and wonders.

Roland rode at full speed into town, urging his horse to a velocity that made the wind fill his cloak like a sail. He imagined himself flying leagues above the earth, soaring over the clouds. One day, he would return to Toulouse and craft verses in the sweet new style, singing of love as resistance to all the world's evils. His father believed he was meeting with Sir Erec to train, but no such meeting had been arranged.

Once or twice a week, Roland fabricated a lesson in order to attend his audience at Lechón Tavern. The people of Rieux loved the songs he had brought back from Toulouse. The young troubadour's success became the success of the tavern itself, and the brewess was grateful. Her business thrived beyond her wildest dreams.

Roland too profited from the venture. He saved his coin in secret, amassing a fortune that he hoped would see him anywhere but Rieux.

Lechón usually lay vacant in the morning, save the occasional lout curled up on a pallet behind the bar. The eaves rustled with the wings of pigeons near the east-facing windows where a family of them nested. The paneled walls were laden with the mounted heads of beasts: several bucks, a boar, and a ram, all haggard and wasting. Recessed nooks containing tables allowed for more private conversations, but Roland seldom laid claim to one. Any given night, these were occupied by gamblers, sell-swords, or otherwise unsavory types. For now, the nooks were empty. For now, the candles in the wall sconces were unlit. An abundance of light poured in from the East, exposing every detail of cracked tables sticky with ale.

Lisette greeted Roland with a cup of brewed herbs and a wrinkled smirk. "There's our Roland," she said as Roland joined Willem at the trestle teak table. Lisette looked similar to her pretty daughter of two-and-twenty, only broader with more freckles and fine lines. She was bundled in a chunky wool shawl that had a smell like something fetid smothered with the perfume of barley and fruit.

"Is your daughter here?" asked Roland.

Lisette finished refilling Willem's tankard to the brim. "Cat is sleeping."

"I must see her."

"You must wait."

"Is she in her room?" He started up, and Lisette pushed him back on his bench.

"I'll not have you pushing into my daughter's bedroom, Roland, not unless you come back with a priest."

"I wrote her a song."

"Oh, did you? The song of Roland?" teased the old hen.

Willem joined in on the fun, pinching his cheek. "Where's your horn, Roland? Leave it on the battlefield?"

"Quiet, Willem," chided Lisette. She returned to attend her cauldron behind the bar. "Cateline worked late last night. I would not expect to see her until the shadows lengthen."

Roland's mood brightened as the rafters creaked with the footsteps of someone shifting upstairs.

"Cat!" he called up to her. Her delicate footfalls gave him hope. Roland grinned at Lisette, who only shook her head as she continued to brew. Cateline soon appeared on the stairwell. Her eyes were sunken, and her dark brown curls lay piled in tempestuous heaps around her face.

Roland skipped toward her, lifting her off the stairs and whirling her. "I wrote a song," he said, stepping onto the platform where his lute hung from a curved nail.

Willem's lips gave a lurch to one side. "May I take my grog to go?"

"Stay, Willem!" Roland entreated him. "I would have you hear my song as well."

Willem leaned his face in his hand. "If I stay, I assure you it is only for the chuckles."

"Cat," said Roland, jumping down to take her hand and guide her to a chair beside his on the stage. "Sit. Help me with the key."

Cat's face glowed. She folded her hands over her threadbare skirt, a dreamy smile on her lips as Roland tuned the lute to his liking. He played the melody.

Cat shook her head. "It is pretty but try this instead." She tuned the lute and played it back in another key.

"I love that," said Roland. He took a minute to figure out the chords. "Yes. Yes! I love it."

"Ready?" she asked.

"Ready."

He finger-picked an overture that sprang like a vine of morning glory. As he sang, his tenor resonated through the hall.

Fairest maid in all Brittany,
Crown of darkening mist,
Cateline, you're a mystery
for too many reasons to list.

Cat bit her lip, closing her eyes as she blushed. This was a good reception, Roland thought.

For though our love may not last the year
At least we know that we tried.
I will live unafraid and free
if I may live by your side.

Cat joined him in harmony as he repeated the chorus. Roland grinned. The woman's ear for music never failed to amaze him. She had never been trained, and yet she surpassed him in her ability to improvise. It should have been another a moment for them, but something was wrong. As the song concluded, Cat stared down at the floor, her arms crossing over her lap. Roland could see her chin quivering, but before he could say anything, she sprang from her chair and ran from the tavern.

"Forgive me," she cried, holding her mouth as she fled.

"I don't think she likes the song," said Willem.

"Cat!" Roland came down from the stage and abandoned his lute on a table.

"Bring her mantle!" cried Lisette, chasing after him as he threw on his cloak. Cateline's mantle hung on a hook near the exit. Roland snatched it and pushed through the door. He sighted her wild hair as she ran down an alley. He pursued her, bending around a passage beneath a bridge, dodging several merchants, and sighting her at last near the well in the town square. The air blustered around them, cutting in under Roland's billowy cloak.

At the well, Cat sat curled against the stones, her face buried on her knees. Roland hooded her in the brown wool, securing it over her shoulders. She wrapped her fingers around its collar, hooking the clasp before returning to her downcast form.

"Cat? Did I muck it up?"

She looked up, whisking her hair to one side and twisting it. "No."

"Tell me what troubles you."

She shook her head, her eyes so bleary that he could tell she was using everything she had to hold back her sorrow.

"May I sit with you?"

She nodded.

Roland sat down on the hard stones, keeping her company in silence as he tried to think of what to say. "Was I really that awful?"

She furrowed her lip, buffeting him on the shoulder. "It was not the song."

"What is it then?"

"I cannot speak the way you can. I haven't the words."

"Speak from the heart, Cat."

"You are so far above me." She met his gaze, her eyes wet with tears, her nose pink.

Roland took her hand in his. Her hands were rougher than those of the ladies of his own class. He loved them more for that reason. Her worn nails had the kind of beauty one could not fake. She had worked hard her whole life, scouring cookware, mixing brews, and carrying platters heavy with half-drunk ale. "You are my love. And for me, that means there is no above or below, all right?"

Cateline leaned against him, touching the crown of her head to his chin. "The people in town have seen us together. They say I am your whore. And I might as well be, knowing we can never marry."

"Never mind what the people here think," he said. "The world beyond Rieux is vast. There are endless stretches of land full of little towns just like this one, not to mention great cities overflowing with people. If we went to Toulouse, we could be anyone we wanted to be." He held her chin, gently pulling her face toward his. "If we married in a foreign land, they would call you Lady Cateline. I would give you servants to wash you in milk and paint your skin with gold. You would wear the finest silks. Your shoes would be threaded with bells."

She closed her eyes, a little smile curling her rosy lips. Roland kissed her softly, and her eyes flashed open.

"Roland!" she chided, looking about them to see if anyone was watching.

"When I inherit, I will leverage my estate to spirit you someplace far from here."

"You imagine things that can never be."

"Push me off then. Make a scene of it. They will say you are most virtuous." Roland seized her mouth. She did not push him off. Several townsfolk walked past the other side of the well, watching their audacious display.

Roland and Cat returned to the tavern, tiptoeing around corners so they could get upstairs unseen. Lisette, they discovered, was down in the cellar getting ready for patrons, and given this opportunity, Cateline pulled Roland toward her room. She bolted the door behind them. Roland arrested her giggles with a kiss, ungirding the knot of her long leather belt.

Every touch—every caress—sent warmth and pressure coursing through him. He would do anything to conjure the blush in her cheeks or turn her skin clammy with lust. They were careful not to yield to baser instincts. Penetration meant confession and it invited unpardonable danger. Still, they mimicked the act, and near the summit, Cat whispered all the things she wanted him to do to her, all the things they both knew could never happen. Roland hushed her, resisting, even as her flower thrummed against his groin. He breathed in the smell of sour mash in her hair, sighing against her head until his urges passed.

CHAPTER 11

There was a kind of life that belonged only to the forest. Its mist-laden grounds echoed with the sigh of the wind. Rock doves crooned in the distance, out of sight where they might not be hunted. Every barren branch, every twig, every fiber of deadened leaves wove into the fabric of that mad place. The forest had a danger to it, a fairy element of all that was unpredictable and cruel. Roland knew that he and his father were merely guests in this unconquerable maze.

They stopped and observed a small clearing where a stag scraped his horns down a tree, clacking against the roots. Food had been scarce, and this was the only beast they had seen in weeks. Roland had a habit of biting his lip when he had a kill in sight. Gripping his bow, he took aim, heart palpitating like he had swallowed a frenzied hare. Steady, he thought quietly. On three. He began to exhale all the tension from his shoulders, letting it melt down his back like wax. The bowstring pulled at the tendon in his hand. He could feel every jitter of his target's heart as it craned its neck in anticipation. The string whipped his bracer as he loosed an arrow. It soared across the divide and pierced the creature's breast. Painless. The stag did not whimper as it fell.

"A perfect shot," Roland whispered to himself as he went to collect his kill. He knelt before the body of the ruined beast, gripping an antler. He unsheathed a six-inch carving knife from his boot. It was a devilishly sharp blade anchored deep in a grip of polished bone. Roland was just cutting into the stag when a voice rang out behind him.

"What right have you to the flesh of that stag!" A shuffle of horses and armor clattered in tow. Roland relinquished the antler, turning to face what he discovered was a party of three knights on horseback. Their armor had seen a great deal of wear. Their faces were stern, ruddy, and freckled from the sun. Their white banners had red crosses stitched over them, and Roland recognized immediately that these were Crusaders. He opened his arms in welcome, showing his hands and bowing his head.

"I am Roland la Flèche-de Beaugency, and this is my father, Sir Ivin. These are our woods."

Ivin held the gaze of the knights, who, even on horseback, were practically eye level with him.

The complainant softened his tone as he said, "My companions and I are returning from Crusade with a larger host just north of here. Our encampment is in dire need of meat. Out of love for Crown and Church, we command you to surrender your kill to us."

"What are you called?" asked Ivin.

"Sir Alain Perth," answered the young man, punctuating his surname with an emphatic nod. "We have been on the road for many days now, so if you don't mind—"

"We do mind. And those bags of meat on your horses' flanks appear full."

"These sacks are filled with the ears of pagans. They are gifts for our Lord to show him our Order's success."

Roland eyed the hessian sacks stained red at the bottom.

Ivin smirked, approaching the bag and sniffing its rancid contents.

"When I helped the Lionheart sack Acre, we didn't let good meat go to waste. The only trophies we took, we kept in memoria res." Ivin tapped his temple.

The knights each looked at one another, unsure how they should respond. "Just give us the stag."

"No." Ivin drew his short sword. The mounted cavalry drew their blades in turn.

"Father," said Roland cautiously.

"Heed your Saracen brat," advised Sir Alain.

Roland felt his blood burn in his cheeks, but he said coolly, "I am a Breton, sir." He said it loud enough so they could hear his speech was exactly like their own. They could not hear him, though, for they were too busy jeering at his father.

"I was slaying Saracens while you were still soiling your swaddling clothes," Ivin returned.

"Slaying their heathen sluts more like." The others laughed more boldly now. Ivin looked at Roland, outrage burning in his eyes.

"You will not speak ill of my mother," said Roland. "She was a Melkite. Her family has been Christian probably longer than yours."

"How they have trained ye to speak the langue d'oïl," said Sir Alain, giddily adding, "It's like watching a hound make letters."

Roland spoke in a level tone, not allowing himself to be riled. "Take the stag and go. Come, Father."

Ivin boomed at the churlish knights, "What cities did you take? Any?" He snorted in the absence of a response. "No. I think you deserted when the Saracen host descended on you. After seeing your fellowship shredded by a hail of scimitars, you fled. Most virgin Crusaders do. And they come back toting whatever tokens they think will redeem their honor with their liege lords."

"I should take your ear too for such insolence," answered Alain.

Neither Roland nor his father had dressed for battle. Roland's mind played through the sequence of events that would transpire if a fight broke out. The men would kill them quickly, go looking for their residence, kill the servants, rape the women, including Rowen, and burn the manor to the ground.

"I'll have yours before the night is through!" cried Ivin, but Roland stepped in front of him.

"Please, take the stag, with our apologies," he said, knowing the escalation of this encounter could not benefit him or his father no matter how things went. His father should have known better than to speak to them that way. A band of knights could have no more honor than a band of thieves, and provoking the ire of such men could prove fatal. These men looked road-weary and like they could use a meal, but they had enough strength left in them to end a pair of hunters in the wood. "My father is old and hardheaded. Accept the stag and be on your way."

"I think not, half-breed," sneered Alain, pointing his sword at Roland's chest. "How about you give me that pretty blue stone you're wearing? And then, we will thank ye for the stag and be on our way."

"The stone was my mother's. I would sooner die than part with it."

"Are you deaf or just a half-wit? It is not you who will die for it. It is him."

The other two knights closed in behind him.

"So choose," said Alain. "Your dead mother's trinket or your father's life?"

Roland removed the chain, flinching at the sound of his father's sigh of disgust. He flung it. The knight, upon catching the lapis, derided him again.

"Coward."

Roland and Ivin took the trail back, moving away from the sound of hateful laughter. Roland pushed himself to keep up as his father charged ahead, lugging all the weight of his bow, quiver, and the bags for meat. "Father, wait!" he called as they crossed the field to their home.

Ivin kicked up a cloud of dirt and whirled to face him. "Are you even my son?" he shouted.

Roland winced and drew back a distance.

"Melkite?" A vein bulged in Ivin's neck, pronged like a thorn. "Melkite, Roland? Your mother was a Turk. Those men insulted her, but you insult her further with your lies."

"I was trying to prevent a fight."

"You think they know what a Melkite even is? All men like that know is 'us' and 'them,' with nothing in between. And do you know what that lapis is worth?!"

"I know."

"Then why would you wear it in the open?! Out of my sight! Before I dash your brains!" he spat the words out so hard he was out of breath before he finished. "I mean it. I cannot bear to look at you. Go! And do not come home until you take back the only thing that remains of your mother." Ivin picked up a rock the size of his fist and flung it at his son's head. Roland dodged, but not without taking a spill on one knee.

He did not bother trying to reason with the old man. He had enough scars: the line on his forehead from the day his father smashed him against the mantle, another over his cheek from a whack from Ivin's five-pound steel gauntlet, and countless lines of scar tissue over his back from the more traditional lashings he received as a child. He took off into the woods, not looking back.

Roland ran for a long while. The woods grew ever dimmer as the sun sank the sky into twilight. An impending storm made that twilight darker than usual, as though an abyss were coming to claim all that remained of the earth.

"I hate him," he whispered to the pines. "I hate him. I wish he were dead. I wish I could be the one to kill him."

Roland wondered how everything in his life had culminated in bringing him here to this forest in Brittany hunting men instead of deer. He missed his master's townhouse in Toulouse, where, at night, he could burn a whole candle down as he wrote poetry with his master's son. The lad, Giraut, who was just a year younger than Roland, had been his closest friend.

Unlike Willem, Giraut had a mind for the texture of words. When Giraut realized that Roland could read Arabic script, he befriended him at once and begged him to help unlock the many manuscripts of philosophy and poetry in his father's library. Giraut understood and respected Roland's boundless love for humanity. He said Roland belonged in a university, not on a battlefield. They drank wine and created verse together. Sometimes, they played music for coin in the streets. That year in Toulouse had cultivated Roland's true identity. It pained him, knowing he would probably never return there or see Giraut again. Their only means of communication were through letters sent once or twice every six months.

Tormented by worries, Giraut often wrote on bleak subjects that brought Roland's spirit low. But each year at Christmas time, he would send opium wine, which all but made up for it. "Please enjoy the transcendent bliss of God's love," his letter would say. Roland thanked him by sending dried mushrooms in return, composing some verse or fable to accompany them.

The darkness transformed the wood into a vault of shadows. The music of the forest and its creatures shifted from birdsong to a chorus of crickets and toads. Branches rustled. The soil and pine needles skittered and shifted. All in darkness. The clouds blotting out the stars waxed ever greater, and Roland could feel it in the balmy air that heavy rain was imminent.

He followed the signs of the Crusaders' trail by its broken branches and heavily trodden earth. It grew more difficult to track them the darker it became, but once the twilight was wholly gone, he could smell the fire of their camp. Roland climbed into the trees and moved between them. He was like a fae-born hunter, advancing on the men from behind a veil of foliage.

The three soldiers sat drinking around a small fire, Roland's venison roasting on a spit. Their horses rested nearby, secured to the roots of trees. Roland watched them for hours as they supped and shared a flagon of wine. He came to know them like characters in a play. There was the leader, Alain, who controlled the conversation and spoke the loudest. Then, there was a younger one named Erwan, and the third was called Yann.

They mused on what they would do first when they got home. Alain spoke of plowing his wife while the other two were more focused on seeing their families. They seemed to share a disdain for Alain's manly boasts. Erwan had fears that his family could be dead. And Yann worried he would never know peace again. He wanted to forget that desert of death, which had brought them nothing but suffering.

The men got drunk on their wine and eventually slouched in exhaustion. The lapis, wherever it had gone, was out of sight, but as Roland watched them, he noticed his chain shimmering against Alain's throat.

Yann was tasked with keeping watch while the others slept. He maintained the fire for about an hour before nodding off upright in full armor. As his head sunk down against his chest, Roland seized his moment. He lowered from the tree, sly and silent as a serpent in Eden. He was careful not to spook the horses, for he could see they were only half in slumber.

Roland crawled past them to where Alain lay. The man's breath hung in the air, shuddering as he coughed in his sleep. Roland drew his hunting knife, and the scrape of steel on leather was enough to make his target flinch, but Alain did not wake.

Roland knelt over him, knowing what he had to do and wishing he had time or opportunity to deny himself. There was no going back. In a way that was at once swift and vulgar, he snatched Alain's ear, made an incision beneath the lobe, and sliced upward as he pulled. A wretched, sputtering cry surged from Alain's throat as the air in his lungs burst forth. The horses started up, hooves beating as they whinnied in fright.

As Alain lay reeling in pain, Roland made sure the man could see his face as he ripped the chain from his throat and retook his lapis. By the time the other knights came to his aid, Roland had fled into the shadows.

From behind the trees, he heard Yann and Erwan saddling their horses and helping their companion to his mount. They set out in another direction, away in the dark. Roland felt safe. He knew they had no intention of chasing him. They were, like him, scared out of their wits and disoriented in the dark.

It was another hour before Roland reached home. He went inside through the front entrance, smashing through doors so they rattled the walls and announced his return. The evening shadows appeared darker than ever. Every filament of candle-light was a special kind of demon. In the parlor, logs crackled gently in the fireplace. Roland found his father sitting before the hearth in his deerskin chair, sipping ale from a tankard. Rowen was asleep on the bearskin in front of the fireplace.

"I have retaken what is mine and punished the thief," said Roland, tossing the severed ear so it fell in his father's lap. Blood scattered like darts.

Ivin dropped his tankard, which woke Rowen. "What have you done?"

"I took back the lapis, Papa!" cried Roland, half-mad with his hatred of his father. He flashed the blue stone. "Are you satisfied?"

"You maimed a soldier of Christ?"

"Surely, you jest, Father. He was a thief. You made it clear I should seek revenge."

"I expected a duel, not some barbaric dismemberment."

"Ah! There it is. You think me barbaric. Heathen." Roland locked eyes with his father so he could show him all the fire that burned in his heart. "It is not my actions, though. It is because I bear the face of your enemy."

"You bear the face of my wife."

"I took her from you. There has always been something loathly in me. I am the revenant of every heathen you killed in Acre. That is why you hate me."

"I have provided you every comfort and privilege. You will inherit all that I have. Is that not enough?"

"Nothing will be enough to make up for the eight years that you abandoned us!"

Roland boomed, running upstairs.

"Why must you vex me so?!" shouted Ivin. "When they come for you, they will kill you for this!"

Roland refused to engage his father any further. He continued up the wood stairs, throwing off his shirt. He was shaking so much that he thought his blood would actually boil. He took everything off, shedding it like a snake sheds old skin, skin that no longer fits right, no longer feels right. But even after the sin-soaked garb was off him and he had washed and replaced his shirt, he still did not feel clean. This was not him in his heart, this monster he had dreamed up for his father. This was certainly no part of Rowen.

"Roland?"

His sister's voice sounded far away. Roland fell into bed. He covered himself with his fleece and squeezed the lapis in his fist.

Rowen's arms fell about him. She said nothing, only soothed his anguish, combing her hands through his hair. His frenzy abated, and he breathed deep. It was like a spell had broken.

"My God, Rowen. How will I keep you safe? They will come for me."

"Did you kill someone?"

"No. I disfigured a man I should have killed."

"Be still, Roland."

He broke away from her, moving to the corner of his chamber so his trestle table was between them. "They might come here. They would hurt you. I cannot bring myself to say what they would do."

"God will protect us."

Roland placed his hands flat upon the table's surface, grounding himself. It was impossible to make her see. She could never understand the world of men without living a day in his skin. Could they ever again be as they had been in Antioch? One mind. One flesh. They were too different now.

"Show me that you remember everything I have taught you," he said, cutting across the room to retrieve his batons. He handed one to Rowen and squared his body with hers. "Without moving forward or back, I want you to deflect my attacks by moving only your wrist. Just as I taught you. Show me." He swayed his baton back and forth in an arc, testing her, trying to tap her on the wrist.

Rowen swiped him away like a cat batting a string. Roland went in for a poke and needled between her ribs under her arm. "Damn it, Rowen!" he shouted, throwing his baton in a fit.

"Roland, I remember everything. It is late, and you are in a foul mood."

"And what if they come here tonight? They will kill all our household. Fight me, Rowen."

He retrieved his baton.

"Again!"

Rowen slashed at his chest, which he quickly deflected, using her recoil to seize her neck mid-spin. He snared her in a chokehold, flattening her arms with his baton. "You failed," he said. "Now, they keep you alive long enough to see me beheaded."

"I could have won," she said. "I did not want to hurt you."

"You are trying to make me feel better, but I am not—agh!" Roland buckled as his sister kicked the back of his heel. As he stumbled, she shoved him headfirst to the floor and smacked him on the spine with her baton.

"The first one is dead. Show me the second." She waited for Roland to compose himself. His nostrils flared. He came at her again with renewed vigor. Again, she bested him, knocking the wind from his lungs with the brunt of her baton. As he keeled forward, she patted his shoulder.

"You needn't worry."

Roland took a knee, clutching the fresh bruise on his abdomen. He wanted to commend her, but he was still reeling in pain.

For the next several fortnights, the two rose early and trained intensely in their father's armory, practicing movement and drills. The room was in the back of the manor's west wing. Having once been a ballroom, it had a space conducive to their training with its tall ceiling and wide berth. Rowen's arms improved. Her shoulders squared, and her biceps became more pronounced. She could move with heavy steel as easily as she could with the baton.

One evening, late in February, Roland discovered her practicing after everyone had gone to bed. A blizzard raged outside, its winds rattling the tall windows and snow spattering the glass. Rowen stood a little straighter, craning her neck as she saw her brother watching.

He leaned against the window casing, folding his arms. He asked, "How often are you doubling your drills?"

"Every night."

He paced wordlessly, assumptions and speculations forming.

Something was driving her. Not fear. Not even anger. She would never tell him if he asked, nor would he expect her to.

He approached her and flicked the pendant that hung from her throat. "Where did you get the hunk of carbuncle?"

"Garnet."

"Who gave you that?"

Rowen swallowed, turning away from him. "I would rather keep that to myself."

Roland curled his arms around his upper body, shoulders hunched. He frowned. "Fine. Then I will not tell you the meaning of the stone."

"Fine," she said. She put her father's claymore away, returning it to its wall mount.

"You are in love with whoever gave it."

"So what if I am?"

"Was it Harlowe?"

"No."

"If it was Erec, you would have said. So it must be Harlowe, which would make you a traitor. It would make you my enemy if you married him!"

"Stop shouting! I would never form an attachment to such a horrible man. How dare you even suggest that?"

One of the branches outside tapped against the window glass as the wind battered the trees. Roland could feel his stomach churning with angst. How dare he? How dare she! He hated it when she thrust him away from her inner world. "Who then?!"

"You cannot know everything about me. Not anymore."

Roland filled his lungs, exhaling slowly as he allowed Rowen the last word. The twins knew their battles with each other often emerged from the battles within themselves.

On nights like this, when the snows fell hard and the moors moaned with wind, Roland craved the former attachment they had shared. It had been a comfort, knowing he could always confide in her and she in him. Now, she clutched the garnet pendant like the key to a secret door.

"All I want is to keep you safe," he offered. It was true, but it was not enough.

"There is no such thing as safe."

She did not want to speak to him. She flew from the armory without another word.

CHAPTER 12

With the return of wild irises in March, Roland and Rowen had just begun their seventeenth year. The thaw of winter and the return of green luster to the trees invited birdsong and bugs, a resurgence of life and sound in the world.

The season for morels had begun. The soil underfoot still held a chill in the mornings, even on sunny days. Roland had been tasked with driving a cart into town to have his armor inspected and refurbished. It was a task far too important to entrust to a servant, and the armor was too valuable to risk losing.

Ever since the incident in the forest, Roland had exchanged his mother's lapis for his father's heavy crucifix, a large, silver cross shaped like a spike. His father had given it to him as a child. It was a pendant set with pearls and rubies, and fabled to have been Ivin's last resort in close combat. In moments of desperation, he had thrust it into the eyes of his assailants. The lapis would remain locked away for now.

The wet air clung to the tips of Roland's black hair, twisting it into matted curls. On his way into town, he saw some beggars, but he had only brought enough coin to pay the blacksmith. All he could spare was the apple he had brought for his horse.

"Sorry, Ash. You'll have to do with grass until we get home."

Ash continued to bob his head as he dragged the cart.

When they reached the cobbled streets of the town square, Roland noticed more people than usual, all of them awaiting some spectacle yet to arrive. They had constructed a platform in the heart of the village. Roland left his horse in front of the forge, hopping down from the cart to investigate.

The little town of Rieux had not seen public executions until recently. Its population was small and insular. Naturally, humiliation took place at the stocks. The local magistrate was fond of demeaning signage to string about a person's neck.

I cheat at dice.

I sell my body for coin.

Then, on the word of several holy dignitaries describing rampant devil-worship and orgiastic sin in Languedoc, the magistrate allied himself with the Church, eager to protect Rieux from heresy. "The rot that comes from within," they called it. Spiritual corruption began in the mind.

Most of the shops remained shuttered, but the blacksmith was up. He thrust charcoal on the fire, working the bellows to breathe life into the forge. Roland unloaded his cart, entrusting the man with adjusting his father's armor to fit his smaller frame. After being parted with both his measurements and his silver, Roland thanked the man for his trouble.

"Good morning, Roland," called a voice from down the lane. In her brown coif, Roland looked right past her, not recognizing his own girl. Cat, with her soft lips and grave, dark eyes, bobbed her head to him, her arm hooking a basket laden with herbs.

"Cat. I did not see you. What is happening here today?"

She pointed into the square where men in white robes gathered at the foot of a platform. As Roland recognized the red crosses extending down the length of their vestments, his heart caught fire. "Crusaders are enlisting men to retake Jerusalem. Today, a heretic will be cleansed of his sin, a troubadour spouting lies about the Church. He will be sent to God."

"Sent how?"

"They will press him with stones and burn his body at the stake."

"Oh, I see."

A cold sweat formed on the back of Roland's neck. He did not claim to know the one true way to worship, but the threat of mob violence against his own person was an ever-present horror.

"I'm sorry, Cat, but you don't mean to bear witness to such a ghastly spectacle, do you?"

"Not for pleasure," she said. "I made these to sell." She gestured to her flat basket with the long handle.

Roland surveyed the many bundles of dried herbs, recognizing meadowsweet and sage.

"Nose gays settle the nerves," she said. "Will you buy one?"

"Ah. No. I wish I could, but I only brought coin for the armorer."

Cat bent and handed him one anyway. "A gift then."

The jailers brought the heretic forward in a cart. He was a frail, thin man, perhaps thirty years of age. He looked rather wolfish with his head of wild black hair and his overgrown beard. The burns on his feet suggested he had already been tortured, but his face no longer seemed to register any pain.

Roland touched his lips to the feathery edge of the herbs, inhaling notes of earth and spice. "I should not have come today," he whispered.

"I'm glad you did. My mother is in Nantes. I will be quite alone tonight."

"Why has Lisette gone to Nantes?"

"My cousin is sick. She is helping my aunt care for her. Will you visit Lechón tonight?"

"I will."

The jailers chained the heretic to the floor of the platform so he lay supine. Willem's father, the magistrate, laid a board over his body and set down the first boulder to secure it against his chest.

The crowd waxed on all sides. Roland found the eyes of someone he had seen before. At first, he could not place the man. And then his heart sank in his chest when he saw his missing ear.

He remembered those eyes crinkling with scornful laughter. And it became evident, as Alain's eyes locked with Roland's, that the recognition had dawned on him as well. Roland pulled up his hood.

"I have to go," he said to Cat, ducking into the crowd.

"Hey!" shouted Alain. "I know you!"

His call was lost amidst the jeers of the turbulent crowd as the heretic was loaded with boulders.

Roland dipped below arms, shoved people out of his way, and sprang into a hard sprint. Soon he breached the edge of the mob. Forget the horse. And the armor. There was no time to fetch Ash, even if he did cut his harness and let the cart fall. People knew him and knew his family's horse. Someone would bring Ash to the house before sunset. Roland passed the city gates and thought he must surely be safe from capture, but as he glanced over his shoulder, he saw Alain closing the gap between them.

Roland leaped onto a cart full of hay. It teetered beneath his gait as he used it to climb the city wall. Alain pursued. He was like a leopard in a tree, climbing the stones with ease and traversing the narrow edge with confidence. Roland surrendered as Alain grasped him from behind with a blade at his throat.

"I have you, Mohammat," said the young Crusader.

"I am a Christian, you fool."

A blinding impact thwacked the back of his skull, and Roland fell from the wall, his vision going dark as he tumbled into the bushes below.

When he awoke, he found himself in the back of a cart, jostling over the uneven roads outside of town. His hands were bound in front of him. Black hessian covered his face, but through some small patches where the fabric was worn and thin, Roland could see that bastard Alain was driving the horse through the forest. After a time, Roland recognized the horse to be his own sweet Ash. Alain had seized Roland's horse and cart as his own.

"That was foolish of you to take my ear. You saw what they did to the troubadour in Rieux today. We'll do much worse to a fiend like you."

The lad went on to describe a host of grotesque killing procedures, likely ones he had already witnessed. On the long ride out of town listening to violent narratives about his future, Roland considered that he might as well try fighting the instant the man stopped the cart. If he died for it, it would be better than being boiled and peeled like a chestnut. He just had to decide when to make his move.

All his schemes evaporated as he heard a great cacophony of activity around him, a blacksmith striking an anvil, some distant chatter, and the baying of hounds. Escape would not be an option. Roland was thinking about his sister and how he had failed her. She would be furious with him for getting himself caught. And he was not ready to die. There was so much he had not done, so much he still hoped to discover, to write, draw, wish, and yearn for. He might have found his way back to God.

The cart rattled to a stop.

"What is this?" said another voice.

"The heathen cur from the woods," said Alain. "I found him in the square."

The second man's spittle struck Roland's shoulder.

His weight tilted the cart as he came closer. Roland braced for a clout, but the Crusader only ripped the sack from his head. Roland could now see that he was in an encampment of canvas tents, destriers, dust, men, women, and children. By the look of their pale garments sewn with red crosses, he ascertained they were pilgrims on the road to Jerusalem. Almost immediately, he saw the cart containing a full-grown African lion. Wooden slats reinforced by metal wire hardly seemed adequate for containing such a large beast. Roland had never seen one in the flesh. Its depictions in the illuminations of bestiaries hardly did it justice. And when he heard the eruptions from the beast's throat, he was astonished at how a lion's roar resembled thunder more than any earthly thing. It made his hair stand on end. Alain wrenched up the collar of Roland's shirt and launched him over the edge of the cart.

Such Christian charity, Roland thought, as his wrists burned under the ropes binding them.

"This is the Saracen who maimed me!" shouted Alain who stood astride the cart's edge.

A pair of templars grabbed Roland's shoulders and pulled him to his feet. The pilgrims hissed and threw little stones. "Deus vult!" they chanted. Suggestions to "Hang him slow!" or to "Cut off his head!" bubbled up from the agitated crowd. But it was another call that broke through them all and ushered in a powerful silence. The roar of the lion split the air.

The crowd parted as everyone veered to see the lion walking along the perimeter of its cage, creaking the wood with its immense weight.

"Let the lion have him! The beast has not eaten in days!" shouted Alain. He grinned exuberantly at the people's cries of approval. Roland was pushed forward, made to walk to the back of the encampment where a pit had been dug ten or more cubits deep. The templars cut his binds and knocked him into a tumble. Roland was careful to tumble well as he descended into the pit. Around the edge, the templars had placed large stakes to prevent a person from climbing out. There was no escaping without help, and Roland's bravery began to falter as a grisly realization dawned on him. He would die in this pit.

He took a deep breath, backing away to the muddy wall as the shadow of the lion's cart fell over him. Today should have been a day like any other. He was not ready to meet God in the jaws of a monster.

A man overhead worked a pulley, and a row of stakes lifted, revealing a sloped ascent. Roland might have escaped, but the cart holding the lion came through. He felt as though the ground beneath his feet had shifted. His legs gave out.

The spikes came back down, sealing the cart in with him. Then, that same man pulled at a rope to lift one side of the cage. The lion crouched, its tail flailing. Then, it sprang forward.

Roland skirted the edge of the pit, moving to put the cage between him and certain peril.

The lion lunged around the side.

Roland climbed the bars, but the animal climbed faster, reaching the top and swiping at him from above. Some spectators screamed, alarmed by the cat's vicious agility. Bestiaries could not have prepared Roland for the reality of facing a lion. The beast moved more like a serpent than a small cat, winding its body and striking with a speed that made time seem to unravel. There was something chimeric about its power, something so monstrous it was the stuff of nightmares. All those illuminations of goat-headed, snake-tailed lions became at once preposterous and visceral.

One bite from that enormous cat would crush Roland's skull. One perfectly felled hit would slash an artery.

Large as it was, though, the lion was undeniably malnourished. It had a ragged mane, bleary, desperate eyes, and ribs that showed through its loose skin. Roland could not help but feel pity for the beast, even as he imagined his flesh joining the contents of its stomach.

The lion emitted another low rumble. Roland dropped and rolled under the cart. He thought about those instances in which he would watch the barn cat playing with a mouse, biting its limbs off one by one, pinning its tail just to make it squirm a little longer before it swallowed the critter alive. Was there ever any hope for a mouse?

The lion's enormous paw batted the back of his shirt, ripping the fabric as well as his flesh. Roland reeled, clenching his teeth. Again. The claws struck his shoulder this time. He could not hide here. He rolled out from under the cart, loosing a battle cry as he let his torn shirt fall away. There on his chest was the bejeweled cross his father had given him. It glinted in the sun pouring down through the trees. And then he remembered a story. Not those he read in bestiaries about lions being incarnations of the Father, the Son, and the Holy Spirit. None of his poems or songs mattered now. It was the story of killing, the story of being resourceful in the worst way.

Roland wrenched the cross from his person, gripping it like a cross guard.

"Lord Jesus," he said. "I know I am not worthy, but I need you, brother! Lend me your courage that I might prevail!" This last part was swallowed by his own scream as the lion emerged from beneath the cart and tackled Roland to the ground.

The Crusaders above unanimously gasped as the beast covered Roland's body. They waited silently for the lion to move to reveal the hideous scene of carnage they so craved. But all they got was a sea of red blood unfolding like a rose beneath the lion.

The lion slumped forward. Impaled through the heart and hopelessly defeated, he fell down on his side. The blood-drenched man beneath emerged, brandishing a gem-studded cross that dripped gore down his arm. The people gathered around the pit were so quiet; the only sound thrumming in Roland's ear was that of his own heartbeat. A woman wailed.

"Ave Maria!"

Calls to the virgin exploded around her, echoing each other. "Ave! Ave!" they shouted. The men beat their shields, echoing, "Deus vult!" Roland could taste the iron of the beast's blood rolling down the back of his throat. It congealed on his chest and arms. He thrust his cross high and bellowed, "I am a Christian! Falsely accused!"

A murmur of prayer enveloped the crowd. Roland joined them, demonstrating knowledge of the Lord's Prayer in Latin:

Pater noster qui es in caelis es sanctificetur nomen tuum
veniat regnum tuum fiat voluntas tua sicut in caelo et in terra

panem nostrum supersubstantialem da nobis hodie
et dimitte nobis debita nostra sicut et nos dimisimus debitoribus nostris
et ne inducas nos in temptationem sed libera nos a malo.

A cold hush punctuated the prayer. The onlookers waited for someone to decide. Roland waited for whatever came next. For the first time in his life, he believed in his salvation.

CHAPTER 13

Caked in blood and reeking of death, Roland could not go home. It would stir the superstitions of the servants, resurrecting old worries over the haunted marshes and Clement's curse. He steered Ash to town, towing the rickety cart. His wounds ached as the cart rattled over the cobbled lane. Roland, slumped in the box seat, pulled up in front of Lechón Tavern. He released the reins in exhaustion. The moss-green paint on the doors was chipping away. The sign depicting a cauldron squeaked on its iron hinges as a dull breeze disturbed it.

Roland eased himself down from the driver's box. As far as his injuries went, they were more of a nuisance than they were disabling. His shoulder felt numb after working the reins, and his back stung terribly, but he had enough strength in him to stable his horse.

The bug-eaten door to the stable swung open, and Cat came through. She screamed when she saw him.

"Easy, Cat!" Roland cried, turning so she could see it was him. "It's only me. And this is not my blood."

"Are you in need of a room?"

"I am."

"Go inside and wash. I will finish up here. Go."

Roland remembered that she was tending the tavern alone. Fortunately, it was a slow night with only a few men playing dice at the tables. They certainly noticed the man covered in blood and they drifted over to him as he dug through cupboards looking for Cat's dingy old wash basin.

"What happened to you?" inquired the tailor.

"I fought a lion," said Roland, knowing they would not believe him. It seemed as unlikely as if he had said he fought a dragon.

"A lion, Roland?" The mason's skepticism was met with the other men's scattered chuckles. Roland removed the sopping red tatters of his bloodied shirt, showing them the shoddy stitchwork on his back and shoulder. The men got close, scrutinizing the wounds and sounding out in amazement.

"A lion!" Roland roared, scrunching his hands into claws.

Ever the troubadour, he recounted the tale for them, beginning with his encounter in his own forest when the men robbed him of the stag. No part of his tale required embellishment. He showed them his father's cross, which still oozed a trail of blood down his chest.

Cat came in, arms heavy at her sides, jaw slackening with a yawn. As Roland's tale continued to unfold, she found a stool and leaned in on her knees. When Roland spoke of the lion, her eyes went wide.

"We close now!" she shouted at the end of his fantastical tale. "If you haven't a room here, you can stagger home to your wives." The men gathered their cloaks and packed up their dice, though one of them complained that his wife had died, and Cat should have remembered that.

"Wait," said Cat to one of the men, a younger lad with a round face. She handed him a coin. "Ride to the manor," she said. "Bring Sir Ivin."

"No," Roland interrupted. "No, it is late. Tell my father I was delayed but do not tell him where I am. I will return tomorrow."

"I told you to wash, Roland!" said Cat with force. "And you. Bring his father."

"Do not bring my father! I will ride to him tomorrow."

"You are in no condition to ride!"

As the tempest raged between them, the lad looked from Cat to Roland and back again. "What is it you want me to do?"

"Ugh!" she groaned. "Tell Sir Ivin his son was detained, but all is well." The lad departed in haste, shutting the door with a bang.

Lechón was quieter than Roland had ever seen it. He had never heard the popping of the fire or the voices that came in from the street as though the timbered walls were made of paper.

"You still fail to bathe."

Roland gave a firm nod. "I will fetch the water," he said. It was a novelty for him to bathe without servants. The whole process seemed quite tedious. After making three trips to the pump and filling the cauldron to heat by the fire, Roland's arms were burning. He tended the pot by the hearth.

Cat leaned into the counter; her brow decidedly arched. "Are you heating your water?"

"It is freezing in here."

"So you bathe by the fire."

"In cold water? I think not."

As soon as his water began to steam, Roland tipped it into the basin and undressed. The water warmed his ankles. He did not mind Cat watching as he dipped the wash rag and drew it up and down his limbs.

Cat pressed her lips. She came around the bar and collected his clothing in a bucket. As he washed, the waters went dark with blood. Tendrils of warm water flowed down his back, helping him to feel calm at last.

Cat brought towels to warm by the fire. She came close to him, taking the rag and wringing it out over his chest.

When he was clean, she wrapped him in the towel she had warmed. It should not have surprised him that she had men's clothing stored upstairs, but he was amazed at how well the tunic fit.

"So," said Cat, putting tankards and trays away into cupboards. "I suppose your next song will be for the lion."

Roland looked away. A small part of him still mourned for the beast. "Yes. I think so." He began to sing softly as he played with the lines:

Clasped in the lion's maw,

Prey beneath his claw,

129

I clutched at my cross
and to Jesus, I prayed.

He watched Cat hop up on the bar, combing through her curls with kitchen oils and braiding her hair into a crown that wrapped twice around her head.

She vocalized softly.

He could never win,
The lion had him pinned,
When Jesus the jouster,
Came to his aid.

Roland chuckled and sang the phrase, "O Christ, my chevalier," as he retrieved his lute from the nail on the wall, divining a new melody from what she was singing. As she went on harmonizing with him, he could not stop smiling.

Lord of sweet victory,
Lend me thy chivalry,
I'm yours to possess.
So fill me with breath.

Together, they wove a tapestry of music so perfect that it was almost as though they had been working on it for months. Maybe, without knowing it, they had been. They had been learning each other's rhythms, familiarizing themselves with each other's voices and intonations, living together in poetry. Throughout the winter, they shared comfort and warmth and belief in a love that surpassed the limitations of their class.

Roland set the lute on the bar, yielding it so he could hold Cat around the hips. Her smell, her soft lips, the taste of her mouth, all of it filled him with heat. His brain flooded with want. He threw her patchwork skirt over her thighs, groping her luscious limbs and pulling her into him.

Their music was halted, lost beneath a more carnal symphony. Roland helped Cat lie back over the length of the counter. Beneath her skirt, she had nothing on, which made it all but too easy to have at her treasure. Oh, this was a sin, one of many forms of sodomy worth the harrowing of Hell. Roland used his mouth, touching her nymph-head with his tongue. In her ecstasy, Cat banged the back of her head against the counter.

"This teasing must end, Roland. There are herbs, and I have learned them all."

She gripped the edges of the counter on each side of her head.

There was nothing more satisfying than the feeling that came just before the act. Knowing each other at their most vulnerable, they would understand each other in a way people seldom understood another person. And in this knowing, they would become each other's responsibility, each other's problem.

"I only want to keep you safe."

"If I wanted to be safe, I would not have asked you here."

CHAPTER 14

Rowen begged her father to ride to town. All day long, she had sensed that something was not right. Nobody believed her, though, and for hours, she thought of ways to sneak away from the manor without being seen. There were too many servants. They watched her closely and prevented her leaving.

When Roland did not return in time for supper, her worries were vindicated. A messenger came at last, announcing that Roland had been delayed and would ride at first light. For the rest of the evening, Rowen committed herself to prayer in the chapel, pacing between the walls. At some late hour, she collapsed in exhaustion against the stone floor. In the morning, she awoke in her bed, still wearing her clothing from the day before. The housekeeper, Emilie, came into Rowen's chamber and opened the shutters to wake her with the sun.

"Your brother is home," she informed.

Rowen rose like a gust of ocean air. She pushed past the housekeeper, padding down the stairs without slippers. Anna was boiling water by the hearth, and Constance came in from the kitchen with a bowl of porridge.

There, at the long teakwood dining table, were Roland and Cecile. Constance placed the porridge before each of them.

"Lady Rowen," said Constance.

"Lady Rowen," said Anna. "Are you hungry?"

"No."

The servants bobbed, each returning to the kitchens.

Cecile smiled to her granddaughter, daintily holding a spoonful of porridge and blowing over it. Roland did not look up. He devoured his vittles.

"Where is father?" asked Rowen.

"Hunting," said her grandmother.

Rowen could tell something of significance had taken place. Roland was different. He was never this quiet. She instantly knew the places where he was hurting, for she could feel them in her own flesh.

"I was so worried," she told him. "I knew it before anyone else that something had—"

"Nothing happened," he interrupted. "The armorer took longer than I thought he would. It got dark, so I took a room in town." He continued to shovel porridge into his mouth.

"Oh, fie on ye, Roland! You know not what it is to worry, or you would never cast me off like this. By the time you sent the messenger, I had wasted hours believing you were carrion for crows! What happened? Is Ash all right?"

Roland tilted upright, swallowing his breakfast. "Ash is in the stables."

"What happened?" she asked again, frustration pricking her heart. He did not answer fast enough to her satisfaction. "Roland!"

"Why should I tell you anything?" His face was strange to her, his eyes wild and black as the devil's. "Who gave you the garnet, Rowen?"

"You are wounded!" She pulled the collar of his shirt. "Badly!" she added when she saw the deep gash in his shoulder.

Roland jostled against her grip. "Unhand me!"

"These stitches are horrendous. I must correct them."

"They are fine! It will mend."

"I will not let you be marred with hideous scars!"

"Maybe I want to scar! Why don't you go and pine for your secret suitor!"

Rowen shrieked like a hawk, tackling him out of his chair.

"You madwoman!"

"Stop that, children," said their grandmother, though she did nothing else to intervene.

As they had done when they were seven, the twins began to wrestle, each insisting they were right.

"I will tell Father you are lying!" Rowen growled.

"Then I will tell him you are hiding a suitor!"

Roland tried to escape beneath the table. Rowen wrenched him back, pulling his collar away from his nape. She cringed to see the three slashes scoring his back, each one sewn like a jagged smile.

"What in God's bones?" she cried. "Were you attacked by wolves?"

"A lion!" He freed himself as she let up on her assault. "The Crusaders found me, and they tried to feed me to their god-forsaken lion! There! Are you satisfied?"

"A lion?"

"My!" cried Cecile. "And you escaped?"

Rowen summoned the servants. A joint stool was placed before the fire, and as Roland finished his porridge, Rowen snipped away his stitches and cleaned his wounds with vinegar. She ordered the servants about to bring clean strips of linen. As she worked her needle through the tender edge of each wound, connecting the folds more evenly, she extracted every detail of Roland's abduction and his encounter with the lion.

"Now that you know everything, you will tell me who gave you the garnet."

Rowen stalled her needle, shaking her head. "This again?" She tutted at him, making him wince as she pushed the needle in with a little too much force.

Roland flinched. "A garnet is a stone men choose to secure a marriage. It signifies commitment."

Rowen deflected, "According to whom?"

"Every lapidary on the continent. Right, grandmother?"

"It is true," she confirmed. "In fact, your grandfather gave me a garnet when I was twelve years old to ensure I would marry no one else before I came of age."

Roland clenched his teeth, growling as Rowen pierced him again with the needle. "Not so deep, Rowen! I'm a person, not a tapestry!"

"I beg forgiveness," she said in a voice that was not begging at all. "Tell me more about the garnet's meaning. It will distract you from the pain."

Roland acquiesced, twisting his eyes shut as Rowen tied off the thread and cut its tail.

"The garnet is the stone of Mars, the god of war who loved Venus with all the fire of the red planet. It is known to inspire courage."

"Courage?"

"Courage to love. Courage to propose. Courage to marry your brother's enemy."

"If you wish to be rid of Harlowe, you should face him in the tournament and avenge Sir Edmund. Harlowe is no lion."

Roland twisted, touching Rowen's arm that held the needle. With this gesture, he stayed her hand.

"Tell me true. Is it from Harlowe?"

"If you think I have any interest in marrying Harlowe, then you are truly not my twin," she said calmly.

"Then why the secrecy? I would not care who you wanted unless it were him. Were he a commoner, I would not care. Were he married, I would support you."

"Perhaps it is from father, a token for his favorite child," she teased.

"We both know I'm the favorite. Right, grandmother?"

Cecile frowned. "Leave it alone, Roland. Let your sister have her secret."

Roland threw back his head and groaned. "You really will not tell me? Why, Rowen? Why?"

"Because it makes you wax so very wroth!"

CHAPTER 15

At a breakfast celebrating the festival of St. George, the great hall of the chateau was bursting with guests. The stones echoed with conversation and song as guests reveled and minstrels noodled ambiently on their lutes and fifes. Three long tables were decorated with pale blue runners and a king's ransom of silver trays and candelabras. Fragrant herbs and fresh lavender mingled with the aroma of roast meat and freshly baked bread. Platters laden with succulent lamb shank, spit-roasted capons, and pigeon pies heralded the end of lent. Copious pitchers of wine and trenchers packed with cheese littered every table. More servants than usual attended the guests, their work orchestrated under the watchful eye of Amarys's stepmother, who was expected to impress the many errant chevaliers that filled the hall. These men of noble bearing beckoned the servants to refill their goblets, loudly toasting their host, their hostess, and the lady whose hand they hoped to win.

Amarys came down, her presence greeted with a hush. She was amazed by the amount of people in the hall. Not a single seat lay empty. These knights had traveled far to lay eyes on the maid of Rieux, a thing that at once invigorated and appalled her. Her cloth shoes matched the silence of the hall as she proceeded toward the little stage her father had prepared.

She held her lyre in her lap, plucking the strings as she had practiced. She had played the same songs all her life, no longer needing to think about them as her fingers moved. Instead, she surveyed the faces in the crowd. There were a great many young men, dashing warriors in the flower of youth. Her father had warned her about these youths he referred to as "slathering wolves." Many errant knights were second sons whose only path to fortune would be found in abducting heiresses. For this reason, Amarys's father kept her confined to his stronghold, only allowing her outside to go to Mass or visit her mother's tomb, always in the company of at least two male chaperones. Seeing all these well-built men assembled before her, she could not help but dream of meeting one in a flowery meadow, weaving love knots and tasting sweet sin on each other's lips. Her lyre's sweet melodies hid all the lust burning in her chest.

She searched until she found the lovely visage of her rose. Rowen and her roguishly handsome brother, Roland, were both in attendance. Roland's indigo stockings accentuated his well-developed calves. He wore excellent sleeves that were like the wings of a brocade bluejay, and the fabric fitted to his forearms was of a fetching crimson. At another table, Amarys's cousins and uncle were seated, her cousin, Harlowe, among them. She tried not to look at him. As she finished her song and the hall applauded, she went to sit with her friends. Her father, intercepted her, taking her on his arm and walking her in another direction. They went around the tables, greeting their guests and accepting compliments on Amarys's beauty and musical talent.

"Has she had her first blood yet?" asked one of the older knights. "I am willing to compete, but only if she can give me an heir by next Spring."

Clement nodded politely, ushering his daughter to the next table. There was Harlowe on his best behavior.

"To the maid of Rieux!" he cheered, raising his beaker. "You played beautifully, cousin. Any man would be truly blessed to have your music fill his halls."

Amarys would not give him her words. She would not waste any breath pretending to like him, not for anyone.

Harlowe went on to brag to the other knights, "Her family often spends the summer with mine."

Amarys dropped her father's arm and went to greet Rowen. "My rose!" she called, inserting herself between the twins. Roland slid the furthest down the bench, which made Amarys laugh. "Do not move on my behalf, Roland. I would like to know you better. You are, after all, the brother of my favorite person in all the world."

Roland tore into his lamb, hardly looking up from chewing. He sloshed it down with the entire contents of his wine goblet, holding the silver over his shoulder for a serving girl to replenish.

His apathy vexed her. "Where is your lapis, Roland? I have not seen you without it for as long as I can remember."

"I do not wear it anymore for fear that someone will try to steal it."

"Oh my. Do you accuse me of coveting your lapis?"

Rowen shook her head. "Do not engage him on this subject. Just leave him be."

"Haven't you enough men here to hold your attention?" Roland muttered, biting into another shank of lamb.

Amarys pursed her lips. "Are you jealous, Roland?"

"Your wine tastes like grass," he said, "and your lamb is overcooked."

"I am sorry you are not pleased with the mountains of flesh laid before you," she returned. "I assure you; I had nothing to do with the murder of these lambs nor their lackluster preparation."

"Perhaps not, but you had everything to do with that musical performance."

"Roland!" Rowen reached across Amarys's lap to hit him.

"If one could call that music," he added sharply.

Rowen clasped herself on the forehead as though she were in a fever. "We should not have come."

Amarys started up but she could not draw herself away from her argument with Roland. "My other guests assured me that I played beautifully."

"You did," Rowen agreed. "Roland is being unfair."

"No," he said. "I am simply the only one with no desire to flatter you. To an untrained ear, any plucking of strings is pleasant enough, but your performance lacks passion and precision. I heard you drop several critical notes, and there was not enough wine on this table to make up for it."

Amarys's mouth hung quite open.

Roland chugged his beaker of grassy wine and gestured for the servant to replenish his cup. "Leave the pitcher," he told the serving girl, which she obliged. "I swear these beakers are made for mice!" he cried.

"Would you wager you play better than me, Roland?"

Roland turned to her and filled her glass before filling his own again. "Oh, little friend," he said, chuckling. "Were I to fill this hall with music, you would have no one left to fight for you in the tourney, for they would fall in love with me anon."

Amarys burst out laughing, gesturing to Roland as though she could not believe his pride.

"Amarys, I apologize for my brother's offenses."

"No. Do not apologize. I will call his bluff." Amarys put her lyre into Roland's hands. "Play for us, Roland!" she said loudly enough that all the table could hear her. "Come! Your hostess commands you." Amarys rose from her seat, shouting over the noise of the hall. "Everyone! Listen!"

Their many voices lowered and tapered off. Amarys spoke again but more gently. "I invite my neighbor, Roland of Antioch, to play my lyre for your entertainment. And anyone who thinks they play better may follow him."

Roland stood, carrying Amarys's lyre to the little stage where she had played before. He bowed, his foot sliding behind him, one arm clutching the lyre to his chest, and the other sweeping back like a sword.

"Our Maid of Rieux has played the Chanson de Guillaume. Allow me to follow with the Song of the Dragon."

Amarys returned to sitting next to Rowen, linking arms with her. "What is the matter with him today?"

"I mustn't speak of it."

He began to weave an intricate melody, one that captured something of the trilling of sparrows in Spring and something of the nightingale. Amarys and Rowen exchanged whispers.

"You really will not tell me? You know all of my secrets. Why not tell me yours?"

"It is not mine to tell. It is his."

What followed was a performance that people would talk about for years to come. Among the aristocracy, Roland's talents were unknown, and many people returned to their conversations in a softer tone, not expecting much of his performance. That is, of course, until Roland's progression of notes increased in tempo.

Amarys's heart pounded as she watched Roland's deft hands strike faster than the bite of a viper. Between his energetic solos, he returned to the same sultry refrain, his dark eyes holding Amarys's gaze as if to challenge her directly.

"He will never tell me," said Amarys, sinking into the spell of his thrall. "He does not deem me worthy."

"You are worthy. If he knew you, he would realize that."

"He has no wish to know me." Amarys stopped herself from saying more. Ever since her friendship with Rowen had been wrought by their fathers, Amarys had been intrigued by the character of her companion's handsome brother. She rarely mentioned him directly, having noticed that whenever she spoke well of Roland, Rowen either diminished the compliment or told a story of her brother's bad behavior.

Roland's fingers danced across the strings. Some people in the crowd applauded prematurely. Some of the men at Amarys's own table whispered of how it was impossible what he was doing.

"Like one possessed," someone said in a hush.

Roland stood halfway through his performance, his melody climbing. Absorbed in his practice, he nodded with every note that afforded a dramatic emphasis. The strings hummed with his fastidious finger-picking, and upon his final repetition of the refrain, a riotous ovation followed. Roland returned to the table, relinquishing Amarys's lyre and patting her on the back.

"Pity I don't give lessons," he said.

Amarys scoffed and stared wide-eyed at Rowen who made a face like she had just drunk something distasteful. Maybe she had tried the wine, which Amarys could admit did taste rather like grass. Hardly knowing what to say next to either sibling, Amarys excused herself and left to go make conversation with the other guests. No matter where she went, Roland was the subject of every conversation.

"I never knew your son played so well," her father was telling Roland's father.

"Part of mastering the sword involves sharpening the mind with music," explained Ivin, folding his hands on the table like he had planned the whole thing.

At another table, the visiting knights inquired only after Roland. How long had he been Amarys's neighbor? Where did he come from? Perhaps he had been right, she thought, churlish lout that he was. His music had made all of them wretchedly enamored.

She considered, for a moment, the movements of her own heart. Of all the men presenting themselves to fight in the tourney that summer, only one continued to occupy her thoughts. Perhaps, if she asked him, or if she told him what it would mean to her, he would consider fighting.

Roland and Rowen seldom left each other's company, but at one point, their father borrowed Rowen to introduce her to Harlowe's father. Roland started in the direction of the exit, and Amarys stopped him behind a wide stone pillar.

She came in fiercely, intercepting his path like a bird of prey. "I have a question," she said sharply.

"Good, because I have one too."

"Oh," she stammered, a little shaken by his quick response. "I only wanted to ask... well, what is your question?"

Roland tilted his chin, smirking. "You first." The perfume of wine was on his tongue. The drink had made him playful.

Now, she was embarrassed. She had lost her edge. "Are you planning to fight in the melee?"

Roland answered flatly, "No."

As much as Amarys wore a mask of indifference, his response had wounded her. "Of course," she said. "I assumed as much. I only hoped..." Amarys felt nothing like herself as she bungled the exchange. Tripping over her tongue, she began to back away.

"I am not a knight," he offered, his tone softening. "And I do not wish to marry so young."

"Ah, yes. Neither do I!" she cried, a little more frenetically than she should have. Cognizant of that, she lowered her voice. "Sorry. You said you had a question."

"Yes." He indicated his sister at the far end of the hall. "I was wondering if you knew anything about Rowen's necklace." Like a lamb among wolves, Rowen stood between Harlowe and his father, the Viscount. "Was it a gift from a suitor?"

"No. I gave her the garnet."

CHAPTER 16

Rowen heard her name whispered like the scrape of a whetstone. The sky outside her window remained dark, the sun still nestled in its roost. Roland crouched at her bedside.

"Rowen, wake up. Get dressed and meet me outside."

Roland tossed a bundle of fabric at her. She unfolded several garments: a tunic, hose, and a cloak.

"This again?"

At least this time, they were clean.

"I will wait for you at the servant's entrance." Roland was gone before she had finished rubbing the sleep from her eyes.

She did as he bade her, concealing herself with the cloak, for she did not want the servants to catch her dressed as a boy.

Outside, Roland kicked his feet off the edge of a cart loaded with armor. Shrouded in darkness, the twins made their way to the cover of the forest. The sky was just beginning to pale with the arrival of morning.

"Where are we going?"

"We are nearly there."

They wound between trees, picking up the wheels of the cart whenever they caught on a root or a dip in the earth. Roland explained to her as they walked.

"I know you to be superior with the sword, but it recently occurred to me that you haven't trained against a man in armor. If you are to protect yourself, you must learn how the body feels and moves in armor."

They reached a grassy clearing concealed by woods on all sides. "Here we are." He lifted long mail chausses from the cart.

"You intend for me to wear that?"

"You cannot understand an armored man's vulnerabilities unless you experience them yourself." Roland began buckling his arming belt around his sister's wan frame. "Legs are first," he said, helping her step into the chausses and attaching them to the belt. The armor was heavy, but as it clasped her body tightly, it made her feel dense and sturdy. Everything changed, though, when he dressed her upper body, fastening plates snugly to a wool gambeson. The chainmail and gorget hung heavy on her bones. Then he added pauldrons and bracers, belting the boiled leather as tightly as it would go.

"Your arms are much thinner than mine, but apart from that, my armor fits you."

Rowen stood buried, sweating a deluge down the front of her helm. Surrounded by forest in all directions, she could hardly stand to lift her arms. All those rings and rivets heated her muscles with fast-pumping blood. Roland placed their father's bastard sword in her hand. She clutched it eagerly, but the blade's weight pulled her forward and cut the dirt. Rowen tensed her core and lifted with the strength of her legs, holding the blade up a full heartbeat before it came crashing down. She could only manage to drag it across the soil.

"How are you supposed to hold it with all this weight on your arms?" she lamented.

"A man's arms have more strength, but if he has a heavy weapon, he will tire more quickly."

"Do we fight now?"

Roland held his chin. "No. Let's start with some basic movement."

The twins aligned themselves as each other's reflection, practicing movement, Roland with his walking stick and Rowen with steel. What she usually accomplished with ease and alacrity, she struggled to replicate in armor. She felt as heavy as a boulder as she lifted the sword in the four positions called out by her brother.

"Ox!"

Rowen slid her left foot forward and drew the blade up above her ear.

"Plow!"

She lowered the blade to her hip and aimed its point at Roland's heart. He came over and adjusted her grip, showing her how to bring pressure against the cross guard to balance her hold.

"Fool!"

She slid her foot back and brought the sword's tip down. Already in this first phase of movements, she was exhausted. Beneath the weight of leather, chainmail, and plates, she could not breathe deeply enough to recover. Her face burned. Her legs trembled beneath her. She planted her boots deep into the earth and held firm.

"From the roof!"

She lifted the sword over her head as if to slash vertically, grunting as she held it firm.

"Again!" he shouted. "Ox!"

Rowen shrieked, sinking her blade into the earth like a fang. "Enough."

"Keep going!" said Roland.

She hissed between gasps, kneeling in the dirt. "I'm not as strong as you."

She removed the flat-plate helm, too exhausted to even stand. Her body shivered like she was freezing to death in her own sweat. A black gauze seemed to blur her vision. She would faint if she pressed on.

Roland stood over her, shouting down at her. "Don't give up!"

Her face burned sanguine. She rose to her feet.

"Fight me." Roland handed her a training sword and stepped back, preparing his own. Then he came at her.

Rowen shouted an expletive, staggering against a tree and whipping herself behind it.

"Hold!" she called out. "Fie, Roland!"

She dropped her wooden sword. "Get me out of this before I throw up in your helmet!"

Her shoulders weren't built for the yoke of knighthood. She could not expect to move in her brother's armor the way he did.

Roland began to unfasten her arms. She panted, catching her breath. Roland lifted the mail coif over Rowen's head, placing it in the wagon.

Now, she had enough wind in her to scream, "I hate this body!"

Rowen rarely shouted and hearing her volume at such a height had surprised Roland enough to stop his process.

"I hate these arms! These legs! I hate this shape that I must call myself. Why are we not one flesh, Roland? Why must I be this weak, misshapen version of you?"

Roland waited for her to finish. He nodded as though he understood. It was moments like this when Rowen remembered he was with her, not against her.

The siblings traveled to a nearby creek, where Roland rinsed his face. The shallow stream sent slivers of light undulating across its dark, glassy surface. It babbled and the sound put Rowen more at ease.

As she removed her hauberk, it caught on her tunic. With Roland's help, she managed to unhook it. Roland gathered the links in his arms and loaded the mail into the cart.

"You have been hiding more and more from me these days," said Roland.

"You have hidden from me for years. I have been alone for years!" she emphasized. Roland handed her a bliaut that he had brought from her wardrobe. She donned the delicate garment to cover the tunic and hose.

"I never wished to hide from you. I only wanted to spare you the burdens of my life. I want to be trained as a troubadour and not a knight. I want to marry a lowborn girl and leave this place."

"The butcher's wife?"

"No. A tavern girl. Her name is Cateline."

"Is she the reason you will not fight for Amarys?"

"It is my turn to ask you something. And you must answer."

Rowen dipped her hands into the cold stream. She washed the sweat from her puffy, blushed face, combing back her hair and braiding it neatly into a fishtail.

"Are you in love with Amarys?" he asked. "The garnet came from her. She told me."

Rowen clenched her teeth, striving to conceal her impulse to react. Her brother could see it. And she knew he could see it. She had not wanted to tell him anything about the garnet because every shred of her feeling for Amarys burned gently at the corners of his mind, those hidden places where Rowen abided. Her desperation became his own.

"You asked me to fight for her because that is the closest thing to fighting for her yourself."

Rowen could see the hurt in his eyes, eyes that were the same brown as her own. There was no hiding from him.

"You said no."

Roland slumped against a tree, planting his foot against the trunk. "Fie, Rowen," he said. "I used to think it looked easy: the joust, the knights charging at each other on horseback. You have seen how difficult it is to move in armor. There is nothing easy about fighting in a tournament. And going up against Harlowe? I don't want to end up the same as Edmund."

"I understand."

Roland pushed off from the tree, shrugging. "If only you could be her champion." He adjusted the armor in the cart, centering it. "Those brutes vying for her hand would get tired; they would give up. And she would seem less and less a prize. But what is she to you?"

Rowen thought anything she said would sound perverse aloud. She watched the water trickle down the smooth river stones as its currents pulled it south.

"Rowen."

Rowen caught her tears on her sleeve. "Please, Roland! It is a wrong that I would leave unspoken."

"Wrong? No. There are errors in us both, but that is not one of them."

"We must get back to the manor." Rowen wrapped her fingers around the cart's handle, towing it over the bumpy terrain. She forged a path through the woods. Roland chased her and seized the cart away.

"Rowen, stop," he said, struggling with her for the cart. "Let me pull!"

Rowen finally relented and followed behind him, sniffling and covering her eyes with her sleeves.

"Listen," he said. "People are what they are, Rowen. They want what they want.

And sometimes, we want to be what society says we cannot be."

"I must confess, but I fear Father Gerard will remove me from her company!"

"Why would you confess? No. Do not do that."

"Until I do, I am divided from God."

"God?" he spat. "God took our mother before she could even hold us in her arms. God would see Amarys married to her cousin, beaten, and raped behind closed doors."

"You must not speak of things that are so real to me."

"Why should that be more real than those of asking me to marry the woman you love?"

A breeze cooled the sweat running down Rowen's back. The leaves hanging over the path bobbed gently. Several of them fluttered as they fell.

"I am so afraid, Roland, for I have never felt like this before. These feelings have come to rule my body, forcing me to suffer bitterly when I cannot be near her."

The twins returned through the forest toward the manor. They came out of the wood. The amber and green grass of the meadow hummed with cricket song. The clouds had parted, and a blue sky opened up above them. The twins trudged through the tall grass and made their way home.

They quieted as they approached the manor. From a distance, they could see a procession of men in white robes. Their billowy garments were stitched with body-length crosses. They were departing, and the twins' father, Ivin, along with the domestics, held the enormous pelt of what must have been Roland's lion.

"The Crusaders have brought you a gift," said Rowen.

"Fie."

"Roland!" shouted their father, livid. "Upstairs. Now. The women will mount your trophy."

Rowen watched Roland follow their father inside the manor. As she came closer to Emily and Constance who were holding the pelt, she struggled to believe what she was looking at. The beast was so strange, its coarse fur as radiant as spun gold, its massive head at once regal and savage. There were the claws that had shredded her brother's back. There were the dagger-point teeth that might have torn the meat from his bones. Had Roland really faced down such a terrible beast with nothing but his crucifix?

Rowen watched as her servants worked to mount the pelt in the dining hall, angling its ferocious head downward for all to see. The women balanced on a ladder and bickered over how to attach the nails. Feeling useless to them, Rowen followed the stairs to the tower room where her grandmother stayed. The old woman was at the warp-weighted loom, her withered hands tangled in fine thread.

Rowen placed a second chair beside her. She worked with Cecile, passing the weft over and under the warp threads. Her additions were often imperceptible. It was a humbling practice.

When they came to Rieux, Cecile had brought her loom, an enormous frame taller than Ivin. In her free time, she worked diligently on the tapestry that her ancestors had begun. The thing was only partly done, being a work so insurmountably large, Rowen could only hope that her own descendants might live to see it worked to completion. Cecile had tried six times for a daughter, hoping to have some help completing the tapestry that had been in their family for generations. The woman had been taking care of children since she was fourteen, raising her boys up to be warriors, watching them die senselessly in skirmish warfare with the Byzantines. Roland and Rowen might have had a good many cousins had any of their uncles not been men of action.

The tapestry was more than half done. It was an image of a red deer fenced in and surrounded by orange trees. No matter how Rowen might have altered the tapestry's plan, the fence was already woven, its size too enormous for her to remake within a single lifetime. Monotonously, she wove on, following the design, fiber by fiber.

Rowen startled as a powerful wind battered the window. Cecile groaned, rising from her seat and staggering across the open the rattling leads. The old woman muttered, her wrinkled face hardening like stone.

Rowen continued weaving, picking apart the threads with her nails and winding some over one finger. She worked the threads in and out of each other, continuing her seemingly insignificant section. Cecile sat down in the chair beside her and watched her weave, nodding slowly in approval and offering advice when she could. After some hours passed, Cecile grew tired and stood.

"Poor creature," she murmured, running her faded fingers over the vibrant tapestry. "Look how she wishes for freedom."

"Perhaps we should name her Rowen, hm, grandmother?"

"Nay, you silly girl. Do not give away your name so easily. One day, it may be all you possess."

Anna came in with a taper and began lighting various candles about the room. The sun was sinking now. Rowen shook the stiffness from her wrists as it dawned on her just how long she had been occupied by this labor.

Outside the chamber door, the floorboards creaked. All the blood drained from her face. She looked up as it opened, standing when she saw Roland.

"Oh, hail Mary. It's only you," she whispered.

Roland said nothing in reply. He came in, his shoulders slumped, arms hanging at his sides.

There was fresh blood on his cheek and so much swelling that his cheekbone looked malformed. Rowen let the weaving fall from her lap, and she met him on the other side of the room, holding and inspecting his face.

"How could he?"

Roland withdrew. "I lied to him about the lion. All is forgiven now that I have given him what he wants. I told him my intention to fight in the tourney. He has promised me his banners, his armor, the shield bearing the family crest, everything. He is so proud of how eager I am to spill Christian blood in the summer games."

Rowen cried aloud, grasping his hands. "You will fight for Amarys?"

Roland knelt before her, pressing her hands to his forehead. "I will fight for you. Let that be clear. I do this for you. Not her. I will marry her, but I will never lie with her."

As quickly as he had come in, he stood and left. Rowen was left stunned. She realized, she thought, the weight of the boon he was granting her. He would never be able to marry for love. He would never sire legitimate children.

Cecile murmured something from bed. Rowen had forgotten she was there. She went to her bedside, taking her frail, cold hand in her own. "Grandmother?" she said. "Are you awake?"

"Men," she hissed, clearing her throat and hacking in an attempt to restore her voice. It was raspy no matter how she tried. "Roland is more like Ivin every day."

"Did you hear all that he said?" asked Rowen, her blood turning cold.

"I heard enough," said Cecile.

"Please, Grandmother, you must never breathe a word."

"Hush now, child. I may be old and weary, but I am not a halfwit." She frowned. "We women often fall in love when we should not, but we must always remember our place in the tapestry of God's divine providence. Remember, you are finishing a story of thread whose beginnings and ends you will never understand. What becomes of the love between you and Amarys ten years from now? What do you hope to gain? What are you willing to lose?"

Cecile's hand tightened around Rowen's wrist. Her blue eyes quivered. "Whatever you choose, make sure you understand the cost."

CHAPTER 17

Roland enjoyed the company of his friends beneath the Grim Tree. Propped up against a rock, he practiced his ode to the lion, hoping to refine the bridge and make it more elaborate. Beside him, there was Willem, his girl, Artemie, two other squires not yet elevated to knighthood, Arnault and Costi, and Sir Erec. The last cool days of Spring were upon them, the pale flowers falling away as the days grew sunnier. The forest foliage had thickened, which helped to obscure their midday gatherings.

Artemie was telling a story about a barn owl while the boys gambled. Erec did not participate, for he had only joined them so he could explain the stranger parts of the knighting ceremony to Roland.

"I have to slap you," he said, chuckling. "It is the last blow you must receive without retaliation."

"Can I retaliate now?" asked Roland, flashing a dimple in his smirk.

"Come at me, brother."

"No. I want you pretty for tomorrow."

"Of course," said Erec. "Your sister will be in attendance, after all."

"Which reminds me..." Roland checked that the others were still engaged with Artemie's story about the barn owl. "...I recommend you distance yourself from her, at least until after the tournament. You are competing, no?"

"I have no choice."

"And if you win?"

"The games are rigged in Harlowe's favor."

"You would do well to win the Baron's daughter. She is an heiress and, from what I understand, you need an heiress."

"Do not concern yourself with what I need." Erec's mouth drew taut.

Roland felt like one stringing a bow with his own patience. "I must, though, for you have concerned yourself with my sister."

"There is an understanding between us."

"The only understanding that matters is the one between you and me."

Artemie and the others paused, and the men bayed in a low, resounding, "Oooo."

"Protective," tittered Artemie.

"Ha!" Erec laughed to preserve a sense of levity. "There's the retaliation."

"I am only offering counsel."

"Counsel that wounds!" There was choler in his tone, subtle but present. "Are we not friends, Roland?"

"You know the love I bear you."

"Then you know that I would never betray you. That is all I will say on the matter."

"That is all I need to hear."

Roland played ambient chords, subtly telling Erec that all was well between them. He continued to play even as he noticed Cateline come around the bend with another girl from town.

They seated themselves on the edge of the wall, backdropped by every shade of moss that tangled deep into the cave.

The girls wore plain, undyed bliauts and their hair hung loose down their backs, adorned with naught but a simple cord around their crowns. Together, they inspected the clusters of mushrooms along the cave wall, deciding they were poisonous and leaving them alone. As a subtle cue, Roland began to play the melody to the song he had written for Cat. He waited for her face to reveal some recognition. It seemed to make her smile, but she did not look at him.

Mutually, in their present company, the lovers pretended not to know each other.

And Roland's friends ignored the girls' presence. At first.

"What pretty maids," said the squire, Costi, interrupting Artemie.

Humbly, Cat bowed her head.

"Does it speak?" teased the squire.

"Good day, milord," said Cat.

"Good day, little apple." Costi took a silver ring from his pile of winnings, concealing it behind his back. "Pick a hand. One hand holds a ring, which you can keep if you guess right. Guess wrong, though, and you must pay me a kiss."

"No, thank you," said Cat. "We must be going."

"What's wrong?" asked Costi. "It is only a kiss."

"We are foraging," she explained. "My mother is waiting for us."

Costi chuckled mirthlessly. "Just pick a hand, girl. The game is hardly complex."

"Leave them, Costi," said Roland, slinging his lute over his back as he stood. "Will I see you at my vigil tonight?"

"I would not miss it."

Cat blinked, sitting straighter and trying to speak with the same courtly manner as Roland and his friends. "Master Roland. Are you to be knighted?"

"He is!" answered Willem. "He killed a lion with his bare hands! I mean, Lord Jesus helped him and all, but still! He had no weapon! Plunged a crucifix through the animal's heart! Instant death!"

"You needn't remind them, Willem," said Roland. "Everyone already knows."

"But do they know about the pelt? The Crusaders gifted him the pelt! It hangs at la Flèche manor. Our very own knight of the lion!"

Roland was beginning to dislike the association. He had stopped playing music at Lechón because all anyone ever wanted to hear anymore was his song about the lion. And the pelt, while it made his father proud, loomed as a reminder of Roland's harrowing experience in the pit.

"When is the ceremony?" asked Cat. "May we attend?"

"Ah, no," said Willem. "Every plate is spoken for, I'm afraid."

"Of course." Cat clutched her basket, taking her friend by the hand. "We should go. My mother will wonder where we've gone."

"I will take you to her," said Costi. "Lest some fawn intercept you in the wood."

"We will be all right," she insisted. "Good day. And congratulations, Master Roland. I admit, I am surprised. I thought you loathed the Order."

All this time, Artemie and Willem had been murmuring to one another, but everyone stopped talking when they heard what Cat had just said.

"Is that true, Roland?" Costi pried. "Do you?"

Roland shrugged. "Sometimes, I drink too much at Lechón and say all manner of things I do not mean."

"Well, that ends now," said Erec.

Cat and her friend bid farewell again and left swiftly. Costi looked at Arnault who nodded, whispering, "Let's go after them."

Roland blocked their path as they tried to go. "They're my father's tenants. You will leave them be."

"Come now, Roland," Costi whined. "In the flower of youth, such maidens wish to be embraced. They would not have come to the Grim tree otherwise."

At that, Artemie slid a little closer to Willem, eyeing the other men carefully.

Roland held firm, refusing to break eye contact. "Leave them," he repeated.

Costi shifted awkwardly to one side, resting his palm on his sword hilt.

Willem spoke to break the tension, "One of those girls is Roland's lover. Just leave it alone."

Costi and Arnault hooted at that. Roland groaned. "Shall I tell them one of your secrets then, Willem?"

"Oh!" Costi chortled like a beast. "Why don't you just join me, Roland? I'll take whichever bitch you haven't rutted on."

Roland flung himself at Costi, eager to throw a punch. Erec jumped in, though. While he kept Roland back, Willem shoved Costi to the back of the cave.

"You cur!" Roland shrieked as he flailed against Erec. "You should be gelded, you licentious dog!"

"Roland," said Erec sternly. "You will have to abandon such vices after today. A knight must keep himself pure."

"To Hell with all of you!" spat Roland, pushing Erec off. He left the cave where his friends continued to holler and laugh. Hiking through the forest brush, Roland moved the vines aside with his bare hands. Prickly nettles burned under his fingertips as he did. He growled at the invisible barbs, wiping his hands over his vest. He followed signs of human activity, broken twigs, strained branches, and crushed flowers. It troubled him how easy it was to find Cat and her little friend. Willem had been right to reveal his attachment to a commoner. Costi and Arnault might have only captured them for kissing, but then again, they might have done a great deal more.

"Cat!" called Roland, catching her from behind.

She turned, her state heightened. "Forgive me, milord. I should not have intruded!"

Roland seized her, kissing her deeply in front of her friend.

"Oh my!" the friend cried, laughing when she saw how Cat returned her lord's affection.

Cat drew back, eyes glistening. "I thought perhaps—"

"No. I have wanted to see you."

Cat handed her basket to her friend. She embraced Roland, couching her head on his shoulder. "Then I can breathe again."

"Listen," said Roland. "I am being made a knight, which means I must withdraw for a time. But I will return. You must only wait for me. Will you? Wait?"

"I would wait a thousand years." They kissed again, supposing themselves in their own little world, though the friend continued to ogle them unabashedly. Roland blinked, remembering her, and he drew back from Cat, bidding her farewell before he sprinted in the direction of home.

A gentle buzz emanated from the grasshoppers of the field. Making his way down the sunny paths of the forest, he thought of his time in Toulouse and a question Giraut had asked him.

They had been listening to a woman troubadour play for them at dinner. The windows were open, allowing the voice of the city to mingle with the lady's harp. Entrenched in candlelight and cool night air, Roland had looked down the length of the table at his host family, the patriarch, the wife, and the children who were all nearly grown. Giraut and his two sisters listened attentively to the lady's intricate song. Every one of them was an accomplished musician, and still, they were so impressed that not a single word passed their lips until the song was ended.

As their gentle accolades commended the lady's efforts, Roland, without thinking, said aloud, "I wish this was my life."

And Giraut returned, "If that is your wish, why should you ever leave us?"

They would have kept him on. It was his choice to return. Yes, in Toulouse, he had a father who did not beat him. He had a brother who understood music as language in the same breath. He had a city brimming with creativity and culture. He could never say he had been happy there, though—not truly—for how could he be anything without his sister?

At home, in his bed with the posts that were carved with the bodies of lions that were not lions, Roland tried to sleep and could not sleep. He kept thinking about what Cat had said about his loathing the Order of chivalry. She was right, of course. He had to remind himself that none of this was for his father. He would marry Amarys to settle her on Rowen, he would love only Cat, and they would go to Toulouse to escape the gossip of town. They would have music and beauty and freedom from the realities of Rieux. All would be well in the end.

That night, during the Feast of the Ascension, Roland watched his friends and family enjoy course after course as he fasted. It was a humbling practice that forced him to look outside himself and appreciate how society continued to churn without him. As a knight, he would be responsible for them in a way he had never considered before. It would be his duty to protect them at the cost of his life. Dwelling on this, his heart sank like lead, for he knew there was a great deal he would never be willing to do for them. He would never forsake Rowen, even if they marred her with the labels of Sapphite and enemy to Christendom. He was willing to defend Rieux from invaders, but he would never be a conqueror. Thoughts of such falseness within himself made him doubt the sanctity of this ceremony, this thing that so many of his friends dreamed of all their lives and seldom achieved.

At the end of the revelries, Clement, Ivin, and their inner circle of knights guided Roland down into the belly of the chateau. A thin layer of moisture on the stone floors glistened in the candlelight. At first, the rooms he passed through looked unassuming. One woman worked a pump as a long chain of servants collected water into clay vessels and moved in the same direction as Roland and the knights.

The bathing chamber was cool but not cold, well-insulated by its small size, its proximity to the earth, and the thick stone walls containing it. The servants undressed Roland and assisted him up some steps and into a tub, a massive circular bowl made from the planks of old barrels. The water's cold embrace enveloped him, shocking the doubts from his mind.

Father Gerard blessed the water and announced that Roland was cleansed of all sin. The men draped Roland in silk robes the color of starlight and took him to the chapel. He made confession, and they sang a mass for him. He maintained a stoic countenance as he knelt before the altar and took the sacrament. When the service ended, Father Gerard blessed each and every article of Roland's armor.

"Bless this sword in the shape of the crucifix that signifies our Lord. May you vanquish the enemies of Christ."

"Bless this lance, O sacred lance, whose timber does not bend for it signify the knight's battle for truth."

"Bless this chapel-de-fer, symbol of shame; may it protect our knight's crown and teach him in the sanctity of his high office that he must always remember the ground and the baseness of his origin."

The great tedium of it all wore on Roland. Was he really going to bless every article?

"Bless this hauberk..."

"Bless these chausses..."

"Bless these spurs..."

"Ah! The collar! Most sacred symbol of obedience!"

Roland tilted now and again into exhaustion, breathing deeply and resuming an erect posture. His spirits lifted to see Father Gerard and some of the village youths leading Ash into the chapel. Gerard dabbed Ash's nose with holy water.

"A knight's horse symbolizes his courage. He is his most cherished partner, his constant companion whose body constellates with his own. This most honorable beast elevates a man and makes him a true chevalier."

Roland cleared his throat, unable to help it as he teared up. There was nothing tedious as Father Gerard blessed Ash's saddle and bit.

Sitting vigil left Roland quite alone with his thoughts. His knees ached as he knelt beside the altar and pretended to pray. Various nobles approached and gave him their blessings. Roland thanked them and offered each a commemorative gift, a coin bearing the mark of his arms with the lion passant.

Amarys approached him, her sisters Beatrice and Honora remaining at a distance.

"Did the lion suffer?" the lady asked.

Roland maintained his façade, hardly moving and continuing to wear the false face of chivalry that was demanded of him.

"Not by my hand. I gave him a good death." He put one of his tokens in her palm. "Lady Amarys, the last time we met, I should have thanked you for filling your hall with music. It is not an easy thing to play for others, and you are accomplished at your craft. I regret that I was rude to you. I should not have spoken ill of the sumptuous banquet provided by your family. I hope you will forgive me and, from this day to my last day, consider me your sworn protector and ally."

"I..." She examined the heraldry on the coin, closing it in her palm. "Thank you, Sir Roland."x

The night dragged on. Roland began to suspect this ceremony existed to ensure a man did not sin the following day since he would be much too fatigued to engage in anything but sleep. To go on sinning, as Erec continued to remind him, was to spit on the sanctity of the Order. Of course, some men took that idea more seriously than others. Erec, for now, no longer gambled or engaged in the riotous drinking contests he had previously championed. Edmund, though, had been known to frequent the bathhouse after dark, a place one could buy a woman for the same price as a meal.

What kind of knight would Roland be? A false one? A pretender? He could not escape the memory of his conversation with his father the day he finally submitted.

There was something so deeply personal about being hit by a father who had been absent for the first eight years of his life. The soulless eyes of the tapestries watched on as Roland held his swollen cheekbone, breathing through the pain as it thrummed in his skull.

"It does not bring me joy to strike you."

Ivin often said that. Roland never believed it.

"You should have told me you were abducted. You should have sent for me instead of trying to conceal where you were staying. I already knew about the girl."

"I stopped seeing Tabitha long ago."

"Not that one. This new one. Cateline."

Roland's blood ran like currents under ice.

"They say you write songs for her."

"I write songs for many girls."

"Yes, but you only lie with them one at a time. You are like me in that way. A pity their loyalty to you is so easily diverted."

Roland shook his head, trying terribly hard not to show how his guts twisted inside of him.

"You gave Tabitha no choice," he choked out.

"She chose the husband I provided, and she chose to betray her vows."

Roland quaked, remembering bruises that could not be explained and trysts that could not be kept. The flickering image of his first love's face fled into the shadows of his memories.

"Seeing how the sanctity of marriage is meaningless to you, I have thought of something else for this one. An accusation of heresy goes a long way, and it is a far simpler option."

"If you want to test whether or not I am willing to duel my own father, go ahead. I would rather avoid it, though, for Rowen's sake."

Ivin only smirked, dragging his thumb down his beard. "For Rowen's sake indeed. You would never estrange yourself from the sister you cannot live without."

There was the thorn. For all of Ivin's incredible cruelty, Rowen loved him in the same way that she loved God. Devoutly. Unconditionally.

"I will leave Cat alone," said Roland. "For now. You cannot tell me what to do once I am married."

"Certainly." Ivin's derisive laughter made Roland's skin crawl. "Did you have a lady in mind? An appropriate match?"

"I do. Make me a knight, Father, and I will win Clement's daughter and take back our ancestral lands."

At dawn, Roland awoke from his deep meditation. The official dubbing began. A procession of knights came through the chapel, surrounding him, each of them dressing him in a piece of his armor. Noble families filled the pews. Roland smiled

163

when he saw his sister. And she smiled back.

Had Sir Edmund lived, he would have been the one delivering this rite of passage, but it moved Roland deeply to have his own beloved friend, Sir Erec of Avenport, presiding over him.

Erec wore his best pieces of armor, including a ceremonial yoke gilt of gold and silver.

"Roland La Flèche-de Beaugency, you come before us today, having proven yourself in a valiant battle against a lion. Knighthood is not merely an accolade but a divine calling, one that I know you will honor."

"I vow to uphold the virtues of our sacred Order," said Roland.

Erec placed his broadsword on Roland's right shoulder and then his left.

"In the name of God, the Father, Saint Michael, and Saint George, I dub thee Sir Roland, knight of the lion. Be a man of courage, justice, honor."

Erec leaned forward, putting his lips against Roland's in a courtly kiss of peace.

"Rise, chevalier."

Roland stood as Erec sheathed his blade. As per tradition, Erec smacked him across the face. Hard. The chapel erupted with applause.

Part Three
The Tournament

CHAPTER 18

Midsummer came fast. The days grew hot, and more time was spent indoors, with Rowen attending lessons at the chateau with Amarys and her army of tutors. All the castle's heat rose to the solar, where each woman sat poised like a muse in marble, each with an embroidery hoop and a needle. Amarys sat between her sisters, the slightly younger Beatrice, and the child, Honora. Their Nurse, Marie, led their practice, offering tips for filling in shapes or threading the needle. Amarys removed her veil and went to splash her face with water from a clay bowl. The windows hung open, and they might have invited cool breezes if there were any wind to be had.

As the day of the tourney drew nigh, whether they were alone or in mixed company, Amarys had become increasingly reserved in her speech. Dark shadows framed her eyes, and the corners of her nails were bitten raw. The light that usually glowed in her was absent, and it pained Rowen to see her in such distress. But what consolation could she give?

Rowen's gown clasped her torso like a trap drenched in honey water. She pushed the blunt needle through her embroidery, careful not to press too hard. She had broken two needles already. New needles were procured, but the hard-hearted Marie warned her that if she broke another, she would stick her with it.

Rowen's stitches formed dark veins of gold across a shapely black leaf, rigid silk patterns that reflected her state of mind. She usually found needlepoint meditative and calming, but today, her heart felt heavy. She could hear the hammers banging on wood outside. The men below toiled to assemble the elevated stands around the tourney grounds in time for the event, which was only a month away.

She looked down and away from her embroidery, her fingers resting idly as her mind wandered.

Amarys continued to work on her wreath of gillyflowers, noticing her friend had stopped. "Does the noise bother you?" she asked.

Rowen nodded, returning to her work.

Each time Rowen looked at Amarys, she found her eyes staring back at her and had to force herself not to gaze too long. She didn't need to see Amarys's eyes to remember them. Those blue-green eyes were always with her, imprinted in her mind. They were the color of a sea she had forgotten.

"Rowen, you are very changed," said Beatrice.

Rowen blinked, looking at the sister. "How so?"

"Harder somehow. Have you been eating enough fruit?"

"Oh. Perhaps not." Rowen finished the last stitch in her spiral of dark leaves. "There," she said, holding her design up for the women to see. "I am finished."

Amarys squinted and smiled softly. "Very beautiful. Reminds me of a certain journey we took together." They shared the secret in their smiles, and the others hardly paid it any mind. "What is the gold connecting them?"

"I cannot say. I suppose I thought it looked pretty."

"Maybe it is lightning?" suggested Amarys.

"Yes. Lightning."

Amarys gave a nod and returned to her project, which was only half done.

"I am too hot!" whined Honora.

"As am I," said Marie. "We will take the air. Come, ladies."

"Rowen and I will be down soon," said Amarys. "I need her help with this." Marie led Beatrice and Honora from the chamber. When the girls were alone, Amarys cast her messy embroidery away and turned to face Rowen.

"This will be the last time I see you before the ball," she said urgently. "With all the preparations for the tournament, I am not permitted to entertain again. I have to warn you, though. You must not let Harlowe court you."

"I do not intend to."

Amarys nodded, but her expression remained tense. "I would never forgive myself if any harm came to you." Her voice was a frail, faint whisper, untouched by inflection of any sort. "God forgive me, I will kill him myself."

"Amarys."

"He has already brought his tyranny to Rieux," Amarys spoke with an edge normally reserved for her Nurse when they bickered. "His heart is blacker than ever."

"In what way?"

"I cannot speak of it. But you must be careful. Do not be left alone with him."

"Are you safe here?"

"Oh, he would not come anywhere near my quarters, but my servants do not have the same protections." Amarys sighed, pressing her lips together. "Something happened. For the sake of her honor, I mustn't tell you her name, but she is a maid here. She wears a heavy wimple to hide bruises on her throat. She will say nothing of what happened, but she was at the welcome feast pouring wine for my cousin. She caught his eye, and I saw him follow her out."

It happened to plenty of girls. If they survived, they knew better than to speak of it. All they could pray for was the discretion of their assailant.

"Ad Deum. You cannot marry such a man." Rowen's mouth went dry. She swallowed and said, "My brother has promised me that he will fight for your hand. As his wife, he would let you live however you like. Take a lover. Live abroad. Anything."

Amarys layered both hands over her lips as though she could not believe it. "Your brother said that?"

"Yes. Out of love for me, he has sworn to deliver you."

Amarys leaned into the back of her chair, her hands lowering to fold around her seed pearl necklace.

"He and I are twins. My pain is his pain, you see."

"It is very noble of him that he would fight for someone with whom he has no attachment." Amarys blinked and straightened in her chair. "Forgive me, friend. I did not ask how you felt about this. Do you not want him to fight? I understand if you are worried for his safety."

"No, I wanted this; I pleaded for this," said Rowen, adding, "Amarys, I would fight for you myself if I could."

Amarys nodded, but her mind was elsewhere. "I cannot thank you enough. I will not forget this."

Rowen wanted so desperately to seize this moment. This was the time to tell her everything, to shed all the fear that hindered truth. But the moment slipped her grasp.

"Does Roland fight well?" asked Amarys.

"Yes. He will liberate you easily."

Rowen hated that she could not say it would be her, especially as Amarys's spark revitalized. "Have you done anything to help him like me better? Do you speak well of me?"

"I speak of you all the time," she confessed, bristling. She wished Amarys could somehow pick up on her discomfort. "I have told him you are kind to your servants, that you are the dearest friend I have ever known. I have told him you can make me laugh more than any other person, even him, which is no easy feat. I have sung your praises as though I were in love with you myself."

If Amarys could only feel the wings beating in Rowen's chest. If only she could know the longings burning through her.

"You give me hope, Rowen, but there is more that I must tell you. Nurse revealed to me that Harlowe will be joining us at dinner. He remembers you and is eager to see you again."

Rowen hardened her heart. She made it sturdy like the wood beneath the beating of the hammers outside. "Why?"

"I do not know, but I have made arrangements to protect you." Amarys folded her arms, tilting her smile askew. "I hope you will be pleased."

"What have you done?"

"My knight will see you home. Or rather your knight."

Rowen heard footsteps advancing up the stairs.

"Who is it?"

"Sir Erec. Did you know my sister is in love with him? Practically threw herself at his feet and begged him not to fight in the tournament. He said he had to fight to honor the glory of our house, but he had no intention of winning."

Each footstep filled Rowen's head with anguish and dread. She clenched her embroidery hoop. Her heart was pounding hard enough to make her chest hurt.

"Still," Amarys went on, "He could not return my sister's love. He was already committed to another. But the lady in question was not me. Can you imagine the sort of woman it would take to steal him from a Baron's daughter? Why, she must either be a princess... or a sorceress." Rowen looked up from the floorboards to see those blue-green eyes waiting for hers. "There are no secrets here, Rowen. Not between us."

"There is no secret. I know almost nothing about him."

"Let me help you! His favorite saints are Saint Quirin and Saint Anne. He is reserved, but he speaks true even when he knows it will not win him any favor. Every woman in Rieux is in love with him, and I assure you, none of them have any inkling of his person beyond the gorgeous exterior." She bit her lip, containing a euphoric smile.

Rowen could not speak or swallow.

"My rose..." said Amarys. "I am not angry with you. I only wish you had told me sooner."

"My lady?" Erec stood behind her, having emerged from the stairwell.

"Thank you for seeing her home, Sir Erec."

"Can you not send for my brother?" Rowen blurted, looking between them.

"Sir Roland is not due back for hours. We go to dinner soon where Harlowe is waiting," said Amarys. "I will protect this love between you, but you must do as I say. Go quickly through the East wing and no one will see you."

"I have readied your horse," said Erec. "Biax is waiting below."

Rowen's eyes were burning, her chest pounding. Without saying goodbye, she fled down the stairwell. Erec followed her, trying to match her pace. She nearly tripped on her skirts before she finally bunched them under her arms and broke into a sprint. She wanted to scream, wanted to tear down every tapestry she passed.

"Rowen," he called to her at a subdued volume. "Rowen!"

She stopped at the bottom of the stair and waited for him. Without looking back, she said, "See me home, Sir Erec."

As Erec had said, their horses waited just outside the gate. Together, they proceeded to the forest trail, riding in silence. She rode a length ahead of Erec, keeping a quick enough pace that she could say the wind was too loud for her to speak to him.

She did not want him to see her cry.

The fires that burned for Amarys were overtaking her, raging out of control.

Why was she born a woman? Why was her love so misplaced?

Amarys would love Roland. Of course, she would. Roland could give her life and love in the open. Roland could give her children. Rowen had always known her love could never be reciprocated, her deepest wishes never fulfilled. And still, she had allowed the god of love to sink his arrows in her flesh. Had she learned nothing from Ovid?

Girls, I tell to you what I tell the men: It's a good idea to quench fierce flames; do not let your heart be slave to love.

Love was vulnerability. Nothing made a person weaker than falling in love. She had to fight it, make war on it, carve it out of herself before it made a rival out of Roland and destroyed her.

He had sworn he would never lie with Amarys, but love was unpredictable. What if it struck him, too? Already, Rowen felt herself resenting him. He had his list of shortcomings. He was mercurial and aloof. He indulged in whatever substances could help him escape his own thoughts. A lady risked so much in loving him.

As Rowen and Erec entered the forest, she couldn't hide her tears anymore. It was not safe to ride like this, for she could barely see. Sliding down from the saddle, she asked him to give her a moment.

Erec waited silently, dismounting and watching the horses as she went to stand beneath a pine tree. She held herself about the shoulders and took deep, tremulous breaths. Love's intoxicants had turned to venom. She yearned for more innocent times when she could hear her brother's name without roiling in envy.

What were the cures for this affliction? Ovid had listed many.

Stay away. Starve it. Kill it. Take a lover. Love gives way to business. Be busy, you'll be safe. How does a lady keep busy? Embroidery? Weaving? Everything reminded her of Amarys, from the trees to the sky to the daylight moon.

"My lady?" Sir Erec came to stand behind her. Turning, Rowen held back her pain with gritted teeth. Like a woman stabbed, she felt her knees buckle. She fell against him, breaking open. Her tears drenched the front of his mantle. Unable to close her mouth, she sobbed against her hands, coughing as Erec ran a kind hand over her back.

His arms made her feel secure. Gradually, she breathed through the sorrow and let it go. Even in cloth, his body felt like the hard skin of chainmail. Perhaps she could stand to marry him. Perhaps she could make those other feelings go away, crush them deep within her. It was only for the rest of her little mortal life. Once her body died, her spirit would be freed from all corporeal anguish. Longing. Lust. All of it.

"You heard I am to compete in the melee? It is expected of me. I have no intention to win." Erec had gentle eyes, blue, like her lady's. His eyes seemed to always smile, even when his mouth was stern as it was now. "Please, do not weep. My heart is not easily given or withdrawn."

Rowen didn't know what else to do, so she tilted her face and brought her mouth against his. His lips were thin and coarse, his chin rough. She felt his arms tighten around her back.

Instinctively, she drew away. Erec let her go, but he brought her hand to his lips and knelt. "Forgive me. I am not worthy."

She knelt with him, her knees cushioned by the carpet of wood anemone sprawling all around them. Every muscle in her body stiffened, and her heart pounded so hard, she could feel her pulse in her lips.

"You are, Erec. More than worthy."

Erec held her face, his thumb stroking the corner of her jaw. His open-mouth kiss revealed the full fervor of his hunger. He unstrung his cloak, laying it over the flowery patch of earth and guiding her down on her back.

Each of his deep kisses was punctuated by an eruption of her battered breath. She felt a sheen of sweat forming on her chest. Her limbs felt cold. Her neck contracted as he kissed her there, and she turned her face away.

"Don't be afraid," whispered Erec. "I ache for the day that we are wed, but for now, I will only kiss you."

She submitted to being kissed, tolerating his rough face even as it irritated her skin. Sheltered by trees vibrant with the foliage of Spring, their tryst was everything the poets had said it should be. When Erec had exhausted his desire, he lay down beside her on the cloak. She brought her head to rest on his chest, allowing the steady rhythm of his heart to ground her. Pollen floated in the spears of light piercing the tree canopy. A butterfly landed on a flower, flexing its cobalt-blue wings.

"Erec?" she said, her voice as pale as a dulcimer. "I have fears."

"Tell me, my fae."

"I worry for my brother in the melee."

"Your brother is a fine rider and swordsman."

"Emotions cloud his mind. He craves revenge on Harlowe for Sir Edmund's death. I fear he will be slain."

Erec grew somber, hugging her closer. "You should worry more for Harlowe. He made a great many enemies when he slew Edmund."

"There is more..." she contrived. "My brother is in love with Lady Amarys. When the Baron announced that Amarys would be wed, Roland could not eat or drink for days. For months, he neglected his training and wasted away in despair."

"This hurts my heart to hear."

"It was not until my father made him a knight that he recovered, hoping he might win his lady's hand. But he is at a disadvantage, having fallen so far behind."

"I could train him. Would that give you ease?"

"Would you?"

Erec kissed the top of her head. "Tell him to meet me on the training grounds tomorrow morning. I will be there all day."

"You are the best of men. Thank you." It was strange to her how her voice changed in his presence. She played a role she had seen played by other women many times before, one she used to pity. It was the role of the submissive lamb who meekly follows its shepherd, even as it ambles toward its slaughter.

Her compliment inspired him to pin her down and resume his claim to her lips. She bade him take care, especially as her wrist began to smart under the pressure of his hand. In the back of her mind, she remembered that for all his chivalry, he was still a weapon of war.

She lifted her face to escape his lips. "Please. I fear for my honor and yours."

"As do I," he said, his cheeks flushed. "You awaken a beast in me that I am ill-equipped to contain."

He released her, allowing her to stand and brush the stray leaves from her hair. They guided their horses by the leads through the dense matrix of trees.

Erec's kiss still haunted her lips. How different it had been, his hard mouth, his flavor like rye and stale beer. Howls sounded in the distance, emanating from wolves she could not yet see. There were wolves, but there were birds also. They whistled softly and gave her hope. She could do it. She could bear the pain of watching Amarys marry Roland.

CHAPTER 19

The stones of the central courtyard shone white under the clear sky. Clement's men were committed to building, and a great deal of work had yet to be done. They loaded beams and bags of sand onto wagons. The chateau's construction was halted, and every mason worked diligently to prepare the landscape for hosting warriors from across the continent.

Amarys and her Nurse waited outside the stables on a little bench beneath a shelter. Amarys adjusted the fillet meant to cup her chin, itching where the white cloth touched her neck.

"Stop that," said Marie.

Amarys laid one of her riding gloves in her lap and popped the knuckles in her hand, watching her Nurse's face purse up in disapproval. Before the woman could chide her a second time, she whined, "This is ridiculous! Where is my father?"

Soon after, her cousin, Harlowe, came in through the gate, trotting along on his horse. Amarys sank into her shoulders.

"Cousin," said Harlowe.

"Cousin," she returned indifferently.

"Uncle sent me. He is still occupied with the hunt. He tracked an albino fox far north of here. At his request, I am to escort you on your ride."

177

"I will require a second chaperone," said Amarys curtly.

"Sir Harlowe is family," said her Nurse, Marie. "I think it appropriate that he watch over you."

"These lands are crawling with men bent on abducting me, Nurse! It is not safe," insisted Amarys.

"You will be quite safe with me."

He called for the groom to help him dismount, but nobody came. He slid down by himself, landing with a thud.

Amarys started away from him, marching as fast as she could in her cumbersome, feathery gown. Marie and Harlowe followed her. Her vision was spotty, her lips tingling. She blamed herself, of course, for Harlowe's fixation on her.

It had begun innocently enough. They had been children playing with a length of rope. Harlowe was the thief and she the princess. When Harlowe tied her up, she had to escape. But when his knots improved, the nature of the game grew sinister. One day, when they were older, Amarys could not get out of her bindings. Harlowe, amazed at his skillful work, took advantage by sliding his hand up her skirt, his fingers brushing her thighs.

"A thief would not simply hold a princess for ransom," he reasoned. "He would have his way with her first."

Amarys, at the time, felt curious about such play. "We could pretend," she suggested. "Lift my skirt. Show me how common hands would feel upon me."

Entirely clothed, she and Harlowe had feigned congress against the tree. Strange sensations urged her forward even as her flesh chafed.

Throughout the summer, they would go for their ride and sink down into the tall grass of the meadow, sharing their lips and tongues and touching each other through their clothes.

Surely, it was harmless, being only a game of pretend. Still, the fact that she could never tell a soul made her acutely aware that it was wicked play.

Amarys surveyed the square for a knight she trusted, someone who would protect her. There was Guyon. No. There was Jean. No. Her eyes settled on Erec. He wore a black surcoat, leather chausses, and boots that came above the knee in a wide cuff. He was not mounted. He loaded a wagon with practice swords and armaments. "Sir

Erec!" she called.

Erec looked up. He abandoned his work and answered her summons.

"Will you escort me on my ride with my cousin?"

Squinting and shielding his eye from the sun, he said, "Yes. Whatever my lady needs."

Harlowe came between them. "I would prefer to escort Lady Amarys myself," he interrupted. "We have matters to discuss, given that I plan to win her hand in the tourney."

Amarys withered in faith. If Erec did not support her, all was lost.

"I am afraid I must insist," said Erec, signaling to the stable hand that he wanted his horse. "You forget, Sir Harlowe, that I too plan to compete for this lady's hand. Anyway, today is a fine day for a ride."

Amarys exhaled, relieved.

The three of them went to the stables and had the groom bring Amarys's horse. Erec helped her mount her palfrey, picking her up as easily as if she had been a doll. She avoided making eye contact with her cousin. She already knew this had angered him.

They rode to the forest's edge, tilting East and South and back to the chateau. Harlowe looked bored. As they came back through the gatehouse, he excused himself and said he would be returning to the hunt.

"And I am appointed to meet Sir Roland on the field," said Erec, dismounting and returning to his wagon full of armor.

"You are? May I join you?"

"Yes, of course, my lady. You can help me explain why I am late."

He guided his horse with one hand and pulled a wagon full of armor with the other. Amarys rode behind him, her billowy blue dress draped elegantly against her horse's chestnut flank.

"Thank you for going with me," she said as they went through the portcullis toward the training grounds.

"It was the least I could do after you devised a way for me to steal away with Lady Rowen."

"I am happy to help. I must know, though, when did it happen?"

Erec kept the back of his head to her as they traveled. "It was when I saw her lift a sword to save her brother's life."

"No! Was it that day on the green last summer? I saw you from my window!"

"There are many pretty maids in Rieux, but there is none so fierce in a fray as her."

"Has she kissed you?"

"My lady..."

"That's a yes."

"I loved her before we ever kissed."

"How is that possible?"

"Roland often speaks of her, how she inspires him to be brave, how she calms his temper. Why, she is temperance itself. And she is clever and confident. She is the only woman willing to tell me my faults to my face. And she sings! I have lived so long without a woman's singing. Every night as I fall asleep, I remember when I heard her sing. And I sleep so well, my lady. Better than I have slept in years."

Amarys swooned to see such a worthy man so in love with her Rowen. She may have loathed the dull murmurs of his concussed mind, but she would not have minded the work of forging sons with him had he been her love match. Fortune had smiled on Rowen at last, and that made Amarys glow within.

Erec went on, "I felt at ease with her anon, as though we had known one another for years. Perhaps it was my friendship with Roland that made me feel this way."

"Careful now, Sir Erec. Do not fall into the trap of thinking you can know one through the other. When I was young, I used to dream of being Roland's wife because his sister was so dear to me. They look similar and they are hopelessly devoted to one another, but they are not anything alike."

"How did Roland disappoint you?"

Amarys spat a scornful sound. "By detesting me."

"Surely not," said Erec. "There must be some misunderstanding."

Amarys laughed. "No. We understand each other perfectly. He has told me that I am too eager for the attention of men. He detests my Norman ancestry and blames my father for the decline of his estate."

These indictments gave Erec pause. As they neared the training grounds, he tried to redeem his friend, saying, "Roland often teases those close to him. His bad behavior is part of his defensive nature. The other youths have set him apart all his life, calling him Saracen and heathen. Perhaps he has been coarse with you because you are so beloved by those who have never accepted him."

"That is no excuse."

"No, it is not. I only wish to explain because I really cannot imagine what would cause him to show such rare animosity toward you... except..."

"Except?"

He glanced over his shoulder at her, smiling and shaking his head. "...that he is in love with you."

Amarys furrowed her brow. "Impossible."

"I heard it from the one who knows him best."

Amarys felt her heart spark like a flint. A smile overtook her countenance.

"Ye God," she whispered, bursting into a fit of cackling. "I knew it!"

CHAPTER 20

A thin veil of clouds muted the sun's power, providing a temperate climate for Rowen and Roland as they waited in the training field outside the barracks. Rowen sat atop Biax's saddle, squeezing her knuckles white against the reins. Her gown billowed against her horse's flanks, its color as lustrous as eggplant. She wore many fine stones, including the garnet pendant Amarys had given her. Roland stretched from side to side, his arms extended skyward. These fields were usually abandoned, but more knights than ever were out training for the fast-approaching tourney. A line of three men trained their calves by jumping on and off platforms. Littering the field were pairs of them thwacking wooden swords, wrestling, and going about all manner of hand-to-hand combat. Other mounted knights tilted at straw men in their makeshift lists, their horses kicking up dust. Straw scattered. Wood cracked and burst. The sight of it made Rowen dizzy with joy.

"This is like a dream," she said, catching her veil as it blew in front of her eyes. "I have imagined this place so many times."

"Where is Erec?" muttered Roland. "He said to meet him in the training field, did he not?"

Rowen squinted to discern the faces of the men at work. Erec was not among them.

"He said he would be here all morning." Erec emerged from behind the cover of trees, towing his horse on one side and a wagon full of armor on the other. He was undoubtedly Erec, evidenced by his posture and height. At his side was a mounted lady, her feathery blue skirts undulating like wings as she rode. Her hair was up in a fillet, her face framed by white fabric. Rowen did not recognize her until it was too late to retreat.

"Lady Amarys," she greeted, bowing her head.

"Lady Rowen. Master Roland. What a pleasure to see you both this day." Amarys spoke in a voice of reserve and performative prettiness.

"I apologize for my lateness," said Erec, going to Rowen's side. He took her hand and kissed it. "The maid of Rieux asked me to chaperone her on a ride with her cousin."

"Her cousin...?"

"Sir Harlowe. We gave him a tour of the demesne. It took us longer to get back than we expected. When I told her of my appointment with Roland, she expressed an interest in joining us."

"I did not expect to see you, Rowen," said Amarys.

"Nor I—you," Rowen tried not to meet the eyes of her friend. She looked at Erec instead. "Thank you for this."

"You needn't thank me. Your smile will suffice."

"I am not disposed to smile at present."

"Ride with me," said Amarys to Rowen. "Just around the field. We can watch the action as we take the air."

Wordlessly, Rowen urged her horse to walk. She glanced back to see Erec dismounting to shake hands with her brother.

Amarys joined her side and blocked her view.

"You are angry with me," she said.

"At least you manage to observe this much."

"I observe a great many things," Amarys shot back, cantering ahead to block her path. "You are jealous of your brother, like a mother who will not approve of any woman for her son. But Roland is a man now. It is time to grow up and accept that he cannot be yours forever."

"Have you ever deigned to just ask me what I feel, Amarys?" Rowen skirted her and continued ahead, looking over her shoulder to see Roland and Erec practicing their blade work. She couldn't hear what they were saying, but she could see Erec was correcting Roland's stance. He had him put more weight on his back foot so he could better retreat.

"All right," she cried, exasperated. "Are you angry?"

"I am not angry."

"Right," said Amarys with an air of distrust. "Will you accept my marriage to Roland?"

"I should think so. I am the one who suggested it."

"Then what is troubling you?"

Rowen, for the first time since their meeting there that day, at last, looked into Amarys's eyes. Their souls met for a brief moment, locked in silence. Rowen yanked her horse's reins and rode away to the far side of the field. Amarys chased after her.

Biax whinnied and reared up, growing vexed with his mistress. Rowen stroked his neck. When Amarys reached her, she said, "Rowen, just tell me."

Rowen shook her head. "I do not wish to marry. I would like for you not to push me toward Sir Erec."

"Very well. I did not know that. He did not know that. You have to say what you want, Rowen, or nobody will ever know. You keep yourself so guarded. You pile walls of stone around your heart. And then you shout at us from the ramparts when we cannot find our way in!"

Rowen continued to watch Erec with her brother, learning their dance from afar.

"Are you listening?"

"Yes."

"The day we ate the devil's cap, you finally let the fortress fall away. Please, Rowen, come down from your tower and tell me what it is that you really want."

Rowen turned her face down, flooded with the memory of their love-making. She still remembered the sweet smell of Amarys's hair, the delicate curve of her nape, the way her shoulder blades flexed as she moved against her.

She rode in close enough to declare what she was too afraid to say above a whisper. "I want to tell you. I do. But there is no purpose. Because the one thing I truly want... I can never have."

She clicked at Biax, urging him away from Amarys and back to the training ground. Amarys went to one of the men in the lists, asking a Sir Derrin to see her home. Finally, with Amarys gone, Rowen could focus on the martial activities. And yet, she could not focus. She continued to resent Amarys for her blindness, for her readiness to accept Roland. She wanted to be everything she had been for Amarys the day they ate the devil's cap. She wanted to be fearless, to refuse the will of the Church and take her brother's place in the tournament. She wanted the steel, the peril, the burden of failure. If pressed, she wanted to tell Amarys it had been her in the lists all along. No amendments. No exceptions. She would be the one to save Amarys.

If Amarys fawned over the knight in the lists, it should be Rowen. Three weeks remained, practically an eternity to a girl of seventeen. As Rowen watched her brother, she resolved to fight in the tourney herself. There was nothing else she wanted more. She could never have Amarys. But she could, for just one day, know what it was to ride with a lance in arm and hear the people's roar in her helm.

"Meet me again tomorrow," said Erec as he and Roland concluded their sport for the day. "I'll get you on a horse, show you how to hold your lance in such a way that you will strike a hit every time."

Roland's hair was full of sweat, his cheeks flushed. The knight had worked him hard all afternoon. The sun sank fast beneath the clouds on the horizon, dimming the field.

"My lady," said Erec, turning to Rowen. "I hope our practice was not tedious for you to observe."

"Quite the opposite." Rowen forced a subtle smile, which dissipated almost as soon as it had appeared. "If it does not seem untoward, I should like to try my hand at a bout or two."

Erec looked at Roland, who was nodding. "If it please my lady, so be it," he said. "A bit of light swordplay?"

He handed her his shield and a practice sword. The shield was massively long and heavier than her brother's, but after weeks of helping Roland train, Rowen's upper body strength had improved. She held the shield aloft with ease.

Erec looked pleased with her posture. After scrutinizing her stance, he had no corrections. "Why don't you practice deflecting, and if you see an opening, strike me."

They faced each other. Gave an informal salute. Erec smacked her shield to test her defense, which was good. Rowen practiced covering her left eye with the shield's top corner, a trick her brother had taught her. She appreciated the shield's length, which protected her legs. Deflections of Erec's blows were quite simple. Of course, she could tell he was treating her gently. Like planets aligning, Rowen's knee and arm jutted forward in a perfect lunge, and she poked Erec just under the rib.

"Hoo!" he yelped, hopping backward and grinning. "Nice thrust!"

"She's even more impressive in an actual duel. I trained her myself," said Roland.

Erec appeared to smile, but it was hard to gauge whether he was intrigued or silently judging them. "You can show me more tomorrow," he said. "Is there a place the three of us might be left alone?"

"There is a pasture just west of the manor. Come at first light before the sheep are brought to graze," said Roland. The meeting was agreed upon, and the three parted ways.

The day was dwindling fast. Roland and Rowen urged their steeds to gallop at full speed before the winding path became too dark to see. They made it home without provoking their father's notice and went up to bed with a bottle of wine they stole from the cellar. The two shared notes over drinks. Rowen prodded Roland for every detail of his training. She stood upon the bed frame, balancing and mimicking his elegant postures. He laughed as she impersonated him in the exhaustion of his work.

"I thought you would collapse!"

"Yes, well, Erec demands the impossible! Again and again."

"He worked hard to achieve knighthood so young."

"You like him," spat Roland derisively.

"I respect him."

Roland's eyes rolled back in his skull as he tilted against the wall. "Respect is enough to make a marriage work. Things would be easier for you and Amarys if you were both married."

Rowen sipped her wine, shaking her head gently.

"Rowen. All I want is to protect you. There are worse things than a loveless marriage."

On this note, they blew out their candles and went to bed.

A new day came upon them swiftly as Rowen awoke from a nightmare. She wailed as she had done as a child, kicking the linens from her bed. In a fearful state of wakeful sleep, she momentarily believed that she was eight years old again and the children of Rieux were about to behead her on the same stone where Constance decapitated chickens. Not real. A bad dream.

Rowen felt viscerally aware of her own mortality. She wrapped herself in a wool blanket and nudged her brother awake.

"It is still dark. We had best make our way west."

"What for?"

"Erec is waiting, dimwit. Get up."

Roland groaned, rubbing his eyes. "I should have drowned you as a child."

"Stop quoting our father. Anon!"

The twins dressed quickly, simply, in Roland's tunics and hose. If nothing else, the garb might disguise them from the shepherds should they arrive amidst their practice. Erec was already there with a little cart of armor, and the sun had not even begun to ease the dark of night.

"Good morning, my friends," he greeted them.

"Good morning," said Roland.

Erec handed Rowen his broadsword, which she held with ease. "It's not even heavy for you," he said in amazement.

"I practice drills with my father's sword," she explained.

"Let me show you something." He came round behind her and placed his arms over hers, repositioning her hands on the cross guard. "Turn your wrist. You will use this muscle to bear the weight of it, and you will spare your joints in the process." He looked at Roland. "I have to adjust her hips."

"Why are you telling me?"

"Because I have learned to fear your anger." Erec looked at Rowen, rolling his eyes.

She allowed him to guide the position of her foot to open her hips.

"Your form is excellent, but this might help you as it helped me. One who is tall like us has to lower one's center. Otherwise, a lunge and a miss mean a stumble. And a stumble means death. Let's armor up. I shall play the pell." Erec began strapping his legs with cuisses. Roland dressed both of them in their plates and mail, handing each a heater shield and a blunted sword. "Try to land a death blow," Erec said, bringing up the shield.

It seemed impossible. The shield was so large, and Erec was too tall for Rowen to land a blow on his head. His left was completely shielded, and when she went for his right, he whacked her sword away. When she went for his thigh, his shield came down instantly.

"Don't look at the place you're about to strike."

"You can see where I'm looking?"

Behind his helm and shield, Erec's eyes had all but vanished. And Rowen could barely see out of hers.

"I can see the important things."

Rowen pretended she would hit one place, but then she would hit another instead. After a while, that started to work.

"Good," said Erec. "But you will need to hit harder than that if you want to wear them down."

"It doesn't hurt?"

"Roland hits me a thousand times harder."

He taught her how to channel movement, to strike with a force she didn't know she could muster. She pulled her power up from the earth, forcing him backward like a column of wind. Erec staggered back and caught himself. He ripped off his helmet, grinning.

"That's it!" he cried. "Now, let's exchange some blows!"

He did not hold back, or if he did, she would have hated to know how hard he hit normally. Each of his blows cracked her shield like a bolt of lightning.

At the end of each bout, he gave her some advice, saying what she did well and where she could improve.

"You're quick, but you're nervous, and you burn through your energy. Remember to breathe and plan."

She bested him several times, and each time made her heart beam with pride. He was the champion, and even he could be tricked by the false angle of her attack. She got him twice with the same move and made him groan with frustration.

He had interesting footwork. Sometimes, he went on one foot. Or, he bounced away. At one point, he jumped in the air to land a blow on top of her helm. Ears ringing, Rowen lifted her arm for relief.

"I'm getting tired," she said.

"Once more."

They readied their shields, saluted, and began to circle. It was over quickly when Erec lunged and tapped her leg.

"Watch that," he said.

They trained for several hours with the sun rising behind them. Something startled Roland. He made off with Erec's cart into the woods.

"Who goes there?" called a voice. There were shepherds not far off. As they emerged on the hill, leading their flocks to graze, Rowen made a mad dash in the same direction Roland had gone. She concealed herself in the tall hollow of a tree.

Erec ran after her, toting their shields. He came around the edge of the nook and crammed himself in, his armor pressing hers.

"If they catch us, they will tell my father—"

"Shh."

Leaves crunched under the shepherds' tread. "Leave them to the yeomen and thieves," the one grumbled.

Erec made a silent grin of relief, bowing his head to press Rowen's.

"Roland will likely meet me at the stables."

"I will take you to him."

They walked down the forest path an arm's length apart, and Erec told her all his plans.

"I will win the joust and sell whatever helm or trinket they provide. Then, I will leverage that wealth to pay my way into several tourneys across France. By harvest, I will return to ask your father for your hand. No doubt he will approve that we wed in Spring."

"May Fortune bless you in the lists."

"May I wear your favor at the joust?"

"My father will be in attendance. I do not want him to know about us yet."

"That is wise."

Before long, they reached the stables. As Rowen had predicted, Roland waited there. The twins said farewell to Erec and Roland went to help his sister out of his armor. But she stopped him. It was a quiet day, warm and uncommonly sunny. And Roland seemed in good spirits having evaded the shepherds. No better time would present itself.

"It is my wish to fight in the tourney," she said.

Roland looked puzzled. "Yes," he began with caution. "But that would be impossible."

"Today, as I was fighting Erec, I realized something. I can do this. He was last year's champion, and I held my own against him. My endurance has improved. I can lay on with strong blows. In your armor, no one would know I wasn't you."

"You haven't really trained, though. Not as I or any of these men have done since we were children. The tourney is a fortnight from now."

"I have trained beside you, all this time. I am every bit as strong now. And I am the better swordsman. And let's face it. We both know I want this more than you."

Roland folded his arms. "Why would you ask this? It won't change anything. Say you win. She and I will still be betrothed."

"When all is revealed, I want to tell her that it was I who fought for her. It is my only chance to win her love."

Roland turned his back, cogitating something. "Have you not won her love already?"

"She does not know how I feel."

"Are you telling me that you would risk your life—and mine—for a woman who may not even love you?"

"She pines for Roland. Not Rowen."

"When you showed me the garnet, I thought you had confirmed that she returned your love! No, no, no. This is not good. Once Love's arrows fly, it can be very painful to wrest them away. If she and I are wed, both your hearts will be broken."

"No, Roland. I will accept her choice. I will be happy that she is happy. And you will come to love her. I am sure of it. But you see why it must be me in the tournament. After we have saved her—together—I will tell her how I feel and reveal the role I played."

He leaned on his hands against a table of farrier tools. "A tournament is not a play. You do not assume the role of a knight simply by putting on his armor."

"Will you not help me then?"

"I don't know," he said. "Why should I?"

"Because you know that the sun would never rise for me again if I lost her."

He spun, brandishing a hammer and lunging to strike Rowen across the shoulder. Rowen instinctively dipped away, and as Roland stumbled forward, she pushed him against a wall of horseshoes.

Roland grabbed for his short sword that leaned against the table. Rowen drew her own blade.

"Roland! You aren't armored!"

"Real knights spar for first blood!" he cried, lunging anew. Rowen parried. "Beat me," he grunted, "And you can fight as me." He struck and missed. She shoved him off balance with a well-timed left hook. She wasn't stronger. She knew she wasn't. But there was something in her that channeled enough raw power to fight like Sir Erec.

She tricked his sword into retreat several times. Roland caught her blade with his cross guard and knocked her back against the wood table. Losing her footing, she brought the whole structure down, tools scattering across the hay. She jumped up and charged like a ram, rolling and wrestling him in the dirt. He grappled with her, got her by the hair that hung down from her head. Playing dirty, he managed to wrench her down and roll her beneath him. Her armor weighed heavy now, with her brother bearing down like an elephant.

She remembered him looming over her in a similar posture one of those times they argued over toys. The pair of lions had quarreled over Roland's wooden catapult.

"It is mine!" he had said.

That was the day she headbutted him and cracked loose a milk tooth. Roland, blubbering, had thrust the wooden siege toy into her hand and gone running to tell their grandmother.

Grappling on the ground, she in her armor and he with his muscle unbound by steel, Rowen disabled him in a headlock. She clasped his throat with the crook of her elbow, her other arm bearing down on the base of his skull. Roland went limp, losing consciousness almost as suddenly as she had touched him.

When he came to and had time to collect his wits, he accepted her terms. "You can wear my armor, but we have to be smart about this."

The twins negotiated a plan. Rowen could impersonate Roland, but only for half of the games. He did not doubt she had what it took to win, but there would be times when he had to be seen without his helmet. Also, there would be a real advantage to it if, in each contest, they could ride renewed against their enemies.

Roland built a quintain, a revolving plank of wood mounted on a pole. Rowen got used to wearing armor and riding Roland's horse. She drove Ash forward and practiced hitting the mark with her lance's tip. Her body quickly got lean and hard. She was hungry all the time, so much so the servants began to gossip that she was going to grow even taller.

The night before the joust, a storm flooded the encampment of visiting knights. Ivin invited many of them to stay in the manor, and Rowen was moved into the attic with her grandmother. She crept out in the middle of the night, climbing into her brother's bed as she had done when they were children. Secretly, she supposed this might be her last night in the world. Jousting accidents were an annual occurrence. One year, three out of three brothers had all died in the same night, stabbed and maimed and thrown. There were no guarantees.

"Can I sleep here?" she whispered.

Roland made a soft noise in the affirmative, rolling over to face away from her. Their bodies were thin enough to fit comfortably in the narrow bed. They slept on their sides as still as two bodies in a coffin. Rowen liked to think they would be buried like that, for surely, being twins who came into the world together, they would depart it together as well. She often wondered how life might have been if she were the boy and he the girl, but those thoughts also pained her, for she might never have met Amarys if she were not permitted into her private inner sanctum.

"Roland?" she whispered. "At the tourney ball, you must dance with Amarys and make yourself known to Clement as a serious suitor."

He was quiet for a moment. He said, "Your heart can take it?"

"It must. I know the only way to save her is for you to win the tournament. Just remember that part of the points will be garnered from the gentry's favor, and this is where you can most certainly rise above Harlowe. Emphasize your servitude to the tenets of courtly love. Try not to speak at all of Antioch or Toulouse. Your heart must be here in Rieux."

"I understand."

Rowen realized how fixated she had been on Amarys and the tournament. She asked, "What will happen with your girl in town?"

"I need to speak to her," said Roland. "She will be heartbroken if I become engaged without explaining everything."

"Will she accept becoming your mistress?"

"She will have to."

The twins closed their eyes. They drifted off to the sound of the rain.

CHAPTER 21

The portcullis loomed like the jagged edge of a lion's jaw. Flames pulsed within stone alcoves. They lined the cobbled paths, flickering wildly. The midsummer games always began with a ball, and Rowen's complaints of a headache had been outmatched by her father's insistence that she attend to attract potential suitors. She need only stand and smile, he said. To dance would give too much promise.

The horses pulled up to the grand entrance of the keep, where the stairs mounted toward a pair of riveted doors sized for giants. The casings held the cold, hard faces of angels. Their eyes, un-pupiled and gray, appeared narrow and discerning as they watched Rowen. A throng of idle footmen hopped up, skimming the entry stairs in their cloth dancing shoes. One of them provided a step while another assisted in opening the door. A third offered his hand and helped Rowen dismount.

Roland and Ivin came out behind her. Nobody spoke or smiled. Roland held up his forearm as a perch for his sister's hand. They walked mindfully into the great hall, their father following behind.

The aromas of roasted meat, honey-glazed and charred, saturated the hall. Elongated tables held enough food to sate the appetites of every man, woman, and child in Rieux. Rowen sighted platters of smoked herring, boiled hens, roasted waterfowl, and pork, all of it littered with nuts and sweet sauce. Everyone took their places and sat down to eat. Sir Clement was seated at a banquet table facing the hall. On his left, his three daughters were arranged from eldest to youngest, and on his right were his wife, brother, sister-in-law, and Harlowe. Clement thanked his guests for traveling to Rieux, acknowledged Rowen's father for being a gracious friend and ally, and welcomed everyone to enjoy the feast.

Rowen examined Harlowe carefully. He appeared not to enjoy any of the food. He finished three glasses of wine while sneering over his roast pheasant. Finally, his father took Harlowe's goblet and turned it upside down, waving away the serving boy and admonishing his son.

Rowen dipped her hands in the nearby finger bowl to rinse them clean. Then, she broke bread with the people at her table and initiated a discussion over the stories depicted in each of the tapestries covering the stone walls.

"That one appears to depict scenes from the life of Saint Adela," she noted, proving that she knew her saints and Norman history.

The noble family introduced themselves. The patriarch was Earl of Chester and Lincoln, Ranulf de Blondeville. His lady wife paid a compliment to Rowen who's white bliaut had a flared skirt with panels that looked much like swathes of clouds.

"It is a rare muslin," explained her father, "woven by virgins on the banks of the Nile."

The nobles offered smiles of approval. Dinner was the first dance. Mingle. Exchange pleasantries. Try to appear well-entertained. Everyone who was anyone was at table, prominent families from all over Armorica and France.

The young women at these events were always so nervous, poised stiffly as statues as they waited to be recognized or spoken to. They avoided even looking at the sumptuous platters of food laid across the long table. They knew that to indulge even with their eyes would be remarked upon. Perhaps not immediately, but one day—a day when it mattered.

Rowen did not care. She tore a crust from one of the freshly baked loaves and shamelessly dipped it in her wine. The fatty meats and puddings, for all their decadence, could not compete with an old favorite.

Her father was not watching his daughter gobbling bread. Clement had pulled his chair up beside him. He called for ale for his friend, which was graciously received.

They hoisted horn tankards and drank to the horses.

"May they carry our lads through their blows!" Ivin exclaimed. Their horns collided. Beer splattered the floor.

The musicians assembled on a broad dais edged in braziers. Flutes and strings filled the hall with mirth, inviting people to dance. Roland greeted his fellow knights as they encroached like a rolling mist. The men complimented Rowen's health and beauty and then proceeded to speak with Roland as though she did not exist. All but one.

Rowen swallowed the last of her bread with a mouthful of wine. She avoided Sir Erec's gaze, pretending she did not notice he had left his seat. She had been watching him, fully aware that his eyes had not left her since she came through the door. He looked as though he was about to say something to her directly. And so, she swiftly backed away from the group. She retreated to the floor cleared for dancing where men and women wove in and out of each other's thralls.

It was a grand space framed in pillars supporting the ceiling's rib vaults. Servants carrying candelabras moved about the room, urging the shadows to dance.

Long gold-threaded skirts swept across the floor. The men wore bright stockings well-fitted to their thighs and calves. Lions and leopards ignited on dark velvet capes, coming to life in the candlelight. Erec appeared among them—a hunter pursuing his doe through the trees. Rowen ambled around pillars and tried to insert herself into a cluster of women against the wall. They all stopped speaking to stare at her, for she had never made any effort to befriend them before.

"I like your dress," she uttered, gesturing to the garment of the group's most charismatic member.

The young lady blinked tempestuously.

"Lady Margaret," added Rowen to show she knew her name.

"What is it you like about it?" asked the lady. By the way she spoke, she might have thought herself a queen. Rowen scrutinized the pale fabric. Had there ever been a more unremarkable dress?

"Its simplicity... draws attention to your exceptional bones."

Lady Margaret went on blinking, but she said, "Thank you."

Erec neared. He flagged her with his hand and saw that she saw him. To retreat now would cause offense. To her great relief, the ladies in her company all turned their heads and buried him in a storm of flirtation.

"Why, it's Sir Morning Glory!" teased Lady Margaret. "Climbing ever higher in fame and rank. Will you win the joust again this year, Sir Erec?"

"I shall try," he said, looking past the others, still fixed on his target.

"You look so well tonight."

"As do you, Lady Evelyn."

"Will you trade a link of your mail for a kiss?"

"I would trade a year of my life for a dance with one lady." His charm cut through their assaults, and they quieted, realizing he had his attention solely on Rowen.

"It could be arranged," Rowen tried to counter, her gaze like steel. "They say I am half-fae, Sir Erec."

"She must be," said Margaret, siphoning her frenetic laughter before it revealed all the jealousy broiling in her breast, "to have enchanted our champion."

Erec did not yield. He reached through the circle to offer his hand. Rowen would not embarrass him. She placed her hand in his, following him into the center of the room where she felt so many eyes upon her. It was a spectacle for everyone to see Rowen dancing with the champion. Clement and Ivin had been speaking loudly and drunkenly, but they ceased in whatever they were saying when they saw the two young people press their palms.

The wine pulled at Rowen's senses. Each time they changed direction, she felt a little more off-kilter. If Erec's intentions were not enough, she soon saw her brother dancing with Amarys.

At last, the face that she had sought in every constellation of guests had emerged, luminous and bright, framed in strings of crystal. A single strand of polished beads lay draped across her forehead, and the others cascaded from her temples. The dress Amarys wore was unknown to Rowen. She thought she knew every one of the lady's dresses, the way the moon knows every corner of the ocean. Ermine trimmed the edge of her breast. Its silver border was beset with orbs of turquoise, gems so very like her eyes. Her lustrous hair hung loose, rolling down her shoulders and curling slightly at her waist.

As Amarys and Roland whirled, hands high and pressed, their eyes saw no other.

There was a kind of fervor that held them fixed in concentration. Amarys made a joke, and Roland smiled.

A turn divided their paths. Partners changed. Rowen met the hand of another knight, with whom she whirled and bobbed. She crossed the part of the wood floor where they had painted sharp angles to make the image of a rose. Looking up, she found herself aligning with Amarys. Nimble-footed as a forest cat, Amarys swayed to meet Rowen in the sphere of the rose. The other dancers blurred with the shadows. The tapers formed a ring of stars around them.

"You look beautiful," murmured Amarys as their palms touched. The cool softness of her hand froze through Rowen's fingertips.

"I am sorry for being cold to you."

"I am sorry for meddling." She and Amarys held each other at the waist as they held out their skirts with opposing hands, turning slowly in a wing-like dance.

No matter how much she tried to convince herself she loved Amarys as a sister, she could not deny all that burned in the tender parts of her anatomy as Amarys's bare hand touched her waist. These sensations were akin to those she felt when their lips had touched. She glowed, sensing the warmth of love radiating between them.

Amarys ran her hand down the fabric of Rowen's gown. "So soft."

"My father says it is the softest fabric in the world."

"Your hands are softer," Amarys whispered, stepping out of rhythm to come near. She bobbed in an elegant lilt as she moved on to her next partner, her demure lips too much for Rowen to bear.

She wanted that lady, wanted to strip away her clothes, kiss every part of her soft flesh. She wanted to teach her to crave a touch only she could provide, teach her never to pine for a man for as long as she lived. Forget Hell. Sick with longing, she was already in the throes of damnation.

Rowen turned to see her new partner. When she did, her chest burned with fire. Harlowe clasped her in his arms.

She felt like a bird snared in a trap as they began a jaunty skip across the room. Harlowe had no interest in tempo or grace, only speed. He yanked her like a bag of grain, practically lifting as he broke the circle and swiftly ran an extra lap around the other dancers. All the while, he laughed. Rowen stared in horror, unsure what kind of recourse a lady had in such a moment. At a smaller private function, she would have scolded him, but at Clement's tourney ball, such an affront might be seen as an act of dissent.

She held her tongue yet maintained the coldest expression of disapproval that she could muster. Harlowe went on grinning like a fox as they turned round each other in a square.

"You know I came here to win my cousin's hand?" said Harlowe. "Yet all evening long, this room only hums with the gossip of Roland the Turk and his fine sister."

Rowen was speechless. This was the part of the dance where they had to spin out, the part Rowen often messed up and relied most upon her partner.

"Is your father entertaining offers for you yet?" By the tone of his voice, she wondered what kind of offers he meant. Marital, or something else?

The feel of that man's hand on her waist induced the feeling of a corkscrew slowly wheeling deeper and deeper into her belly.

The spin, like the skip, proceeded violently. Her neck released like a whip. And at the end, Harlowe pressed his lips to her ear and whispered, "If I lose the tournament, you might have a chance to be the next Countess of Rohan."

Rowen imagined his mouth opening against her, his breath pouring into her ears and down her throat. It was all too much. At this point in the dance, she was supposed to curtsy to him. She could not. She looked beyond him to the ornate structures ascending into peaks above the doors. She imagined herself running for the exit, flying from the chateau, and seeking the air of the wild world outside.

The dance continued without her, for she stood there frozen. Harlowe moved on to another lady in the circuit. Erec resumed his position at Rowen's side, taking her hand in his. He noticed instantly something was wrong.

"My lady?" he said. Rowen watched helplessly as the rib vaults melted down the wall. She was falling. Her skirt puffed up around her like a pair of clipped wings. Erec caught her and eased her to the floor. The musicians ceased their play at the sound of Erec's shouting. "She has fainted!"

"Move."

Rowen knew her brother's voice. She leaned toward his familiar embrace.

"Rowen. Can you hear me?"

Her vision was dim, but she was lucid. "Yes. Too much spinning, I think."

"Can you stand?"

"Not yet."

Roland scooped her up from the floor and went with Erec out of the ballroom. By the time they reached a bench, her vision had recovered. The festivities had resumed, and Rowen could, at this point, hold herself up in a seated position.

"Is there anything I can do? Bring her water?" Erec inquired.

"No, thank you, friend. You are most courteous. My sister merely needs some respite from the excitement."

"Perhaps eating would help?"

"Friend—friend," Roland interjected between each of Erec's courteous attempts to aid Rowen. "Let me tend to my sister."

Erec bowed his head and obeyed. He could not appear too desperate to please in the public eye.

The quiet between brother and sister was a welcome interlude. Roland waited for her to explain.

When she said nothing, he asked, "Are you still fit to joust?"

"Yes," she answered.

That was all she had to say. Though it had been completely unplanned, her fainting worked in her favor as it gave her the chance to disappear for the night.

"Harlowe has trapped me," she whispered when Erec was far enough away. Her breath ran away like a wheel. "If he cannot win Amarys, he says he will marry me. Father will never say no to the next Viscount of Rohan. Even if he has to club me over the head to get me to chapel. I must declare myself for Erec!"

"Rowen. Think this through. I can protect you."

"This is the best way. It is the only way." Rowen stood, chasing after Erec. He had returned to the banquet to sit with his fellow men-at-arms. She waited for him to notice her, which he did almost at once.

"My lady?"

Quaking within, she said boldly, "Make it known that I am yours."

Erec's fellow knights heard her say it and looked amongst themselves as if the girl were speaking in tongues.

"I have not yet spoken to your father," said Erec, rising and shuffling her away from the many witnesses whose interest she had attracted. "I need time, my fae."

"I have suitors, Erec. Make it known, or all is lost."

"Very well," he said, and raising his voice to a public height, he asked, "Lady Rowen. May I wear your favor in the joust?"

Rowen unwrapped a silvery white sash that had been tied as a girdle around her waist. Erec knelt, accepting the girdle as a mantle which she draped across his shoulders.

"You may. I pray that it brings you good fortune, most worthy of knights," she said so all could hear.

And just like that, she had been claimed. Harlowe glared from across the room. Her father eyed them strangely. The women in attendance turned their backs and pretended not to notice or care. Simple. Rowen could not believe that was all it took.

Erec returned to table. Ivin came charging at his daughter, clutching her furiously by the wrist and dragging her from the banquet hall. He took her to Roland.

"Lose something?" he shouted, thrusting his daughter at his son. "Did you see what she just did?"

Roland caught her by the shoulders, moving her back so he could shield her if their father tried to strike at them. "It is a tournament, Father. Ladies are expected to extend their favors to knights."

"These are things you discuss with your family," he scolded, his finger pointed at her like a dagger. "This man is unknown to me."

"I wanted to tell you," she said. "Love has clouded my thoughts. I will marry whomever you tell me, but my heart will always belong to Sir Erec."

Ivin paused. The finger lowered. He looked at her as though she were a little girl again. "You are in love?"

"I am," she said. "Sir Erec is a second son, but he is ambitious and determined to improve his prospects. He says he will make his fortune fighting in tournaments. He will ask your blessing when he is worthy."

"This is the man who brought you home in the rain?"

"Yes, Father."

"And do you deem him worthy?"

202

"I do."

Ivin folded his arms, tapping his bicep. "I thought you were bound for the convent."

"I was. Everything changed when Erec professed his love. Do you approve?"

"Not officially." He bit his lip, closing his eyes. "But I am moved."

"Thank you," said Rowen, sitting down on a bench. "Ah, Father. I am very faint. May I retire for the evening?"

"You do not wish to see your brother joust?"

"I wish to, but I am not well. Too much wine, I think."

Ivin left Roland with the charge of finding an escort to see her home.

CHAPTER 22

All knights, married or not, were invited to participate in the joust. In the interest of preserving the dignity of the event, Clement invited Father Gerard to host a prayer at the beginning. When the man of the cloth had finished his Latin verses, the Master of Ceremonies came forth and explained the terms. The winner of the joust would receive a large sum of money and an elaborate golden helmet engraved with dragon wings.

Roland tried convincing Rowen to reconsider her intention to participate. She did not have nearly enough training, and if she were injured, she could hardly expect to fight for Amarys in the melee. His argument went nowhere, for she was determined to have equal claim as Amarys's champion. Giving in to his sister's will, Roland advised her to conserve her energy and focus solely on staying horsed and guarding her eyes from the shards of a broken lance.

"You will get hit," he told her. "And it will hurt."

Safely concealed in their tent, Roland dressed his sister for battle. He moved from her ankles upward, wrapping her knees with thick bands of bracing cloth. He attached chausses and razor-sharp spurs.

"Tomorrow, you will feel it. And remember, I am serious when I say you must not be unhorsed. There is nothing more dangerous. Enduring a fall in all that armor is like perishing under a rockslide." He lifted the mail over her head and guided the links around her narrow form. Around this time, Willem came running into the tent.

The youth shimmered with sweat. He slicked back his wet curls. Willem always stood with his shoulders held a little too close to his ears, but this posture was especially pronounced tonight.

"My God. So she's truly doing this?" he uttered when he saw Rowen.

"We all are," answered Roland.

The belt was tight about her waist, but it helped to distribute the weight of the mail so as to grant Rowen a better range of motion. For the first time since she had begun her training, the rings of mail felt natural. For three weeks she slept wearing the hauberk with the mindset that it would strengthen her body. Her father once told her that this was how he trained his destrier as a young foal to carry the weight of a man in armor. He would attach heavy sacks of grain to the beast's sides, and as the horse grew, it waxed strong and sturdy.

Roland covered his sister's chest in a padded surcoat and began the tedious process of fastening its many buckles and laces. Willem asked, "Are you not afraid, lady?"

She watched her brother's hands fastening with care. "I am not," she said.

"You should be. Did you not see the men out there? Big as towers. I'd be soiling myself if it were me."

Rowen ignored him.

He added, "You know all men, even knights, soil themselves when they die, so if you haven't emptied your bowels as of late—"

"Shut up, Willem," said Roland. "You are not to speak to my sister that way. She may be dressed as a man, but she is still a lady. You are here only to squire and to keep your mouth shut, unless you want your father to learn of your adventures to the bathhouse."

Willem nodded, although begrudgingly and with a heavy scowl. His father, the magistrate, was a pious man and well-respected in the community. Willem, being the eldest of five brothers, risked his inheritance if the old man ever found out about his whoring.

Roland completed the armor with pauldrons, gauntlets, and helm. "Make me look good out there," he said, his voice muffled by the steel shell around Rowen's ears.

"Seriously," said Willem. "And if you're unhorsed and revealed, I knew nothing about it."

"Rowen, you'll be fine. Remember your training. And if all else fails, my horse will win the joust for you." He smacked her helmet and shoved her forward.

Rowen ducked under the tent flap with Willem in tow. Her chest pounded with the vibrations of the deerskin drums. Hordes of guests gathered in the stands, their voices elated and echoing with laughter. The night was windy and damp, alive with anticipation. Willem offered a block and assisted Rowen in mounting her brother's dark horse. When she was in the saddle, Willem handed her a shield on her left and the lance on her right, which she couched under her arm. To her amazement, these instruments were light as air in her grip. She held the lance the way Erec had taught her and rather felt like she was floating as she rode. She was finally living what she had dreamed about all her life. The people elevated on the stands greeted her with exuberant cries.

"Roland!" she heard them chanting, though it was garbled through her helmet. She raised her lance high over her head, rallying the spectators to cheer ever louder. The stands were filled with noblemen and women arrayed in lush, colorful fabrics, beaded and laced to excess. The ladies' veils swayed against the mild breeze that carried the perfume of ash trees. Torches flickered against the people's fair faces, lighting up their teeth as they smiled.

Several men were in the process of carrying a felled knight away on a litter. He lay clutching his helm to his chest, gritting his blood-streaked teeth. A shrill whimper rolled out of him as he arched his back.

"Not so bad. Only a bonk," his squire assured him.

Foam sputtered from the knight's lips, and the whites of his eyes quivered like boiling milk. "Get him hence!" shouted another. Men rushed the litter to obscure the unseemly sight.

The stands hummed with anxious murmurs. Rowen recognized her father sitting beside an empty seat. He kept looking over his shoulder and around the stands. What had he made of her absence, she wondered.

In the central stand, Amarys was seated with her sisters and stepmother. When she saw Rowen's family crest emblazoned on the black metal shield, she rose from her seat.

Their eyes seemed to lock, but Rowen knew Amarys could not see beyond the guise of her helmet. Nobody could. Amarys saw only the person that she wanted to see, the man she expected. Roland.

Rowen's armor scraped with every jostle in the saddle. She could hardly make sense of the voices outside her helmet, but she saw her lady step down to the front of the stands and extend both her hands with a long silk scarf draped across them. Rowen rode toward her, gave a salute, and tilted her lance.

Amarys tied her favor into a loop and sent it sliding down the length of the lance until it found rest at the pommel.

"Thank you, Ro." Amarys's lips mouthed the words. Her eyes caught the light of the torches.

Rowen lifted her lance upright and, with a curt pivot, rode away from Amarys, her face burning like a torch within her helm. She felt ashamed for hiding the truth from her, and more so that it was her brother's name on her lady's lips, her brother's visage imprinted on her mind.

She had to remember that this was of little consequence. She was here to fight. She was here to prove something to herself. Rowen spurred her horse to gallop to its mark in the lists.

The tilt—a low curtain stretched far between two rods—divided the strips of earth where Rowen and her opponent would charge. The rules of jousting were quite straightforward. Land a hit on the opponent's shield. Earn points. And most importantly, in doing this, one must not be hit nor fall from one's horse.

Her opponent's banner showed the heraldry of the Chandos family line: three lions passant on black beneath a golden key on red. The knight wore a cylindrical flat-nosed helm with plumes as black as his horse. They did several preliminary passes back and forth, calibrating their form. When this was done, they readied to joust.

Sir Chandos gripped his long black lance and beat his enormous left pauldron with provocative force. He bellowed a blood-chilling war cry, banging and banging like a madman. The roar of the crowd swelled to an upsurge of terrible sound.

Rowen's steed snorted and reared his head. She reached around his armor and stroked the side of his neck, whispering, "Easy, Ash." There was no turning back now. Her conduct here would follow her brother's name.

The horn sounded, blustering over the murmur of the crowd. Every muscle in Rowen's thin frame tensed. Roland had said nothing would prepare her for that first impact. In preparation for it, he made her ride up and down a lane of dirt and slammed her shield with a club when she passed. Jousting, he contended, was less about strength and more about grit, sucking up the pain and going at it again and again and again.

"You will feel like a yolk that has burst within the shell, but you must charge ahead despite it."

Rowen presented her shield, slammed her spurs into her mount's hide, and launched forward, her lance secured against the arret on her chest.

The two-beat pace of Ash's gallop matched the blood pounding in Rowen's head. Time seemed to stall. The other knight seemed infinitely distant, suspended like a beetle in water. Amarys loomed in the stands, a beam of light amidst the dust of ambush.

Time caught up rapidly all at once. Rowen blinked, and her opponent's lance tip was in sight, shimmering in the torchlight. This was the fleeting moment before her opponent's lance obliterated her. She tried to strike and missed. Sir Chandos's lance flew over hers. As the metal tip collided with her breastplate, it shattered the lance into a spray of splinters.

"Hurrah!" cried the spectators.

The hit was severe, though not as bad as Rowen had anticipated. Lances were made to break, and this one broke well. The force of it quaked in her bones, and she leaned far back in her seat, hooking her feet in the stirrups to stay saddled. She heard Sir Chandos belt an obscenity. Turning, she saw that he was whacking himself in the head with his broken lance. The louse had missed her shield and not scored any points.

They lined up again on opposite sides of the field. Ash flicked his tail and nickered. Rowen breathed deeply, trying to collect herself enough to charge back into certain pain. Again, she rested the base of her lance under her arm with the grapper hooked against the arret.

At the sound of the horn, she charged, roaring as her steed took flight. She kept her legs straight and her body leaned forward, just as Roland had instructed. Her joints tensed. Her armor clattered. Remembering how the knight had positioned his lance, she brought hers above it in a way that would upset his stability. She thought of it like weaving.

Over and under. Over and under.

She brought down the lance and smacked Sir Chandos's shield head-on. Lightning shot up her arm. Pain jarred her wrist as her lance exploded and splinters whirled in the air. A fractured feeling pitched throughout her body, but the triumph surging in her breast carried her through as the marshals called out: "Roland has broken his lance and won a point."

Through the haze of the torch smoke, she could see Amarys stand and shriek for joy. That alone made everything worth it.

Rowen replenished her stave. Again, she and Sir Chandos went head to head in the lists, flying toward each other like angels. Sir Chandos landed a powerful hit that nearly unhorsed Rowen, but she dropped her lance and took up the reins, adjusting her core until she regained balance.

Again, they prepared to do another pass; this was her only chance to defeat him. Sir Chandos beat his lance against his shield, but Rowen realized this was just something he did. The horn bellowed, and they advanced on each other, driving down the line to merge in the center. Rowen leaned forward and anticipated the collision.

She brought her lance down, and with a powerful thwack, it burst.

The recoil shook her in her harness. She had hit the man's shield dead center. The marshals declared her winner, and everyone began screaming her brother's name.

"Roland! Roland! Roland!"

Rowen circled around the lists, thrusting her broken lance high as the people cheered. Her eyes were on Amarys, who was now leaning toward her father to whisper something secret in his ear. Rowen imagined any number of things it could have been, the worst of them ringing the loudest in her head.

There is the man I want to marry.

As the next two knights were introduced, Rowen and Willem returned to their tent behind the stands, hitching Ash outside. Roland had a skin of water for his sister as she came in. She put it under her helm and drank fiercely, barely stopping to breathe.

"How did it go?" asked Roland.

"She bloody won!" cried Willem, for Rowen was too busy chugging water to say anything.

"Holy Mother of Christ! Yes!" Roland smacked her metal shoulders. Rowen plopped down on the edge of a chair, hunching forward as she panted.

"Hurt like Hell," she sighed, setting the water aside to breathe. Everything above her waist was drenched in sweat: her face, back, and hands. Her mail felt cold inside her surcoat. Rowen finished the water, shaking it out to the last drop. Roland brought a muslin scrap to her forehead and dabbed the beads of sweat. "Who's next?" she asked.

"Sir Erec. Let me take this one. He and I have trained together long enough that he knows my technique and form."

"All yours, Roland."

Willem got to removing Rowen's armor and transferring it to Roland. When the laborious work was finished, he was out of breath, and it was time for Roland to get back in the lists.

"Go make your name," said Rowen, kissing his helm. "Good luck, my brother."

Roland vanished on the other side of the tent flap. Rowen had to go on hiding herself in his pavilion, which was devastating because she so longed to see her brother and Sir Erec face off in the lists. But she listened for cues from the crowd as to who was winning. Cries for "Erec" and "Roland" seemed to mingle. It was impossible to discern who had faltered and who had emerged victorious when most of the shouting was completely unintelligible.

An announcement from the master of ceremonies declared a draw. "Both men will advance!" The people cheered. A moment later, Roland and Willem came in laughing.

"What happened?" asked Rowen.

"A draw! Roland should have won, though," said Willem.

"Who is our next opponent?"

The men continued to talk to each other like Rowen wasn't there. It amazed her how much they changed when she was out of the armor. She asked again, clarifying, "Is it Harlowe?"

"The winner from the first set. He sent one opponent flying off his horse after the first course. Cracked his head."

"I should joust again," said Roland. "If we are unhorsed, it would be better if it were me under the helm."

"Is it Harlowe?" repeated Rowen, louder.

Willem threw his arms up. "Yes! Yes! It is Harlowe!"

Rowen saw that Roland understood her intention.

"Let me ride," he said. "You will face him tomorrow."

"I must face him. I must tell Amarys it was me."

Roland yielded to this point, albeit reluctantly. He began the arduous work of disarming himself. His armor hung heavy on Rowen's tired flesh. Her knees trembled, and her stomach reeled, but she held firm, visualizing the work ahead.

"Focus on deflecting his lance. Don't bother trying to strike. You need to save your strength for the melee. The joust doesn't matter."

"Listen to him, Rowen," said Willem. "Harlowe will not be defeated by a novice."

"I hear you," she said.

"Ho, Roland!" Erec came in through the front of the tent unannounced. The three conspirators whipped their heads in his direction. Somewhere in the middle of his praise for Roland's brilliance, Erec saw Rowen dressed for battle below the neck. His exuberance vanished like a cloud of steam. He stood, staring for a moment, and said, "Is this some sort of jest?"

"Erec."

Rowen went to him, her mail ringing with every step. Her hands were dirty, so she tried to conceal them at her sides. "Let me explain."

He continued to stare, too shocked to respond. "I... I cannot hear it." He stepped back, knocking his ankle on the corner of an ironclad chest. Murmuring an incoherent apology, he excused himself.

Rowen caught his arm. "Wait."

"Ma fae." He stroked a wisp of hair from her eyes. "You have to understand. The Baron is like a father to me. It would betray both my houses to be privy to such scandal. Out of love for you, I will not reveal you, but for now, I must break our attachment... and return your favor." He untied the silver sash, sliding it from his belt.

She would not take it. "You gave me your word."

Erec let the sash sink to the ground between them. "I must go before I am made an even greater fool."

He departed. Roland and Willem finished dressing Rowen for battle.

"Forget him," said Roland. "Harlowe is waiting."

Outside, the temperature had dropped, and an eerie mist clung low to the earth. The people had hardly cheered for the last round. Apparently, both knights had been disqualified from continuing, having jousted so poorly that neither of them landed a single hit.

Willem brought the mounting block, and when Rowen arranged herself in the saddle, Willem handed her the shield and lance.

Amarys's attitude had changed drastically from the time Rowen had last emerged to see her. She did not stand for her champion but only gripped her skirts and shut her eyes.

The people took up the chant of "Roland! Roland!" Roland was a popular victor, as he had grown up in these lands. Harlowe was an outsider. His small entourage chanted his name, but even in their deep, resounding tones, the rally drowned in the roar for Roland.

Harlowe's charger was equipped with a menacing chamfron, a faceplate covering the length of its nose. A metal horn jutted out in the center.

Harlowe's pauldrons were similarly bedecked in steel spikes. The face of his helm was open at the bottom, and Rowen could see his mouth curled in a smirk. His confidence made her uneasy. She barely knew the man, but his smile—she decided—imparted all the malice of which Amarys had spoken. Regardless of all that was said of him, the man's soul had a tangibly evil aura.

The lances were readied, the chargers aligned on either side of the tilt. The sky lit up with lightning in the far reaches of the horizon and a low tremor of thunder rumbled.

Rowen decided that if she must die now, she was satisfied to die fighting for Amarys. They would pull off her helmet and Amarys would see the long dark hair. She would see the face of Rowen—not Roland—at last knowing the truth of her silent heart.

Rowen's mind stirred at the sound of the horn. Ash whinnied and thrust into action, soaring down the tilt in a spirited assault. As Harlowe got near, Rowen lowered her lance. She could see as she got close enough that it would be a direct impact. There was no escaping it. The loud noise of collision resounded within the shell of her helmet. A force like nothing she'd ever felt knocked the breath out of her. It was like flying full speed into a wall of solid rock.

Rowen's teeth ached in her gums. She clenched her throat as her stomach sent up a rush of acid. Swallowing her sick, she steadied herself on her horse. Her bones ached with the pulse of each canter, but she maintained her upright posture and raised her lance above her head. The people cheered and whistled.

"Come on, Roland! You've got him!"

Rowen marveled at the realization that both she and Harlowe had split their lances on each other's shields. The first course was a tie.

No more than four courses could be run. She had to land a hit without taking one herself. Her win would take him out of the lists and prevent him from doing further harm. It would give her lady hope. If she could only give Amarys hope for just one night, it would make everything worth it.

Once the lances were replaced and the chargers brought back around, they began again. The hoof beats beneath roused Rowen's blood, and with exhilaration, she struck Harlowe's shield a second time. His lance went right over her shoulder. She could hear him screaming, and as she turned on horseback, she saw him deliver a strike to his squire's head. She flinched at the sound of his gauntlet hitting the man's skull. It knocked him off his feet, and the medics came running to tend to him.

Willem hurried to Rowen's side, brandishing a fresh lance. "Rowen," he hissed, but she couldn't hear him. "Rowe!"

"What?" she said, low and gruff.

Willem exchanged lances, whispering frantically, "That man he jousted before you just died in his tent. Roland implores you to yield at once!"

"I can beat him!" Rowen raised her lance to rally the crowd. Their cheers swirled inside her helmet, but she could still hear Willem.

"Roland says I must reveal you if you will not agree!"

"And ruin us both?"

"He would rather be ruined than lose you!"

"Do as you must, Willem, but remember, you will be ruined as well for agreeing to squire for a girl."

Roused with frustration, Rowen shouted aloud as she kicked her heels into her horse and returned to her mark before the tilt.

Across the lists, Harlowe's spirited horse tossed its head and stamped the earth. Harlowe hoisted a fresh lance from the rack. Again, they rode. Again, he neared. But this time, he aimed directly at the ocularium in Rowen's helm. The wood seemed to howl as it pierced the air. Rowen ducked, dropping her lance altogether but dodging what might have certainly been a killing blow. Having just brushed the edge of the Ankou's cloak, she could hardly catch her breath until she reached the end of the tilt.

"Bastard!" she cursed, bringing her horse back around to her mark. He had made an attempt on her brother's life.

Harlowe spit in the dirt. Rowen stared ahead as she waited for Willem to return her lance to her. He came empty-handed.

"Enough," he stated. "If you do not climb down from that horse and withdraw, I will tell your father everything. You think he will ever forgive you? No. Not something like this."

"Then go ahead and tell him." Rowen hardly cared what her father would think. She hardly cared if he never forgave her. He could resent her for the rest of his days. And even if he learned all the truth, that she yearned for the affections of a lady, she did not care about that either. She finally felt at home in her skin.

Willem groaned aloud in agitation. He fetched her lance and handed it up.

Once more, Rowen and Harlowe drove their horses forward, couching their lances. The gut-wrenching terror of bounding full-speed at a madman with no honor was almost enough to make her spirit leave her body.

Rowen prepared to guard her head at all costs but would go for a strike if the opportunity presented itself. As they neared, a dreadful feeling weighed on her mind.

Harlowe was smiling again. He was open. And yet he was smiling.

Rowen fell for it. She landed a blunt strike at the top of Harlowe's shield—just as he sent his lance straight through Ash's throat. Rowen felt that spear as if it had pierced her own flesh.

"No!" she cried, curling forward as the horse's gallop weakened, slowed, and began to tilt. Ash leaned to one side. He buckled under the weight of his load and collapsed into the dirt. Rowen flew forward, dropping her split lance and rolling some cubits ahead. Her armor clinked and pinched at every impact as she continued to roll out.

A swell of deep voices booing came down from the stands. Everyone knew the father of Roland was Sir Ivin. They knew of his noble sacrifice in the Crusades, knew the valor of his warhorse Godwin, and the young destrier that had been born from his stock. Rowen's thoughts were no longer for her own survival, nor for liberating Amarys, nor even for fleeing before being unmasked. The bastard had to die.

She bit back the anguish and stood, armor clattering like chains. Gazing up at Harlowe on his horse, she removed her gauntlet and threw it down in the dust. A gasp lifted off the crowd.

"Roland! Stop!" shouted her father. She heard him getting closer as he leaped over the side of the stands and came running at full speed despite his bad leg.

Come on. Pick it up, she thought. If Harlowe accepted, she could vanquish him this very night.

Harlowe dismounted. He neared Rowen's gauntlet, but before he could capture it in hand, Rowen's father rushed in and kicked it away.

"No!" he bellowed, shoving Harlowe back. Even without armor, even aged and war-wounded, her father was significantly larger than the other knight. He had always been bold, as his great height and build allowed. Turning toward the beautiful, limp body of their destrier bedecked in silver plates, his eyes filled with hate. Blood gushed from the wound in Ash's throat, pooling massively beneath his glistening, speckled form. Her father pressed his fist to his heart.

Rowen could not console him, not in Roland's armor and not in such close proximity to Harlowe. Her father turned. "I should have never made you a knight," he said, but as he looked on at what he thought was his son, there was a change in his

216

countenance. He stared oddly, tilting his head. He could always tell the twins apart, whether it was in the dark or from a great distance. They were his children. They walked differently, had their own posture, their own little idiosyncrasies.

As Rowen started to back away, her father intercepted her and grabbed her helm by the basket. An instant after looking into his daughter's eyes, he shoved her. "Pavilion. Now."

Rowen picked up her gauntlet and went. Willem followed her, whispering, "Does he know? Hey."

"Yes," she said at last as they exited the lists. "He will kill me for this."

In the pavilion, Ivin had an unnerving calmness about him as he waited for Roland to slide out Rowen's leather chin strap and remove her helm. Her cheeks were streaked with blood. A gash on her forehead bled profusely where the helmet had bit into her scalp. Roland worked to remove her armor. She sounded starstruck, half out of her mind.

"I've killed Ash. I rode him into the point of a lance."

"It was Harlowe who killed the mount," Willem emphasized to Roland.

"Papa," said Rowen. "I cannot express... well, I am only... I am so sorry."

Ivin ignored her. "Roland."

"I know, Father. This was a mad enterprise. We, Rowen and I, had to ensure victory."

"By God's bones, that does not explain why your lady sister is wearing your armor!" Ivin's anger rose with the decibels of his voice.

Willem went to unbuckle the casings around Rowen's arms.

Her head sank forward as she failed to compose herself. She sobbed for Ash, that beautiful destrier, the last of Godwin's line. Willem continued to work. He removed her gorget and draped it on a stool by its leather straps.

"Rowen, you should leave," Willem urged in a soft register, pulling up her chainmail and splaying it on the table with the bracers and helm. "This is your chance. Just go."

"Ash is dead," said Ivin.

Roland nodded. "I know."

Their father clasped his forehead to cover his eyes.

Rowen followed Willem toward the tent flap. Ivin jerked into action. Willem slipped out, but Rowen was snared by her hair and wrenched back.

"Father!" cried Roland. "Before you do anything, think about your love for your daughter."

Their father's hands were trembling as he handled Rowen like a beast, shoving her down on her knees and twisting her hair like a rope around his wrist. "She killed your mother, Roland," Ivin hissed. Rowen clasped her hands over her father's, trying to ease the strain of his pull. "She killed—" He paused to swallow up the name. He always had trouble saying her name. "Saffiya," he uttered hoarsely. "I have seen all the horrors of Hell on the battlefield. Nothing compares to the horror of your sister's birth. You were perfect, Roland. You came out quickly, head-first from the start. Rowen, though, was backward and unnaturally large. Hopelessly caught. When she came forth, she brought a river of her mother's blood. Saffiya was awake the whole time, reaching out and asking, where was her son. She bled to death before we could even place you in her arms."

All Rowen could stand to do was weep. Steel flashed as Ivin drew the knife from his belt.

"No!" Roland flew at him. They grappled for the knife.

Ivin slung his son away. He began sawing away at his daughter's raven locks, cropping them in jagged wisps. In his fury, the knife slipped and cut her scalp, but it hardly gave him pause. He went on sawing until no single strand hung past her chin. He threw her locks down, and they scattered into threads.

"Father!" she wailed, clutching his leg.

"You forfeit the right to call me Father. Your only father is God, and you will submit yourself to the sisters at Redon Abbey and spend the rest of your days on this earth begging His forgiveness." Next, Ivin turned the knife on Roland, "And you, allowing your sister to fight in your stead, you will be dealt with like the devil you are. I shall beat this evil out of your crooked skull."

"He tried to stop me!" cried Rowen. "It was all my fault! It is because I am in love with Amarys that I wore the shape of a man! You must forgive him, Papa. The sin is mine alone."

Ivin sheathed his knife, and the moment he did, the back of his hand whipped across Rowen's jaw. The slap split her eardrum and knocked her against the table that held her armor. A leg snapped off, and all the shimmering fragments of steel bashed and clattered as they fell to the ground.

Rowen tried to stand but could not. She could hardly speak. Her father had only ever struck her with a switch. He had never used his bare hand and never with such force.

Roland attacked Ivin, driving at him like a battering ram. The men rolled across the pavilion, wrestling over plates and scattered mail. In the chaos of arms, Rowen clawed her way out. She snatched her cloak from a chair as she ran from the tent. Hooding herself and dabbing her tears with the hem, she bounded away from the tourney grounds.

CHAPTER 23

Roland drove his knee into his father's bad leg, overtaking him and pinning his teeth in the dirt. Ivin grunted, straining to throw Roland off.

"Why do you hate us?" Roland hissed, wrenching his father's face up to have his answer.

"Hate you? I have housed you! Fed you! Clothed you! I have taught you the ways of this world so you could survive. And the both of you are determined to destroy our good name! I am astonished, Roland, that you would not come to me with such a scandal!"

Ivin mustered an incredible strength, churning like a mountain as he toppled Roland beneath him. Roland used the blunt of his forehead to land a blow square in the old knight's face.

Ivin growled, shoving his son away from him. He stood and staggered through the tent flap. Roland pursued and was soon upon him, riding his back. Ivin whirled around, but again, Roland brought him to his knees. Only now, there were spectators.

Roland and Ivin kicked up dirt as they rolled and fought to pin the other.

"I should have left you in Antioch," Ivin choked out as Roland gained the upper hand.

"Yes, you should have."

221

Ivin thrust his knee into Roland's ribs, knocking the wind out of him and effectively tossing him over. Roland flipped and landed badly on his shoulder. Ivin did not relent. He grabbed Roland's arm in a vice twist behind his back near its breaking point. Roland bowed his head and ceased to struggle; he whimpered under the mounting pressure. If his father broke his arm, he would have to withdraw from the tournament. All he could do was brace himself for the crack.

"I hate you!" screamed Roland.

"A boy should hate his father," said Ivin, hideously calm.

"Let him go!" cried one of the onlookers. It was a girl with her father and sisters.

The father spoke up as well. "It is only a horse, Sire. And it was not his fault."

"Only a horse?" Ivin relinquished his grip on his son and went striding toward the little family. Roland collapsed in a heap, clutching his throbbing forearm.

"Have mercy," said the man. His daughters scattered like seedlings as Ivin came in swinging, knocking the man out cold with one powerful clout. The daughters screamed. Ivin's blow had cracked the man's eye socket.

Roland got to his feet. "Hey!" he shouted. "Leave them out of this."

The spectators fled, one man assisting the young women in removing their unconscious father.

Ivin spit. "What was the plan, Roland? You marry Amarys and be a cuckold to your sister?"

"More or less."

"Why would you want a life of such disgrace?"

"I am already a disgrace, Father."

"Would you wish to extend that fate to your offspring as you litter Rieux's brothels with your issue? Life is long, Roland. Things do change. And one day, when you hold the Barony, you will need an heir to keep the peace. What will Rowen think of that when you must plow her lady's fields? Will she wear the cuckold's horns as well as you do?"

Roland held firm and silent. He had not considered the pain and suffering it would cause to sire bastards out of wedlock, children who could never inherit. He would not give his father the satisfaction of knowing he had struck a nerve.

"Roland," said Ivin, with a tonality that hardly suited him. "I know you can win the melee on your own. And when you put a son in Amarys, you will leave a legacy of peace between our families."

"I promised Rowen I would never lie with Amarys."

"Rowen is confused. Her soul is in crisis, Roland. But you needn't worry. With our help, she will find her place with the good sisters of Redon Abbey. They will set her on the righteous path."

"I will not help you imprison my sister. Disown me if you must. Strip me of these honors. I never wanted them."

"Roland."

"Rowen will never come home again, Father. You have truly lost her this day. She bared her soul to you. And I think, one day, some years from now, you will think about this night and remember how you rejected and shamed her, and you will be filled with such regret, such sorrow, and remorse that your hard heart of stone will actually crack."

Roland returned to the pavilion, not looking back. Inside, he began picking up the armor and laying its pieces on Rowen's cot. The mail glistened in the candlelight, catching it like water catching the moon. It all seemed hopeless now. He could sense himself losing his sister; she was drifting farther and farther away with every movement of Fate's hand.

"Roland?"

He turned to see Cateline coming in through the front of the pavilion. She looked radiant in the dim light, her garments as orange as a maple tree in Autumn.

"I know what Ash meant to you." She grasped his hands.

As much as he had missed her touch, he could not enjoy this. He drew back. "You shouldn't be here."

"I know. Your becoming a knight has changed things between us."

"Things are complicated," he said. "I have no choice but to compete. And I must win."

Cat nodded, wringing her hands against her waist. "You aim to marry the Baron's daughter?"

"I must."

"I hope you will be happy."

"You are my only happiness, Cat. If I do marry, I would naturally take a mistress," he said indelicately.

"You would not be faithful to the woman you are fighting for?" she said unsurely. "Roland, that is vile. It is downright ugly."

"It is the only way for us to be together."

"You spoke of far-off lands and new beginnings—"

"I was a fool. Love made me so. My father will hold his estate for years to come, and I haven't the fortune to support you. If I married Amarys, though, all of that would change."

"And I would be what? Your whore?" she rasped, her voice thinning under the weight of her emotions. "I believed your pretty lies, your songs."

"I fail to understand, Cat. You made yourself my mistress when you gave yourself to me."

"You spoke of marriage and running away. I never wanted to be your whore!"

"Without me, you may have to be somebody else's."

She bit back a sob and swatted at him.

Roland caught her by the wrists as she weakened into sorrow. "You cannot strike at me! I could have you stoned." He spoke not out of malice, but out of true concern that she did not know the danger she might invite if she acted this way with any other man of his rank. "I am the heir to half of Rieux. My father would disown me if I married you. He would see my lands willed to Sir Clement, and—and you and I would be his serfs. Or banished. Neither of us wants that. If you weren't such a fool, you would understand."

Cat began shouting over him. "It should not matter! If we are together, it should not matter! If you love me, it should not matter! You said you loved me!"

Roland wearied of her heightened state.

"Listen!" The shouting match ended with Roland just shouting, "Listen!" again and again. Roland finally dropped to his knees to compel her silence, but she seized the moment of his exasperation to make him listen instead.

"I may be poor, Roland. And I may be a tavern girl until the day that I die, but I am no one's whore."

All his life, he had been warned against playing with lowborn girls, and he had always doubted the rationale, thinking everything could work out in the end. Many prominent men had mistresses. Their wives knew and tolerated it well enough. His books of courtship said that men should make love to several girls for practice, not too many, but several, enough to understand their bodies and to teach their wives to love their duty. As he saw the hurt growing heavy in Cat's eyes, he resented those books.

"Being my whore was the best I ever had to offer you." He did not mean for it to sound as cruel as it did. He was completely serious. All the same, he understood when she stormed out.

He stood there watching the cloth door of the tent. She did not come back. She would not come back. He could hardly believe the woman he had held and kissed so intimately could despise him so. He would never hold her again. And he felt foolish for not assuming things would end this way. He stood there, just watching, waiting for a sign, a shift in the curtain, a shadow through the canvas. The minutes stretched on and on, empty minutes. He began to understand why some men never strayed from duty.

CHAPTER 24

In her mind, Rowen kept returning to memories of her father by the fire, of sitting with him, listening to his stories, and watching his eyes light up when he talked about Godwin. She could have wept, remembering those nights he ran his hand over her hair. It meant so much to be called "perfect" by one's father. He had, on several occasions, said as much. But now, those rare moments they shared were splintered by this new memory, the feel of Ivin's fist smacking her in the side of the head, the knot in her stomach since he had said what he said about her mother.

Rowen's thoughts were fragmented and accompanied by fits of crying; she tried to think of someplace she could hide, a place she could stay without being discovered.

Amarys, she thought. Amarys would take her in. She was the only one who would not surrender her to her father. Amarys was her friend and confidant, the only person in all the world she could trust aside from Roland. Running toward the chateau—chausses and spurs ringing—Rowen drove her legs hard and refused to stop for breath even as her lungs burned, and her ankles throbbed.

Amarys was her only chance. With most of the guards occupied with the joust, the chateau would be relatively empty. Rowen slipped in through the servant's entrance, a submerged door leading through a tight cranny. She would have to be quiet, and as a precaution, she removed the armor on her legs. Carrying her chausses in a metallic lump, she came through an empty kitchen and tread softly down the winding corridors housing the servants' quarters. She froze at the sound of chainmail ahead of her. The torches illuminated the stones with flickering orange light. The silhouettes of two men marched toward her.

Rowen squeezed into an alcove and waited silently. Clutching her chausses to her chest, shutting her eyes, and sealing her lungs, she counted down from ten in her head as the guards passed.

"Well, whether or not he is Sir Ivin's son, the boy doesn't stand a chance at impressing the nobles in the melee."

"He had good form on that mount. I would not say he lacks skill—"

The guards' voices faded as they disappeared around the end of the hall. Rowen inhaled without noise, holding the breath in her lungs a beat. She collected herself before setting out again down the passage. She found the way to the solar and ran swiftly up the spiraling stairs. At long last, she came upon the green door, the gate to the only person in the world who could protect her now. But as she tried the handle, she found it locked. Peering through the keyhole, she could see there was no one inside. Only shadows and slivers of starlight.

Nearby was a gilded window. Knowing she would have to climb to break into Amarys's chamber, Rowen strapped on her chausses. She could not very well leave them unattended on the floor. If nothing else, they might help keep her anchored against the castle wall. She unlatched the window and climbed through, feeling with her boot until she found a narrow stone lip to stand upon. The ledge traveled around the curve of the tower, and gripping the rough-hewn stone, she edged her way around to the grand bench window of the bedchamber. To her relief, it was unlatched and came open with ease.

The chamber was pitch black, all but for some remnant embers glowing in the fireplace. She stowed her armor beneath the bed. Dressed in naught but a laced shirt and braies, she concealed herself in the armoire, curling up amidst velvets and furs.

The narrow cloister smelled of cedar shavings and moth wings, but there was a hint of Amarys's natural scent in the clothes. The smell put Rowen at ease, even in her contortion. She bit her lip, trying not to cry. Everything hurt. Her muscles, her bones, her head, and her heart. She wished she could just disappear and never be seen or thought of by anyone again. If only Roland had come into this world alone.

For a brief moment, she considered that perhaps it was the devil and not God who had made her. Was it as her father said? Had she been a curse on their family? She dried her tears on her sleeves and leaned into the back of the armoire. It was not long before she'd fallen asleep and awoke to the voices of Amarys and her maidservants coming in through the green door.

Rowen had forgotten about maidservants, about nighttime rituals. Amarys would be getting undressed; her clothing would be put away, and—Rowen crept through the door of the armoire as the maidservants were still lighting candles about the room. She tried to slide under the bed, but it was too low to the floor. The women's backs were to her. They suspected nothing lurking in the shadows and merely watched their tapers to be sure they did not lose their flames.

"Ay, me," said one of them, closing the window. "Someone must have left it unlatched."

Rowen rolled onto the mattress and sealed the curtains around the bed just as the first candelabras were being lit. Her heart pounded in her chest. What if they prepared the bed for Amarys? What if Amarys screamed when she saw her?

"Most assuredly, no one was happy with the outcome of the joust, but at least your champion managed to beat Harlowe." One of the maids took Amarys to sit down before she began brushing out her hair.

Amarys scoffed, "Harlowe should have been disqualified for killing Roland's steed."

"Everyone despises him for it. Surely, he will not be declared winner tomorrow after such a dishonorable display."

"I wish it could be so," said Amarys.

Rowen heard the armoire open and close as the maids put Amarys's garments away. The bed curtain swished, and there was Amarys standing in full sight of Rowen. Her eyes went wide. Rowen held a finger to her lips pleadingly.

"Ladies, I am quite exhausted," said Amarys, shutting the bed curtain before anyone else could see beyond it. "Perhaps we might forego our ceremony in the interest of sleep."

The ladies shuffled to the door, one of them uttering, "Yes, my lady. Goodnight." They left the candles and the fire burning. The instant the chamber door sealed, Rowen leaped from the bed and folded her hands in gratitude.

"I swear I had nowhere else to go."

"What has happened?" whispered Amarys, touching the ragged remains of Rowen's hair. "Who did this to you? Oh, Rowen, is this why I did not see you at the joust?"

"Let me speak."

Amarys nodded, waiting.

"On second thought, I cannot tell you. Only please let me hide in your quarters until I think of a plan."

Amarys normally would have pressed her harder, pinched, or threatened unless she explained, but her attention lingered on the loss of Rowen's hair.

"Come, let me wash your face." Amarys went to bring a pitcher and basin, setting them before Rowen on the floor. Dampening a soft, white cloth, she dabbed the blood away from her forehead.

The cloth was freezing cold, but Rowen would not seem ungrateful by flinching. "Thank you."

"It's nothing." Strands of cold water dribbled down Rowen's neck as Amarys washed her.

"Who won the joust?" asked Rowen.

"Jean de Rieux. Though Erec came close. They faced each other in the final joust. Your poor beloved. He was so distracted."

"He is not my beloved."

"You declared yourselves before everyone at the ball."

"He is not my beloved!" said Rowen more firmly. "He has withdrawn his interest. He said so at the joust."

"So you were there?"

"I was there until the moment of Ash's death."

"You know. Tell me true, then. Who was it that ravaged your locks? Was it Harlowe?"

"This is the only damage with which I can credit your cousin." Rowen pulled her collar open to expose the welt beneath her collarbone where Harlowe's lance had struck.

Amarys ran a finger over it, whispering, "Ma chiere." The fire crackled gently, and despite Rowen's bruises and the danger of being found, the touch of Amarys's finger on Rowen's skin conjured a shiver of ecstasy. Amarys looked up, her eyes aglow. "It was you, Rowen. When you rode up to the stands, you saluted and—" She stumbled over her words. "I knew it was you."

"Roland helped me with the deception."

"You could have died!" Amarys's tone cut through like a dagger. "How could your brother do such a thing?"

"It was my idea... I had to."

Amarys's face softened, and it was as though in this moment, she could read everything Rowen's heart had ever concealed. "Your beautiful hair." She brought her hands to swipe away the scraps of Rowen's jagged black hair. "Why did you cut it?"

"My father did it to punish me. He knows everything, and now, I cannot go home."

"Stay with me. As long as you need. I can protect you."

"I will stay tonight, but when I finish the melee tomorrow, I must quit this place forever."

"Rowen," said Amarys. "Your father will forgive you, and if he will not, my family will provide for you. My father knows how much I care for you."

Rowen seized Amarys's hands, folding them up in her own. She had to tell her. She had to make it plain, even if rejection crushed her heart beyond repair. What was the way of the chevalier if not charging at the very thing one feared the most? "Amarys, I could not bear it. Forgive me; I could not. To see you married. To live in your radiance—ever stifled by my own cowardice. You may hate me for saying it, but I may conceal the truth no longer. I love you. And in a manner that endangers us in this life and the next. I love you as Man was made to love Woman, as Erec loved Enide, as Lancelot loved Guenevere. But I am a broken, loathly thing. And I must keep myself away from you—love you chastely and secretly—lest I corrupt you with sin." Rowen's voice quavered, anticipating a shriek of disgust, a pulling away.

Amarys brought Rowen's hands to her heart. "Not sin, Rowen. And never loathly.

I do not care what the church fathers say. God alone will be my judge." Amarys leaned forward and pressed Rowen's lips with a kiss. The room was dark, but in that kiss, Rowen found the brightest of suns. She gathered her lady's hair in her hands and returned the kiss with ardor. Her pulse fluttered as Amarys emitted the faintest sigh.

Verses from Song of Songs spilled over on Rowen's mind as she hugged her beloved close.

"O dove," she whispered.

They moved to the featherbed, closing the curtain to shroud them in darkness. The two continued to imbibe each other's kisses, swaying and trembling. Rowen kissed behind her ear. Their clasping hands tightened; they stopped to breathe, in and out again, as Rowen trailed her fingers up from her knee, along her thigh, up to where she reached the sacred flower of her sex. She touched her there, cautious as any freshly forged lover.

Amarys hid her face against Rowen's neck. A moan caught in her throat.

"Who is this meek and mild maiden?" Rowen teased, pushing back Amarys's hair and kissing her hot cheeks.

Amarys brought her chemise over her head. "I know not what you mean," she said.

"Where is my lady with all her bel acceuil? I crave those wicked things you used to say."

Rowen flinched slightly at the touch of Amarys's hand gliding down the lines of her abdomen.

"I thought you wanted one thing. Not another. Forgive me, chevalier. I would have you use this hard body against me. I would have you hold me fiercely. Take me like a man takes a wife. Make me die a little in your arms."

Rowen milled into her, savoring each triumph as she enticed another moan from her lips. The textures of her body, from her bead-like nipples to the delicate lace of hair between her legs, drove her mad with want. Her body tingled with the agony of bliss, a powerful unraveling. She pleaded that the dawn would never come.

"My rose. Kiss me here and use your tongue." Amarys guided Rowen's fingers between her legs.

Rowen kissed her down to her stockings—soft as lambswool—and caressed her shapely limbs. Amarys heaved, the sound of her dear little sighs washing over Rowen, urging her to go on.

CHAPTER 25

The lovers woke in each other's arms well before first light. The rich, green samite overhead reminded Rowen of the forest. It sheltered them from the eyes of the world. If there was anywhere safe, it was here. Only in a forest of the imaginary could she and Amarys ever find sanctuary. How long could they know bliss? A day? A week? How long before the world returned for them to place them in their proper places, she in the nunnery and Amarys at her husband's side.

Morning birds filled the trees outside with sprightly chatter. The light was still faint, the air imbued with that icy wetness of the dawn.

Shirtless, Rowen laced her chausses and fastened her belts. Amarys reached around her waist, kissing her bare shoulder.

"Don't go."

"I must be on the field before sunrise."

"You've already won. I am yours."

"Amarys." She did love the feel of her lady's name on her tongue, especially since last night, when she might have consigned herself to saying nothing else for the rest of her life.

Amarys touched the teardrop garnet dangling from Rowen's throat. She kissed her between the shoulder blades and whispered, "Let this garnet symbolize that we are wed. Wear it always to tell the world that you are spoken for, my bride, my queen of Carthage."

"Aeneas." They laced fingers. "I cannot stay."

Amarys released her hands and slid from the bed. "Perhaps, then, it is you who is Aeneas."

"I must defeat Harlowe. Roland does not have the stomach for it."

"Leave him to me. When we are wed, it will be easy."

"I could never let you stain your soul with such a sin."

Amarys laughed with an air of spite. She held herself, looking down at her lap. "Did you not believe me when I told you I was no innocent? You think Harlowe forced me to play those games with him? Oh, Rowen. I devised them! I wanted him to sin with me."

"No," Rowen whispered, her voice fading to a wisp. "You were preyed upon."

"Not so, my love. He is a wolf, yes, but I am no lamb."

Amarys had never told anyone before. She explained the nature of the games she played with Harlowe. She had once been very fond of her cousin, but his tempers got worse as they got older and they slowly drifted apart. One summer, when he asked to escort her on a ride, she refused. She went instead to chapel with his mother and sisters, hardly considering it might offend him. It did, though, and in retaliation, Harlowe killed her robin, a show of force to intimidate her back into compliance. Amarys loathed him for it and refused to ride with him ever again. Their fathers insisted they spend time together, reasoning that if Harlowe accompanied Amarys on a ride, they might repair the bond they had once shared. Old fools, thought Amarys.

The pair had gone out through the gatehouse, spurring their mounts to a gallop as they tore across the meadow. Amarys rode ahead of Harlowe at a faster pace. Her mount was unphased by the menace of stones and uneven ground, and she put as much distance as she could between him and herself.

"Are you trying to escape me?" Harlowe had shouted. He pulled a riding crop from his saddle and whipped his horse, giving chase.

Amarys saw him charging. She directed her palfrey to the woods.

"Careful, cousin!" Harlowe's tone had no shred of concern. Only malice. Amarys wove between trees. In the sheltering foliage, the air was crisp with the smell of moss and pine. She passed an ancient stone mile marker, straying from the road. Twigs and spiny stems snagged the hem of her skirts and sliced her horse's flanks.

She was not experienced riding there, and it was not long before her horse tripped over a root and spilled her from the saddle. She cried out, rolling through nettles. Pain smarted as the invisible spikes penetrated the fabric of her dress. She wasn't thrown hard, but the shock left her unable to stand. Then came the real terror.

Harlowe behind her. Amarys screamed.

Laughing, Harlowe slid from his horse with ease. "My princess!" He brought a length of rope from his saddle. "At last, we are alone!"

Something remained so thrilling in it. Amarys shrieked as Harlowe grabbed her by the hair and wrenched her up on her feet.

"No!" she cried at the top of her voice as he pressed her to the elm and fastened rope around her waist. He removed her shoes and stockings, laughing as she kicked at him.

"You play so well," said Harlowe, giddy at her fervor as he pulled his shirt over his head. It was only pretend—until it wasn't. It was only a game—until she felt him like he was really inside of her.

She could feel the heat of his naked chest—she could taste his sweat as his shoulder pressed her mouth—and it struck her that the game felt real because it was—and had always been—real.

"Oh, Amarys." His whisper licked at her inner ear. "Do you want me to stop?"

"No."

Harlowe placed his riding crop between her teeth, rocking her against the tree until she felt his seed bloom inside of her.

"No one plays as well as you do," he said. "Believe me, I have searched."

When the game that was not a game was over, he cut her ropes. She sprang forth like a rabbit from a trap. It would be the last time.

She stayed away from him while maintaining a tenuous peace. If he were willing to ruin her, she would be wed to him at once, but he too would be disgraced. Let him try and prove himself and maybe die in the lists.

When Amarys had finished her story, Rowen hardly knew how she should react. For now, she only listened, occasionally shifting and closing her eyes.

"When I learned he played the game with others—servants, tenants—all against their will—why—I hated that I was ever born. I am ashamed to have wrought such evil in a man."

"You had nothing to do with that. You are not like him. You would never force your lust upon a servant."

"A servant, no, but a friend?"

"Amarys..."

"I tricked you into kissing me. I fed you the devil's cap so I could persuade you to let me touch you. And when it happened, I saw within myself a shade of the man I so despise. If it is anyone's duty to stain their soul with his murder, it is mine, for I have known him most intimately."

"No, it must be me. Today. If he survives, he could marry someone else. He could go on hurting people. It could be me, for all we know. Erec has withdrawn his interest. I have no one to protect me."

"I will protect you," said Amarys, holding her face. "You can stay here. I will restore your engagement to Erec."

"Erec knows I jousted. He will never speak to me again."

"Erec will do whatever my father tells him, and when I am betrothed, my father will grant me a boon. You and Erec will be married. We will be neighbors and spend all our time in each other's company. We will grow old together and raise our children side by side."

"Our children?"

"Yes, my rose. We will have to do our duty. That part is not up to us."

"But... Roland loves another. He will take her as his mistress, he says. He will never lie with you."

"I see." Amarys frowned, suddenly somewhere distant in her mind. "Who is she?"

"Does it matter?"

"No, but... is she a peasant?"

"What should it matter?"

Amarys hesitated, but she said, "People talk, my love. If Roland and I do not

238

produce an heir, they will call him 'impotent' and me 'barren.' And should he take a mistress, they will pity me." The pragmatic Amarys was beginning to surface in the soft lines furrowing her brow.

"Ad Deum." Rowen covered her mouth. "You have always wanted him."

Amarys stared at her as if amazed. "I am pleading with you not to leave these walls because I love you. Let Roland risk his life. If something happens to you, none of it matters."

"I have seen the way you look at him. From the moment I told you he would fight for you, you have adored him. Just once, I want you to look at me that way."

"How must I look at you? Tell me, and I will do it if it will save you. A melee is nothing like a joust, Rowen. It is chaos. It is a blood sport ordained to kill the second sons whose lives are meaningless to this world." Amarys was so affected that she could hardly breathe. "Are you really so led astray by the songs and stories? I should have known you would not listen. I am only the prize, after all. What could I know about your world of violence?"

Rowen dressed and went to stand in the window, looking down on the field below. It was still bare, littered only with tents where the men were sleeping. She looked down to her brother's tent, wondering how he had fared dealing with their father the night before.

"I have to finish what I started. Do you know the safest passage out of here?"

Amarys stood, removing the linens from her featherbed. "You would do best to disguise yourself as a wash woman." She draped a sheet over Rowen, creating sturdy knots to form a hooded cloak. "Down the tower steps to the very end, there is a door to the laundry. Go through a passage and take the third door on the left. The one with birds carved into it."

"I will see you again. I swear it."

Amarys piled more linens into her arms, not looking up.

"Amarys. Please do not be cross."

"Courage, chevalier. At last, you're just like the rest of them."

Rowen worked to bundle the linens tightly around her armor, which she carried out. Without embrace, without farewell, she abandoned the tower.

CHAPTER 26

The swells of tall meadow grass bent in the cold morning fog. The sky shone silvery white, an airy death shroud pulled tight over the face of Heaven. Rowen hiked across the plains, breathing in the ghosts of campfires. She found Biax hitched outside her brother's tent. The white canvas was wet with dew, and rivulets of water slipped down her hands as she pulled back the opening and went inside. Roland and Willem lay sleeping on their bedrolls, each draped with quilts and furs. As Rowen came in, Willem, still dozing, rolled his back to her.

The air was cold enough that Roland's breath hung in front of his lips. Rowen kindled a small fire at the center of the tent where the ashes of a former one had grown cold.

"Rowen," rasped her brother, sitting up. "Father is looking for you. You must not be here."

"Have you given up on me so soon?" Rowen blew gently over the kindling as it ignited. "Like the masked knights of verse, I will ride in disguise, kill scores of men, and leave before the end."

Roland sat up, rubbing his forehead. "This has gone far enough. Our little ruse will be our family's ruin. Trust me to win the melee, and I will see you and Amarys settled in the same household. I will force it."

Willem groaned, awakening to the sound of their voices. "This again? Just take her to the nunnery already."

"Bite your tongue, Willem. I will not have her cloistered."

"This is my fight," she said. "You don't understand. Amarys and I... We feel the same."

He shook his head slowly, not looking up.

"You are certain?"

"We are wed now in the eyes of God."

By the empathy pooling in his eyes, he showed her that he believed her.

Willem, throughout this exchange, packed his clothes into a rucksack. He started to go.

"What are you doing?" asked Roland.

"Oh. I'll be at the bathhouse," he said. "I want no part in this."

"Are you not my squire?"

"Your sister needs help, Roland. Erec had the right idea. I will not interfere, but I also will not help you."

"You betray me."

"You betray the Order."

Willem shrugged and left. The twins felt quite alone now.

"He is not wrong. There is no honor in this, Rowen."

"Perhaps not in the beginning. It was selfish of me to ask you to marry Amarys. This was never the highest good. Now, though, I wish only to slay Harlowe. I understand the full weight of his depravity. If you can win Amarys's hand, you will have my gratitude, but it is more important to me that I wear your armor one last time and kill the rapist swine who embraced my lady by force."

"What are you saying?"

"He has ruined her. And he must die for it."

Roland nodded, his mouth tight. "We will fight together as before. I will ride in so all can see my likeness before the hat goes on. I will appear before Father and the other nobles and allow them to interview me. I will earn points and reunite with you in my tent. We will exchange armor, and then you can earn points in the second half. When your honor is satisfied, you return to me. I ride back out, fully rested, and earn enough points to win."

"Our mother made two of us for a reason, did she not?"

Her brother's eyes were burning with fever for a fight. "*Nahn yad wahida.*"

Rowen gave a nod. "One hand, my brother."

He offered her a cowl to wear while she waited in the tent. Should anyone chance upon her, she would claim to be a fletcher delivering arrows.

With these instructions, Rowen left the tent to hide amidst a nearby copse of trees. She watched from a distance as her father came down the road to the encampment. He prepared Roland in his armor and helped him mount Rowen's white palfrey. Rowen tried to listen to the conversation between them, which was sparse.

"The Mohammat ride smaller horses. It makes them swifter to strike and evade."

"How fitting," said Roland. "Biax tolerates me well enough."

"He will serve you better than a destrier you've never worked with... Any sign of Rowen?"

"No."

Little else passed between them. The townspeople were lining up around the vast fences that extended toward the edge of the forest, where sprawling meadows converged with a maze of trees. Roland rode out to find formation amidst the other knights and the squires, where the streaming banners flickered on the wind, where knights lined up on horseback, side by side, two rows facing one another. Rowen climbed one of the trees and found a vantage point that gave her a clear view of her brother with the other knights. Their armor looked dull in the low morning light. Their horses' limbs were wet with dew.

"Roland!" shouted one of the knight marshals, flagging him down. Roland trotted Biax over. He would have to explain the absence of his squire.

As he conveyed that information, the marshal shook his head, his face flushing. He shifted uncomfortably. Speaking harshly, he seemed to admonish Roland.

Amarys and her father stepped forth onto the green, dressed in rich velvet and glittering gemstones. Clement carried a chain of gold plates encrusted with rubies. Amarys carried a sash of pale lace. They stood before a row of wooden chairs where the nobles of Rieux and neighboring Baronies were seated.

Clement addressed them first. "Welcome, my esteemed guests, to the tournament that will ensure my daughter is wed to the noblest of chevaliers."

Amarys spoke next. Her back was stiff, her voice projecting over the field with emotions painfully contained. "There are thirty-four champions contending for my hand. Over the course of two hours, you shall watch them perform in hand-to-hand combat. Each man will come forward and present himself. Your scores will be taken into consideration with the points garnered later on the field. You may, as a collective, ask each man two to three questions. At noon, you will each select a favorite and a second."

Two of Clement's men carried tall chairs to place behind the row of nobles. Clement and Amarys were seated, and on the field, the knights began to spar. As the knights paired off and performed their prowess of arms, Clement called each of them to come before the nobles. He let the older men go first, which made sense logically, as these men would be more tired after battling in the sun for an hour. One by one, they answered the nobles' questions. As the sun got higher, more ladies flitted wicker fans to cool themselves. Servants brought pitchers of honeyed water to refill their goblets.

"Will Sir Erec of Avenport please present himself?" called Clement.

Erec clinked forth, taking a knee and removing his helm. Behind him, the shouts of battle raged on.

"Sir Erec," addressed one of the Barons. "Can you tell us why you became a knight?"

"Yes, my lord. Since I was a child, I have always loathed injustice. God makes each of us with a plan in mind. Some men are better suited for war. Others are builders or have a strong connection to the divine. No matter what purpose God has in mind for us, I believe we should treat one another with respect and goodwill. When I see a knight taking advantage of a farmer because he has strength and the farmer cannot defend himself, I am angered, sire. I became a knight so I could defend the small folk who cannot defend themselves."

The nobles whispered and were pleased with his response. "May I ask," began a noble lady, "Who inspires you on the field?"

"Roland of Antioch," said Erec without pause. "He has many talents and shows no fear in battle."

"Thank you, Sir Erec," said Clement. "Go drink some water before you return."

In time, they called Harlowe. Rowen watched and stewed over each of his answers.

"Why do you wish to marry Lady Amarys?" asked one of the nobles.

"I have known the lady since we were children," said Harlowe, the picture of courtesy. "We spent our summers together, inseparable from a young age."

"What will you give me?" interjected Amarys, rising from her chair. "Should we be wed, what will you give me on our wedding day?"

"A title, for one thing," said Harlowe, and the other nobles laughed. "Most importantly, though, I will give you something that no other lady has ever possessed. My heart."

The nobles applauded. Harlowe was dismissed and allowed to return to sparring. Roland was summoned next. He knelt and bowed his head, removing his helmet so all could see his face and countenance. Upon seeing the helm come off, Amarys brightened. "Roland!" she cried aloud in a voice tinted with a great many emotions.

"Roland La Flèche-de Beaugency, son of Sir Ivin of Antioch. What does chivalry mean to you?" asked a Baroness.

Roland, kneeling, mussed his hair as he thought. He squinted up at her. "The lady has asked what chivalry means to me. This is a good question, and it is one my father asks me daily. Chivalry, for me, is a promise made to the people. If someone is wounded, imperiled, or in any way distressed, I am there to protect in any capacity that I can. Chivalry means my life is no longer mine. It belongs to God and the Order."

"What is it that you love best about fighting?"

Rowen began to worry. Roland would surely falter here.

"Milady, it is difficult to say what I love best about the thing that comes so naturally to me. Fighting gives me purpose. It protects the people I love. When I go out on the field and hold my sword aloft, there is nowhere else in the world that I would rather be."

"I have a question," insisted Amarys. Everyone craned their necks to face her. "What will you, Sir Roland, give to me when we are wed?"

"I will give you the keys to your cell," he said. A hush fell over the nobles. They ceased their private whispers and listened. "I will give you the world. Wherever you want to go, I will take you. However you want to live, I will support you. What else could one give to the lady with everything... if not freedom?" The nobles smiled, some of them nodding. "I will move the stars and planets for you. Whatever it takes."

Amarys stepped forth with her lace. She laid the sash into her champion's hands. "I choose Roland for my favorite in the melee. Wear my favor with pride and do not dash away thy life."

"As my lady commands."

Amarys kissed her fingertips and extended them toward him. "All my blessings to you, Roland. Ride to victory."

Roland held her favor aloft, letting the white lace undulate on the breeze. He tied it to the pommel of his sword. Clement called Harlowe back and laid his chain of gold and rubies over his shoulders, declaring him his favorite. The other nobles declared mostly for Harlowe, a few divided between Roland and the other knights.

When those points were awarded, Lord Clement announced how the rest of the tournament would proceed. "For the rest of the day, until the sun sets, our knights shall do mounted combat. Should ye require sustenance or arms, ye may return to thy tent, but pay heed. Yon smoke pillars mark the edge of the perimeter. None may venture outside these lines without yielding his stake in the competition."

Rowen looked toward the East and saw the streaks of black smoke climbing the gray sky. There was a good bit of forest within the perimeter, enough to lure Harlowe into unfamiliar territory and take advantage of him amidst the trees. She knew every footpath of the forest, and she wanted revenge.

"Points shall only be garnered either with knockout, capture, or unhorsing. Death by misadventure shall garner no additional points. The execution of a fellow knight's mount will result in a significant loss of points—" Here, Clement narrowed his eyes at his nephew. "—so mind the horses. Marshals shall attend the knights to observe their conduct. While prowess in battle and capture will earn you points, upholding honorable conduct shall also be taken into account. Let's have a clean fight and send everyone home alive in nomine patris!"

Amarys crossed herself. She dropped her hands to her belt and lifted a pale hunting horn to her lips. A deep, resonant howl emerged. Both rows of knights roared like fiends and slammed their spurs into their horses' flanks. Rowen held her breath as Harlowe went charging at her brother, eager to finish the rivalry that had arisen the night before. Roland yanked Biax's reins and spurred him forward, but not before the sea of steel enveloped him. Swords collided in a matrix of impact. Roland veered into a sharp pivot, ducking as Harlowe's sword grazed his back.

Rowen held her breath.

Her brother drew his sword and bludgeoned Harlowe across the shoulder. The blade recoiled like a baton that had struck a gong, and it hardly affected the man, but Roland had hit him hard enough to spook his horse. The beast whipped its head violently as it snorted and bucked.

Another mounted knight came flying in, engaging Roland in a dance of steel.

Rowen should have been exhilarated, but instead, she felt sick in her core to see her brother's life so imperiled. She studied the field, the tactics, the activities of the marshals traversing the perimeter on horseback. They tallied points as blows were doled out and banners snatched. She did everything she could to distract herself from strokes that came close to ending Roland's life. Harlowe lost interest soon enough. He focused his energies on his weaker opponents in order to garner points. With a steel-cased mule kick, he unhorsed one of the men. Another he cracked over the head with his sword hilt, causing the lad to go limp in the saddle.

Roland stole the glory as he rode in, dismounted, and engaged the felled knight in combat. Several swift movements later, he had managed the first knockout of the melee. The maidens in attendance were screaming with delight, all except Amarys, who instead appeared to be smiling and sharing a knowing look with her father.

The glory did not last. The crowd grew quiet as Harlowe rode up behind Roland. His gray horse reared, alerting Roland to Harlowe's presence. He quickly pivoted into a handspring as the brute's sword came sweeping down. Rowen hated to watch, but nothing could have torn her eyes away at that moment. Roland stuck the landing, his armor hardly shifting, for it fit his every measurement. He whistled to Biax, who was as quick and light-footed as the wind itself. The white steed circled him, and Roland mounted as gracefully as one climbing a stair. The beast cantered some distance from Harlowe until Roland brought it round to meet his enemy in the center of the fray.

Their blades collided. Their horses shrieked and stamped the earth in a tight circle.

Something upset Harlowe's balance, either the unlevel ground or the wobbling of his saddle. From all Rowen could tell, Roland's attacks had little effect. But he shifted in his seat quite suddenly and went entirely—and unforgettably—horizontal, hanging by his stirrups.

Roland reached out to help him but was swatted away. He managed only to grab Harlowe's helm. The flat-top helm popped right off, and Roland found himself carrying an unintentional trophy. Peals of laughter rose from the stands. Amarys covered her mouth, unable to hide that she was laughing hysterically with all the rest. The horse dragged Harlowe away from the action, panicking at the crescendo of applause and the chorus repeatedly shouting, "Roland, Roland," with tenacity. Then one man exclaimed in a voice like a cannon: "Roland, Son of Rieux!"

Those three words changed everything. A powerful cry rose from the people, and a group of Breton lords rallied the cry, "Our son of Rieux!" Many others joined in, but the Norman families grew quiet, turning to Lord Clement for guidance. Surrounded by his daughters, his nephew humiliated, he had nothing to offer them. And then, against all odds, the Normans joined in chanting "Our son of Rieux" with the rest of them. Rowen could not believe what she was hearing. All her life, her brother had been Roland the Turk or Roland of Antioch. Never had he been anything but an outsider. Yet here in the tourney, he was granted his birthright. He was the son of Rieux, descendent of the original Breton nobles and heir to Clement's holdings.

Roland rode to the dais where Lord Clement and his daughter were seated. Ladies clasped each other and held their breath as Roland laid Harlowe's helm gently at the foot of the platform. Tread carefully, thought Rowen, remembering all that could transpire if Clement perceived this as an insult. The Baron did not look happy. Civil war brewed behind his eyes. Rieux in flames. The chateau in ruin.

Clement almost grabbed the back of Amarys's dress as she rose and went to Roland. He was not fast enough. Amarys bid him to remove his helm, "That I might thank you for the gift." Roland did as she asked. To the amazement of all, Amarys leaned over the rail and kissed him as fiercely as a hawk seizing its prey. The chants for Roland dissipated as a rising howl of approval enveloped the crowd.

Rowen could not shut her eyes, suspended in the nightmare of a kiss that lasted far too long. Fire burned in her skin. She reminded herself it was all an act, part of Amarys's plan to de-escalate the Breton-Norman tensions playing out. Still, the thought of them making vows before God enraged her. Had she really imagined she could let her brother marry Amarys?

Clement snatched his daughter back like a toy, but instead of looking angry, he seemed almost relieved. He observed the crowd, his disbelief apparent. How popular this couple had become with them. Who could have imagined that a Breton-Norman alliance could be achieved with a lad of Roland's reputation?

Harlowe fixed his saddle in the distance, having finally detached himself and caught up to his horse. Roland fled the field in the direction of the tents. A knight was quick on his heels.

Rowen squinted to make out his colors. Red, white, and green with a lion passant. That was the heraldry of Clement de Rieux. It struck her to the core when she realized who it was. The only other man with half a claim to being the son of Rieux.

Sir Erec.

CHAPTER 27

Roland rode harder. He made a tight turn to see his pursuer. Erec had followed him all the way to the edge of the field. One of the marshals was just starting out that way to observe them at a distance.

"Roland!" shouted the sanguine knight. "Is it you there or your imposter?"

Roland put up his hand for peace that they might speak a moment. He sheathed his blade, and Erec did the same. Each rode in, close enough to talk and far enough to flee in a skirmish.

"The only imposter is you!" cried Roland. "You never loved my sister. Your love is as fickle as the seasons."

"You lied to me. You endangered her. What else should I have done?"

"To love her, you must accept her as she is. You cannot keep her from combat."

"I cannot betray her to Clement nor betray Clement out of love for her."

"No!" Roland shouted. "Do not speak to me of love!" He drew his sword, urging his horse to widen the gap between him and Erec.

"You should have told me!" Erec's voice drowned in the wind roaring through Roland's helmet. They rode in a vast circle, holding their blades out like talons. Roland spurred his horse to action. His palfrey was a quicker beast, and as he gained on Erec, he stood in the stirrups like a demon taking flight. With one foot atop the saddle, Roland soared through the air.

The knights collided. They clasped, falling together against the hard earth, lost in the dust kicked up by their horses. Roland landed on top of his friend, and when he looked at him, he saw his helmet had spun. Except it hadn't.

The veins in Erec's neck twisted like ribbons down a maypole. Blood vessels burst in his eyes, purple and crimson blooming as he blinked rapidly. Roland's extremities went cold.

"No," he stammered. "No, no, no."

"R-Rowen." Erec clutched at Roland's vambraces as they clung to one another's arms. "Tell her."

"Tell her what?" Roland squeezed Erec's hand.

"I will... I still..." Erec's mind was a broken thing.

"Tell her what? Tell her what?"

No further words ever came. Roland felt a pressure building in his chest. His ears hummed; he crawled away from the body, from his friend, from this thing, this body of his friend. He began to wheeze as memories lay on like a whirlwind of blows.

There were so many things that could push the soul right out of its sleeve: the prick of infection, a fall, a fever. It happened quickly. And there was never enough time to reflect on why it had to or what it meant.

Roland vomited on the grass, his eggs from that morning in a rancid pile with the blood rolling out of Erec's body. It wasn't right. Roland's brain smoldered like raw steel in a forge. Erec was a great warrior. The best. Why did he fall like that?

Roland ripped off his helmet. He smashed his fists into his head, screaming as hateful thoughts swarmed his brain. Why couldn't she just marry him? Why couldn't she just follow the rules and accept the love of this perfect man? Was her hunger for Amarys really so much more important than the lives of everyone else?

Already, Erec's voice hounded him, howling in his skull, *You should have told me!*

Roland, on hands and knees, clawed at the dirt, letting the tears fall. The marshals signaled the medics who came to collect Erec's body. None of the other knights swooped in to engage. They ceased their battle, watching from afar.

"Vile sport," Roland wept, hoping someone would hear him. "What games!" He rose sharply, throwing his handful of dry earth in the direction of the nobility. "What daring feats!"

Taking his horse by the leads, he returned to his pavilion, where Rowen waited.

CHAPTER 28

Rowen's time had come to wear the skin of the warrior. But in her heart, she felt herself withering as she thought about that kiss. She had not seen Erec fall. Her thoughts were still only of Amarys. As her brother entered the pavilion with his helm tucked under his arm, a rush of fire flooded her chest.

"How could you?" she demanded.

Roland was silent, his cheeks stained with dirt and tears.

He began removing his pauldrons. Rowen peeled away his hauberk and removed his gambeson. The twins turned, and Roland began dressing her.

"You enjoyed that kiss far too much." "Did you not see what just befell?! Erec is slain! Just now, on the green!"

Rowen felt her very spirit knocked from her bones. It was as though she were looking down at the top of her own head. She breathed, holding herself firm. "No," she uttered. "No. It must be a mistake."

"No mistake."

"The medics will see to his wounds."

"I watched him die."

Rowen held her chin.

"We fought upon the green. I knocked him from his horse and broke his neck."

255

"Why?"

"Why? Because that is what happens!"

If there was blood in her veins, she could not feel it. Her face and limbs felt utterly exsanguinated.

"No," she stammered, her breath tight in her chest. She fell to a chair, her head swimming.

Roland wrenched her to her feet and finished belting the gambeson.

He brought the mail over her head and adjusted it to lay evenly.

"He spoke to me before he died. He still loved you. He would have married you. He was only angry that you left him in the dark. And as for kissing Amarys, I will have to do a great deal more than that when we are wed. I will have to look upon her in her shift and lie beside her at night. We may have to perform some rendition of the carnal act to convince our families we have consummated the union."

Rowen inhaled slowly, containing the beast of emotions clawing its way to the surface.

Roland finished setting the coat of plates. "Get out there. Earn some points and return before noon."

She donned the helm. As much as she wanted time to process Erec's death and mourn her part in it, there was no time. She rushed from the tent and mounted her palfrey. Biax, her light-footed and agile friend, knew her at once. The horse carried her over the green to the mounted warriors, who continued to chase and bludgeon one another. The scene was more chaotic up close. With many scores of knights competing, it was difficult to discern the best way to engage them.

She rode past what appeared to be Erec's helmet. His body had been carried away, but there was blood smearing the stubbled green where he died. She could not dwell on the loss. Not now.

It was not difficult to find her target. Harlowe's face was fully exposed, his chestnut hair sweat-pasted to his skull. Rowen squeezed her horse's flanks, leaning forward as she charged her rival. Harlowe sneered, a flash of amazement in his eyes as though he could hardly believe Roland was coming at him with such renewed vigor. Rowen stood in the stirrup, drawing her sword and sweeping it above her head.

Racing in on the palfrey he had given her, she flew at Harlowe like Perseus.

Another mounted knight intercepted her, but she made quick work of him, circling him in sword-to-sword combat until he leaned awkwardly, lost his balance, and fell from his horse. Another mounted knight came swooping in, twirling a flail. Encased in armor, Rowen felt like steel itself. She thrust her hand forward and let the chain encircle her arm. Then she ripped it from his grasp, pulling him from his mount. Both men were out cold. The bottom of one's helmet shed bright blood on the grass.

Rowen suppressed the feeling of guilt and regained the pursuit of her enemy. She advanced until she could smell the sweat of his horse. She thought she had a clean shot at his throat, but then he leaned back in the saddle, dodged her sweep, and clobbered her gut with his polearm. Clever. He had used her speed against her. The stick might as well have been a wall. It took her right off the palfrey, launching her into a heap of clattering armor. The fall was worse than the blow. Her plates pinched through the layer of wool. Her helmet resounded with a terrifying hum like a hive on the brink of bursting.

Biax recoiled, nearly trampling her. She rolled out of his dust, jumping to her feet and trying not to visibly stagger. The ladies in the crowd screamed.

Where was her sword? She found it on the ground, took it up, and slid it into the sheath on her back. Humiliated and desperate, she chased down her palfrey. Biax was rattled, but he had enough savvy to return for her. She had to escape; she could never best Harlowe in an open field. He had the advantage of experience, and her only hope was to bring him to the place she felt most comfortable. Biax understood. Rowen was only halfway up the stirrup as the horse broke into an open gallop.

The percussive clamor of battle was behind her. Rowen clung to the saddle and rode as fast as her mount could manage, hardly slowing as they entered the maze of the woods. With subtle leans, she guided Biax between the trees, urging him with the pressure of her thighs to run at a quicker cadence despite the obstacles. They had to trust each other. And in doing so, they outpaced Harlowe.

Biax paid no mind to the brambles and snags tearing his hide. He had all the determination of Rowen herself. They charged in the direction of the smoke pillar. Rowen felt the pull of the earth as the ground became softer. She blinked hard, clinging to the horn and steadying her heart and her head. Why couldn't she hear Harlowe behind her?

Doubt darkened even the strongest of hopes.

She rode until she came to the Grim Tree, that thick, bent trunk whose roots clung like veins to the mouth of a shallow cave. She dismounted and tied her horse's bridle to one of the Grim Tree's low-hanging branches. She hid behind the massive root wall of a felled oak.

Using the hilt of her sword, she punched a hole through the clay that clotted the roots together. She removed her helmet so she could see the forest floor in all directions. All she had to do was wait. Harlowe could not stand to let an insult go. He would come for Roland.

As she waited, Rowen contemplated the loss of Erec, telling herself none of this was her fault. But then she remembered the bond of chivalry. Willem's words repeated in her head: You betray the Order.

There came a sound of movement behind her. Before she could turn to look, the hands of her enemy were upon her. Harlowe held her arms, gripping just above her bracers.

"What's this?" His voice sent a shiver through her loins. "Lady Rowen, sister to my rival." His hands were crushing her flesh. She bucked against his grip, trying to tear free. "Are you helping Roland cheat?"

Before she could answer, Harlowe encircled her waist. He disarmed her, tossing her sword to the ground and clutching her around the ribcage as though she were but a cat in his arms. She tilted her head back to glare into his cruel, unfeeling eyes. His coarse hand closed over her throat. "If you want to play at war, I'm willing to oblige," he hissed, brandishing a hunting dagger.

Already, she could imagine how they would find her the next day. Throat slit. Corpse ravaged by bugs.

"You die this day," she choked out.

Harlowe thrust her away. She landed against the dried leaves of the forest floor. "Little witch," he sneered. "Your curse means nothing."

To her surprise, she saw genuine fear in his eyes. She had inadvertently discovered his fear of magic. "You will bleed like a woman," she said. "And no one will come to save you."

"Stop speaking!" he shouted.

Rowen began to recite what little Saracinois she knew with determination and zeal. Who was this person speaking through her? She could not know, but even if her curses were not real, she would take Harlowe's power away by denying him the pleasure of her fear. Channeling the voice of her mother, the words of her ancestors, she compelled him to lower his knife and back away.

Rowen stood to meet his eye. "It was I who bested you in the joust."

"Impossible."

"I bear the welts of your lance. You will find no such mark on my brother's chest. I am your challenger, Harlowe." Rowen threw down her gauntlet, echoing the challenge from the joust. "Take it up and fight me. My father will not intervene."

Harlowe gave her a sideways glance. "Hardly seems fair."

"We are more evenly matched than you think."

"Why do this? What do you hope to gain?"

"The same thing as yourself. The lady, Amarys."

He nodded. "So she corrupted you too. The little witch. Still weaving her webs." Snorting, he bent at the hip and retrieved the gauntlet, lifting it over his head and then flinging it away. "All right," he said. "Pick up your sword but leave the helm. This ends when one of us is dead."

Rowen did as he bade her, squaring her shoulders with her blade in plow position. She made a mental map of every tree in the vicinity of ten paces. These were her soldiers. She dug her boot into the earth, grounding herself. She thought of Amarys, of holding her in the warmth of her bed. To defeat Harlowe, she had to recede into the calm of that sanctuary, that peaceful, firelit room where God's judgment could not penetrate. Protecting that sacred place meant removing Harlowe's head.

Mustering the will to kill, Rowen charged at him, whipping her sword at his neck. It bounced off his pauldron, further deflected by his own blade. He made a try for her head, but his sword landed in the flesh of a tree. Again, he tried, and again, she leaped between her soldiers and evaded his blade. Soon, several of the trees bore the wounds of his wrath. Rowen began to hope again. Harlowe was getting fatigued each time his sword slammed into another tree, or he stumbled through a cluster of nettles. But her luck could not last. The knight adapted, tricked her into thinking he was in pursuit, when really, he knew to pivot and meet her head-on at the other side of a tree. There, he clobbered her jaw with the back of his gauntlet, knocking her flat on her back.

Rowen tried to roll, but the edge of Harlowe's sword came down on her chest. It felt as though her heart exploded beneath the force.

"How's that?!" he bellowed.

Rowen flipped onto her belly and tried to crawl, but Harlowe grabbed her by the legs and pulled her back.

"You really thought you had me!" He laughed heartily. "Let me fuck some sense into you." He grunted as he worked to contain her beneath his weight, pressing her so hard into the dirt that she got mud along the side of her face. Rowen fought with everything she had, but she could not escape him. Harlowe clutched his sword, pulling at her chausses. She thought he was about to force himself on her but quickly realized he was planning something else. He was preparing to sodomize her with the fat hilt of his blade.

Rowen wriggled enough to free her arm and smash his nose with her coude, the steel plate on her elbow. The bones crunched and bled down his lips. He grunted, shielding his face. She stole this chance to get out from under him and back on her feet. While he was snorting up blood, she shoved him and stole his hunting knife. Ducking his grasp, she stabbed him deep in the thigh, ripping out gore as she withdrew the blade and plunged it in again.

"Maybe I'll fuck some sense into you!" she screamed.

Harlowe kicked her away. Blood gushed from the wound, but his body seemed to deny the effect of that gaping hole. He kept slinging expletives as he clutched at the wound, his face growing redder, his eyes tinged with fire. He went behind a tree, one that he had scarred deeply.

"Marshals!" he shouted. "A woman!"

Rowen looked frantically for her helmet. She did not realize when the tree began to bend beneath Harlowe's weight. The came a loud crack. Harlowe shouted for he had been leaning up against the tree when the support failed. Before Rowen could understand what was happening, the timber came crashing down. The tree crushed her gorget like tin. The garnet beneath the steel plate punctured her flesh just beneath her jugular notch. Some of her mail embedded itself in her skin, opening her like a vat. And Harlowe's full weight smashed her ribcage.

Rowen gasped for breath, the tree pressing her neck like a stem. Harlowe lay atop her. All the world hushed beneath a spell of silence. She watched the leaves leap up around her, fluttering slowly, as though she were underwater. Harlowe pushed himself up and rolled onto his back, trying to tourniquet his leg with his belt. Storm clouds darkened the sky through the tree cover, and the earth was cold against her back. Rain. The tourney would be cut short.

"Amarys," she whispered, straining to breathe. The garnet's chain was painted against her neck with her own blood. There was so much blood on the soil. Was it all hers? She could not be certain, for an ocean of it swelled beneath Harlowe as well.

"Medic!" cried Harlowe. But where were they? It was just Rowen and Harlowe dying alone in the forest.

Rowen wondered bleakly of death. Would she feel the embrace of the mother she never knew, the woman whose last words denied her very existence? Or would she only feel the elements slowly pulling her apart?

Harlowe squeezed the strap around his upper thigh. "No," he wept. "We are both going to die."

The realization of death made Rowen inexplicably giddy. She no longer knew if she was in her right mind, but she suddenly felt the irresistible urge to laugh. And so she did. She laughed out loud, long and hard. Her laughter was immensely curative, as it seemed to open her lungs. She tasted the metallic fragrance of her own blood bubbling in her throat. She saw how her laughter baffled Harlowe. The man began to scream. In the end, his terror worked in her favor because, despite all her longing to live, she could not stop laughing long enough to call for help.

CHAPTER 29

Outside the tent, the noblemen of Rieux were discussing something, their faces weary. The servants lit torches to light the medical tents. The crowds had been sent away without answers, a victor to be announced at the feast that evening. Ivin and Clement knew all the details now, and they had to spin a narrative that would satisfy the nobles. Amarys moved past them, for the instant she heard what had happened, she had run through the rain to find the surgeon's tent.

Rowen was laid on a pallet just an arm's length from another that held a body fully draped with linen. Roland was seated on the ground beside her, holding his face with a trembling hand. He looked at her with an expression that conveyed there was no hope. Never had Amarys seen such a grim countenance.

Rowen's chest plate was grotesquely concave, and Amarys could hardly understand how the girl could still draw breath in the narrow shell that remained of her chest. Amarys fell to her knees, afraid even to touch her lest she end whatever miracle was keeping her alive.

"Amarys," whispered Rowen.

"Harlowe did this?"

"A tree. The forest gives, and the forest takes," said Roland. "Harlowe bled out before the marshals reached them. Rowen cut him deep, but then there was some

263

kind of accident. The surgeon says the armor is keeping her alive, but she'll be gone by morning."

There was so much Amarys wanted to say, but she could barely speak through her sorrow.

"Amarys," said Rowen. "We won. Harlowe will never have you."

"What does it matter? If we cannot be together, it was all for nothing. Don't you understand? I would have been the devil's wife if I could have kept you in this world!"

"Amarys," Roland admonished her. "She's going soon."

Amarys kissed her gently, her tears falling into Rowen's eyes.

"Do not be afraid," said Rowen. "You will find solace in each other." She reached to take the hand of her lady and the hand of her brother and place them in one another.

Amarys pulled her hand away. "No. You cannot ask this!"

"It's already done, Amarys," said Roland. "Our parents know everything. Your father said he would contain the secret and declare me the victor of the melee."

Amarys wanted to scream, but her beautiful knight was really dying now. Rowen's breathing grew increasingly shallow and frail. Her eyes wandered over the ceiling of the tent as though her sight had left her.

"Roland!" cried Rowen with urgency. "How will I find you again?"

Roland squeezed his sister's hand, pressing his face to her knuckles. "You needn't search. I am with you always."

Rowen tried to sit up, but it was something her body could no longer manage. Roland leaned over her, kissing her cheek and guiding her back to rest.

Rowen touched the edge of his ear. She held a lock of his hair, relaxing against the canvas cot. "You were my mother and father both. You loved me like a child. Anyone else would have condemned me to Hell. But you did not." Her eyes rolled back in her head as she seized.

Amarys covered her mouth, whimpering as she witnessed Rowen's neck contracting under spasms.

Soon, all the tension slunk from her muscles. Her jaw slackened. Her eyes closed. All the war that she had waged against the world drifted away, and a mask of calm fell like gossamer across her brow. Amarys and Roland lost all composure. United in anguish, they held each other, if only to keep from chasing Rowen into the next life.

CHAPTER 30

Roland had usurped his father's throne. The imposing chair in front of the fireplace had always been off-limits, but that did not mean anything now. The room blazed with an oppressive warmth; Roland had beads of sweat flecking his brow. Three greyhounds reposed at his feet, each of them gnawing the bones from supper. Two of them snarled as the tread of Roland's father disturbed the stairwell.

Ivin came forward, balancing on his cane as he hugged a gold-plated chest beneath one arm. He sat across from Roland, making a noise of soft frustration, something like a sigh.

"You were right," he said.

Flames danced in Roland's eyes, which could not have been pulled from the hearth for all the gold in Brittany.

"Roland?" His father set the chest on his knee, arranging his cane to rest against his chair. "I was wrong to condemn her. And now, I have nothing but regret. The loss of her presence has cast our house into darkness."

Still, Roland said nothing.

His father opened the chest, uncovering a pocket of red velvet where a pile of gold rings glittered in the firelight.

"These are from my service to the Lionheart, a ring for every battle," Ivin

267

explained. "I intended for you and Rowen to divide them equally upon my death. I would like for you to have them now."

He took one and placed it on his son's finger. Roland's arms were limp, his muscles wasting.

"This pain is not forever," said Ivin.

"Who was my mother?" said Roland flatly, hardly stirring from his statuesque torpor. "Rowen is dead, and I am a ghost. Why keep it from me any longer?"

Ivin sat in the chair opposite him. "When I married her, I was not the man you know today. I was young and foolhardy, and I made a mistake in marrying the girl who came out of nowhere."

"Who was she?"

"I cannot tell you. You are too close. You are a knight, Roland. Champion of Rieux. Betrothed to Lady Amarys. You have achieved all that we could have ever wanted."

Roland rose from the chair, ambling upstairs. Pausing between weak attempts to climb one stair at a time, he said, "I killed my friend. I led my twin to her death. And I traded true love for an heiress's coin. Is that what you wanted?"

Ivin did not answer.

"I thought so," said Roland, continuing his climb.

It would have been easy to sink into his cups and stew in the depths of anger and self-loathing, but Roland had no will to escape his suffering. He refused all food. He spent his days near the place where Rowen had perished. He walked the grounds where he had spilled Erec's blood. He spoke to their phantoms, begging forgiveness that never came.

His beard grew haggard and long. His frame waned, and his cheeks became sallow and gaunt. After a month, his clothes—like his skin—hung from his bones to the effect that people no longer recognized him. His own servants would turn him away from his own door, assuming he was a beggar. He would start to go without objection, until they would see their mistake and bring him inside.

After several boisterous attempts, Ivin gave up on trying to reach his son. Roland did not respond to his father's verbal assaults, and any sort of clout would have broken right through his knobby limbs.

Roland had become a body without a spirit. In the way he had withdrawn from

God, he withdrew from all the world. Even his grandmother could not reach him. Cecile had no idea what had really happened, as no one would tell her. They kept her confined from the truth, and as much as she asked about her granddaughter, all anybody would say was that she was gone and would not be coming back.

"Who will finish the tapestry?" Cecile had asked. "I will not finish it in time."

Lies and strange stories filled the town. They said Rowen had committed suicide. She may as well have, thought Roland, for his father had told him—with an heir of righteousness—that Rowen had been sent off on a corpse wagon to be buried next to dogs and thieves. Unhallowed. Unmarked. Unwritten.

"Poor creature," gossiped the women at the well, not knowing it was Roland loitering nearby. "They say she and Erec were secretly betrothed. That is why Roland sought him out in the tourney. Erec was a second son, and the family did not approve. When her brother slew her love, Rowen could not live with her grief."

Roland mustered what little strength he had to stand. "Lies!" he cried. The women turned, several of them carrying their water away in fright. "Erec was my friend!" he roared, snatching away the woman's bucket and slamming it so it broke into splinters. "You know nothing! You shut your mouths, you stupid fools!"

A gentle hand touched his bony shoulder. Through tears, he could see the familiar look of concern. Cateline held him and told the women, "What happened in the tourney was an accident."

The women backed away cautiously as Cat led Roland away from the scene. He was weak and struggled to walk for very long before leaning into her.

"Roland, what has happened to you?" A whimper escaped her lips as Roland collapsed against her. She assisted him back to Lechón Tavern, where she had him lie on the pallet behind the bar.

He must have fallen asleep, for he soon stirred to the savory aroma of stew and spices. Cat and her mother worked over a bubbling cauldron, bickering softly over what it lacked and what would help Roland recover best. Marrow, they finally agreed.

Roland felt a cup at his lips. "No," he whispered, turning his head.

"It's either going in your mouth or over your face."

Too feeble to get up and go, Roland submitted and drank the broth. His headache subsided, and his body craved more. He reached for the bowl, but Cat drew it away.

"Uh uh uh," she tutted. "Too fast, and you'll make yourself sick."

"Why are you helping me?"

"I would help anyone in such a strait."

For the next few days, Roland lived there at the tavern, sleeping next to Cat in her room. She cared for him and brought him liquid meals to break his fast gently. The first few days, he could barely hold a conversation with her, but on Sunday, he was well enough to go with her and her mother to church. People whispered, but Cat seemed not to care. She wanted him to get well. Most days he just stared up at the wood ceiling, tracing the tree rings with his mind. But the tavern girl never gave up on him.

One day, one of Clement's servants visited to inquire about Roland's situation.

"He is grieving. Only time can heal this wound." Roland could hear Cat's voice through the wall, but the messenger was more soft-spoken. "He will be well enough to marry your master's daughter in the Spring, but you must entrust his care to us. Your doctors will not do him any good. This is a malady of the heart, and its only cure is the company of his kin. Now, return to the Baron and leave us be."

Roland pulled his bedcover over his head, cozying into the rare feeling of comfort he had always found in this place. They really were his kin. Hearing those words come out of Cat had its own curative effect. The next time she came in to bring him a cup of soup, he gave her the ring from his father.

"I want you to have this," he said, placing it loosely on her finger. "You will sell it and use the money for whatever you like. You have been so good to me, though I am completely undeserving."

"Stop," she said, setting the wood tray beside him on the mattress. "I do not want your money."

"I will pay for room and board. I will not take it back. Throw it into the sea if you are too proud."

Cat sighed, tucking the ring in her apron pocket. "Why did you do it, Roland? Why did you try to follow your sister to the grave?"

Roland blew over the surface of his broth. Its steam emitted a heavy, earthy aroma. "Living without her is like living without my soul."

"Has anyone ever told you how my father died?"

Roland was embarrassed that he had never asked. He always assumed Cat had been born out of wedlock and avoided the topic of her father as a courtesy.

"He took his own life. Like Rowen. He could not afford the Baron's taxes, and he knew we would not survive the winter with what little grain we had, so he hanged himself from a rafter in the cellar. Mother says it was an act of love, dying so we might live." Cat blinked back tears, swallowing. "Can you believe he thought himself of so little worth to us? I felt pangs of guilt for every ration I took, every morsel of food that my father died for. I had to eat when I could not bear to eat because if I starved, my father's death would be for nothing."

"Rowen did not die so I could live."

"That is beside the point. My point is that Mother and I got through it. And we got through it when in the Spring, the Baron had us removed from our home. He seized our assets as recompense for the loss of his miller. With nothing more than a pot and a head full of knowledge, Mother began brewing. She pulled us out of poverty with her labors. I am proud to call myself her daughter. Whereas your maid of Rieux should die of shame for her father's cruelty."

"Cat," said Roland. "Had I not sworn to Rowen that I would marry Amarys, I would forsake her in an instant."

"I do not fault the daughter for the sins of her father."

He owed it to her now to tell her the truth. After swearing her to secrecy, he revealed every last part of his sister's story, from her love for Amarys to her masquerading as him in the tourney.

Cat listened without judgment. It softened her anger toward Amarys to know that she had lost as much as anyone. When Cat understood that Roland had truly never planned to consummate his marriage, she began to forgive him. He could not forgive himself, though, for he was still condemned for the death of his friend.

"His death was not your fault," she told him.

"Still, he is gone, and I remain. How can I balance the scale?"

"The scale was balanced when you lost your sister."

"No, that was the price she paid for Harlowe. They took each other's lives, while I, on the other hand, killed a man and walked away with everything! I should be dead, too! I should be with Rowen!"

Cat held his shoulders. Roland took a deep breath, calming all that raged within him.

As days passed, Clement sent more servants to inquire about Roland's health. He finally got strong enough to send them away himself.

Then, one day, a letter from his father came. It had been penned in Latin. It read:

My son,

I will tell you who your mother was. As you know, she was called Saffiya, and for the final year of her life, she lived with your grandmother in Antioch. I neglected to tell you how we met.

After suffering great losses in the Battle of Hattin, our scattered forces retreated to Tyre. The men under my command came upon a troupe of entertainers out of Damascus. They offered us stories and wine in exchange for protection, which we accepted. Saffiya emerged, playing her strings, singing her pretty songs in Saracinois. Her voice entranced us. For the duration of her song, we were all enthralled.

When her performance ended, my men felt it was owed to them to enjoy her. She tried to refuse their advances, but the men would not relent. I ordered them to let her go. They did not listen. Our pact with the jongleurs was broken, and there was something about this particular injustice—this particular woman—that broke through my loyalty to the Order. Perhaps, after witnessing such incredible cowardice and defeat at Hattin, I had lost faith in my men. I slew the bastard who was close to having Saffiya. I abducted her and fled.

We returned to my home in Antioch. I did all I could to help her feel safe. It took many weeks for her to trust that I would not harm her. I remember that it surprised her when I spoke to her in her own tongue. This language was the bridge that eventually brought us together.

Saffiya was the daughter of a court physician, a Jewess who had abandoned wealth and privilege to pursue her love for music. She had betrayed her family, and she could not go home. Her real family was the band of entertainers that had perished in the skirmish with my men. I took it upon myself to protect her until she found another troupe, and as time passed, we fell in love.

Living together with this woman, learning her stories and songs, I gave my whole heart to her, and she, in turn, converted to Christianity and became my wife. We lived quietly together in Antioch, praying my men would not seek me out for the treachery I had done. For years, I believed they had all died, as many of our forces did following the fall of Jerusalem.

Around the time that Saffiya passed away, those men came looking for me, and that is why I abandoned you and Rowen for so many years. At least, that was the reason at first. I stayed on with King Richard because he inspired me to love the Order again.

You must forgive me if I embellished or obscured your mother's history. I did not want for you to think of her as a jongleur or vagabond, nor to think of yourself as anything less than the heir to our family's great legacy. You have always demonstrated her talent for music, and after seeing you so despondent for so many months, I thought it might revive you to know who you truly are. You are both my son and hers. You are a Christian and a Jew, a Breton and a Turk. You were born to wander, to sing the songs of distant lands, to fight for a better world, and to preserve peace.

After losing Saffiya, I lost sight of what she would have wanted. I cared more for duty than my own children. Only now do I begin to remember what should have always mattered.

Come home, my son. And I will tell you everything.

After reading his father's letter, Roland asked Cateline to bring him his lute. Tuning it and practicing scales each day seemed to steady him and remind him who he was.

"There lived a noble bard, and he loved a lady fair," he sang from his bed. "His head was full of wool, and his lady didn't care." It brought real joy for Cat and Lisette to hear their bard returning to his old self. Roland's fingers quickened the melody and wove down familiar paths. Cat and Lisette began to dance, spinning and jumping around each other in a circle.

Through his songs, Roland found his love of life again, even when he played laments. He composed a canso. He did not have a name for it or any words to express all that he was missing, but playing its sad and lilting melody helped him feel closer to the half of himself that was missing. The song became a favorite in town.

Music and the company of friends began to heal his broken heart. In composing and playing music, he found his way toward a kind of forgiveness. He forgave his father. He forgave Rowen. And, with the utmost difficulty, he forgave himself.

A man without a soul,
a wandering troubadour
will take to the sea
and search every shore.

Noon and night, the tavern bustled with patrons, many townsfolk eager to hear the son of Rieux sing and play. During his matinee, Roland spied an unexpected spectator. Cat did not look happy to see Amarys, maid of Rieux, presenting herself at Lechón Tavern. She arrived in the company of Sir Guyon and her Nurse. Roland stopped playing in the middle of his song, announcing to his audience, "My betrothed, everyone. Well, it was nice knowing you."

The patrons laughed. Roland came down the stairs of the stage to meet her. She was standing in a compact posture in the middle of the tables, eyeing her environs suspiciously. With her hands folded and her gaze brazenly set on Roland's face, she addressed him.

"Do you no longer wish to marry?"

Roland pulled her away from the center of the action. He asked her Nurse, "May I be left alone with my betrothed to speak plainly?"

The Nurse scowled, shaking her head with a stern motion.

"Please. You may stand watch."

"Stay where we can see you," said the Nurse.

Roland led Amarys to a dining nook where the sound was quite insulated. The murmur of the crowd provided some additional noise dampening. They sat on either side of a table, him leaning forward and her folded up like a swan.

"There is a rumor," she explained. "They say Roland lies with a tavern girl who wears his ring on a chain 'round her neck. I do not know what to believe, but if you do not wish to marry me, will you please explain that to my father?"

"There is no affair," he said plainly. "Crush any rumor with truth. Cat is caring for me in my grief."

"I only wish to preserve my dignity." She looked away abruptly. "My God. You have the same eyes as Rowen."

Roland flinched and looked away. "I never meant to take your dignity. I intend to fulfill my sister's dying wish."

"I release you from your promise."

Roland felt his shoulders tightening. "Only she can release me from it."

Amarys leaned in. "No, Roland! She is dead! I am the one being married! Why should we fulfill a promise made in grief? I was never included in the discussion of my own fate. You should have told me what Rowen was planning. I knew nothing until it was too late to stop her. I could have helped you."

Upon this, she stood. How she shone like a crystal in the sun. Something about this woman in all her vicious glory made Roland feel more cleansed than he had after any confession. Her words struck like arrows made of lead, and Roland wanted more.

He snatched her wrist, urging her, "Stay."

"Unhand me."

"I beg of you, cruel goddess, lay on me again."

"Excuse me?"

"It is well known how the wicked crave God's punishment. Assail me with your tongue's sweet venom, for everything you say is true."

"You want me to insult you further?"

"With all my heart."

"This I can oblige," she said, returning to her seat. Softly but with intensity, she railed against him. "You knew this sport was deadly, and you gave your sister, a woman with barely any training, total access to your horse and armor. Still, even with her inexperience, she surpassed you in skill. Clumsy, lazy, drunk fool that you are. Had you actually attended your lessons with Sir Edmund or any of the knights your privilege bought you, you might have acquired the finesse to win the tournament yourself. You might have even spared Sir Erec in the melee. But no, like a careless knave, you flung yourself at him and broke his neck. And the people loved you for it! Roland, son of Rieux! Let us give him a tourney crown he did not earn, a woman he does not love, and the Barony for him to neglect. Oh, rose of chivalry. Valiant Sir Roland."

For the first time since his sister's death, he felt something besides grief. It was hunger. Raw, all-consuming hunger for the abuse of this ruthless harpy.

"Finally, someone who hates me as much as I hate myself," he said. He tried to kiss her. Before he could, she touched his chin, her breath catching against his. "Roland."

"Do not relent now. You were doing so well."

"There is no justice in this. I am so sorry."

"No. Do not apologize," he said. "Everything you say is true."

Amarys looked to see if her Nurse saw them touch. They were just beyond her chaperone's line of sight, and now, the Nurse was drinking ale with Lisette.

"Did it really help?" asked Amarys.

"It did. I am in your debt."

"Will you return the favor? Call me what I am."

"You are sure? I will not hold back."

"Lay on." The words taking shape upon her rose-colored lips made him ache for her. It was enraging to find himself so allured by the woman who had wrought his present misery.

He tried his hand at her cruel craft. "I am not now, nor have I ever been convinced that you are any of the things my sister said you were. She said you were clever and kind and noble." He touched Amarys's throat with the tip of his middle finger. Amarys swallowed. She blinked, flinching a little but letting him go ahead. "I find you to be conceited, childish, hopelessly immoral. And I seem to be the only one who sees what everyone else ignores."

"Is that the best you can do?"

"You were drawn to my sister's innocence."

"I loved her."

"You? Love? No. Not Amarys, always flirting. You love to be desired, to make others jealous. You made Rowen doubt herself when you kissed me at the melee. That is why she placed your hand in mine as she was dying. You used her. You took a pious, kind, and quiet girl, and you turned her into your agent of violence as you passed your quarrel with your cousin onto her. Most people look at you, and they see only an ornament, a pretty heiress to be wooed and won. For this reason, you think yourself immune to others' judgment. But when I look at you, I have always seen beyond the mask. And you might be the most evil she-wolf I have ever met."

He was better at this work than he thought. Amarys broke eye contact. Her body went as still as marble.

"I am sorry," he appended. "I spoke to wound."

"No, Roland. I am grateful. You see me for what Fortune has made me."

She had never been so vulnerable with him before. It was stunning.

"What has Fortune made you?"

"Your wife? Someone else's? Fortune has no place for girls like me outside of marriage. I cannot read or fight or do much of anything. Perhaps this is why you have always hated me—"

"Amarys—"

Her eyes rejoined him. Before he could refute her, she went on, "—but if I had the choice, Roland, I would choose you—not just for your promise to let me live how I like—but because you have so much you can teach me—I..." She stopped, her lips drawing shut. The glacial semblance of control hardened her face. First vulnerable, now afraid, this Amarys was unknown to him, but her longings were a currency with which he was well-acquainted. "Do not doubt that I loved her."

"You should not care what I think."

"I did love her."

"I know."

"But I wanted you."

"I know."

He hated that she had said it, but he could not fault her for trying to bridge the gulf between them.

They stared down at the table, their whispers softer than anyone could hear. "I must tell you something before you commit yourself to me. My mother was a Jewess. It must never be made known. I am only telling you because I want you to know what you risk in marrying me."

She nodded. "You will have to tell me the story behind that one day. It changes nothing."

"You are impossibly tranquil over this. You do not need any time at all to come to terms?"

"No. You are the only man who can give me a child with her face. I will marry no other."

CHAPTER 31

Everything hurt. There was a wheelbarrow. A stench of meat and excrement. A cloaked figure pulled back his hood to show that he was missing his head. Edmund? No. The head was there, after all, his eyes as red as molten steel. Wrong champion. It was the Ankou. Or was it Erec?

For a long time, all Rowen knew was darkness mingled with agony. Is this damnation? She fancied, for a moment, that she had become a field of thorns sprawling across a meadow. Like serpentine vines, she would cover heaths and craggy cliff sides, prickling the globe. Nettle and hawthorn seemed to twist through her bones, reclaiming all that flesh that raged against the very language that defined it: girl, child, insignificant, frail, weak, thing. Her soul seemed to vanish amidst the ooze of words.

"Is this a dream?" Her whisper was like the freezing wind through the underworld, hollow and thin.

"Shhh." An ancient man pressed a finger to his lip, coming into the light of a candle. She could see his forehead was heavily marred with the shape of the crucifix, a crimson cross edged in scar tissue. "Save your strength."

Rowen closed her eyes. She imagined Amarys still cradling her face with her hands, kissing her eyebrows, her eyelids, her cheeks, and her mouth.

"Where are you, my love?" she moaned deliriously.

"You're close to death, my child. Be tranquil."

"Are you an angel?" she asked, half to Amarys and half to the creature looming over her.

"I am no angel. And you are beyond saving. That you are speaking now is nothing short of a miracle."

His breath tasted like metal and something so sweet it was rancid. He sorted his surgical instruments on the table beside her. She could hear them scraping and clicketing against the wood.

"What are you doing with those?"

"You were bound for a pauper's grave, but the undertaker brought you here."

"To what end?" she asked.

"That I might understand the human anatomy. I pay for bodies. They don't usually wake up and talk to me. God must have some reason for granting you this last repose. Have you a sin to confess?"

"Too many to count."

"I could fetch a priest that you might be absolved."

"Do not bother. I am the devil's creature."

"Ah, well, you would probably be dead by the time I fetched him. Your ribs are broken. One of them punctured your lung. You had a hunk of rock shoved mere pouces from your heart."

"Is it still there?"

"No. I removed it. Consider it my payment for winning you this last chance to appeal to God."

"Please. I wanted to be buried with that stone."

"Let's hear your confession first."

Rowen winced, too weak to fight him. "Very well," she said. "I corrupted earth's most perfect flower. I lay with a woman and knew her fully. I lured a good man to his death and murdered another in cold blood. Give me up to the soil. I am undeserving of your medicine."

The physician ignored her and proceeded to apply dense mud to the seams of her wounds. "It is not my place to judge, and since you are alive, I must do all that I can to help."

Rowen felt weak in the chest. She could hardly bring herself to speak again.

The stranger told her the story of his life. He was the son of a Benedictine monk and a woman whose circumstances brought her to relinquish him to his father's monastery. At the age of fourteen, he went to Salerno to study medicine. There, he treated pilgrims and soldiers of Christ, eventually joining the Order of the Bloodcross Knights and bringing his knowledge of medicine to the battlefield. Recently, he had returned home to impart his medical knowledge to the monks who raised him. He lived in the forest, though, on the edge of town, a place where he could conduct his experiments with some privacy. He was a learned man in possession of a great many medical texts, some of which he was gifted so he might extend his knowledge to other physics. His name was Bartholomew. And he said he was very pleased that he had been granted the chance to talk to a woman who might have been in the earth without his intervention.

"Is my prattle a nuisance? Should I stop?" he asked.

Rowen's whisper scraped like fingernails on stone, "Not at all."

Bartholomew described how she was when the undertaker brought her. Upon examining her, he quickly realized she was just barely alive, breathing very faintly, her heartbeat so dim it would have been undetectable to an untrained ear. Never had he seen anyone survive wounds like hers, but for the purpose of learning and because he felt it his duty to do all that he could, he attempted to save her. He washed the gore from her wounds and pulled out two of her ribs...

"As though ye were Adam," he said. Then he stitched her up like an old boot and had been treating her with a medicinal balm used by physicians in Salerno.

"God will have to do the rest," he said. "You will be weak for a long time, and you will need to wear a brace to compensate for the bones I took out."

"I must survive," she whispered, careful to take slow, shallow breaths that did not cause her ribs to expand too much.

The physician cared for Rowen throughout her period of healing, which was much longer and more trying than she could have imagined. His dwelling consisted of a single room with a hole in the ceiling to vent the fire. It was large, but there was nowhere to sleep except in his bed. He was building a platform for her... slowly. As much as she wanted to speed him along, she was not ready to help with the build or much of anything, really. She could barely crawl from his bed to the hearth to fill her clay bowl with broth. Between the choice of his bed and the dissection table, she didn't mind sleeping next to a stranger.

She would not tell him her name for fear that he might inform her father how to find her. She claimed not to remember.

Each breath made her chest feel like it was full of thistles. Even eating was difficult to endure. She had to force herself, swallowing one bite at a time in the interest of healing. She asked Bartholomew to take a letter to a man named Willem, which he tucked into a saddle bag before setting out for supplies.

Rowen had covertly asked Willem to "send her brother straightaway," careful not to use any names or details that Bartholomew might use to solve the mystery of her identity. She expected Roland would arrive any day for her. Each passing hour spent waiting for the arrival of his response or his presence itself filled her mind with worry and dread. Had something happened to him? Had her father intercepted her message? When a month passed with no reply, she pressed Bartholomew for details.

"What became of the letter I gave you?" she asked, tearing a piece of bread from the iron spike nestled against the fire. "Are you certain you put it in Willem's hands?"

"You must forgive me."

"Oh no. To whom did you give it? A servant?"

"No."

Bartholomew told her he had not sent the letter at all, and would not, until she told him her name and explained what kind of trouble she was in. Initially, Rowen's condition had indicated she would not survive the week, but now that many weeks progressed and she continued to improve, Bartholomew wanted to be certain he could trust her before he went delivering messages to noblemen in Rieux.

"Go on, child. Let's start with your name."

Rowen chewed her broth-infused crust and swallowed hard. "I told you. I don't remember."

"Do not lie to me. When you first spoke to me, you listed a number of sins on your head. You remember those well enough."

Bartholomew had proven himself to be pure of intention and as having her best interest at heart. Though she could not imagine him revealing her to her father against her wishes, she still resisted coming forth with her name. She no longer wished to be called by that silly name, the name that cast her as being any less than Roland. Going forward, she wanted to be christened anew. What name to take, she wondered.

"Explain why you were bound for an unmarked grave. I only need to know that you will not steal from me or cut my throat in the night. How else can I let you stay here?"

Rowen rubbed the soot from her eyes. "I am no criminal."

"You are a sinner, though, as you said yourself."

"I loved someone," said Rowen. "I murdered the man who would have married and abused her. I am not a thief nor an outlaw."

Bartholomew sighed. "To think you nearly died with such a sin on your head." He stared at her, his eyes like dew-laden poppies. "God spared you... that you might cleanse your soul of this sin. Do you still refuse to see the priest?"

Rowen looked away, her jaw clenching as she adjusted on her stool. "No priest would absolve me. I cannot be anything but what God made me. Even if I confess, these feelings will never go away."

Bartholomew shook his head as a firelit grin broke across his face. "We all have thoughts we wish we did not. God made you the way you are for a reason, perhaps to test you."

"I have had these conversations in my own mind a thousand times. There is no helping me. I am a monster."

As winter dragged on, Rowen heard news of the wedding between Roland and Amarys. It would be better, she thought, for Amarys to go through with it. She was not like Rowen. She could love men as well as women, and she had been very fond of Roland in the beginning, even if it was mostly just the idea of Roland that enthralled her. If Amarys could be saved, Rowen knew she should let it be so. If Amarys were married and content, perhaps Rowen could remove the temptation to sin with her again.

Asceticism helped to wash away her longings. Far from the comforts of her father's house, Rowen learned what it was like to be poor. Upon finishing her bed,

Bartholomew covered the frame with a mattress stuffed with straw and rags. Was this really her life now? The scarcity of food and warmth was harder than she had ever imagined. Day after day, it continued to weaken her body and fog her mind. Bartholomew never had any meat, and most days, they filled their bellies with runny pottage and meager rations of onion and broad beans.

Their clothing always stank of smoke and soot from the fire. It made Rowen's hair and skin feel dry and dirty. For a time, her lips became inflamed from dehydration, burning when she licked them. There were no servants to draw a bath, no basins of cool water except those she filled herself. And in her recovery, she was too weak to carry water back from the pump. Simply walking more than a few strides could leave her out of breath.

She relied heavily on Bartholomew's labor. The man was kind, but he was also old and had his limitations. Still, he had the benefit of his medical knowledge. He made a balm for her lips. He taught her simple habits of keeping clean, covering her hair with a coif, brushing the soot from her clothing with a boar's bristle brush, and washing her hands frequently and before every meal.

The two of them shared many conversations as they prepared food or cleaned together. Rowen was getting stronger, and Bartholomew began to give her more responsibilities, like mixing teas and medicines or bringing wood for the fire. One day, the wood was too much for her. Though it had not snowed in weeks, the earth was still frozen. The cold went right through the soles of her thin shoes. The pads of her feet burned with frostbite. She was close to their hut when her legs collapsed beneath her. Her bundle of sticks went everywhere, and her ribs ached too much to lean over and gather them up again. That's when the tears came. Rowen felt the overwhelming impact of how far she had fallen.

She missed her grandmother, and it broke her heart knowing she would never complete the tapestry. She missed her brother, too, and her remorse for Erec's death still gnawed at her. She should have missed her father, but she was still angry with him for too many things. Her memories of the joy she shared with Amarys were mingled with incredible shame. Though in her heart she knew it was better for them to never meet again, she still wished she could hear her beloved's laugh just one more time. She wished she could hold her and feel the softness of her cheek against her own.

Bartholomew came running out of the hut. He gathered up the sticks, tucked the bundle under one arm, and helped Rowen to her feet with the other. It was absurd, an old man assisting a young woman in such a way, but her pride buckled under the weight of necessity.

The physic brought her inside where she collapsed to the floor near the fire. He gave her a clean towel to dry her tears and laid a consoling hand on her shoulder. "There, child. You will get your strength back in the Spring."

"I used to think I was a warrior. Now, I am nothing."

"Oh, just wait, child." Bartholomew laughed gently, patting her shoulder as if to snap her from these dark meditations. "We are not creatures of our own design! We do not pen our own stories. That duty belongs to God alone. And in the mind of Providence, our stories have a purpose we will never live to comprehend, but faith compels us forward. Into the unknown! Into the pain! Into the loss of all our vanities! Embrace your new life, girl. I know everything looks bleak in winter, but I have lived to see enough Spring-times to know a person's life can change in a moment."

"How can I begin to believe in this life when I have lost everyone and everything I fought for?"

"God brought us together for a reason; I am sure of it. Nothing heals a broken heart better than a new horizon."

Maybe the old man was right about God having a plan for her, but Rowen could not begin to look forward to a world without the people who mattered most to her. How could she live without her brother? Who even was she without him?

When she could not sleep because of the cold or the bites on her ankles from bugs in her straw, she imagined herself with Amarys. She would talk to her love in whispers, talk to her for hours until she fell asleep. She made bundles of tansy and lavender to repel insects, and those reminded her of Amarys, too. Sometimes, in the morning, she would pen letters to her brother with excerpts he should read aloud to Amarys, but she always burned them before the day was through.

Save her, she kept telling herself. You promised to save her, not condemn her. Choose pietas, that profound duty owed to the divine that places the whole of the world before the desires of the flesh. No matter how many times she considered what course of action to take, Rowen knew she had to speak to Amarys before the wedding. To let it go ahead while she yet lived would be the ultimate betrayal.

One evening, Rowen found Bartholomew in his surgery, where a human carcass lay stretched on the table. Rowen surveyed his coarse features, his wrinkled brow, his black beard, and his abundance of hair. "Who is he?"

"An outlaw."

"A bit young, no?"

"Pity."

Rowen could smell the contents of the man's intestines mingling with the scent of herbs and wax. With steady hands, Bartholomew made a precise incision down the center of the man's breastbone, opening the chest cavity to show Rowen what lay beneath. She saw the placement of the heart, the lungs, the stomach, and many other organs she knew even less about. Bartholomew described different wounds she might see on the battlefield, different ways of assessing who could be treated and who should be left for carrion. With each incision, he illuminated new secrets of the flesh.

"What a liver!" cried Bartholomew, pulling out a lobe full of scars. "This man died of rotgut!"

"How do you know?"

"Do you have a better theory? Tell me! That is part of the fun."

When he was done examining the body's organs, Bartholomew asked Rowen to sew the man up. He commended her for her even stitches.

"We must name you," he said. "I cannot go on calling you 'child.'"

Rowen nodded, washing her hands in the nearby basin. "Long ago, my grandmother told me my name might one day be all I possessed. Now, it is true. You have given me so much, and if my name is all I have to repay you, I will give it willingly. I am Rowen La Flèche-de Beaugency, Sir Ivin's daughter who is presumed dead."

Bartholomew smiled. "I learned your name months ago, Rowen." He retrieved something from his pocket. Rowen's eyes flickered in astonishment when she saw the garnet pendant catch the light.

"My necklace! I thought you sold it."

"No. I kept it for you."

"But this was your payment for saving my life."

"Your honesty is worth more to me than any coin."

As winter receded and the warm sun returned, Rowen found herself waking each morning with renewed feelings of hope and radiance. She began talking to the people at the market, people she would have never met before, much less spoken to. Interacting with them challenged her perspective on peasants and, by extension, her perspective of the world. She had always thought women like her maid Anna had dull, unimaginative minds and weren't worth her time. But seeing the people at the market and trading wool for bread and eggs revealed a very different truth. They talked about all kinds of interesting things, their tricks for trapping birds, spices one could sprinkle on an herb garden to deter rabbits, and secret places where wild blackberries grew. The mothers knew how to wrap babies to their backs in a way that would make them nap in the afternoon. A milkmaid knew the herbs that would ease the pain of monthly courses as well as those that would reduce bleeding.

The world of their knowledge astounded Rowen, and she looked forward to her conversations with the farmers who foraged most of their nutrition in the wild. These people laughed and teased and enjoyed their lives. They were clever. They sang songs. The young people climbed trees and buildings and would chase each other for fun, leaping over branches or beams as easily as running across an open field. An old woman whittled animals for the young ones, telling them stories about each creature, where it made its dwelling, and what plants it found distasteful.

It made Rowen wish she had been closer to her servants and made more of an effort to get to know them and ask questions about their lives. But more critically, it made her realize there was a great world beyond the scope of her understanding, people with knowledge to impart, and distant places that could reveal the myriad ways that people worshiped, loved, and lived. As much as she wanted to face her loved ones and reveal herself, she let the days slip away, always questioning whether this was the right course of action.

At last, the wedding day arrived. Rowen was no closer to knowing what she wanted. Some spirit animated her. Perhaps it was God. She covered herself in a hood and moved in the direction of the chateau. On her journey, which she made on foot in sole-worn shoes, she considered how she would approach her love and what she would say.

"Amarys. I did not die. I did not know how to tell you, but I am here now. I will go anywhere with you. If not, I will become a healer and seek God's forgiveness."

Perhaps Amarys would be unreachable. If she could only find her brother, she would beg him to help her one last time.

The wedding festivities were open to the people of Rieux. The servants bustled through the corridors as they carted and carried platters of food to the great hall. They draped fantastically long table runners, intricately woven tapestries depicting notorious lovers of myth and legend. Bowls of halved pomegranates and small platters piled with honey-dipped apples adorned every table. Pitchers of wine were carried to the tables in preparation for the great feast. Rowen followed the lull of the holy choir singing in the chapel. It resonated on a higher plane. As if it had been orchestrated by angels, Amarys came through the hall.

Dressed in a gown of rose-colored silk with gold lattice overlay on the sleeves, she held the hands of both her sisters. She was crowned with emeralds and pearls, and her hair was tightly bound in the same gold net containing her forearms. Rowen was dressed in men's clothing, her mantle affording her a disguise. She had nabbed a pitcher of wine to drink, and when she passed Amarys, she looked no different from any other wedding guest.

Amarys wore a long string of pearls wrapped twice about her neck, her cross shimmering against her breastbone. Her soft eyes and the sweet, forlorn expression written deep within them transfixed Rowen so entirely that she forgot to call out to her as she passed. She followed her to the entrance of the chapel, watching helplessly as Amarys greeted her guests. Roland, meanwhile, came in beside her and brandished a lute.

He played a song from Toulouse, one that he had learned when he lived there.

Amarys filled the hall with her sweet voice. Roland joined in, his tenor complementing her with a haunting cadence. Rowen listened long to the pull of that serene song, her heart breaking with every note.

They were beautiful together. Everyone could see it, and soon, every cheek was stained with tears. When had it happened? Had she stayed away too long? Their performance revealed a bond formed over many nights of practicing and perfecting the harmony. Amarys was nervous at first, but as she looked into Roland's eyes, the tremor in her voice eased. His subtle smile showed how charmed he was by his little bride.

Rowen slipped away. She staggered into the study, her chest aching as though it had been crushed with a hammer. The world was spinning. Heavy tapestries depicting griffins and dragons whirled in a menacing attack. She jostled a chess table that was midway through a game. Its enamel armies tipped, but she caught the table before throwing them over.

The door opened behind her. The voices of ladies followed. Rowen concealed herself behind a heavy curtain, covering her own mouth with her hands. Amarys and her sister Beatrice came in, shutting the door and giggling together.

Beatrice spoke first. "You are so lucky! To marry a man who sings like Orpheus and fights like Achilles!"

Rowen could not see them through the curtain, but the hesitation in Amarys's response gave her hope. "Come here, Bea. When you come of age, I promise, your fate will not be determined by a silly tournament."

"My heart will always ache for Sir Erec," said Bea, a twinge of true sorrow shaping her tone.

"He was the best of knights. Promised to the best of ladies."

"Does Roland still blame himself?" Their voices went so low that Rowen could not hear them at all. Then, they came closer to the window, just within earshot.

"Yes," she whispered. "Let us not speak of dreary subjects on a day of celebration."

"You are happy with your match? No?"

Rowen's stomach turned. She thought she should reveal her presence at once, but what Amarys said next snuffed that impulse entirely.

"I have loved him for a very long time," she confided. "He felt the same, though he pretended not to." Her and her sister's voices faded as they returned to the hall.

Rowen's legs might as well have been made of straw. They could not hold. She went down, curling over her knees and smothering her face with her cloak.

She had been willing to die to free Amarys, willing to let her brother die. And all this time, Amarys had loved Roland. Truly. Deeply. Shutting her eyes, Rowen mourned the loss of the life she had sacrificed.

The voice of Father Gerard echoed through the castle walls as he spoke of matrimony and God's will for man and wife. Unable to bear it, Rowen crawled out from behind the curtain. Wrath supplanted sorrow. At a lectern, she flung piles of unbound folios across the floor. In her anger, she wished Bartholomew had let her die.

On a round marble surface near the door, she found a prayer book and a statuette of Saint Lazarus. She took the garnet pendant and wrapped the chain around the idol's throat.

"Saint Lazarus, who conquers Death, convey my message. I am alive, but I am no longer hers, and she, no longer mine."

Rowen would not hear the vows. She would not say goodbye. Outside, the sky dulled to an amber hue as the sun sank on the horizon. She had every intention to leave as quickly as possible, but as she traversed the courtyard, she discovered something completely unexpected. Her horse.

Biax was hitched to the well, his silvery mane decorated with violets and red ribbon. He was attended by a pair of peasant girls who were weaving the remainder of their flowers into fairy crowns.

Rowen was much too dirty to pass for a servant, which might have allowed her to lead her horse away without frightening the girls.

There was only one way to go about it. She approached Biax head-on, sliding her palm down his velvety nose.

Bold as a chevalier, she swung herself onto her horse's back. "Ya!" she shouted, kicking Biax into a leap for freedom.

The girls screamed, scattering petals as they ran. Rowen leaned into Biax's quickening flight, her heart pounding in her throat as they galloped beyond the portcullis.

As they charged across the meadow, Rowen pulled the flowers from Biax's mane and cast them away. They floated behind in a swirl of color.

"Can you feel the wind, Biax?" She laughed, wiping the tears from her eyes. "We are the wind."

CHAPTER 32

A wedding should have been a day of pleasure and beauty that one could hold like baubles in one's heart for a lifetime, but Amarys hardly took any account of the roses adorning every table or the abundance of candles that glittered like stars. The music of the minstrel's dulcimer only made her sicken with remembrance of the one she had lost. And as it came time for her and Roland to go to their marital bower, they both adopted a serious countenance.

One of the bedchambers had been decorated for them, a room large enough to host fifty or more witnesses. Its elaborate rug, woven of red and yellow wool, came from Antioch. Bed curtains of sheer gauze contained an immense mattress upon which a scattering of rose petals resembled blood.

Father Gerard blessed the bed. The servants undressed man and wife, removing all but their crowns of flowers and draping their wedding garments gently over a bench. The unsettling presence of their families was enough to persuade them into bed together, where they performed their duty quickly and without noise.

When everyone except a single servant was gone, Roland and Amarys just lay there in the stew of their mutual violation, staring through the bed canopy at the ceiling.

"I promised her I would never lie with you," he said.

"I think she has released you from that promise," returned Amarys.

They listened to the chambermaid putting things away and settling in to sleep upon the pallet on the floor.

"Did it hurt?" he whispered.

"A little."

"I have been with others, you know."

"So have I," said Amarys. "I played the virgin well, though, did I not?"

Before he could answer, Amarys put a finger to her lips. She sat up, slipped between the bedcurtains, and went to the bench holding their wedding clothes.

The servant dozed silently on the floor, unaware as Amarys retrieved Roland's lapis lazuli. It was as heavy as a river stone. Even in the dark, where the only light came from a dwindling candle, the lapis burned with blue heat.

Amarys returned to her husband, toting the chamberstick so he could see she had taken the lapis. Roland blinked rapidly as she straddled him and held her candle between them.

He looked similar to Rowen. They had the same forehead, cheekbones, and lips. Amarys had always found him beautiful. How many years would she gaze upon his face and be able to remember the softer, lovelier Rowen that had lived? Ten? Twenty? Would she or Roland even live that long?

Now that she could see him, he could see her too, and his eyes went immediately to the stone that fell just above her navel.

"You cannot keep it," he said.

"Why not? You get to keep me."

Roland ran a thumb from her ribcage to the crease at her hip, where his fingers opened and trailed ribbons down her thigh. Amarys felt her blood come alive at his touch.

She tipped the chamberstick, spilling a line of wax over his chest.

Roland inhaled through his teeth.

"That is how it felt for me," she said. "On each thrust."

He pressed his lips, biting back a moan as she dribbled another bit of wax on him. "I tried to be gentle."

"I wish you hadn't."

Roland's lips parted with the whisper of a smile. He blew out her candle. The hiss of bedlinens accompanied a loud clattering sound as the brass chamberstick tumbled. Roland bit her neck, pulling her skin between his teeth. Flecks of hardened wax fell from his body. He was nothing like Rowen in how he made love. But then, there was no love here. Only need.

She felt his length, felt the rending pain mingled with swells of desire. Fastening herself like a knot around him, she called out the wrong name in the dark. His skin had the same softness, the same smoothness as Rowen's. Her heart ached with remembrance.

After pleasure had crested and flown, her legs would not stop trembling. With all the pain she still carried, there was also the pain that Roland had poured into her. It was too much.

Gripping her hair, he seized her lips with an impassioned kiss, their first since the melee. Something broke his fervor. He hid his face in her hair, his tears cold on her neck. He exhaled like she had pulled the last breath from his lungs.

"Amarys," he sighed, falling away, lying flat on his back.

Amarys blinked back tears, her eyes burning like embers. She frowned, holding her breath. Even after all these months, she still felt shattered.

"Can I tell you something?" he asked.

"Of course."

"Today, I felt a presence. Her presence. Not a spirit, though. It was as though she was really here."

"She could not have been," said Amarys, encasing him with her arms.

"I know. It is just that... when we were children, and she would spy on my lessons, I always knew. I never saw her or heard her. But I still knew. We were of one mind. One hand, we used to say. I saw the world through her eyes as much as she saw it through mine. And today, as you and I were singing in the hall, I felt her heart break within my own chest."

"Roland... We saw her die. We saw them carry her away under a cloak."

"I cannot deny what I felt. And moments later, Biax was stolen."

Amarys touched the curve of his shoulder. "You want it to be true. So do I. Anything to deny what this bleak and barren winter has made us confront again and again. She is gone. And she is never coming back."

Amarys did not want to think of Rowen. On this night, all she wanted was to fade into Roland's arms. Sleep did not come for her, though. Roland dozed beside her, and outside, a storm assailed the tower with wind and resounding thunder. Every time Amarys came close to sleep, a ghostly moan would jar her back into the waking terror of her grief.

Troubled by thoughts of Rowen, she donned her robe and stirred her servant from slumber. As much as the servant entreated Amarys to return to bed, she insisted she could not. She needed to make a prayer for the dead. She could not rest until she did. A guard was summoned. Another servant brought a candle and followed her to the chapel. Roland slept, unaware.

The floor was like ice through her slippers. The chapel's immensity felt somehow magnified in the darkness. All but for Amarys's single taper, there was no light to be found.

Amarys knelt before the altar, whispering her prayers as she worked the beads of her rosary. Her servant left her there, eventually returning and waiting behind her in the pews. The groan of the doors interrupted her "Hail Mary," and Amarys craned her neck to see Father Gerard coming in, a book of hours tucked against his ribs. He came to perform a commendation for the dead.

He spoke in Latin, wishing rest and eternal light for the souls of the deceased. Amarys repeated each phrase after he said it. When the prayers were done, Father Gerard handed something to her, something hard and cold and precious: a red teardrop on the end of a chain.

"I found this in the library," he said. "I remember when your father gave this to you. Has it been missing?"

Amarys knit her brow, lifting her palm to the candlelight. She nearly said, "This isn't mine," but as the burgundy fire within flashed before her eyes, she remembered everything.

She remembered receiving the garnet after recovering from the fever that nearly killed her. Her father had been so worried, and when he gave it to her, he had said, "A treasure for my treasure." And that had been Amarys's intention when she gave it to Rowen. Treasure for my treasure. She remembered the garnet hanging over Rowen's heart the night of the tournament ball. She remembered Rowen sleeping next to her, remembered telling her to wear it always for it meant that they were married. And she remembered the blood coagulating on the silver chain as Rowen lay dying. She had sent her to her grave with it.

"Where did you find this?" she demanded.

"Someone draped it on the statue of Lazarus. Was it stolen?"

"No. No." Amarys tried to make sense of it. Had the gravedigger brought it back? Or perhaps a graverobber?

Amarys slipped away from Gerard, carrying her candle into the library. The priest shuffled after her.

In the study, the statuette of Saint Lazarus stood silently upon the marble table. Amarys scrutinized the figure.

"It was just there upon the saint's throat," explained Gerard, "as though someone left it to be found."

Amarys saw the folios scattered wildly across the floor. An inkwell had been toppled, its black stain just left to sprawl and harden. "Who did this?" she asked. "It was not like this earlier."

"I do not know."

Amarys would not believe it at first. She remembered going in there with her sister. She remembered crossing herself to Saint Lazarus on her way out. There was no garnet then.

"Oh, God!" Amarys cried, tightening her fingers around the stone. She broke through the doors that led into the stone courtyard, wailing, "Rowen! If you are still here, you must come to me now!"

The storm still raged outside, but it was nothing compared to the tempest within her. "Rowen!" Amarys climbed over the stone partition surrounding the courtyard's garden. The flowerbeds swelled with rainwater. Lightning flickered endlessly, its screams of thunder bursting all around.

Amarys slammed herself against the hazel tree corded with honeysuckle. The white blossoms drooped in the rain and came down like snow.

Shutters along the timbered walls clattered, the many eyes of the chateau opening and bearing witness. Amarys fell down on her knees in the mud, gripping her thin clothes about her shivering frame. "He isn't you. He could never be you." The storm swallowed up her voice.

Father Gerard called to her through the haze. She could not hear him, though.

"Send for Roland!" he commanded the servants within.

He stepped out in the rain and pleaded with Amarys to come inside. She shouted over the percussive storm for him to leave her there.

"You will be struck by lightning!" cried Gerard.

"My love will save me! Like Lancelot, my love will come for me!"

Roland came through, disheveled and dazed. Slipping through mud, steadying himself against stone pillars and tree limbs, he fought to join Amarys and Gerard at the base of the twisting trees. Gerard wiped the rain from his eyes. "Help me lift her!"

"Just go!" shouted Roland. "Please, just leave me with my wife."

Reluctantly, Father Gerard returned through the doors to the library. Roland knelt close to Amarys, leaving space between them. The rain drenched his bedclothes.

"If you cannot sleep, I will stay awake with you," he said. "Only come inside."

Amarys released her grip of the tree, going at once to Roland. He held her fast against him like she could blow away with the sweeping gale. She lay her fist in his hand, her fingers so cold that she could barely open them. With effort, she surrendered the garnet and showed him the marvelous and horrible truth.

"She lives."

EPILOGUE

By the hearth of the physic's hovel, Rowen tended her humble vittles in the cookpot and felt blissfully numb. She clutched her coarse-spun wool around her shoulders, her stomach growling as she waited for the stew to boil.

Burn away this old cage of flesh, she told herself. Rowen is nothing. A memory forgotten. A kiss stolen in preparation for a husband. Rowen lies in an unmarked grave.

Bartholomew came in from the garden and dropped a few thin carrots into the pot. Rowen stirred them in with the onions and parsnips, sighing as the water began to bubble.

"Are you still angry?" she asked.

"You stole a horse."

"He is my horse. I have only reclaimed him."

"Have you considered my suggestion? The horse would help you on the road."

He was marching South on Crusade. Following the murder of a papal legate, Pope Innocent III had excommunicated the Count of Toulouse and called for a holy war on Cathar heresy in Languedoc. This was the call Bartholomew had anticipated for years, and he wanted his apprentice at his side.

"If I went with you, could you guarantee the men would not use me badly?"

"We are Crusaders, child. Our Order exists to uphold the tenets of our faith. The Bloodcross Knights obey the laws of God and protect all pilgrims traveling to Jerusalem."

"My father told me stories. It would seem that not all men who take the cross are so devout."

"I cannot speak for all men, but I can speak for the fellowship of our Order. We would keep you safe."

"I struggle to see myself healing when God has made me so well for battle."

"Should our encampment be compromised, you could use your skills to defend other healers."

Rowen extended her arm to touch his hand. "If this is the path to repaying you for all that you have done for me, I will go."

Bartholomew patted her hand gently. It was a gesture she found beautiful for it reminded her of her father in those rare moments of tenderness between them. "If you prefer to return home, I will help you confront your family."

"No," she said. "It will be my life's honor to heal the wounded soldiers of Christ."

The choice was hardly a choice. It felt like destiny as she rode out with the Order of the Bloodcross Knights.

They were unique as an Order. When they took the cross, they took it in the most literal sense, searing its image into the flesh of their faces. The brand was optional, but Rowen wanted everyone to know her love for God the instant they saw her, especially if hers were to be the first face a soldier saw upon awakening after a battle.

Near a cliffside, a clan of Crusaders gathered for the initiation of a girl who had risen from the dead. Most of the men bore the brand of the cross on their foreheads, but several had opted for their cheeks. Rowen stood before a brazier, her hair flicking like dark fire. Her spine held firm inside a leather harness fastened tight, a vested contraption that kept her ribs upright and her chest flat.

As they waited for the physic to light the brazier, some of the other warriors spoke amongst themselves. "You will have to kill without hesitation," one said to another.

"I know." The man was clean-shaven and had more scars than most men his age.

"They will not be Mohammats this time. They look and dress like us, but they are nothing like us. They must be sent to Hell, their cities and farmlands burned."

"Farmlands?"

The rest of the men glanced at one another, uncertainty written on their faces.

"We kill whomever we are told to kill. All is done in the name of God. If your commander tells you to kill a woman…"

"I'll kill women," said the man unflinchingly. "Man. Woman. Child. In war, there is no difference. Anyone can take up arms for the devil." He looked at Rowen. "Just as anyone make take up arms for Christ."

"To face Hell's army, you have to be ready for the unimaginable."

"I will do as my commander orders. I will trust his judgment as I trust God."

"What about you, girl?" the leader asked of Rowen. "Will you take up arms against heresy if you are so commanded?"

"I will."

His face was like stone, unmoved either way. He gave a nod, assuming a proud posture as the brazier filled with fire.

Bartholomew lifted a hot iron from the flames, blowing over the brand of the cross so it glowed like carbuncle. "Kneel."

Rowen went to her knees in the grass.

"Be one with the cross," he said. "In the name of the Father, the Son, and the Holy Spirit."

Rowen closed her eyes. The press of iron stung only at first. Then, it was obliterating. She allowed the pain to fill her lungs like cold air. The image of the cross burned in her mind's eye as Bartholomew seared its likeness into her forehead. When it was done, she rejoiced, having burned the edges of her soul without once crying out.

"Deus vult," said the Brotherhood.

God was with her—now—there—in the sign of the cross. Holding a tremulous fingertip to the cross that blistered above her eyes, Rowen whispered a prayer.

"O Lord, Jesus Christ, Good Shepherd, son of God. Give me the courage to walk the righteous path of Crusade. Amen."

BIBLOGRAPHY

Aquinas, Thomas. *Summa Theologica* (On the Power of God). Translation by English Dominican fathers. Westminster, MD, 1952.

Asbridge, Thomas. *The Crusades: The Authoritative History of the War for the Holy Land*. Harper Collins, 2011.

Aucassin and Nicolette. Translated by Ivin S. Sturges. Michigan University Press, 2015.

Backman, Clifford R. "Arnau de Vilanova and The Body at the End of The World." *In Last Things: Death and the Apocalypse in the Middle Ages*, edited by Caroline Walker Bynum. University of Pennsylvania Press, 1999.

Barney, Stephen A., W. J. Lewis, and J. A. Beach, eds. *The Etymologies of Isidore of Seville*. Cambridge University Press, 2006.

Bartlett, Ivin. *The Making of Europe: Conquest, Colonization, and Cultural Change 950-1350*. Princeton University Press, 1993.

Biblia Sacra Vulgata. https://www.biblegateway.com/versions/Biblia-Sacra-Vulgata-VULGATE/

Binski, Paul. *Medieval Death: Ritual and Representation*. British Museum Press, 1996.

Boethius, Anicius Manlius Severinus. *The Consolation of Philosophy*. Translated by David R. Slavitt. Harvard University Press, 2008.

Bynum, Caroline Walker. *Holy Feast and Holy Fast: The Religious Significance of Food to Medieval Women*. Berkeley: University of California Press, 1987.

Capellanus, Andreas. *The Art of Courtly Love*. Columbia University Press, 1960.

Cohen, Jeffrey Jerome. *Medieval Identity Machines*. University of Minnesota Press, 2003.

Davis, Adam J. "Medieval Understandings of Charity: From Penance to Commerce." *The Medieval Economy of Salvation: Charity, Commerce, and the Rise of the Hospital*, 33–78. Cornell University Press, 2019.

Dinshaw, Carolyn. "A Kiss is Just a Kiss: Heterosexuality and Its Consolations in Sir Gawain and the Green Knight." *Diacritics* 24, no. 2/3 (1994): 205–26.

Duby, Georges. *The Chivalrous Society*. Translated by Cynthia Postan. University of California Press, 1977.

Elias, Norbert. *The Civilizing Process: Sociogenetic and Psychogenetic Investigations*. Blackwell Publishing, 2000.

France, John. *Western Warfare in the Age of the Crusades*, 1000-1300. Psychology Press, 1999.

Gilchrist, Ivina. *Medieval Life*. Boydell and Brewer, 2012.

Gillingham, John. *Richard I*. Yale University Press, 1999.

Grabar, Oleg. "The Shared Culture of Objects." *Byzantine Court Culture from 829 to 1204*, edited by Henry Maquire, 125–29. Harvard University Press, 1997.

Hanawalt, Barbara A. *The Ties That Bound: Peasant Families in Medieval England*. New York: Oxford University Press, 1986.

Heng, Geraldine. "Cannibalism, the First Crusade, and the Genesis of
Medieval Romance." *Differences: A Journal of Feminist Cultural Studies*, 10,
no. 1 (1998): 98-174.

———. *Empire of Magic: Medieval Romance and the Politics of Cultural Fantasy.*
Columbia University Press, 2003.

———. *The Invention of Race in the European Middle Ages.* Cambridge University
Press, 2018.

Herdam, Ayaal, and David J. Smallwood. "The Queen from the South: Eleanor
of Aquitaine as a Political Strategist and Lawmaker." In *Strategic
Imaginations: Women and the Gender of Sovereignty in European Culture*,
edited by Anke Gilleir and Aude Defurne, 159–80. Leuven University
Press, 2020.

Houppert, Karen. *The Curse: Confronting the Last Unmentionable Taboo,
Menstruation.* Farrar Straus and Giroux, 1999.

Jacoby, David. "Silk Economics and Cross-Cultural Artistic Interaction:
Byzantium, the Muslim World, and the Christian West." *Dumbarton
Oaks Papers* 58 (2004): 197–240.

Keen, Maurice. *Chivalry.* Yale University Press, 1984.

———. *Medieval Warfare: A History.* Oxford University Press, 1999.

———. *Nobles, Knights and Men-At-Arms in the Middle Ages.* London:
Bloomsbury Publishing Plc, 2003.

Khanmohamadi, Shirin A. *In Light of Another's Word: European Ethnography in the
Middle Ages.* University of Pennsylvania Press, 2014.

Kinoshita, Sharon. *Medieval Boundaries: Rethinking Difference in Old French
Literature.* University of Pennsylvania Press, 2006.

Kostick, Conor. *The Social Structure of the First Crusade.* Brill, 2008.

Llull, Ramon. *The Book of the Order of Chivalry.* Translated by Noel Fallows.
NED-New Edition. Boydell and Brewer, 2013.

Maalouf, Amin. *The Crusades Through Arab Eyes*. Translated by Jon Rothschild. New York: Al Saqi, 1984.

Magnus, Albertus. *Albertus Magnus, on Animals: a Medieval Summa Zoologica*. Translated by Kenneth F. Kitchell and Irven M. Resnick. Revised edition. Columbus: The Ohio State University Press, 2018.

Mandeville, John. *The Book of Marvels and Travels*. Translated by Anthony Bale. Oxford University Press, 2012.

Marie de France. *The Fables of Marie de France: An English Translation*. Edited by Harriet Spiegel. University of Toronto Press, 1994.

Menocal, Maria Rosa. *Shards of Love: Exile and the Origin of the Lyric*. Duke University Press, 1993.

Ovid. *The Lover's Handbook: a Complete Translation of the Ars Amatoria*. London: New York: G. Routledge; Dutton, 1923.

Ovid. *Metamorphoses*. Edited by Rolfe Humphries and J. D. Reed. Translated by Rolfe Humphries. The new, annotated edition. Indiana University Press, 2018.

Silence: A Thirteenth-Century French Romance. Translated by Sarah Roche-Mahdi. Michigan State University Press, 1999.

Sir Gowther. The Middle English Breton Lays. Edited by Anne Lascaya and Eve Salisbury. Kalamazoo: Medieval Institute Publications, 1995. TEAMS.

Vaughan, Theresa. *Women, Food, and Diet in the Middle Ages: Balancing the Humours*. Amsterdam University Press, 2020.

Warren, Michelle. *History on the Edge: Excalibur and the Borders of Britain 1100-1300*. University of Minnesota Press, 2000.

If you want to support this book and help others learn about it, please leave a review on Amazon and send an email to megmerriet@gmail.com to let me know that you did. When I reach 100 reviews, you will be entered into a sweepstakes to win a free hardcover copy of the sequel.

Coming Soon

KNITBONE

Visit parkwoodpress.com for details
or follow us on Instagram @parkwood_manor_press